ROTTEN TO THE CORE

TALES OF DARKNESS AND FATE: BOOK 1

LIZ CAIN

ANNE K. WHELAN

CLAN WHELAN
PUBLISHING

**For every young person
who thought life was a fairytale.**

Life often doesn't work out how we think it will and there's
nothing wrong with that. We all have strengths we are yet to
know, have faith in yourself and be the wonderful individual
you already are!

To Kerry

Happy reading

Liz Cam

PART I
THE RISE OF THE QUEEN

CHAPTER 1

RAINA

I took a deep breath, staring at the elaborate frame of the mirror that hung on my chamber wall. Carefully my eyes followed the trails of ivy leaves and flower petals intertwined around the silver surface.

"Mirror, mirror, on the wall..." I muttered. My nose wrinkled as I tried to remember the rest of the rhyme my grandmother used to tell me as a child. My heart still ached at her loss, even though it was nearly twenty years ago. I shook my head, raising my hand to touch the elaborate design with my eyes avoiding the reflective surface.

"Raina?" Kiara's shout echoed along the passage outside my room. My hand jerked away as if burned and I closed my eyes. I turned to face my chamber door as my handmaid strode through, smoothing her pinafore with her hands.

"I'm not a girl anymore." I scoffed. At twenty-eight I was considered an old maid in the town, but Kiara had been my handmaid since I was born. I stepped away from the mirror, and Kiara glanced over my shoulder, frowning.

"Still having the nightmares?" She stepped around me and reached for the silvery surface.

"Don't." I pulled her hand back frantically, breathing a sigh when her fingers didn't touch it.

"It's just a mirror, Raina." Her brow creased when she looked at me. "You should not be afraid of looking at your own reflection."

"I can't explain it," I replied. "When I look at myself, I don't see *me* anymore." I cringed when she stepped back toward the mirror.

"I just see myself," she answered, smoothing her hair down and peering at her reflection. "This mirror has been here for years. Why now?"

I peeked up and smiled at her reflection. It looked normal, her dark gray hair neatly in a bun with soft brown eyes meeting my gaze. I shook my head, shrugging one shoulder.

She turned to face me. "What is bothering you? Is it the king's visit today?"

I wrinkled my nose. "No, nothing like that. I just have this bad feeling when I look at my reflection...a darkness in my face. It's not my face...but it is me." My eyes glazed over, becoming unfocused as I looked through Kiara. My stomach clenched as dread washed through me and I shivered.

Kiara snorted. "You've been reading too much from your grandmother's journal again."

I thought about the old tome I hadn't read through in years. I might could find the mirror rhyme. The journal held wild stories that my grandmother used to make up and tell me as a child. Kiara turned, gesturing toward the door. "Let's get you some fresh air. You've been in this room too long."

I sighed. "Of course."

Stepping toward my chamber door, I straightened my back. Head held high, I made sure my mask was in place before I took that first step.

"That's my girl," Kiara spoke softly as we approached the main part of the house.

Holding my breath, I walked down the stairs, my eyes drifting over our large entrance hall. It was covered in family portraits along one wall, displaying my mother's family for all to see. My mother scrutinized each step as I descended the stairs, so I held myself straighter and kept my chin high.

I gave my mother a curt nod and a small curtsey as I reached her, my posture and form perfect, as I had been taught. We were one of the richer families in the area, and my mother had high expectations for how I should act. I paused as her eyes narrowed; she stood with my father and her own handmaid. She examined the simple pale blue gown I wore, one with few embellishments but a flattering style. I kept my face blank under her scrutiny, not daring to breathe until she looked away. Kiara's brief touch at my elbow was a comfort when my mother didn't speak.

My shoulders relaxed slightly, and it was an effort to hold my posture. I approached without a word and stood stiffly behind my mother, returning my father's small smile. We all faced the door and waited in silence. News of the king's arrival at our home had come the evening before. I managed to stop myself taking a deep breath, not wanting to draw my mother's attention. Rumors were spreading through the kingdom like a plague; the king was looking for a wife.

I could practically feel my mother's excitement at the prospect of him picking me. I'm sure she wished she was younger and unmarried. I nearly rolled my eyes. As was tradition in the kingdom, he would visit every eligible woman of noble birth. We hurriedly entered the small sitting area used to welcome guests to the house, taking up position near the ornate fireplace.

I heard the heavy footsteps of our butler as he approached the door to the house. A system of bells had informed us of the king's arrival at the main gate. I tried to swallow, my throat constricted and mouth dry. I could feel my heart beating hard against my chest, and my stomach was in knots.

"Don't say a word, girl," my mother whispered harshly over her shoulder at me. "Let us do the talking."

I nodded, not meeting her eyes. I strained to hear the door open to the house and the voices in the hallway. I was surprised my parents hadn't turned to face me. My heart pumped faster and so loudly they must have been able to hear it.

"His Royal Highness, the King of Lestoria," Frederick our butler announced, stepping aside and half turning to face the door. His bow was so deep I thought his nose might touch the floor. I took an involuntary step further behind my parents and bowed with them. All I saw was a pair of large hunting boots enter the house. I scrunched my eyes closed and remained in the bow, my stomach twisting.

"Please rise." The king's voice was deep and rich, sending a shiver through me. I held my position a moment longer, rising only when my parents had.

"It is such a pleasure to have you visit our home, my king." My mother stepped forward, and I had to stop myself from taking a step behind my father. I needed to get a grip on myself. I was behaving like a shy teenager. I watched as my mother continued to simper at the king.

"Kiara, send for some refreshments," she called to my handmaid. Kiara caught my eye, giving me a small nod as she quickly left her position near the door. My father took a step forward next.

"It is good to see you, sire," he gave another small bow and grinned when the king offered his hand. "How has the hunting been near the palace?" The king smiled at my father as they clasped wrists.

"It is good to see you, Henry. We have missed you in court these last few years and alongside us outside the wall." The king's smile seemed genuine, and I allowed a small frown at their friendly exchange.

"I'm too old for that sort of dalliance. I'm sure you've been faring well without me," my father answered.

"We have seen an increase in skirmishes, but we are holding them back," the king told him. My heart stopped for a second as I realized they spoke of the attacks outside the walls. Rumors of the fight against monsters that fed on blood had circulated the kingdom over the years, but my father had never spoken of it.

The army had been holding them back from the kingdom as long as I could remember. It was forbidden to talk about the attacks, and most of us within the walls referred to them as hunts or hunting expeditions. I sneaked a glance at my father. I hadn't known he was part of the skirmishes.

He cleared his throat. "I would be no use to you these days, I'm sad to say."

"Nonsense, man, you're barely older than me." The king was being kind. My father was close to sixty, and his body was failing him while the king looked to be in his early forties. A warm sensation started in my middle at the kindness he was showing, though I could feel my mother seething from across the room at the lack of attention she was getting. I frowned as memories surfaced of my father saying he had grown up with the king, but I must have been mistaken. "It always has seemed too easy. My father always said it was harder to push them back before the vampire king disappeared."

Vampire? That was the first mention I had heard of the attackers being named as vampires. I swallowed nervously and looked at my father. His face was blank, but when he glanced at me, I saw a flash of worry in his eyes.

"That is good news. However, I'm happy at home with my family. You remember my wife Eleanor?" I smothered a laugh when my mother allowed her perfect expression to fall into a scowl behind the king's back.

"This is our daughter, Raina," my mother spoke before the king could answer, approaching me and giving me a small shove to take advantage of the pause in conversation. I caught the stumble before I could trip forward and gave a small curtsey.

"It is a pleasure to meet you, sire," my eyes looked up into a beautiful smile and kind eyes. My face heated, a blush creeping into my cheeks, but I couldn't pull my gaze away. His black hair was slicked back over his head, though a small portion had come free and fell near his eyes, which were the color of rich milk chocolate. His beard was neatly trimmed, causing my attention to draw to his lips. My blush deepened and I managed to pull my gaze away.

"The pleasure is all mine, Raina. Would you mind accompanying me to the seat? Please sit with me." He arched an eyebrow at me, his lip twitching when he glanced over my shoulder toward my mother.

"Of course." I took his hand, following his lead to the seats near the window. I loved this spot with a view of the main gates and a large oak tree.

"Why haven't I seen you in court," he asked.

I cringed at the question. I hated court and avoided going with my parents, to my mother's dismay. Since my father had quit the court, my mother had been pressuring me to return so she would have an excuse to attend.

"I'm—"

"She's shy," my mother interrupted me. "She prefers to keep to herself, though she has had considerable training in court etiquette."

The king frowned but didn't say anything. I dropped my

gaze to my hands, neatly folded in my lap. I tried not to think about the handsome man before me and why he was here. The silence stretched uncomfortably, and my stomach clenched when I looked up to find the king watching me. He smiled, looking thoughtful as he studied my face.

"No matter. It's my loss for not having met you before. I find some of the events tedious myself." His casual tone surprised me, but not as much as the wink. "I'd like to invite you to meet my daughter, Niveus. She's coming into her teenage years, and a woman's influence is sorely needed in her life."

I found myself nodding and rose as he stood. "Of course, sire. I would love to meet her."

"It is settled then." The king glanced up at my father, who gave him a nod.

"It would be our pleasure to lend you our daughter for the visit. Eleanor will agree," my father said.

Kiara entered the room carrying a tray of sweet tea and lemon cake. It was a favorite of mine, and she was trying to help me feel more comfortable. I rose from my seat, but my mother beat me to the tea, pouring it out for the four of us. I sipped mine slowly, allowing the warmth to spread through me. I barely spoke as my mother regaled the king with tales of my accomplishments. I almost started to believe them.

"You aren't leaving?" my mother's cry pulled my attention back to the conversation. My body relaxed as the king rose and strode to the door.

"Forgive me, Eleanor, but I have further business in the kingdom. Your refreshments were delicious," he said.

My parents bowed, and I belatedly stood and followed their action.

"I will send an invitation to you." His eyes met mine, lingering.

"Yes, sire," I said softly, my cheeks burning under his gaze.

With that, he swept out the door with our butler hastily following, only just beating him to the house entrance. I let out a breath and rose from the bow. If he wanted me as a companion for his daughter, he couldn't be interested in me as a prospective wife. The butterflies in my stomach finally settled, allowing me to breathe easier. Kiara removed the tray of cakes and tea on the small table in front of me before she gave a shallow curtsey and left.

"Excellent," my mother said, rubbing her hands together and gazing out the window into the distance. "This looks very promising." Father took the seat opposite me, recently occupied by the king.

"What looks promising, my dear?" He turned to mother.

"If he wants Raina to meet Niveus, he obviously thinks she is suitable as a potential wife," she answered, grinning. "Not that you did much to help, child," she sneered at me.

"I am not a child, Mother," I snapped, regretting it immediately.

"What did you say?" Her voice turned cold.

"I'm sorry, Mother," I mumbled.

"Then stop behaving like you *are* a child," she snarled at me. "If you went to court more instead of moping around the house, you would be suitably married by now. You're too old to be living with your parents and not have a family of your own. Still, if you hadn't kept to yourself, the opportunity to marry so high would not have been available to you. It is a shame he already has a child as an heir."

We had this argument every day. It would never matter what I did because she wouldn't be happy. I sighed, biting my tongue so I didn't argue back. I hadn't been like the other ladies at court, pining after the men in the room and desperate for a husband of their own. None of them had anything else to talk about, so I had avoided going to court when my parents went and refused to attend now.

"Wouldn't it be marvelous," my father spoke. "Lucas hasn't been the same since the late queen passed. I know he loves his daughter and was surprised to hear he was looking for a wife. But he is a wonderful friend and would be a perfect fit for you, Raina."

A twinge of guilt curled through me at the look of hope and joy on my father's face. I reached for my tea, belatedly realizing it had been cleared.

"Exactly." The glee in my mother's voice grated through me. "It would certainly raise our stature among the nobles. It's about time they stopped looking down on us."

"They don't look down on us," my father said.

I struggled to swallow as they continued to talk. I saw my mother roll her eyes and wondered how I could leave the room.

"I knew you had to amount to something one day, Raina. You are my daughter, after all. Now let's hope you don't ruin this for us." She swept out of the room, the smile still on her face.

"Don't worry," my father said to me. "She's just excitable. Whether the king wants you to be his wife or not, it is your choice if you want to accept or reject him. Though you would make a handsome couple."

My face heated at the thought of marrying the king. He was an extremely handsome man and had aged well. "How can I say for sure when I don't know him, Father?"

"You learn about each other once married. That's always been the way. I barely knew your mother before we moved in together, and look at how happy we are," he answered.

I stopped myself from rolling my eyes. My father was oblivious to my mother's faults, and I truly believed he loved her. I, on the other hand, despised her. I had been closer to my grandmother. My mother had barely tolerated the relationship I'd had with her mother. I thought she must have been jealous as Grandmother had ignored her once she married my father.

"I have business in the kingdom tonight. Once the invitation from the king arrives, we can make arrangements for you to meet Niveus." He smiled at me, standing quickly. "It would be nice to see you settled and happy, Raina. I worry about you here by yourself all the time."

"I'm not alone. I have Kiara and my books," I said. He smiled before leaving the room. I sagged into the chair, finally able to release my stiff posture.

My head abruptly turned toward the mirror as I entered my chambers, as if it had called my name when I walked into the room. I narrowed my eyes at the sight of a shadow moving across the reflection, but when I blinked it was gone. Slowly I took a step toward the mirror, bracing myself. I shouldn't fear a mirror or my own reflection. The shadow grew larger as I drew near, and my reflection came into view.

I wore the same style dress, but in the mirror it looked darker, almost black. All the color had drained from my face making my eyes stand out starkly against my pale skin. The room looked dreary over my shoulder and the shadow flashed in the background, so fast I would have missed it if I had blinked. I refused to tear my eyes away.

Taking a deep breath, I studied my face. Shadows were present under my eyes, which looked entirely black. The dark blue no longer shined in them, like the black center had melted toward the edges. My skin was pale, almost translucent, and my expression was hard. I could see no warmth or kindness. I closed my eyes, turning away to study my chambers. They were once again bright and comforting, nothing like the gloomy reflection. I took a deep breath and slowly walked over to my vanity.

I crouched, pulling open the bottom drawer and staring at the journal my grandmother had left me. The leather-bound book was fastened with a pure silver clasp. I caressed the pattern of her family crest, raised on the leather surface. She had died when I was eight, yet I still missed her. Mother had been vocal about the relationship we had, but Grandmother had always stood up to her. I think in some ways it was one of the reasons she was so dismissive of me, especially after Grandmother died. Her mother hadn't paid her much attention as she grew up but visited with me often as a child. Kneeling on the floor, I opened the journal, smiling at the memory of my grandmother reading to me.

"Mirror, mirror," I murmured as I thumbed through the pages, my brow furrowing. It was more of a collection of short stories and letters than a journal, stories grandmother used to tell me. My heart skipped a beat when I caught the word mirror on one of the pages near the end. I gasped at the image on the page, a beautiful sketch of the mirror on my wall. The words were written in the center where the reflection would be. I flattened the page, frowning when the words faded so that only the word *Mirror* was visible. Carefully I tilted the book so I looked at the sketch at an angle and the words appeared again.

> *Mirror, mirror on the wall,*
> *Show your secret to stop the fall.*

I shook my head, squinting at the words and wondering how I had never noticed them before. I spoke the words slowly, rolling my eyes at my grandmother's rhyme. Stop what fall? When I finished, a strange feeling washed over me, like the feeling when you remember a dream that had been floating on the edge of your memories.

"Well now, who do we have here?" a man's voice cut through the silence in my chambers. I stumbled to my feet, whirling around in a circle to see who was there. The room was empty.

Movement caught my eye. The mirror had gone completely black, and the surface shimmered. As I watched, my breath caught when the blackness settled into the same dark reflection of my chambers. I edged closer, my heart pounding when I saw the dark figure standing near my bed in the mirror. I whirled, looking at my bed behind me, my eyes widening when I saw no one there. I quickly turned back to the mirror, gasping when I saw the man staring back at me with a smile.

CHAPTER 2

RAINA

"*I*s this real?" I whispered.

"I can assure you, I am real," the man in the mirror spoke. "May I introduce myself?" He quirked an eyebrow at me.

"Y...yes," I stammered and then straightened up as my mother's training kicked in. "Yes, sir." I curtsied at the reflection, pushing confidence into my voice.

"So polite," he said. "My name is Damien. What shall I call you?" He gave me a bow in the mirror and I studied his face. Clean shaven, with shoulder-length brown hair and a straight nose. His face looked too perfect. His eyes were a brown so dark, you could barely see any depth to them.

"My name is Raina," I curtsied again, internally rolling my eyes when I realized I'd just done that. "How can I see you in my mirror?"

"I was trapped here by an evil witch," he told me, his tone somber. I fought the urge to frown and took a step forward, just as he took one too. Slowly I moved toward the mirror until he faced me, as if he was my own reflection.

"What did you do to get trapped there?" I asked.

LIZ CAIN & ANNE K. WHELAN

"I can't tell you that," he said. "How do I know I can trust you?"

I frowned. "That is a good point." I looked at my grandmother's book, picking it up and showing it to him. "How did this book help you appear?"

He narrowed his eyes at the book. "Where did you get that?" Suspicion laced his words.

"It was my grandmother's. She used to read it to me as a child," I answered.

"And is Constance still around to read it to you?" he said stiffly.

"No." I bit my lip. "She died when I was eight."

I saw him visibly relax, reaching a hand up to touch his lips. "I'm sorry for your loss," he said hesitantly. "She was always good to me. She was trying to help me."

My eyes widened. "Help you how?"

"My brother was power hungry and wanted to steal the throne from me. It was mine by right," he growled. "But he took it and bribed a powerful witch to trap me in here." He dropped his hand.

"Wait, you're the king's brother?" I shook my head. "That can't be right. He doesn't have a brother."

"Who is the king now?" he said.

"King Lucas."

"I am his great uncle. His father was on the throne the last time I spoke with Constance." He scrubbed his chin and started to pace before he halted and looked at me again. "You look familiar...Raina did you say your name was. I used to speak to a child in the mirror called Raina."

My heart stopped in my chest, and that sensation of remembering a dream tickled the back of my mind. I gasped, taking a step back. Something unlocked inside me at his words, and I remembered playing near the mirror as a child. I had an invisible friend.

"But that was years ago. I couldn't have been more than five." I bit my lip, looking up at the handsome man in the mirror. "My grandmother was helping you?" I shook my head. That didn't feel right. The king had been friends with my family for years. I tried to remember if my grandmother had ever mentioned anything about the king, but the more I tried, the more the memories trickled away.

Damien's eyes sparkled. "You have grown into a beauty, my dear. Constance always spoke fondly of you."

I felt the heat flush into my cheeks and dropped my gaze. When I peeked up at the mirror Damien looked thoughtful.

"If my grandmother was helping you, why are you still trapped?" I asked. "How could she help you?"

"I'm not sure. I haven't spoken to her in nearly twenty years. She stopped summoning me." He shrugged.

I inhaled slowly. "She died around then. Just didn't wake up one day. I always liked this mirror, so my mother let me have it after she passed."

At least that's what I now remembered. The mirror had seemed perfectly normal until a few days ago. Then it had started to feel like a darkness leaked from it, the images not reflecting my room but slowly becoming dreary. I took a step back, unsure if I believed the man in the mirror.

"Wait, please don't leave," he begged. His hands reached for me but then slowly dropped.

"The mirror feels dark to me," I said quietly. "Why did it change?"

"That's part of the curse. The mirror has started to change, which means it is all finally coming to an end...this curse," he said. "I can feel the mirror draining my strength. I don't think I can hold out much longer. I don't blame you for not believing me. It was nice to see you one last time, my sweet Raina. I always did enjoy our conversations. "

His words cut through me, and I stepped forward again.

"Wait." I reached for the mirror as he turned away from me. An echo of the same phrase vibrated within my chest. A memory from my childhood. As I touched the mirror a gold flash stole my breath. The room in the mirror brightened and Damien stumbled within the frame. When he turned, he no longer looked pale and drab. His clothes looked brighter and his cheeks had more color.

"Raina, I…" his words trailed off. "What did you do?"

"I don't know." I looked down at my hands. They didn't look any different. "I just remembered something my grandmother said about this mirror feeding on energy. She always told me not to touch it. I'd forgotten she'd told me that." I squirmed wondering why I had been drawn toward the mirror. I hadn't been able to stop myself when I reached out to touch it. I remembered begging my mother as a child to let me take it home without knowing why.

"Thank you," he said with wonder. "I truly was on the edge of fading and you brought me back." He reached up to touch the mirror, blanching when he couldn't reach for me.

"You're welcome." I smiled at him. "I don't like seeing anyone in pain. Can you explain to me what happened with your brother?"

"My younger brother was second in line, but he disagreed with my policies. I had most of the council backing me, and he didn't like that. He tricked me, offering a meal together before the coronation—a *peace* offering." He paced the small chambers on his side of the mirror.

"That's awful." I swallowed hard. "I didn't know any of this." I tapped my chin.

"Yes," Damien said. "You won't have heard any of it. The victor can write history as they please. If you ask the family, they will tell you I was the evil one. I just wanted to keep the kingdom safe. What he wanted to do would cause the kingdom's fall."

"What did he want to do?"

"I…" he hesitated. "I will tell you, but I don't have the strength right now."

I watched as his image faded. "Damien," I cried. "Stay with me." I reached for the mirror again and his image sharpened once more.

"You can't keep doing that, Raina," he said. "I believe it is what drained your grandmother in the end."

I gasped, snatching my hand back. "Why?"

"The curse should have ended me a long time ago. It was always a race against keeping me alive long enough for the family's hold on the curse to fade. With each generation, it weakens but I weaken with it."

A sudden realization hit me. "The king's father passed away last week. It was one of the reasons the king is looking for a new wife. My mother thinks he wants to find someone to look after his daughter." My stomach churned when I remembered the king's invitation to visit his daughter. Could he truly be considering me? He was handsome and seemed pleasant enough. I shook my head to rid myself of the distraction.

"That might be why my prison has finally drained of its strength. The death of the last king means I might finally find peace." Damien closed his eyes.

I opened my mouth to speak, sadness swelling at the look on his face. I snapped it shut at the sound of footsteps approaching my chambers. I glanced at the door, hurriedly stepping back from the mirror. I quickly glanced at it before my eyes shot to the floor. Damien was nowhere to be seen, and the mirror reflected my room as it had before the shadows had appeared.

"Raina, there you are. We need to buy a suitable dress for when you visit the king and his daughter." My mother hurried toward me, grabbing my wrist in a painful hold.

"Mother, you're hurting me." I yanked my wrist back.

"Don't behave like a child. You're a grown woman who has long overstayed at her parents. It is about time you marry and stop being a burden to us," she snapped. Tears stung my eyes as I followed her, biting the inside of my cheek to keep them in check.

"I have a closet full of clothes. Why do I need another dress?" I muttered, instantly regretting my words when my mother turned on me.

"You will behave yourself, Raina. This is a great opportunity for the family. If the king chooses you, it means you will have everything you've ever wanted. We will also be elevated in the eyes of the other nobles, which is what we deserve." Her eyes flashed angrily. I kept my mouth shut and nodded meekly, feeling like a teenager rather than the woman I was. Kiara came around the corner up ahead, curtseying as my mother passed.

"Good, you're here. What took you so long?" my mother said as she strode past her.

Kiara wisely did not speak, and I bit my lip when she rolled her eyes, falling in step next to me. My mother's hand-maid held our coats near the door, handing mine to Kiara before helping my mother into hers. I gave Kiara a small nod of thanks discreetly when I heard my mother shouting outside.

"Maybe this is your chance to finally escape *her*," Kiara whispered as she straightened my collar.

I sighed. She was right. It would be my chance to escape her. She constantly complained about me being a burden but had chased off any man who had come asking for my hand in marriage. I hadn't been interested in any of them, but it would have been an escape. I turned, straightening my shoulders, and walked stiffly out the door toward the carriage my mother had called for.

I watched trees and farmhouses fly past our carriage on our way back from the dressmaker. My mother had scared her into a rush order, which would be ready by tomorrow. I had barely registered the clothes and swatches as they were passed to my mother. My mind had drifted to Damien and the last glimpse of his face that had looked so sad. Years trapped in a mirror, what a waste of a life. I sighed sadly, wondering if I'd see him again. When I touched the mirror, a connection had opened to it, at least I thought it had. I was suddenly anxious to get home, and my left foot tapped under my dress.

"Stop that, Raina. It is unbecoming," my mother snapped before returning to her journal. She had been writing in it since we left the dressmaker. As our house came into view, excitement bubbled up from my middle. I tried to keep my face blank, slowly leaving the carriage, and controlling my pace so as not to rush into the house. I waited until Kiara and my mother's handmaid had removed our coats before I spoke.

"May I be dismissed?" I was careful not to meet my mother's eyes as I spoke, portraying the meek woman she wanted me to be. I held my breath, as I always did, waiting for her to speak.

"Fine, hide in your room with your books. I have things to do anyway. I will call you when the invite from the king arrives," my mother answered.

I heard her sniff as I carefully turned and walked to my chambers. They were on a landing, several steps up from the other bedrooms on the first floor. Gently closing the door, I did something I normally did not dare and turned the key in the lock. I listened at the door for any footsteps on the landing. Tension left my shoulders and I took a deep breath before I rushed to the mirror.

"Damien," I whispered, not daring to speak louder. "Damien, are you there?" I drooped when nothing appeared in the mirror. My eyes darted around the reflection, searching every corner for a trace of him. I closed my eyes for a moment and then checked again. Nothing.

Turning, I sat down on my bed and put my head in my hands. He had seemed so sad, and I remembered him being nice to me as a child. I tried to remember if my grandmother had spoken about trying to help him. If he was truly gone, the king's father had damned him to a lonely life in the mirror, and he had never had his freedom. I knew how that felt. My mother kept me here, trapped in a solitary life.

"Your mother always was a bully." Damien's voice broke my reverie and I leaped forward, smiling at him in the mirror.

"Damien!" I reached for the mirror, jerking my hand away before I touched him. "I thought you were gone."

"Nope." He smiled at me. "Still here." He gave me a grin, which made my insides melt. When he smiled, it was with his whole face. Not the reserved smiles I'd seen at court, which never reached anyone's eyes.

"I'm so glad." I shifted my weight on to my other foot.

"I would do anything to stay in your company, Raina. Even if it means I'm trapped in this mirror forever," he said. He lifted his hand as if to reach for me but then dropped it again. My neck flushed hot and heat infused my cheeks. "You have a lovely blush my dear."

I cleared my throat. "I need to ask you some questions."

"Anything for you." He bowed, lifting his head so his gaze never left mine. What was it with this handsome man that made me feel giddy?

"Tell me more about what happened with your brother," I

said. I was hoping I could figure out how the king's family were involved. Lucas was so kind, and it was hard to see his family in the role of the villain, especially when they were so linked to my father's family.

"He wanted to call forward dangerous forces and try to control them so he could get a better handle on the kingdom. I believe there was rioting over taxes at the time, but as the eldest, I should have been crowned. It was my problem to deal with. I planned to lower the taxes for the middle and lower classes." He paused. "Of course, this was not popular among those in the court, but some good men in the council had come around to my way of thinking. Your grandmother told me that my brother had them executed after I was trapped."

That sounded like a conversation I'd once had with my father when he tried teaching me about economics. My mother put a stop to those lessons when she found out, but I remembered his teachings.

"What do you mean by dangerous forces?" I asked, my pulse quickening when I realized what he might be talking about.

"What do you know about the myths of the vampires?" Damien had started to wander around the mirror room as he spoke.

My heart lurched at the mention of vampires. "I only heard my father and the king mention them for the first time yesterday," I said, my eyes widening. "They've always mentioned going on hunts outside the wall."

Damien put his head in his hands, scrubbing them down his face when he looked up. "I failed," he said, barely above a whisper. "I fought for so long to make sure they couldn't be released, but my brother…"

"You're saying your brother released them?" My skin

broke out in a cold sweat as I thought of all the reported kidnappings and deaths among the lower classes.

"I told him they couldn't be controlled. If we are still fighting to keep them at bay, then everything I sacrificed fighting him was for nothing." He started to pace again.

"Could you stop them now? If you were free?" I put a hand on either side of the mirror, trying to catch Damien's eyes. He stopped mid stride and turned to face me.

"How can you free me?" Damien paused and then quickly leaned forward. "Of course, if you summoned me, you must have your grandmother's power. She never managed to figure out how to free me, though."

My shoulders drooped. "What power?"

"Your grandmother was a powerful charmarutha. Like a witch but much more complex," he told me. "She was working to undo the curse put on me by my brother's crone of a witch."

"Charmarutha." The word was foreign on my tongue. I looked at the journal I had left on my bed, grateful my mother hadn't noticed it earlier. I picked it up and caressed the family crest.

"How can I have power? Surely I would have seen it by now?" I asked.

"An charmarutha's power doesn't develop until woman-hood. Mid-twenties with the guidance of an elder," he said. "I imagine your grandmother planned to teach you. Normally it would be your mother, but your grandmother didn't trust her with the gift."

"I can try to read my grandmother's journal, and you can tell me everything she told you. I don't know about having power, but surely that's better than not trying at all."

"Raina, you are a marvel. My sunlight in a world of darkness." Damien gave me another smile, clasping his hands together. His eyes sparkled with hope. "We can only try."

"Do you still want the throne?" I asked. If he was the rightful king, this could make Lucas's life difficult. I felt a pang of guilt, realizing I was talking about saving a man's life. I shouldn't be worried about what the king would think. He fought against the vampires to protect the kingdom. "Maybe we could ask the king for help. He fights for the kingdom against the force his ancestor called forward."

"No, I just want my freedom. If my brother is dead, there is no need for me to be in power. Most of my legislation was to stop him from releasing the vampires, but if they're already released I will join with my great nephew and try to fight them. The best way would be to send them back where they belong before they were summoned by my brother."

"I can ask the king for help when he invites me to meet his daughter," I said eagerly.

"I would keep my existence a secret for now." Damien frowned. "He might have been told a different story. As I said, the victors write our history."

I nodded. "Are you sure? He seems like a good man, and I'm sure he wants all the help he can get fighting the vampires." I shivered at the word.

Damien shook his head and then gave me a quizzical look. "Did you just say you were going to meet his daughter? Are you close with the king?" He cocked his head. Another blush rose to my cheeks and I looked away, not wanting to meet Damien's gaze. "Ah, your blush is lovely. You've taken a liking to him?"

I sighed. "The king is looking for a wife. He stopped by yesterday to see me, at least that's what my mother thinks. He asked me to come and meet his daughter Niveus."

"And you said yes." I saw a flash of pain in Damien's expression, but it was gone so fast I thought I must have imagined it.

I shrugged. "I don't like the idea of marrying someone I

don't know. I don't even know if that's what he wants. All he's asking is for me to meet his daughter."

"You must like him if you said yes. It might work in our favor, actually." He reached up to scratch his chin.

"How do you mean?"

"If the king trusts you, hopefully he will trust me when I'm free," Damien said.

The warmth I'd started to feel around Damien's presence wilted inside me. I'd started to feel an attraction toward him, but he was just another person pushing me toward the king. I took a deep breath and mentally shook myself. I barely knew Damien, and he had been trapped in a mirror with no one to talk to for many years.

"I'll do what I can to help you, Damien…but I won't marry him to make him trust you." I spoke firmly. Even if my mother disowned me, I wouldn't marry just for her sake or anyone else's.

"That's not what I was saying." He looked horrified. "I realize how that sounded. I don't want you to use him. Of course, you need to make up your own mind."

I relaxed. "Thanks for saying so."

"I'll try to remember what your grandmother needed. I know the last thing was power from your family line. She didn't have enough herself to free me." Damien looked around the mirror. "But you might. Already I can feel power within the mirror just from a few touches. More energy than your grandmother could provide over a whole year."

"I didn't know I could do that," I said. "I will try to learn as much as I can. My grandmother must have left more books. I will find a way to free you."

"Thank you, Raina." Damien gave me a warm smile.

CHAPTER 3

RAINA

*W*hen the invite from the king arrived, my stomach was in knots. I hadn't managed to eat much since the conversation with Damien. We had talked late into the night as he told me stories about the court when he had been the crowned prince and how his subjects had adored him. It was easy to see why. He was so charming, charismatic, and handsome. I blushed when I caught myself thinking about his face, the curve of his lips, and his strong jaw. Sometimes when he looked at me, I thought he felt the same way.

"It's finally here," my mother sang as she entered the sitting room. Kiara had just brought me some lunch, though I hadn't touched it. I reached for the gold-embossed envelope with my name written clearly across the back. My mother ripped it open without looking, scanning the card inside. Her eyes gleamed as she devoured the words until she reached the end.

"Hmph, signed by his head of staff," she scoffed. "A little impersonal for a future wife."

I peered over her shoulder.

Raina Walton
You are cordially invited to attend a celebration.
His Royal Highness King Lucas Albus requests
your presence at noon on Thursday.
You will be one of twelve ladies in attendance
Signed
Harold Beacon
Chief of Palace Staff

My mouth was dry, making it hard to swallow as I took in the words. I would be one of twelve invited to meet Niveus. Part of me felt relieved. This way I could make friends with the family, but there wasn't much chance of me becoming his wife. If I could befriend the most likely candidate, I could still get close to the king. My attention snapped back to my mother, who eyed me critically.

"I knew you would need that new gown." She clapped her hands together. "Now let's call the salon in town. They must have someone available to come and do your hair for tomorrow. *Lara!*" Her screech made my ears pop as she called her handmaid into the room.

I saw Kiara cover her ears from the corner of my eye and stifled a laugh as my mother left, shaking my head when Kiara came toward me.

"I hope her vocal cords explode one of these days." She put a hand on my shoulder. "Are you okay? You're looking rather pale."

"Just nervous," I said.

"No more shadows in the mirror stopping you from sleeping?" she asked.

I shook my head. "No," I answered too fast.

She narrowed her eyes at me before glancing at the door. "Don't let her bully you into acting like her. Be yourself and he will love you." She smiled sweetly at me.

"*Raina!*" my mother yelled.

"I better go," I said. "I don't see why he would pick me over the others. I bet they all attend court regularly."

"You don't give yourself enough credit," Kiara said, winking as she left the room.

I found my mother in the kitchen. Her face had taken on an ugly red hue as she shouted at the chef. The poor man held a wooden spoon between them, as if to ward her off.

"I don't think we need a chef for tomorrow, Mother," I said, stepping into the room to intervene.

"I want him to prepare you something magnificent tonight so you have your strength. Why are you still down here? Up to your room and get that handmaid of yours to draw a bath."

"It's barely afternoon. I don't need to bathe yet," I said.

"Do not question me, girl. Your appearance leaves a lot to be desired, and you'll need all the help you can get." She turned back to the chef.

I threw him an apologetic smile and disappeared up the steps to my chambers.

Kiara was waiting for me. "Come on. It'll do you good to have a nice relaxing soak away from her for a while. I got you another book from the library, another adventure one for you."

"Thank you." I grinned at her. I loved adventure stories, but my mother had burned all the ones in the entire estate when I first took an interest in them. Dramatic, I thought at the time, her reasoning was they weren't good for young ladies. Instead, I was given books like *How to Win a Husband*, and *Ten Ways to Treat Your Man Well*. I had dropped several of those in the bath by "accident" while reading them.

As I leaned back into the warm water with a sigh, I started to read about a lost prince and his quest to rescue his friend. The prince made me think of Damien, and I found myself rereading the same page several times before I gave up. I looked across at my grandmother's journal, which I'd picked up before I came into my bathing chamber. Flicking through the pages, I tried to remember each story and which may be relevant to Damien's curse. I found the page with the mirror and nearly dropped the book. Water sloshed over the bath as I sat up quickly. New words had appeared in the image of the mirror when I tilted the book slightly.

Mirror, mirror on the wall,
I call the spell book to curse them all.

Curse them all? What was my grandmother doing? I looked around the room, leaning forward and peeking through the doorway in case Kiara was coming back. I leaned back and braced myself.

"Here goes nothing," I murmured and read the words. I looked up expectantly when I'd finished, but the bath chamber remained silent. I frowned and looked over the page again, peering at the words. A loud thud made me jerk and I barely held on to my grandmother's journal for the second time. I looked over the side of the tub and saw a thick tome lying on the chamber floor.

"What the—" I blinked a few times to make sure it was real. With the same cover as my grandmother's journal, the book with its yellow pages looked like it had been written hundreds of years ago.

"Raina?" Kiara called from my chambers. I gasped, struggling to lean over the tub toward the large book. The water spilled over as I finally connected with it and gave it a shove. The tome slid easily across the floor and under a cabinet storing all the bathing scents. I stared after it. That should have been harder.

"What is all this water?" Kiara exclaimed, and I turned quickly to face the doorway.

"I slipped," I answered lamely.

"The book I got you is soaking wet." She bent to pick up the adventure story next to the tub. I stared with sorrow at the drenched book. It hurt my heart a little to see its bedraggled state.

"I'm sorry, Kiara. You know that's not like me," I said.

"How did you slip? Surely you can get out of the tub without falling over yourself at your age." She chuckled.

"I'm not that old," I grumbled. Kiara picked up a towel and draped it over my shoulders as I climbed out. I glanced at the cabinet across the room, only just peeking at the edges of the large book. I longed to dismiss Kiara and retrieve it, but if my mother saw her, she would send her back to make sure I was ready for tomorrow.

"I don't know what else I need to do to get ready," I told her, following that line of thinking. "I won't be leaving until late morning."

"Let's just humor her. It keeps you out of her sights for the rest of the day. Probably better for you. Let's just hope she doesn't want to move into the palace with you once you're married to the king," she said.

I stopped dead, blood draining from my face at the thought. "You don't think she would?" Horror washed over me.

"Of course she will try to move into the palace with you. I'm surprised she hasn't tried to marry the king herself," Kiara answered, raising an eyebrow. "Could you imagine her as a queen?"

I shuddered, shaking my head at her. "I don't think the kingdom could take it." I walked behind my dressing screen and slipped on a delicate silk bathrobe. I loved the way it caressed my skin, though I rarely ever wore it. I looked at the mirror, my stomach clenching when I didn't see Damien or any sign of shadows in it.

I spent the next few hours trying not to cringe as Kiara applied one beauty treatment after another until I was thoroughly plucked and polished. My eyes kept wandering back to the mirror, not sure if I was happy that there was no sign of the man in the mirror.

"If men had to go through all the treatments ladies do for courting, I'm sure there would be no one to court," I remarked as she put on the final treatment. The hour was late, and I hadn't been able to think of much except the book hidden under the bathroom cabinet. I stared at the ceiling while Kiara continued to fuss over me, counting under my breath to distract me.

Finally, she spoke. "I think that's all for tonight. I don't think your mother will be bothering you, so try to get some rest. I'll be in early in the morning to come and get you ready."

"Thanks, Kiara. Goodnight," I said too quickly. Lying on the bed I couldn't see her but could feel her gaze on me. Tension hung in the air as if she knew I was hiding something. I gently bit my lip and waited, hoping it was all in my head.

"Goodnight," she eventually said, closing the door softly as she left. I listened as her footsteps drifted away down the corridor. I kept counting under my breath in case she came back. After three hundred, I let out a breath, rising slowly from the bed. I quietly padded toward my chamber door, listening for anyone on the landing. Turning the key, I looked over to the mirror on my wall and swallowed my disappointment when I still didn't see Damien there. I sighed, moving toward the bathing chamber, and retrieving the thick book.

Running my hand over the surface of the book, careful

not to lean over in case any of the mask on my face dripped on it, I traced my finger over the familiar crest. It was larger than on her journal and more worn. I would recognize it anywhere. Carefully I opened to the first page and gasped at the written message.

Raina, my dear child. If you are reading this, you have discovered our family heritage by yourself. This is the way of things in our line. You must discover your birthright before you can start your training. Now the power will be yours. If you're reading this, I am not there to guide you, and I'm sorry you will have to walk this path alone.

Thank the gods your mother was never interested in my stories! With all my love, Grandmother Constance

My heart swelled at the message. My mother had stopped me seeing my grandmother, and I wasn't allowed to go to the funeral. My father had kept her journal for me, and I had always been grateful to have something of hers. Now I knew what it had held, and it meant even more that my father had defied my mother to give me such a gift.

The words shimmered before disappearing, my eyes widening as more words appeared starting with "The legacy of the charmarutha..." I carefully started to read, devouring every word.

"Learned anything interesting?"

I started at Damien's words. The light in my room had lowered as each candle had burned out, and I was now using the last one on my side table. "Damien." My heart gave a funny flutter as I saw his face appear in the mirror. "Where have you been?"

"I needed to conserve some energy," he said. "Is that what I think it is?"

I noticed the gleam in his eyes when his gaze fell on the large tome in my hands. "It's my grandmother's I guess. Maybe it can help you." I grinned at him. "I'm hoping she had written something about your curse."

"If the answer is anywhere, it will be in there." His eyes closed, and I could see the relief in his face.

My stomach twisted. "I can't promise anything, but if I can help you, I will."

"What have you learned so far?"

"Mostly the history of our family, various tales of powerful women and the creation of the lamia," I said, touching my face. I turned away from the mirror when I realized I was still wearing the mask Kiara applied before bed.

"Don't turn away. You're still beautiful even if you're hidden underneath a thick cream," he said softly behind me.

Laughter burst from me. "Don't be silly." I rose from the bed and hurried to my bathing chamber, scrubbing my face in the basin with cold water. As I thought of Damien waiting for me, my stomach fluttered, and giddiness swelled through me. Once the mask had been removed, I picked up a brush to neaten my hair and looked myself over in the mirror. Happy with my appearance, I smiled and rushed back into my bed chambers. Damien's smile brightened when I entered, and my heart fluttered at his handsome face.

"Hello," I said shyly.

"Hello, Raina, you're looking beyond beautiful this evening." He gave me a little bow, and I had to stifle a giggle.

"Stop saying that. You look well yourself," I said.

Damien winked at me and seemed to relax. "It is rather

late, my dear. I hope you aren't planning on reading all night. Even if the reading is as interesting as your family grimoire." He eyed the book behind me.

"Grimoire?" I turned to look at the book. "I thought it was the history of our family, a written account."

"That is what it will be for now, until you are ready. This is your grandmother's spell book, and it was passed down through your family until it reached you." Damien reached up and brushed a hand through his hair as he spoke.

"How do you know so much about my family?" I asked. He'd known my grandmother, but she hadn't told me anything about the power in our family. The more I'd read the more curiosity burned through me.

"I was working with her to free me from the mirror so I could stop my brother and the vampires invading our kingdom." He turned to walk toward the window in the mirror's reflection, the twin to mine behind me. I cocked my head, wondering what he could see through his window. "I spent many years conversing with her and learned a lot."

"Does that mean I could learn to use the power?" I frowned, looking over my shoulder at the large book. Damien's answer made me turn back to face him.

"Of course, Raina. You can do anything when you put your mind to it." He smiled at me and I felt my insides quiver.

I shook my head to shake off the feeling. The draw to Damien was a nice distraction, more than nice if I was being honest with myself, but it made my heart ache when I thought of the king's invite to meet Niveus. I dropped my gaze, sighing.

"You're too kind," I said, my voice quiet.

"What is wrong, Raina? Would you prefer I didn't bother you?"

"No," I said quickly, looking back up into his face, which was now right in front of me. "It's just…I'm meeting the king tomorrow…or later today, I guess…and I don't know what is going to happen. My mother thinks he will want to marry me."

"What do you think?"

I shrugged. "That there will be others younger than I am, who will make a more appropriate match. I won't be pining after him like the others."

"Nonsense, the king would have to be a fool not to see your beauty. Inside and out." Damien looked thoughtful.

"You're too kind." My face heated, and I was tempted to fan myself.

"How about we teach you some magic? Will that make you smile." Damien's eyes pierced mine, and I could almost feel his gaze penetrate through to my core.

I nodded, picking the book up from my bed. "Where do I begin?" I flipped through the pages.

"You need to want to learn something. The book will follow your wishes." He gave me a sly grin. "You are now its mistress."

"Is it alive?" My eyes widened as I turned to a new page, and writing slowly appeared before my eyes.

"In a way. It is linked to you. Only you will be able to read it, which is good considering your mother." He chuckled. I grimaced at the thought of her finding the book. "We could start with a concealment spell. One that would allow you to hide the book and call it as you need it. That way you can hide it from your mother. You'll need to accept the power first."

I skimmed the words on the page. It seemed simple enough. The page was beautifully illustrated and described how to use the power within me. I ran my finger under each line, concentrating on feeling the power inside me.

"I just say these words and I will have the power?" I looked up at Damien.

"If that is what the book wants from you," he said.

"I need to drop some blood on the mirror at the bottom of the page." I continued to read, cringing when I reached the part at the bottom about the blood offering. I took a deep breath, fetching scissors from my sewing materials across the room. Glancing down, I started to read the words.

"Power of my ancestors, rise through time and distance across the skies. Come to me, a daughter of fates, settle here. Let the power be mine." I bit my lip as I used the scissors to cut my finger, a single crimson drop beaded on the end. I tilted my hand over the book, allowing the drop to fall onto the page.

Nothing happened.

I looked up at Damien. The mirror was empty, showing the reflection of my bed chambers. I sighed, wondering if I had just made a fool of myself. Gathering up the book, I looked out the window at the haze of light seeping into the distance. Sunrise wasn't far off, and I still needed to sleep. I walked over to my vanity, opening the bottom drawer, and attempting to cram the book inside. When it didn't fit, I looked around and settled on my closet. I would have to hide it among my shoes at the bottom and hope Kiara didn't find it.

Turning toward my bed I stumbled, hurriedly reaching out for the bedpost to support me. Dizziness threatened to overcome me as I took another step. Something unlocked inside me, and heat washed over me, building slowly at first but speeding up until my body pulsed and a buzzing started in my ears. Damien called from a great distance, and I sat heavily on the bed, reaching up to cover my ears. Squeezing my eyes shut, I cried out as the heat built higher, and pain prickled my skin with each pulse. I opened my eyes to stare at the mirror as a shadow crossed the reflection but Damien did not appear. My sight blurred and darkness edged my vision.

"Help," I called out, but still Damien did not come. I couldn't hold my body upright, so I let it fall onto my bed. Curling into a ball and holding my hands to my chest, I prayed I didn't burst into a million pieces. The heat continued to lick at my insides as I imagined myself bursting into flames over and over. When it felt like I couldn't take another second, I felt darkness take me under, and the world faded around me.

CHAPTER 4

RAINA

"*Raina!*"

I opened my eyes groggily at the shrill voice. My whole body was shaking, and a dull pain had settled behind my eyes.

"What?" I cracked an eye open to see Kiara hovering over me. "Kiara? What's wrong?" Kiara's face was pale, her eyes rimmed with unshed tears. Alarm echoed through me when I saw her.

"I couldn't wake you," she sobbed. "I was shaking you and you wouldn't wake."

I reached for her. "I'm fine, Kiara. I stayed up really late and didn't get much sleep." Kiara wiped her eyes and sniffed.

"Are you sure you're okay, my lady? You were cold to the touch. I thought you were dead." She visibly shook herself and cupped my face with both hands as her eyes searched mine.

"I'm okay," I said soothingly. "I was just tired." I smiled weakly at her. She still held my face in her hands. "Shouldn't I be getting ready?" I gently tugged her hands until she let go. I looked around the room, my eyes automatically finding the mirror. I wilted a little when I didn't see Damien. Kiara had taken a step back. She looked around the room and started arranging objects on my vanity.

"What time is it?" I asked, slowly rising from the bed. I wobbled a little on my feet but managed to stay standing. I closed my eyes, trying to push through the fog in my mind. I glanced toward my closet, thinking about the book I'd hidden there.

"Almost eight. Your mother wanted me to get an early start, but when I couldn't wake you…" she trailed off.

"Please tell me you didn't go and fetch her," I groaned.

"No but I nearly did. You scared me, Raina." Her hand trembled as she reached for a brush.

"I'm sorry, Kiara. I didn't mean to. I'm okay. I promise." I gave a bright smile while my stomach churned. I wondered if I'd managed to release the power within me. I hoped so after all the pain I'd felt before I'd passed out.

"Here, sit," she beckoned me forward. "Let's get you ready. Your carriage leaves at eleven."

Kiara fussed over me, applying rouge and eye makeup over my face. I still looked deathly pale when she finished. My skin made my eyes appear bright, the only color on my face. She had twisted and pinned my hair into an elaborate style. I preferred it plain but my mother had insisted she do something more intricate. Once Kiara had finished, I could feel the pins pulling on my scalp and cringed.

"It's going to be a long day," I murmured.

"Nonsense, dear, you look beautiful." She leaned in. "You could always spend your time with Niveus if you want to avoid the king. Rumors are she has a wonderful temperament, and I know you love children."

She squeezed my shoulder and left my bed chamber. Heaving a sigh, I turned to face the mirror for the thousandth time, hoping for a glimpse of movement or a shadow.

Carefully standing, I approached it, letting my fingertips skim across the surface.

"Damien, I hope you can hear me," I whispered. "I'll gain the king's trust. I can ask him to help you. I know he will when he knows the truth."

"Here we are." I started as Kiara came back into the room, carrying a billowing gown of purple with red shimmering through the material. I swallowed hard, staring at the size of the large skirt.

"Doesn't that seem a bit much." I grimaced as she approached my dressing screens.

"Not for you." She beamed and looked at me expectantly. Reluctantly I followed her behind the screen, grateful to my handmaid for being there for me.

"How much longer will this take?" My mother tapped her foot, peering out the window of the carriage. I held my tongue. We were one in the string of carriages entering the palace grounds. I saw more than twelve, and I suspected that ladies who didn't have an invite were trying to talk their way into the gathering. I sighed, resisting the urge to reach up and scratch at my aching head from my elaborate hairstyle.

"This is ridiculous. Do they have no class?" She scoffed as another carriage was turned away. We were still early, fortunately, but neither of us had expected to be trapped in a warm carriage on one of the hottest days of the season. I pulled out my fan and started to waft it at my face. I could feel myself starting to sweat in my dress.

"That is not how you fan, my dear." She snatched the fan out of my hand. "Like this, you need to draw attention to your bosom." She carefully fluttered the fan near her chest. I bit back a groan, taking the fan when she handed it back and following her example.

"Better, you have wonderful assets, and the king needs to have his eyes drawn to you if you hope to capture him as your husband." She pulled back the curtain, looking out the window again.

Inwardly I groaned; since we had left our home, she had not stopped giving me advice on how to win the king over. He was handsome, I would give her that, but I did not know him, and I had always been perfectly content by myself. At one time, I would have gladly accepted a marriage proposal, but my mother drove each candidate away for one reason or another.

I braced myself when the carriage jolted forward, and my mother exclaimed as we continued. I fanned myself harder, not daring to look out the carriage window. My stomach fluttered, and my mouth suddenly felt dry when we pulled up to the carriage entrance. The door to the carriage flew open and a well-dressed footman held out his hand.

"Invitation," he demanded. My mother smugly handed over the card, and I kept my gaze straight ahead. "Welcome to the palace, Miss Walton. Will Mrs. Walton be your chaperone today?"

I gave myself a mental shake and nodded politely.

"I will," my mother answered him when I didn't speak. She reached for his offered hand and exited the carriage. I followed with the help of another footman, and they led us toward an ornate entrance. We were greeted by a butler dressed in black formal wear. Not a speck of color was on him.

"Please follow me, Miss Walton. My name is Asher and I will be your butler for today. If you require anything, please do not hesitate to ask." His lips quirked up into a half smile. There wasn't a brown hair out of place, and he had kind hazel eyes. He didn't look more than seventeen but held himself in a mature way.

"Thank you, Asher. Please call me Raina." A flash of surprise crossed his face before his smile widened, and he nodded.

"This way, please." He bowed and gestured down the corridor. My mother glared at me as she took a step forward, and it was an effort not to shrink away from her offered arm. She gripped it tightly as we followed Asher, my head spinning with all the twists and turns we took before the corridor ended and opened out into a large room.

"Are we the last?" my mother asked Asher.

"No, ma'am. One more is to arrive. Please help yourself to refreshments while we wait. I will be over in that corner if you need me."

I watched him walk over to one corner of the room, which was lined with ten other butlers. I scanned the ladies near the refreshment table and my eyes widened. They were dressed impeccably, matching the luxurious room we were standing in. Their gowns were every bit as elegant as the one I wore, and I was suddenly glad my mother had ordered a new one. Though none matched the unusual coloring or shimmer of mine, they were all beautiful.

"None of them look like they're over twenty-two, Mother." I quickly looked between them.

"That gives you the advantage of maturity. You're closer to the king's age." She narrowed her eyes at the competition and then pulled me toward them. "I can see I'm not the only mother joining as chaperone." She nodded toward a group of older women gathered at the far end of the room.

"I shall join the ladies?" I cleared my throat. "I mean, I shall join the ladies." At least it sounded less like a question the second time.

"Good, I can see Mrs. Peterson over there. Aurelia must be here. You'll remember her."

I remembered a spoiled young girl who used to visit around fifteen years ago. She barely spoke to me the entire time, and I was happy to ignore her, reading in the library all day. She hadn't been eleven and acted more like a sixteen-year-old. I took measured steps toward them, some turning to look me over before turning back dismissively.

"But she's so old," I heard whispered before I reached them, not sure who spoke. The comment made me smile, and the butterflies in my stomach lessened. They were right. I was much older than all of them, which meant it was less likely for me to be picked.

"Ladies." I gave them a small nod as I joined them, letting my smile deepen as I made eye contact with each one of them. I realized now why the attendance number was so low. These were ladies from the ten wealthiest families in the kingdom. My parents were well off, but these families were practically royalty themselves.

"Raina." Aurelia returned my nod. "Do you know the other ladies here?"

"No need for introductions." A girl with red hair sniffed. "We are after all in a competition here."

"Fair enough," I said, reaching for a glass of water on the table next to them. I sipped and smiled politely, though the conversation did not continue. Taking the hint, I moved down the table and admired the room we were in. A large crystal chandelier reflected light above us, making the room appear bright and accentuating its size.

Walking slowly, I studied the paintings on the wall, mainly landscapes of large lakes and forests. I nearly missed a step when I came upon a painting of two men. They were strikingly handsome and looked so similar, they must have been brothers. I smiled, letting out a slow breath when I recognized Damien as one of the brothers.

I ran my eyes over his face, enjoying the opportunity to study his face without speaking to him. A thrill of pleasure surged within me as I thought about talking to him that first night when I had barely slept as he told me stories of his life in the palace and listened intently as I told him about my family. I glanced back at the group of young ladies, thinking the king would probably choose one of them. If only I could talk to the king and ask him for help on Damien's behalf. I sighed, if the king had been told stories about Damien from his family, he probably wouldn't help.

"I like that one too." A young girl about twelve years old stood next to me. "I always wonder what they must be talking about in that painting." She pointed up at it.

"It's a very interesting one." I gave her a warm smile. "My name is Raina."

"I'm Niv." She bobbed a curtsey as I did the same.

"Nice to meet you, Princess," I said and frowned at her informality.

"Just call me Niv." She scrunched her nose. "I hate being called Princess."

"I can only imagine." I laughed, and my heart warmed when she giggled with me.

"My father will be joining us soon, but I thought it would be fun to sneak in and see all the ladies first." She told me, her eyes bright as she looked across the room at the chatting girls who hadn't noticed her.

"Who do you like so far?" I bent a little, leaning in toward Niv so she could talk quietly.

"They all look pretty in their dresses," Niv whispered. "The red-haired lady looks mean, though."

I gave an exaggerated gasp. "Tell me it's not so."

She giggled again. "Why aren't you over there with them?" Niv asked. I gave her a shrug.

"I wanted to get the lay of the room first." I gestured to the paintings. "I find the art here fascinating."

"I suppose it is, but when you see if every day..." She grimaced.

"I guess that's partly what I mean. I stare at the same paintings every day in my father's house, so it's nice to see something new." I gave her a wink, and she grinned at me. Out of the corner of my eye I noticed that the ladies had turned to face us, the final lady had arrived while I was distracted. As they started rushing toward us, after seeing Niv, I stepped in front of her protectively so she wasn't swarmed.

"His Royal Highness King Lucas," a loud voice rang out, halting the ladies. I let out a breath, belatedly remembering to drop into a deep curtsey as the king entered the room.

"Please rise," the king's voice echoed around the room. I heard footsteps as I straightened and felt the blood drain from my face. The king was inches from me smiling at his daughter. "Hello, dearest, when did you sneak in?"

Niv blushed. "About fifteen minutes ago." She fidgeted next to me but smiled up at the king.

"The princess was kind enough to show me the paintings in this room." I shocked myself when the words left me. The king turned to face me, and heat flushed through me. My entire body started to warm, and the tightness of my dress pressed in on me.

"Miss Walton, I'm so happy you accepted my invite." The king took my hand, pressing a kiss to my knuckle. His eyes never left mine, and he held on longer than was appropriate.

"Please call me Raina," I insisted, my heart thundering loudly in my chest. The king finally dropped my hand.

"Raina," he said, barely above a whisper.

"You can call me Niv," Niv said next to me. "I know I already said you could, but now father knows you can too." She took her father's hand and I saw him give it a squeeze. Behind the king, I could see the other ladies glaring at me. I pressed my lips together so I didn't laugh.

"You better not neglect your guests, my king," I gave him another curtsey. "I will take my leave so you can better acquaint yourselves with them."

The king frowned and nodded at me. "Indeed." I felt his eyes follow me as I left to find my mother. I spotted her in a corner with the rest of the chaperones, watching me walk across toward her.

"He went straight toward you," she said excitedly. "You should have seen the look on the other girls' faces."

"Mother, people can hear you," I whispered harshly, pulling her into a corner of the room.

"That was a good idea, engaging Niveus before he arrived." Her eyes gleamed. "You might be useful for something after all."

I sighed, watching the king talk to each of the invited ladies. "I am what I am," I said wearily, wondering if she would treat me worse if I didn't marry the king. As I continued to follow him, Niv kept turning to give me a wave every few minutes, and my heart warmed. It would be worth marrying the king to get to know her better. I returned her wave.

"Stop concentrating on the girl and concentrate on catching the eye of the king. She will have no sway over his decision," my mother snapped. "Now get back out there with the other girls, and stop standing here gawking at them." I hid my eye roll by walking away from her and taking my time to join the others.

"After some refreshments, I will take each of you for an

informal sit-down with your mothers to get to know you better," the king was telling the ladies.

I sidled up to the back of the group and tried to listen. A tug on my hand caught my attention, and I looked down to see Niv. I gave her a smile and a wink, turning to face the king again. Niv tugged my hand again; I looked down at her with a frown. She jerked her head toward a nearby door, giving my hand another tug. I looked across the room to see my mother engaged in an animated conversation. Giving Niv a nod, we slipped out, careful not to catch anyone's attention.

"Are you feeling okay, Niv?" I asked.

"Yes, but I was getting a bit bored. I thought you might like to see more paintings." She grinned at me and pulled me further down the corridor. I felt lighter the further we got from the room full of eager ladies.

"Close your eyes," Niv told me as we approached a large double door. I did, only peeking once as Niv pushed the doors open and led me inside. "Open them...now."

I gasped, whirling in a circle as I gazed upon the walls completely covered in beautiful artwork. I saw portraits, landscapes, and sculptures in the center of the room as well as an entire area dedicated to paintings of horses.

"Do you like it?" Niv asked, pulling me toward a painting of a large lake with a tree overhanging it. "My mother painted this one."

"It's a marvel, Niv. Thank you for bringing me. Much better than being back in that room with all those ladies." I bit my lip when I realized what I'd said.

Niv looked at me. "It's okay. It was getting rather crowded. Wasn't it? I wouldn't want to be Father right now."

The minutes rushed by as we examined the paintings, each one with a story Niv hurried to tell me. It wasn't until a cough resonated around the room that I let go of Niv's hand and looked back at the door.

"Your Majesty," I curtseyed, stumbling in my haste. "I'm sorry, I couldn't resist…" my voice trailed off.

"I wondered where you both got off to. Your mother wanted to send out a search party. She's an interesting woman." The king chuckled.

"Father, I'm sorry for stealing Raina away." Niv ran to him, wrapping her arms around his waist. I lowered my eyes, staring at my hands.

"I…" I wasn't sure what to say.

"It's okay, Raina. It's nice to see Niv smiling." He strode closer. "I'm afraid you missed your allotted interview with me and your mother, but we could have it now. I can ask Asher to go and find her."

I noticed he remembered my butler's name. "That's okay. I would rather talk to you and Niv alone." Niv smiled broadly to be included.

"Both follow me then." The king gave me a small bow. I followed him out into the corridor and across the hall into a small sitting room. A maid appeared behind us carrying a tea tray. After placing it on a small table, she retreated to a corner of the room.

"You're well-prepared," I said, reaching to pour myself a cup.

The king waved my hand away and served me himself. I reached to help, but he waved my hand away again.

"Now, lovely Raina," the king remarked, and I smiled at the compliment. "Why do you want to be queen?"

My eyes widened and I took a sip of my tea, trying to remember the answers my mother had drilled into me. After a moment, I placed the cup back on the table.

"Honestly?" I asked.

"It is always better to be honest." The king raised an eyebrow at me.

"I don't want to be queen." I bit my lip. My mother's head would have exploded if she heard me say that. "I am quite content in my life, though I would have liked to have children. My age doesn't make me a desirable prospect among the nobles."

"You're not that old." The king poured Niv a small cup, adding three spoons of sugar.

"I understand you're looking for a wife. Did you not find one among the other ladies?" I gave the king a small smile, only cringing slightly at my audacity.

He chuckled. "They're all fine women." The king finally reached for his own cup. "Niv, dear. Can you give us a moment?" Adoration for his daughter shone in his eyes. The young girl nodded eagerly, putting down her cup after she took a huge gulp of tea.

"Come on, Peter," she pulled one of the men standing in the doorway from the room. I saw another maid in the hallway step in behind them, and my eyes drew back toward the king.

"As you have been honest with me, I will be honest with you." The king took a sip of his own tea. "I would have happily remained unmarried, but Niveus is a young lady, and I can see she is missing a mother figure in her life. I have been hoping to marry to find someone for her."

"I don't understand," I said. "Why don't you hire a governess or a tutor?"

"I have to admit that I am also lonely, so Niv suggested I look for someone for myself." He sighed. "I don't think I'm explaining this well. I have seen the way you are with Niv. You've barely met, and I can already tell she adores you. The other ladies didn't give her a second glance once I entered the room."

"That is their loss." I tried to will my stomach to settle, reaching for the tea again. I scrambled to think of something to say. I hadn't expected the king to be so open and show such a vulnerability. I opened my mouth to speak at the same time as the king.

"Go ahead." He gave me a handsome smile.

"No, that's okay. I'm not sure what I was going to say." I shook my head, closing my eyes for a moment.

"I like you, Raina. I've heard from the servants that you have a good reputation, and you were so sweet with Niv today. I'd like to get to know you more." The king rose, starting to stroll around the room. He paused. "I don't sit still very well."

"Then I shall join you." I rose and circled the room with him. A glass door stood near the window that I hadn't noticed.

The king opened it. "Care to join me in the garden?"

I nodded. We walked silently while I thought about his words. The roses were arranged in a small maze, though not even knee high.

"If I'm correct, you want me to stay here with you, letting us get to know each other. And you're looking for a lady to marry?" I swallowed thickly. "Are you inviting any of the others?"

"No, just you. I don't want to rush into this although it may seem that I do after visiting all the eligible nobles. Don't think I'm only keeping you here for Niv's sake. I've found you very endearing, and it won't be a hardship getting to know you. I can already tell." He turned to meet my eyes, stopping me on the path. "Your openness is refreshing. Tell me what you're thinking."

I stared up into his face. "I don't know what to say...I adore Niv. She's so charming and full of stories. I can see myself quite easily loving her as a daughter. But..."

"But…" he prompted.

"I had given up on the idea of marriage, and as handsome as you are…I don't know you." Nervously I bit my lip. When he reached up to curl a piece of hair behind my ear, I stopped breathing. His eyes burned into mine, and I couldn't look away. I leaned into his touch as his fingers caressed my cheek.

"Then come visit for a week, and get to know me." His lip twitched as he watched my face.

"Raina?" I groaned at the sound of my mother's cry and turned to see her coming from another doorway of the palace.

"Only if my mother can't accompany me," I whispered quickly, taking a step away. My stomach flipped at his rich laugh.

"Agreed," he whispered back.

"Where have you been?" my mother shrieked. Her eyes suddenly darted to the king, and she composed herself and bobbed a quick curtsey. "Your Majesty, apologies. I was worried about my daughter."

"Understandable," he said politely. "I believe your daughter just accepted my request to come and visit us here at the palace."

My mother's eyes widened, and I held back a laugh at the delighted look on her face.

CHAPTER 5

RAINA

"*H*ow very clever of you to see a way to the king through his daughter," my mother said, repeating herself for the tenth time on the journey back home. "I think it was risky to disappear completely and miss your interview, Raina. You should have discussed it with me first, but it looks like your gamble paid off."

I didn't answer, staring out the window with a slight frown on my face. My thoughts flitted between happiness and confusion. Could I marry the king? Would he be the same as his ancestor, or was he the good man he appeared to be? I hadn't seen any signs of cruelty, only kindness. He obviously adored Niv, who was a delight to be around, and he fought against the vampires trying to invade the kingdom.

My thoughts turned to Damien and how he made me feel when I was with him. Even if he was trapped in a mirror, I had opened myself up to him and felt more comfortable than I had with any other person in my life other than Kiara. I liked the king, but he didn't make me feel the same as when I was around Damien. In my heart, I knew he was a good man from the way he spoke to his daughter and the staff in the palace. They respected him in return.

"Are you listening to me?" my mother snapped.

I turned to face her and gave her a small nod. "You need to take this seriously, Raina. This is for the good of the whole family. For once in your life, think of others and not just yourself." She crossed her arms and leaned back in the carriage. I knew her silence wouldn't last long, so I was relieved when the carriage pulled into our estate. I sighed, the tension in my shoulders finally releasing as the footman helped me out.

"Raina," my mother called after me. "Get your things together for when the king's carriage picks you up tomorrow. I still think I should be coming with you."

"You always tell me how busy you are here, Mother. The king thought Kiara would make a suitable chaperone, and it would give the wrong message if you had to coddle me." I smiled at her sweetly.

My mother gave me a hard look before she turned, walking toward my father's study. I turned to see Kiara, wide eyed behind me.

"What is she talking about," Kiara asked.

I grinned. "We are moving into the palace for a few days." Kiara's eyes grew wider than I thought possible, her eyebrows rising.

"What?" she stammered.

"The king has invited me to stay with him so we can get to know each other." Despite my misgivings, a bubble of excitement grew in the pit of my stomach, and my face started to ache from smiling at Kiara. "I could do with a moment. Why don't you pack your things and then come up to my room?"

"Sounds wonderful." Kiara turned in a daze, walking

away in a wobbly line toward her quarters. I gathered my skirts and climbed up the stairs to my chambers.

"Did you have a good day?" Damien asked as he finally appeared. The relief at his face in the mirror made me dizzy, but I'd managed to stand before the mirror.

"Yes," I gave him a bright smile, which dimmed quickly. "I spent most of the afternoon with Niv." I bit my lip.

"Something on your mind?" He raised an eyebrow.

"The king has invited me to the palace for a few days." I looked down at my hands, the excitement dissipating.

"Are you not happy about that?" Damien questioned. "I would have thought you'd be excited to get away from your mother."

"Yes but…" I trailed off. "What about you?"

"Bring my mirror with you. Surely they allow you to bring some personal items." He tilted his head. "Actually, that will be perfect." He strode across the reflected room.

"The king is hoping to marry me." I shivered, thinking about being a queen in the palace. I trembled and pushed the thought away.

"Do you not want to marry the king?" he asked.

"I…don't know," I said lamely. "I do like him, and he's very handsome. Niv is so sweet and welcoming, but I don't know him. I know—" I cut myself off.

"Oh is your heart elsewhere, my dear?" Damien leaned close to the mirror. "Do tell."

"I…" I took a deep breath. "I like you, Damien." My face flushed as I admitted that to him.

"I worried that might happen." He sighed, raising a hand to brush it through his hair.

"Do you not feel the same?" Horror washed over me and my face reddened.

"I am in a mirror, my dear. I have been trapped here for

many years. I can't think about returning your feelings." His voice was low and a flash of pain crossed his face.

"But we can get you out the mirror. I know we can!" I clenched my hands into fists.

"Do you know if you managed to accept the power?" He looked hopeful, and his eyes gleamed.

"I…" I hadn't had time to think about it. Kiara had woken me this morning, and then I'd been swept away to spend the day at the palace. I frowned, trying to remember what had happened when I said the spell. I had been in so much pain followed by nothing but blackness.

"It hurt," I said quietly, which was less than the truth. The pain that had clung to me, gnawing through me, had been agony.

"That just means you will be all the more powerful." He smiled sympathetically. "You won't have to go through that again. This is good. This means the power accepted you, and the fact that you survived means you accepted it. It could still take you years, even decades to help me."

"You mean I could have died?" Shock rolled through me. "Wait, decades?" Each revelation hit me like a hammer.

"No, I knew you were too strong for that," he said, looking proud. "Your grandmother had decades and couldn't find a solution."

"I promise you it won't take that long." I was determined to help him. Somehow I could feel that I would.

"You can't put your life on hold waiting for me. The king sounds like a good man. You should consider his proposal." Damien turned from the mirror.

"He hasn't proposed. We are just getting to know each other." I paused. "What if I can release you before the king proposes?"

He scoffed. "I'm sorry, dear. But with how kind and beautiful you are, I don't see you having much time. You remind me of someone I once knew, someone I hurt. I cannot do the same to you."

My mouth turned down, and my insides simmered with disappointment. I couldn't meet his eyes as his image blurred and wobbled. I blinked rapidly to hide my tears. "You have a chance at happiness. You should take it. You came in here with such energy when you returned. Imagine feeling that way every day. I can teach you how to use the power, and we can be friends." He put his hand up against the mirror.

Reaching up, I put my hand over the imprint of his, and my heart clenched when I realized this was the closest I would get to touching him.

"I just want to help," I said.

"And I want you to be happy. Why don't you fetch that grimoire, and I can teach you some spells?" He dropped his hand.

"Yes, please." I pulled myself together, giving him a smile. I knew he was trying to distract me and found it even more endearing.

"As lovely as that dress is, and you look stunning in it, you may want to take it off before spell work." He chuckled.

I looked down at the dress. "My handmaid is packing. She won't be back for a while and I can't remove it myself."

"Then I will be able to admire your beauty in it for longer," Damien said.

I strolled over to my closet, carefully arranging the boxes to retrieve the book.

"Didn't you mention a spell where I could hide the book and call for it when I needed to?" I carried the book to my bed, sitting down on the mattress.

"Yes, well remembered. That would be a great one to begin with." He gestured to the book and I opened it. "Remember, the book will give you the spells you need when you need them."

I marveled at how much he knew of my family's power. Turning the first page I thumbed through the history that the book had already shown me. Coming to a blank page I concentrated on it, willing the words to appear. Nothing happened.

"Why was this so easy yesterday?" I sighed.

"You need to see it. Imagine it and know the words are there," Damien advised. "Don't think they will appear. Know they will appear.

Bleary eyed, I stared out my window the next morning. Damien and I had worked on the spell for hiding the grimoire until Kiara had come to help me pack. I'd finally gotten out of my dress, and my belongings had been taken downstairs to await the king's carriage. I glanced over my shoulder at the blank wall where the mirror used to hang. It had been taken down late in the evening the night before.

Kiara had certainly been confused at me wanting to take it and was even more surprised when I insisted. But Damien and the mirror were now accompanying me. My mother had been up to my chambers to try and persuade me that she would make the better chaperone. Fortunately, my father had talked her out of it.

I'd practiced the new spell until the early hours of the morning, finally being able to hide the book in the "unknown," as Damien called it, and able to call it at will. A twinge of disappointment that Damien hadn't been there to see me accomplish it had caught me. I would be able to show him when we unpacked in my chambers at the palace.

"How exciting!" Kiara exclaimed, bursting into my room.

I managed a smile as she busied herself helping me get

ready. "You're quiet today," she said as she brushed my long hair. "Didn't sleep well?"

"It was a bit of a struggle," I lied.

"Too excited, I imagine. I'm sure we will have a busy day, and you'll sleep well tonight."

I sighed, thinking about the day ahead. I thought of spending more time with the king, trying to quell my disappointment at Damien's reluctance. I put the idea of the two of us together away in a hidden part of my mind. I wondered if I could figure out how to free him before the king proposed and whether Damien would change his feelings for me. In my heart, I knew he didn't return my affection for him, and I shouldn't hope that he would.

"Maybe I should give the king a chance," I said aloud to Kiara.

"Maybe you should, dear. I know you weren't keen on the idea of your mother pushing you toward him, but you were glowing yesterday and seemed lighter than I've seen you in years. That can't be a bad thing." She turned me in my chair to cup my cheek. "You deserve happiness. You have a kind heart and a beautiful soul."

"Thanks, Kiara. I'm just glad you will be there with me. You'll love Niv and the king is…" I thought of the king. He didn't seem to be how Damien described his father. "He is a good man."

Time passed quickly, and before I knew it, Kiara and I were in the king's carriage and on our way to the palace. The carriage was much larger than ours and more opulent, and I pulled back the curtain on the window, looking out into the busy streets of the kingdom.

"What would be expected of me as the queen?" I asked Kiara.

She gave me an encouraging smile. "I'm not entirely sure, probably organize and host events with the king. Raise

Niveus to be a proper lady." She laughed at my grimace. "Be a wife to the king and regent when he is away," she continued. I shifted in my seat, uncomfortable with my lack of knowledge.

"I feel like I'm out of my depth. I don't want to be a trophy in a marriage. I want to be an equal," I said, shaking my head and closing my eyes.

"You could always ask him. From what you've told me he appreciates your candor," she suggested. "You wanting to be equals is probably why you aren't already married, and you shouldn't change yourself for this marriage. Like you didn't with the other suitors."

I mulled that over as we finally entered through the palace gates. My eyes widened when I saw the king and Niv waiting for me at the palace carriage entrance. Niv was bouncing on the spot in excitement, wearing a blue gown with a rose pattern intertwined along the bodice in black stitching, and I couldn't help my grin at the sight of her.

"Raina," she squealed when the carriage door opened. A thrill of excitement shot through me as the king took my hand, helping me step down. I could feel the heat from his body as the step down brought me close to him, a blush rising in my cheeks. He wore simple clothes, like the day we had met.

"Your Majesty," I took a swift step backward, curtseying.

"Come now, there's no need for that." His brown eyes twinkled when I looked up into his face. "No formalities during your visit." Niv grabbed my hand, hesitating slightly when I turned to her.

"I'm so happy you're here." She smiled shyly, her enthusiasm dampened. I crouched down, boldly pulling her into a hug.

"It's good to see you again." I smiled when she threw her arms around my neck. My nerves quieted as I marveled at how right it felt to be here. Straightening up, I turned to Kiara. "This is my handmaid, Kiara. She has been with me my whole life."

"It's a pleasure," the king said to her, inclining his head.

I laughed when Kiara shifted on her feet, starting to curtsey and stammering her thanks. She blushed and chuckled with me.

"Kiara!" Niv threw herself into my handmaid's arms. "It's lovely to meet you."

I glanced up at the king, biting my lip at the intense look on his face. I could tell he adored Niv, and seeing her happy influenced him. He turned to catch me watching him, and I gave him a smile, which he returned. My heart thudded in my chest when he didn't look away.

"Father, can I show Raina around the gardens?" Niv asked.

"Maybe tomorrow, dear heart." He didn't turn away from me. "Let Raina and Kiara get settled in their rooms first. I've arranged for us all to sit down for lunch, and we can plan then." He finally looked away, releasing me from his captivating gaze. My entire body flushed with heat, my skin feeling too tight.

"Raina…" Niv stepped forward, taking my hand. "I helped pick out your rooms, I really hope you like them."

"Why don't you lead the way to them?" I suggested, finally catching my breath. I offered her my hand, which she eagerly took. We walked through the palace entrance, and I was delighted to see Asher waiting for us. My face broke into a smile, which he briefly returned with a bow.

"Miss Raina."

"Please call me Raina, Asher," I reminded him.

His smile returned when I remembered his name. "Yes." He paused. "Raina."

Niv continued to lead me through the winding corridors

of the palace, and my head spun at the distance between the entrance and the sleeping chambers. The king followed closely behind me, and I was aware of his every step. I turned to look over my shoulder and saw Kiara following chatting to Asher.

"How will I ever find my way?" I cried in mock shock.

"I still get lost sometimes," Niv whispered to me.

"I have no hope then," I whispered back.

"We can explore together." She giggled.

My heart warmed. It really might be worth marrying the king just to have Niv as my daughter. Finally, she ran toward a door, letting go of my hand.

Clearing her throat, she turned with a curtsey. "Your room, Raina." She gestured grandly toward the door.

I returned her curtsey. "Why thank you, dear Niv."

"Allow me," the king, who had followed us without a word to the room, took my hand and reached for the door. A tingle spread up my arm from our clasped hands. I swore that if I continued blushing, I might catch on fire. The king turned, catching my eye as we walked into the room. I almost forgot how to breathe, barely seeing the room around me.

"I hope you like it." Niv took my other hand, and I returned her squeeze. I tore my gaze away from the king. I was in a large receiving room with two couches and a dining table. The windows were so large they took up most of one wall. I could see four rooms leading off from this main room.

"I hope you'll feel comfortable here," the king said, his voice making my body tremble. It was so deep and rich.

"I'm sure I will," I said not daring to look at him. I looked at Kiara who gave me an encouraging nod.

"Here is your room." Niv pulled me away from the king, making me let go of his hand, which I hadn't realized he still held.

"Kiara, these are yours," I heard Asher tell my handmaid

as Niv and I entered a grand bed chamber. A four-poster bed, larger than I'd ever seen, barely took up any room. The room was a deep blue, which I would have thought too dark if not for more large windows taking up one wall. I loved how the light streamed through, making the room cozy. Another wall was taken up by large bookcases, all empty, and my heartbeat sped up with he thought of filling those shelves.

"An adjoining door here goes to your dressing room. The other one leads to the receiving room." Niv showed me. "And here is your bathing chamber." I gasped at the sight of the bathing area. There wasn't a tub. I could step down into the floor into a sunken area, which was the epitome of luxury. "Father had a clever engineer who has done something with the pipes. It blows bubbles at you when it is full."

My eyes widened. "I look forward to seeing that." She led me back into the bed chamber and stopped before she led me back into the receiving room.

"I'm really glad you're here." Niv turned to me. She toed the ground with one foot.

I lowered myself to her eye level. "I am too, Niv."

She grinned at me, showing all her teeth. "I didn't like the other ladies. I know Father wants to find a wife…" She bit her lip. "I hope it is you."

"Niv, whether your father and I marry…" I struggled to continue. "I would always like to be your friend, if you'll have me."

She threw her hands around my waist. "Always."

I patted her head, a slight furrow working its way onto my brow. I took a deep breath and held her. The king opened the door quietly, giving me a quizzical look. I gave him a reassuring smile, still holding Niv, which he returned. Holding his child, staring into his eyes, I was overcome with a feeling of being home. I suppressed a flash of guilt as I thought about Damien, torn between my feelings for him and what I felt for the king. Niv looked up at me, noticing her father at the door.

"Come, dear heart, let us give Raina some time to make herself at home," he said. Niv quickly reached for his offered hand, turning back to me.

"Bye, Raina. See you at lunch." She waved as they both left. The king's stare lingered on me until the door blocked his view. A shaky breath left me as I heard the door to the receiving room close.

Kiara appeared at my bed chamber door. "I could get used to this," she announced. "He looked entirely enthralled by you, my dear."

"I…" My head spun.

"You look enthralled by him too," she exclaimed.

CHAPTER 6

RAINA

"*Y*es, there looks good," I said to Asher. He gave me a nod and let the mirror go.

It had taken some arguing with Kiara, and eventually I had given in, letting her hang Damien's mirror in the sitting room leading off from the receiving room. The sitting room was smaller than the others, a private area for me to retreat to when I wanted privacy. The rooms were larger than the upper floors of my father's house, which I tried not to think about. When Asher and Kiara left, I gave the mirror a small caress along the ornate frame.

"I will help you, Damien," I whispered. I longed for him to appear, wanting to show him that I had learned the spell to hide the grimoire. Maybe then he would believe I could free him. I just needed to get the book to tell me how. My grandmother had been trying for Damien, but deep down, I knew I was supposed to free him. Why else would I have discovered the power?

"Raina," Kiara called. "We need to get ready if we want to be on time for the lunch." A thrill of excitement spurred through me at the thought of seeing Niv and the king again.

I dressed in a pale blue gown, not dissimilar to the style Niv had worn earlier. Glad to get out of the clothes my mother had insisted I wear to meet the king, I felt more myself in simpler gowns and was grateful she wasn't here to express horror at what I had chosen to bring with me.

Asher led us down to the lunchroom, and I was surprised to see it was a smaller room on the ground level with large doors opened to the garden. I closed my eyes, breathing in the scent of the roses just outside the door. The table Niv and the king sat at was small and intimate. Nothing like I'd imagined for a royal lunch.

"Raina," Niv cried as I approached her and the king. He rose from his seat as I came forward, only returning to it once I was seated.

"Good to see you both," I said, looking between them. "I'm really happy to be here." I realized just how much I meant it.

"We are happy to have you here too," the king said, pouring me some tea. I felt his knee brush mine under the table. I swallowed hard, my mouth suddenly dry.

"Thank you," I said breathlessly.

"Do you like riding?" Niv grabbed my attention. The king's knee stayed in place leaning against mine as we talked.

I could barely remember what we said during the lunch. Niv chatted away and I tried to pay attention, but the close-ness of the king distracted me. I didn't look at him the entire meal, but it didn't matter. I was so aware of his presence and felt his eyes on me the entire time.

"Time for your lessons, Niv." An older woman entered the room. She was tall and thin with a high-collared dress in black. She didn't look my way, looking at Niv expectantly.

"Do I have to?" Niv groaned.

"Yes, dear heart. If you do well, I will take you riding later this afternoon. Raina can join us," the king said.

Only then did I turn to him, and my stomach flipped when his gaze bore into mine with an intensity I didn't expect. My breath caught so I nodded, not trusting myself to speak.

Niv leaped up from her seat. "Promise?"

The king laughed. "Of course. Now get on with you so I can spend some time with Raina." The king's hand brushed mine as Niv left the room, and he turned to me.

"You are so good with her," he said. Taking my hand, his thumb stroked my knuckles and I stared at the caress.

"She is wonderful," I replied.

"Would you join me in the garden?"

"Yes," I said, my heartbeat uneven as we rose. The king still held my hand as he led me out the doors into the garden. I walked slowly next to him, not daring to turn and face him. I could feel the tension building as we walked away from the palace, neither of us speaking. Shivers spread slowly from our clasped hands, through my arm and down my body.

We approached a large wisteria some distance from the palace before the king spoke. He ducked under the deep purple vines of flowers cascading down. Pulling me with him, he suddenly turned me to face him.

"Raina, you are a wonder." The king sounded awed, and my heart thundered in my chest.

"Your Majesty, I—"

"Please call me Lucas." He reached up and stroked my cheek with his knuckles. I realized how close we were but couldn't pull away. His hand reached up into my hair, cradling the back of my head. My stomach clenched, and I could barely breathe, let alone speak as he stared at me.

"I wanted to find a mother for Niv, but the way you are with her..." He shook his head. "I never imagined how it would make me feel. You are beautiful, inside and out."

"I..." I took a step back, the king following me. My back

met the large trunk of the wisteria, and the king took another step toward me, our bodies flush against each other.

"Tell me to stop if you don't want this or are uncomfortable, and we can go back." He leaned closer.

I swallowed and took a deep breath. My chest heaved, and searing heat shot through me when Lucas glanced down briefly.

Red rose in his cheeks, and I smiled at him, biting my lip. He groaned. "Raina, please tell me what you are thinking. Tell me to stop if you need me to."

"I can't tell you to stop," I said breathlessly. "I just can't think right now."

"I know what you mean," Lucas said, leaning down and pressing his lips to mine.

The kiss was soft and sweet. My body tingled when I felt his lips, soft but firm against mine. I closed my eyes, sighing. The king swiped his tongue against my lips, and I parted them without hesitation, moaning when Lucas plunged his tongue into my mouth.

I reached up and ran my hands through his hair, the silky strands falling between my fingers. Lucas wrapped an arm around my waist, pulling me tightly against him. Heat shot through me, and I gasped into his mouth. Lucas broke the kiss, panting. I looked at him, my heart racing as we both breathed heavily.

"I want you," Lucas said, his voice deep and husky. "I never thought I would feel this way again."

I swallowed hard. "I have never felt this way before." I blushed at my admission, our bodies still entwined and the bark from the tree digging in my back. His forehead pressed to mine, and I closed my eyes, longing for him to kiss me again.

"It's going to be very easy to fall in love with you," he said.

My eyes shot open, looking into his. My mind halted as his words echoed through me, and my breath caught. Damien's face came to me, and I couldn't help the slight shake of my head. Lucas took a step back, letting me go. The sudden loss of his closeness felt cold, my body flushed with heat doused.

"It's so sudden," I said lamely, dropping my gaze. His hand was back on my face, and the cold departed as he came close to me again. His lips met mine for a second, and then he stared into my eyes.

"You're right. I'm sorry I got carried away." He kissed me again. "Have dinner with me tonight. We can take this as slow or as fast as you'd like. But I want to get to know you, Raina." His thumb caressed my cheek and I sighed, leaning into him.

"It's not that I don't want to spend time with you," I tried to explain.

"You don't have to tell me." One side of his mouth lifted into a half smile, which made him look even more handsome. "I understand."

His other hand brushed up my waist, making my entire body tighten in a pleasurable way. I leaned forward and kissed him deeply, the urge overcoming me, and he pushed me back harder against the tree. When he broke the kiss, he groaned.

"I need to leave. Otherwise this may go further," he said.

Almost every part of me wanted him to stay, but the small part that thought of Damien gave him a small nod. I found myself alone under the dim purple canopy of the tree. Reaching up I touched my tingling lips. I stared after the king, more confused than ever. Damien had said I had until the king proposed but that had happened so fast. I pushed away from the tree, my legs trembling as I walked back to the palace.

"She suits you," Lucas commented as our horses walked forward along the country lane.

I smiled, loving the feeling of riding instead of being in a stuffy carriage. After dinner last night, Lucas had invited me to go riding with him today. I'd been given a stunning pure white mare to ride, the perfect contrast to his black stallion.

"She is lovely, though Niv might object if I steal her." I chuckled, stroking Beauty's mane.

"Very true," he said, smiling. "I will have to get you your own horse."

"That's not necessary, sire," I told him. "I will be home in a few days." I swallowed my sadness at the thought of having to return home. Dinner last night had been perfect. We had talked late into the night, and he had shown me to my room. Before leaving me, he had leaned in for a kiss but quickly stepped back when Kiara opened the door to my rooms with her eyebrow raised. My cheeks had burned so much that I thought I might catch on fire at the twinkling look in her eyes.

"You could always stay longer, and please call me Lucas," he reminded, reaching across the gap between us and taking my hand gently.

My knee bumped his as our horses continued to stride forward, behaving well considering how closely together we rode.

I bit my lip, smiling. "I think my mother would try to come and visit if I stay too long." I was finding it hard to breathe with his hand caressing mine.

"We can't avoid your parents forever, Raina." He paused. "Do they not treat you well?"

My smile fell from my face. "My father treats me very well. My mother…has high expectations.

"Ah, I understand," Lucas said. "You don't have to talk about it."

"It's just…" I sighed, trying to think of how I could explain. "My father loves me. I sometimes think my mother resents me for being younger and more beautiful than she is now. She was a beauty in her own right, but my parents had me late, and I think she's found me lacking."

"I can't imagine why," he said, his thumb stroking circles on the back of my hand. The gesture soothed me, and my shoulders began to relax as my breath slowed. I told him stories of studying with my father and couldn't help confessing my mother's horror at the reading materials he gave me. Lucas laughed when I described the books she had given me to read instead and how they had come to unfortunate ends in my bathtub.

"Your father was always a good man. Brave, honorable. I never did understand his adoration of your mother," Lucas commented.

"I don't either, but Kiara tells me they were very much in love when they married," I said. "Did you spend a lot of time with my father when he was in the king's guard?" I didn't look at the king when I asked. My father rarely spoke of his time hunting with the king and his father.

"Yes, he was very close with my father. It's why I'm so glad we get along so well." He lifted my hand to his mouth to kiss it. I turned my head to look at him, and he looked into the distance as if his thoughts had drifted away to another time.

"Is it really worse than it used to be?" I frowned, worrying my lip at his sudden withdrawal.

Lucas sighed. "Yes, the vampires' numbers have grown when they should be dwindling. They've become especially violent this week, more determined. They've been getting closer to the walls with each attack, and my men are tiring."

I stared at the wall at the edge of the palace grounds. The palace sat to the west of the kingdom rather than the center. That is where most of the attacks came from, the large forest at the base of the mountains.

I squeezed Lucas's hand. "You will defeat them."

"I wish I had your faith," he said. "We do not have the weapons we used to. My father never spoke of it, but I'm sure when I was a boy he had a witch who fought with him."

My breath caught at the mention of the witch. "A witch?" I looked ahead, trying to keep my face blank.

"Yes, an older woman who could fight them with her magic. She used to stop the attacks before they started. Saved many of my father's men."

"What happened to her?"

"I've been trying to remember. She disappeared. I'm sure she was connected to one of the noble families, but my father kept her existence a secret. Even from me."

"He must have had his reasons," I said, thinking about the story Damien had told me about the curse of the mirror. Could this witch be the same one who imprisoned him? That would make her too old, of course, but maybe she knew the witch who had cursed him. "Have you tried searching for her?"

"Yes but it has been many years. My father's journals haven't been found either, which makes me think he hid them on purpose to prevent her being found."

"You think magic could help with the fight against the vampires?"

"Yes, even if it was while working with my men. We wouldn't lose as many and the vampires wouldn't gain as much ground. We are lucky they only attack at night," Lucas said.

I nodded but didn't speak. If I could develop my own powers to help the men when they fought the vampires... I let the thought trail off. I had barely scratched the surface of what I needed to learn and didn't want Lucas to get his hopes up. If I didn't become as powerful as Damien thought I could be, I would only disappoint Lucas. The stables came into view around a corner of trees, and I stiffened when I saw my mother waiting for us.

"She didn't wait long." Lucas chuckled.

"I'm surprised she didn't come sooner." I laughed with him, though more nervous than amused.

"Raina, my dear," my mother called. "I have been looking everywhere for you."

"Welcome, Mrs. Walton. It is a pleasure to see you," Lucas said as we drew close to the stable. He quickly dismounted and waited for her to give him a small curtsey.

"Call me Eleanor, please. The pleasure is mine," she preened.

I hid my eye roll as I dismounted, giving Niv's horse a pat on the neck and a kiss on her soft nose.

"Surely it would have been more appropriate for you to ride side saddle, Raina," my mother scolded, eying the saddle on the back of Beauty.

"Nonsense," Lucas said, coming to my rescue. "I admire Raina's skills with riding. She is a credit to her family and has been impressing me with her accomplishments since she arrived."

I fought a grimace. "She was saddled this way when I got here, Mother." I leaned in to kiss her cheek, and she sniffed, obviously at the smell of horses lingering on me.

"Shall we go inside for some tea?" Lucas asked, gesturing to Harold, who was directing the stable hands to collect our horses.

"That would be a lovely idea," my mother turned and started to walk back to the palace.

I fell in step with Lucas, whose mouth came so close to my ear that his breath made me shiver.

"Was that a bit too much gushing on my part?"

"A little but I forgive you," I said, grinning at him before I followed my mother inside.

~

"The weather has been rather wonderful this year," my mother continued her monologue as Lucas and I sipped tea with her.

Neither of us had managed to steer the conversation or get a word in after she sat down and started speaking. "It has resulted in a wonderful harvest. Though I do wonder if we should be expanding outside of the wall to increase our food stores."

I blanched at her comments. She often expressed her disgust at the huge wall surrounding the kingdom and how it limited the growth in size and wealth. My father was usually around to censor her outbursts, and his presence was sorely missed today.

I opened my mouth to say that I wasn't sure but stopped when I felt Lucas's hand on my knee. He gave it a squeeze, and I caught his eye, smiling at his amused glance. I let out a breath, relieved that he wasn't offended by her opinions. I lifted my cup to take a sip of the sweet tea.

"And of course, a late summer wedding would be too perfect," my mother gushed.

I spluttered, nearly spitting my tea out at her words. I had been distracted and not realized where she was going with the conversation.

"A wedding, Mother?"

"A royal wedding. Are you simple, child? Your father and I have been waiting for an announcement." She smiled at me.

I opened my mouth but nothing came out. I looked at Lucas apologetically.

"Raina and I are taking our time getting to get to know one another. Surely you don't want to put any pressure on us, Eleanor," he said.

"No, of course." She lifted her cup to sip her tea, but her eyes narrowed on me when Lucas turned to the door.

Harold stepped into the room, bending to whisper in the king's ear.

"Ladies." Lucas rose. "You must excuse me. I have urgent business to attend to."

The urge to grab on to his hand and pull him back so I wouldn't be left alone came over me. I took another sip of tea.

My mother waited until the door closed. "What are you playing at, Raina?" she exclaimed. "How have you not managed to secure a proposal from him yet?"

"It has been one day," I commented.

"You only have a week. Do what you must to secure this marriage," she told me. "I will be very disappointed if you don't. In fact, if you aren't engaged I won't allow you back in the house."

I cringed, knowing she wasn't joking. "Yes, Mother." I could see myself falling in love with Lucas, but how was I supposed to know by the end of the week?

"Good," she said, placing her cup down on the table. "You should suggest inviting us to dinner before you are due home. It is only proper for the king to ask for your hand, and it will give His Majesty time to do so."

"I shall show you to your carriage," I said, rising from my seat. I would make sure she left the grounds and didn't try to stay the night. We walked in silence back to where her carriage was waiting for her. I kept my posture straight and head high. My mother surprised me by leaning in to embrace me before she stepped into the carriage. I should have known better.

"One week, Raina," she whispered harshly in my ear, letting me go abruptly and alighting without looking back. I stood staring at her carriage until it was on the road.

CHAPTER 7

RAINA

"*D*amien, please," I whispered, willing him to appear in the mirror. It had been several days since we arrived at the palace. I spent every day with Lucas and Niv. It had been perfect, and I could easily see myself making a life for myself here. Lucas was charming, self-assured, and very patient with me. I was most of the way in love with him but something still held me back. I knew if I talked to Damien, I would know what to do.

I had tried to get Damien to appear a few times, but he was still absent. I worried that moving the mirror had somehow broken his connection to me. Niv would be arriving soon so we could go on our daily ride. She had suggested walking, but I had been unable to pass the wisteria without thinking of the king, causing my heart to skip a beat each time I glanced in its direction.

I looked at the reflection in the mirror, but all I saw was the room I was in and my own face. I needed to speak to Damien before I saw Lucas again. Tomorrow would be my last night at the palace, and Lucas had agreed to invite my parents for dinner. He was looking forward to spending time with my father. Was Damien purposely staying away? Anger washed through me at the thought. My hand crashed against the surface, a sudden anguish causing me to act. I saw him in my mind, imagining him in the mirror.

"Damien," I demanded. "Appear." Shadows lifted from my hand, swirling in the reflection. My own image swirled in front of me, becoming masculine and dark. Damien appeared, looking gaunt and pale.

"Yes, Raina, I appear at your command," he said weakly, though his eyes held amusement.

"Where have you been," I cried, wincing at my voice and looking quickly to the door. I looked back at Damien when no one entered.

"Worried about me?" he asked, lifting an eyebrow.

"Yes," I said, throwing my hands up in exasperation. "I thought you said you would be here for me during my visit, and I haven't seen you. I was worried."

"I'm surprised to hear that. The servants have been talking about how you disappeared with the king into the garden a few days ago," he sneered.

My body seized up in shock. I didn't know what to say and blanched at the look on his face.

"It is true then," he said, sounding hard and cold.

"Didn't you tell me to give him a chance? That we couldn't be together?" I said, clenching my hands into fists. I refused to be embarrassed.

"I didn't say to throw yourself at him." Damien frowned and then sighed. "I'm sorry, Raina. I can't help it. The thought of you being with another." He smiled at me.

"I don't know what to do," I yelled, turning, and pacing the room. "I thought this was what you wanted."

"It was unfair of me, Raina. Please forgive me. I have been stuck in this mirror too long. If he makes you happy, of course you should be with him," he said. "I'm beginning to think I should let go, leave you to your life, and fade away."

"No," I said, rushing to the mirror. "I have been trying so hard to find the answer. I know I can find it." I gestured and the book appeared in my hand. I was so practiced that I only had to think the words of the spell and the book appeared.

Damien looked impressed. "You've been practicing," he said.

"Yes and I've been reading about your curse." I fingered the edge of a page. "It's not completely revealed, but I believe it shows there is a way to break it."

"I will only stay if you promise me something." He folded his arms across his chest. "Marry the king. You deserve to be happy, and we can still be friends."

My heart broke at his words as the last hope of being more than friends dissolved. Conflicted, I looked up into him.

"One condition," I said, holding up a finger. "Tell me you don't feel for me what I feel for you. Then I will let go of my own feelings and tell Lucas how I feel about him."

"I don't. I can't." He grimaced. "I can't get in the way of your future, Raina. I will accept you trying to release me only if you seek your own happiness first."

I watched his face, sensing that if I told him that I would choose him first he would disappear and leave forever.

"Okay," I said softly. "But we work on this every night, only if you promise that will I accept."

"Deal." Damien reached as if to shake my hand and then shook his head. He looked better after our conversation.

My eyes widened as I realized I'd just agreed to see where it went with the king. I reached for the mirror and put my hand flat against the glass. Damien reached up to meet my hand and took in a shuddering breath.

"You don't look good, Damien," I whispered, though as I spoke he started to look stronger.

"I need to conserve my energy, and you shouldn't keep feeding me yours. I will talk to you tomorrow," he said. His image faded, leaving me staring at my own reflection, my hand raised to meet my own.

The dinner with my parents had been a disaster. Even my father hadn't been able to keep my mother from making several insulting comments about the state of the kingdom. It was one thing for her to criticize my actions and behavior but another completely to openly remark on how the king could run his kingdom better. I shuddered as I entered my room, relieved to finally be away from her. I had barely spoken to my father, but he looked happy enough, and I could see his relief when my mother retired for the evening.

Lucas had insisted they stay so they weren't traveling home late. I was glad he was getting to spend time with my father without my mother's presence but also a little jealous that I wouldn't get to see him this evening. I approached my sitting room, determined to make the time alone useful. Damien was waiting for me.

"Let's work on holding large amounts of your power today," he said, smiling wider when I entered still in my gown. "You look ravishing, dear Raina."

"Thank you, my lord." I curtseyed and giggled at his playfulness tonight. "I'd be happy to oblige." I'd been practicing with the grimoire as much as I could, but having someone who knew more about the power than I did would help.

I called the book to me. "Where shall we start?"

Damien was patient with me while I practiced simple

spells: lighting a candle, creating a breeze, and moving objects around the room with a gesture of my hand.

"Good, Raina," Damien said. "Do you feel tired?"

I shrugged. "Not really. It's coming more easily."

"The more you practice, the more your power will grow. You're doing great," Damien told me, smiling so that a dimple appeared on one side of his mouth.

I couldn't help but compare his features to the king. You could tell they were related. Their bone structure was the same, but Damien's features were darker. I looked away from him and concentrated on creating a ball of fire from nothing between my hands.

"Excellent," Damien said.

"It is more egg shaped than a ball," I said, scrunching up my nose and releasing the fire. It disappeared into a wisp of smoke, leaving behind a faint musk.

"You'll rival your grandmother in no time."

"How did you meet her?" I asked, taking a seat in my favorite chair. I rearranged my gown, curling my legs up underneath me.

"She found my mirror, and using her power, she managed to bring me forth, the same as you." Damien clasped his hands behind his back, moving within the mirror around the small room.

I looked through the glass, watching him. "But it was on my wall." I laughed. "How did she come to have the mirror?"

"Inherited from her mother," he said, shrugging.

"I wonder where she got it." I frowned, looking out the window across the garden. The sun had set, but a mellow tinge of flaming clouds still lingered close to the silhouette of the wall. I thought about the witch Lucas had told me about. "I wonder if my family knew her?"

"Who?" he asked.

"Lucas…the king mentioned a witch that used to work for his father," I said.

"Yes, your grandmother," Damien told me.

I frowned. "Oh. I thought it might have been the witch that trapped you for Lucas's great grandfather."

Damien laughed, throwing his head back. "She was quite a force, that one. The spell weakened her, and she didn't survive much longer."

"Did she have any children? Maybe I can find them and they can tell me about the curse?" I asked. Damien opened his mouth to answer but snapped it shut, jerking his head toward the door.

"Raina?" Lucas called as the main door to my rooms opened.

"In here," I called back, rising from my chair. A glance at the mirror told me Damien had disappeared. I breathed out a sigh, smoothing my dress as Lucas strode in.

"There you are, my dear," he said, approaching me and reaching for my hands. I smiled up at him; nervously my eyes fell on the mirror behind him for a moment. My stomach clenched and my heart fluttered when he clasped my hands.

"Did you enjoy your evening with my father?" I asked, my breath catching when he leaned down and captured my mouth with his own.

"Very much so," he answered when he pulled away slightly. He was still close enough that our breaths mingled and I couldn't help smiling at him. "Your mother on the other hand…"

I laughed. "She's a horror," I said, giggling when Lucas nodded fervently. I continued to smile as he stared down at me. He reached up, his fingers entwining in my hair and cupping my face.

"It is a miracle you turned out as you did," he said softly.

I closed my eyes and leaned into his hand, trying not to think about Damien watching us in the mirror. Unable to resist, my body gravitated toward Lucas, pressing against him. "Will you stay with us for a little longer? Don't go home tomorrow."

I bit my lip. "I would love to stay longer. If I could, I would stay here forever." The words came easily and my eyes widened when I realized what I'd said. "I mean…"

Lucas stopped my stammering explanation with a kiss. "I might hold you to that."

I lost myself in his kiss, no longer thinking of Damien watching us. I protested when Lucas pulled away from me, bidding me goodnight and telling me he would see me the next day. I watched Lucas walk from the room, my heart beating rapidly until I heard the outer door close. I bit my lip, my face heating as I approached the mirror searching for Damien. I pushed away my embarrassment when he didn't appear, and I hoped he'd given us privacy when the king and I shared our kiss.

No matter how much I called and yearned for him to come to me in the mirror, he didn't appear. I sighed and left the room to get ready for bed. I struggled to sleep that night, my body trembling and agitated after his caresses and touches. I understood now why some women struggled to wait for their wedding day to give in to their urges.

"It is unusual," Lucas said, peering closely at Damien's mirror. I entered my sitting room from the door to my bed chambers, my heart speeding up as he examined the frame. "I believe I've seen something…it's very familiar." He shook his head.

I wore riding clothes, having to unpack them after telling

Kiara that we wouldn't be leaving today. "It was my grand-mother's," I told Lucas, waving my hand at it.

Lucas turned. "Hmmm, you look well today, my dear." He was next to me in a heartbeat, pulling me close. "I shall have to make sure that you ride more appropriately today. Astride a horse wouldn't be acceptable to your mother."

I giggled at his teasing tone. "Maybe you should ride more appropriately, sire."

He shook his head, his gaze falling back on the mirror. "I swear I've seen this before."

I swallowed hard, giving his hand a tug. "Come, let's make the most of this beautiful day."

Lucas nodded but reached up to touch the elaborate frame of the mirror. The need to yank his hand away shot through me, and I reached forward quickly.

"Ouch," Lucas exclaimed, pulling his hand away before I could reach it.

"Are you okay?" I grabbed his hand, looking between the frame and the shallow cut on his hand.

"Just a scratch," he reassured me, raising his finger to his mouth and sucking on the injured digit. My brow furrowed when I spotted the crimson drop on the gold frame.

"A piece must be damaged," he said. "I can get it looked at if you'd like." I shook my head distractedly as I stared at our reflection. The flash of an image of Damien appeared, over-laying the king's reflection, but was gone when I blinked. I reached for the frame, nearly jerking when Lucas caught my hand.

"Let us not have two injured hands." He kissed my fingers and pulled me toward the door. "I agree. We shouldn't waste this beautiful day." He didn't let go of my hand until we reached the stables, and my stomach didn't stop somer-saulting the entire way.

The mirror had never cut me. I wondered if it was

damaged. The thought made me turn cold as I thought of Damien disappearing because I hadn't been careful with it. I longed to run back to my room and check that he was still there.

"Are you okay?" Lucas asked me. "You've gone pale."

"I am well," I said, giving his hand a squeeze.

"That is good. I have something to show you." He pulled me forward, the stables now in view.

An incredible, large stallion pawed at the ground with its front hoof, his coat gleaming black in the sunlight.

"He is magnificent," I said, letting go of Lucas's hand and slowly approaching the large horse.

He shook his head gracefully and snorted as I approached, eyeing me curiously. He lowered his head to my hand and blew hot air onto my fingers. "You're very handsome. Aren't you?" I crooned, stroking his silky coat.

"He likes you," Lucas commented.

"I like him," I stroked down the horse's neck and sighed when he bowed his head into my chest.

"Then he is yours."

"I couldn't possibly accept him as a gift," I said, awe creeping into my voice and my eyes widening. I shook my head, watching Lucas over my shoulder but keeping my movements calm so as not to spook the horse.

"Nonsense. It is the least you deserve. Your father agreed he would suit you," Lucas said, coming up close behind me. His hand reached to stroke the horse's neck with mine and I leaned into them both.

"Would you like them both saddled, sire?" the stable hand called from behind us.

"Please," Lucas answered.

I named the horse Trident. He was a dream to ride, despite his playfulness and tendency to shy away from bright flowers. I was grateful to my father for teaching me to ride astride a horse instead of side saddle. He had approved of Trident, knowing that I would be able to handle a spirited horse. We flew across the fields, keeping up with the king's equally elegant stead. I could have stayed out riding with the king forever, the rhythm of hoof beats carrying us away from my parents and the rest of the kingdom.

The sun had risen to its peak by the time we returned to the castle, the horses breathing heavily. My legs trembled as I dismounted causing me to lean into Trident slightly. The horse turned to nudge me, and I gratefully gave him an apple from my riding coat that I'd saved for after our ride. I watched after Trident as he was led away by the stable hand and felt Lucas come to stand next to me.

"Don't worry." He put his arm around me. "You can see him tomorrow." I grinned and turned to him, my heart skipping a beat when I looked him in the face. His normally sparkling eyes were dull, his skin clammy and cold to the touch when I reached up to check.

"Are you unwell?" I asked gently.

"Just tired. I have been pushing myself too hard, and Niv will chastise me for it I'm sure," he answered. "Come. We are meeting her for lunch."

I took his offered arm, biting the inside of my cheek and watching him carefully as we made our way inside the palace. My mind kept casting back to the drop of blood staining the gold frame of Damien's mirror.

"I'm sure your father will be feeling better soon, Niv," I reassured the young girl as we walked through the palace gardens. She had been talking about her lessons when she asked me whether I thought he would be better by the evening. The palace physician had reassured me there was nothing to worry about, and the king had just been working hard recently. He went out most nights with his men to thin the numbers of the vampire horde. It couldn't be anything to do with touching the mirror. I hadn't been back to my rooms yet and hadn't been able to ask Damien.

The existence of the evil creatures that plagued the kingdom didn't seem real to me, as it was for most of the kingdom. Lucas and his men fought them night after night to prevent them from coming inside the walls. I had taken that for granted for most of my life, not realizing the cost to the palace.

"I hope so. He has something special planned tonight," Niv said, drawing my attention back to her.

"Does he? And what might that be?" I said, reaching to brush my fingers along the leaves of a nearby tree.

"It's a surprise." Niv giggled, turning to me with a mischievous grin. "Race you back to the palace," she challenged, sprinting ahead of me.

"That's cheating," I called after her playfully, lifting my skirts and racing after her. I was laughing so hard my side ached by the time we entered the large glass doors into the parlor we had dined in earlier. I gasped as I entered, my breath catching at the sight of Lucas on one knee in the middle of the room. He was surrounded by flowers—from apple blossoms to roses.

"I told you he had a surprise." Niv grabbed my hand, bringing me toward Lucas. "We both have a question to ask you."

I studied Lucas and was relieved to find the color had returned to his cheeks. He looked as well as he had the day I met him—handsome with a kind face and eyes that pierced me to my soul.

"My dear Raina, last night you said you wished you could stay here forever. I'd like that too. Would you accept my humble request and be my wife?" Lucas's smile made my chest tighten, his gaze expectant.

I swallowed thickly, my mouth dry. I could see myself with them both, as a family, and the idea made my heart soar. For a brief moment I thought of Damien but pushed the thought of him away. He had made his feelings clear.

"I will." The words came out breathy, barely above a whisper. I nodded slowly and Niv squeezed my hand. Lucas rose from his position and pulled us both into an embrace.

CHAPTER 8

RAINA

"You're sure the mirror didn't injure him," I said for the third time.

"Yes, Raina. The king is unharmed. The frame must have been damaged over the years and he was unlucky enough to touch a sharp fragment," he reassured me.

I sighed, shaking off my worry. Lucas had been well the rest of the day. The physician must have been right, and he must be tired after so many nights outside the wall this week. I'd asked Lucas about the attacks, though he hadn't told me much.

"Is there anything I can learn to help with the vampires?" I asked Damien.

He frowned at me and scratched his chin. "Why would you want to know that?"

"I have all this power, and you've said it will grow, but I feel useless right now. Could I do anything to help?" I sat down, growling in frustration.

"You will be plenty useful, Raina. Give it time and patience," Damien said.

"We don't have time," I insisted.

Damien watched me thoughtfully. "Fire. That will help." He sounded reluctant as he spoke.

"I can already form fire," I said, pouting.

"Not the fireballs we've been working on. Fire so hot it turns the body to ash."

"How do I do that?" I asked, leaning forward in my seat.

"You'll have to check in your book. That is the only way to learn. Remember, *know* that the knowledge will appear and it shall," Damien said, turning in the mirror and pacing around the small room.

I called the book to me. "I feel like I'm always using my grandmother's grimoire. Will I ever get to the point where I don't need to call it every few minutes," I grumbled.

"Yes and that will happen very soon." Damien tilted his head. "From what your grandmother said, with every spell you perform, your power grows, but so does your connection to it. It will become easier to use. You won't need to say words or use them as a crutch. Your power will manifest at will."

I mulled over his words. "I just have to *know* it will happen and it will."

"Precisely."

I watched the blank page in front of me, and as Damien said, the words appeared with much less effort than even the day before. "You're right. This is getting easier." I studied the spell and raised an eyebrow.

"What is it?" Damien asked.

"It calls it blackfire. But the color will change according to the personality of the bearer," I answered.

"Interesting." Damien shrugged, looking uninterested as if he wasn't really listening.

I snorted, used to his moods during our teaching sessions. He no longer helped that much, more directed what I needed to ask of the book and provided moral support. I couldn't imagine feeling so powerless and trapped. I shuddered when I realized that was what my life had been before I met the king.

"You're procrastinating," Damien commented, his attention back on me. I shook my head slightly and started to read the words on the page again. I raised my hand and started to picture the flames around my hand. A flash of the wisteria tree from the king's garden entered my mind as I thought and the fire around my hand flickered to a dark purple. I smiled at the color change, enjoying the shimmering tinge.

"Beautiful," Damien said, watching the flames swirling around my fingers. My skin tingled, though I didn't feel any heat. I told Damien as much.

"That is because it's so hot it feels cold. You must be careful with this, Raina. It can be extremely harmful."

"I will be careful," I said, letting the flames dissipate and my hand fall. "Why is it called blackfire?"

"You know as much as me."

"I think you know more," I said, looking up and smiling at him. "You knew to look this up to begin with. Did my grandmother show you this?"

"Not your grandmother. No," he said, looking behind him. He fidgeted with his hand, his fingers twitching. I had never seen him look so uncomfortable. "I've only ever seen this used once and the results were devastating."

"I thought you said it was for fighting against the vampires." I rose from my seat and approached the mirror.

"It was used on the vampires but there was...collateral damage. Children were lost." I raised my hand to cover my gasp. "My brother was trying to control the creatures and he failed."

"That's tragic," I said. "I will be careful and only use it as a last resort. I promise."

91

"Good," Damien said, though he didn't look relieved. In fact, he was grimacing. "Let's see it again."

I lifted my hands, speaking the words to bring forth the blackfire. My brow creased in concentration as the lavender color of the wisteria tree, in the form of flames, danced around my hand. The color deepened to a darker purple.

The door suddenly opened. I froze, releasing the blackfire as Kiara walked into the room. She stiffened when she saw me and paled. "Raina? What was in your hand?"

My hands shot behind my back, and I knew I looked guilty. I resisted the urge to look at the mirror, instead noticing the grimoire still sitting on my chair. I bit my lip, looking back at Kiara. Her head snapped to the large book and she frowned.

"Your grandmother's grimoire," she said quietly. My heart jumped in my chest as I watched her approach it. "How did you reveal it?"

I coughed. "Her journal had a verse in it, and the book appeared when I read it out loud." I watched as Kiara sat heavily in the chair, holding the grimoire. She slumped, her breath shuddering as she inhaled deeply.

"I had hoped you wouldn't discover it, but you're too clever, Raina," she said slowly.

"You knew," I said, taking a step toward her with clenched hands.

"I knew it was possible. I raised you, after all."

I sank into the chair opposite her, placing my hands in my lap and picking at my nails. I took a deep breath and looked up at Kiara. She was staring out the window, her eyes distant and sorrowful.

"Why didn't you tell me, Kiara?" A tinge of desperation lined my voice. I needed to know. I could have had the power earlier, been stronger and more capable by now.

"It isn't the way of things." She shook her head. "Your

grandmother told me you would have to discover the secrets yourself. Otherwise your power could be corrupted."

My blood turned cold at her words, and I kept my face blank. Still not looking at the mirror I spoke. "What do you mean corrupted?"

"If you are guided to the power, it won't entirely be your own."

My heartbeat raced in my chest, and I wondered if Damien's help and hints would corrupt my power or if I had discovered enough by myself. I opened my mouth to ask her but decided against it. Did she know about Damien? Would she know that my grandmother was helping him? She was looking at the grimoire, so I risked glancing at the mirror. Damien was shaking his head vehemently, holding his hands up. I looked away quickly so as not to draw attention to him. I would just have to trust him for now.

"Can you help me now?" I asked her. My heart sank when she shook her head.

"You must complete tests before I can reveal anything."

"Why do you know so much?" I smiled at her, trying to reconcile her with the woman who raised me.

"I can't even tell you that," she said, tapping her fingers on the grimoire.

I reached for it, tugging harder when her hands tightened on it. Reluctantly she let it go.

"I suppose we will be having a more in-depth discussion in the future, Kiara." I waved my hand and the book disappeared. I didn't even have to think of the words. It was a moment before I realized I had done what Damien said I would. I had willed it with my power.

"Looks like you've passed the first test. That conversation will be sooner than I thought." She gave me an encouraging smile as she stood and walked over to me. Giving my shoulder a squeeze, she kissed me on the top of my head. "I'm here. Let me know how you progress."

"I will."

~

"You could have had a longer engagement and a beautiful wedding. A large wedding. This small ceremony is an insult to our family," my mother said, huffing. She did not speak quietly, and my concern grew as she walked me down the corridor. I wished she would keep her voice down.

She had repeated the same phrase every few minutes, even with my protests that we had been engaged several months now. I had tried to explain that I didn't want a big wedding, but she would not hear of it. I adjusted the roses in my hand as we approached the small hall ahead where we had agreed to have a private ceremony. I wore a long simple gown with a high neck and long sleeves. Kiara had made it for me, spending every night over the past week creating it. We hadn't spoken much since the conversation about my power, but the love she had for me was sewn into every stitch of this dress. My mother hated it, and I couldn't treasure it more. My father waited for me outside the hall door, his face breaking into a huge smile as we approached.

"You look beautiful, Raina." He leaned down to kiss my cheek. "He is a lucky man. You will make a fine pair."

"Thank you, Father," I said, returning his smile. A rumble broke the air and I shook my head. "Shame the weather doesn't agree."

"If you had waited until next summer, you could have guaranteed the weather." My mother sniffed. I rolled my eyes, biting my lip to stop the laugh bubbling up when my father's mouth tightened to fight his own amusement.

Neither Lucas nor I had wanted to wait another year. The

months we had spent together during our engagement were long enough. The only dark spot in that time together was the never-ending vampire attacks.

"Shall we?" my father said, offering his arm. I took a deep breath and nodded, my heart fluttering and giddiness spreading through me as we pushed the door open to the small hall. I smothered a gasp when I saw the room.

When Lucas had shown it to me, it was kept simple. The furniture had been removed, making the space look larger. Niv and Lucas waited for me with Harold, who would preside over the ceremony. We had both been happy with no further guests, though we had felt compelled to invite his advisors and the council. My smile grew at the look on my mother's face when we had told her that we wouldn't be inviting the whole kingdom. Lucas had insisted on those present to ensure they saw me as an equal once we were married. He wanted the whole kingdom to know that my word would hold equal weight to his.

It wasn't hard to keep smiling as I approached Lucas, surrounded by apple trees. I didn't know how he had done it, but he had put an entire orchard in the room, each planted in an elaborate marble pot. They lined my path to him and his daughter, who was grinning at me holding her own bouquet of roses to match mine. I tried to remember not to race toward them, taking each step with care. The dress trailed behind me along with my parents accompanying me. I saw Niv flinch as a loud boom echoed through the room. Rain started to patter against the windows, the sky darkening.

"Don't worry," I whispered to Niv, pulling her in for a hug. "It's just a thunderstorm."

"You look beautiful, Raina," Niv whispered back.

My arms tightened around her before letting her go and turning to Lucas. I took a moment to admire him. I was used to seeing him in his hunting clothes, less formal and still handsome. But dressed how he was now... no words could describe him.

"Raina," he said simply.

The sound of my name made me shiver. His eyes fell to my mouth when I bit my lip, and I could see a hunger in them. I could imagine it reflected in my own gaze.

"Sire," I finally said.

"Lucas to you now, my dear," he said, taking my hands. His lips lingered on my fingers for a moment though his eyes never left mine. I let out a laugh when Harold cleared his throat. Lucas didn't drop my hand, turning to face Harold. I did the same, reaching out to take Niv's hand on my left.

"Shall we begin?" Harold asked.

He didn't drop his usual stiff demeanor, but I could see a hint of amusement in his eyes. I could barely remember the ceremony as Harold asked my father to formally give me away and Niv for permission, as Lucas's only family, for the union to take place. I stared at Lucas, the smile never leaving my face while I repeated the appropriate words when prompted.

I blushed furiously when Harold finished the ceremony, saying, "You may kiss your wife."

Lucas grinned at me and leaned in for a deep kiss. My whole body flushed as he pressed into mine. Thoughts of my parents, the king's men, and Niv disappeared, and I longed to make the moment last.

"Sire!" the call shattered our moment. Lucas broke the kiss, pulling away from me but not letting go of my waist. His brow furrowed, and a look of anger flashed across his face.

"Yes, Brigsten," he snapped.

"You're needed. Urgently," Brigsten said, his eyes wild and sweat apparent on his face.

"Go," I said gently, pushing down the disappointment. "He would not have come if it wasn't urgent."

"I will return to you as quickly as I can." Lucas held both of my hands and gave them a squeeze. He gave me a hurried kiss before striding from the room with Brigsten apologizing profusely as they left.

"That was rude," my mother exclaimed.

"He wouldn't have left unless it was important." My father gave her a stern look. My mother huffed at him, standing straight and holding her chin high. I did not miss the worry on my father's face. I caught his eye, and he shook his head slightly.

Worry gnawed at me, making my stomach clench and my chest tighten. I glanced at Niv, who was fidgeting and looking at the floor. Walking over to her, I put an arm around her shoulder.

"Let's go and do something to distract ourselves," I said, pulling her from the room and letting her lean into my side. I didn't glance back at my parents.

"Did you like the apple trees?" Niv said quietly.

I gave her a smile. "Yes, they are beautiful."

"They were my idea. Father said they can stay in this room as it's so light and they will be a symbol of your marriage." She grinned at me.

My heart warmed at their thoughtfulness, and a pulse of love for their welcome of me into their family seeped through me.

"Then I love them even more."

"Thanks, Raina," Niv said, throwing herself into my arms.

The weather had cleared, so we had dressed ourselves in less formal clothes and gone for a ride. It distracted us enough that we both started to worry a little less. Only a little.

"You're welcome," I said, looking down at Niv. She was tall for twelve, so I didn't have to look far. It wouldn't be long before she surpassed my height.

Asher had come to my rooms before I left to collect Niv. Lucas had requested that my belongings be moved to his rooms. My hands had trembled while I instructed Kiara what I would need. The mirror, of course, would come with me.

"What shall we do now?" Niv asked, looking up at me uncertainly.

I grasped for any ideas of what else we could do to distract ourselves.

"What would you like to do?" I asked her.

"Not my lessons." Niv wrinkled her nose, skipping toward the palace. "I could show you more galleries or the library?"

My heart leaped at the idea of going to the library and Niv showing me around. "Sounds perfect," I told her.

The library was empty when we entered. I could barely hold back my glee at finding shelves upon shelves of books going back as far as I could see. I looked up to the ceiling to try and gauge how large the room was but couldn't see from here.

"This is incredible, Niv," I said, and awe tinged my words.

"I don't come here much, but Kiara said you liked books," Niv said, grabbing my hand and pulling me along. "She told me to show you where the adventure stories are." Niv winked, and we turned down into a section of books deeper in the library.

"This is wonderful, Niv," I stared at all the shelves, neatly arranged and numbered with a complex color-coding system. "You could get lost here."

"Madam Beatrice always does," Niv replied. "She's the

librarian. If you ever want anything, she can help you find it. Here we are."

Row after row of books. I was in paradise. "Do you like to read, Niv?"

"Not really. I can't seem to sit still long enough."

I laughed. "I see." My fingers brushed over the shelves of books, their aroma surrounding me. My shoulders relaxed and I sighed contently.

"You look happy," Niv commented. "I'm glad you're happy with us." She looked at the ground and I took both her hands into mine.

"What is bothering you, Niv? You look very pensive."

"I just want you to know that I don't expect you to replace my mother. I loved her very much but when you came here, it made me realize that while I still love her, I have room in my heart for you too. You're not my mother, but I'd like it if we could be friends."

"I would be honored to be your friend, Niv. I will do my best to be here for you whenever I can. You can always talk to me." I reached to cup her cheek. "I can't wait to see the incredible woman you will grow into."

"My father chose well when he invited you here." She grinned at me, making it easy to return the grin.

No part of me could have imagined ever having been invited to become part of a more wonderful family.

CHAPTER 9

RAINA

iv whirled around the room as I got ready to meet Lucas for dinner. I hadn't been able to sit still all afternoon, and I felt like a swarm of bees had infested my entire body. After the wedding yesterday and Lucas's quick departure, I had been wondering when I would see him and know why he had been called away so urgently.

Every nerve within me vibrated as I pulled out each gown and laid it on the bed. Niv's presence eased the feelings mildly, but I felt like I was going to explode any second. I sat down on the bed and put my head in my hands. Niv's touch had me looking up into the young girl's face.

"Are you unwell," she asked.

I shook my head and took her hands. "I'm nervous," I said simply.

"There's no need." She grinned. "Father adores you and I can tell you love him too."

I held back my laugh. I knew I loved him, but to her eyes it must seem that simple. I still felt conflicted about Damien, and this caused a churning of guilt at Niv's words. I pulled her in for a hug. But Lucas and I were married now. I shouldn't be thinking about Damien.

"Never stop being yourself, Niv." I squeezed her. "Hold your ground and never change."

She hugged me back. "I love you too, Raina. I know we will be happy together, all three of us."

Kiara entered the room. "My goodness, ladies. Will you ever be ready?"

Niv and I giggled as we pulled apart and looked at the dresses. She helped me pick a beautiful black gown with silver thread interwoven into a starlike pattern across the skirts. It was fancy for a dinner, but Niv dressed in a pale pink masterpiece just as grand. When we were dressed, Asher applauded as I twirled Niv around the receiving room.

"The king awaits you both," he announced, and my heart fluttered.

We walked down the corridors to an area of the palace I had never been to before. Niv held my hand and gave it a squeeze as we arrived at the room where we were to dine.

"You're going to love this," she said, smiling at me.

"I'm sure I will," I replied. I reached up with my other hand to smooth my hair and took a deep breath as Asher opened the door. Niv ran into the room, letting my hand go and leaving me to follow. I braced myself before taking my first step into the room.

The entire room was made of glass, a conservatory on the roof of the palace. The sky was so clear with so little light around us that a blanket of stars twinkled like diamonds above me. I froze, staring up into the sky and trying to pick out each individual sparkling light.

"Magnificent, isn't it, my dear wife?" Lucas stepped up next to me, and it was an effort not to turn to him as I stared up at the star-laden night sky.

"Yes," I breathed. "You have shown me such wonderful places within your home."

"Father," Niv called, coming to stand between us. "I have missed you."

"I have missed you too," he said, so close to me now that I felt the words penetrate my entire being. Niv took each of our hands and led us to the candlelit table in the center of the room. The king pulled out my chair, and I finally looked at him. He smiled broadly, his eyes searching my face, and I couldn't help but smile back. I saw him relax as I took the seat he offered. His fingers trailed over the back of my neck as he moved away to take the seat opposite me.

I barely ate as we talked. Niv mostly told us both what she had been up to since the wedding. I smiled as she spoke of our time together. Every time my eyes met the king's, my stomach flipped, chasing away any hunger. Eventually Niv quieted and the king looked over my shoulder at one of the maids.

"Bedtime, dear heart," he said, giving her a nudge.

Reluctantly she rose out of her chair, looking between us.

"Night," she said quietly, smiling at both of us.

When she left I stared at my plate, not daring to look up.

"Am I that hideous now that we are married that you can't even look upon me," the king asked.

"No, sire," I whispered, still staring down.

He rose out of his chair and came to my side before dropping to his knees. "I told you to call me Lucas. We are married now," he said, leaning over and inhaling deeply, close to my neck.

I gasped. "Lucas," I said softly.

"I haven't been able to stop thinking of you." His nose trailed up my neck until his lips kissed me gently. "Every moment I was away from you, I wanted to be back here. I'm sorry I had to leave yesterday."

"Me too." I told him truthfully. He reached up with his hand and turned my head so his lips nearly met mine. "What called you away?"

"Not now. I will tell you, but I have other things on my mind now."

I gasped as he captured my mouth. I kissed him deeply as he moved, finding myself sitting in his lap with him in my seat. I didn't remember him lifting me onto him. I wasn't close enough, needing to feel him against me. I shifted my position until I straddled him, my skirts flowing around us. His groan vibrated through me as I moved against him in the chair, feeling his hard erection against my core. I couldn't stop myself leaning in to kiss him again.

His hands were in my hair, making me moan as he pulled me closer. My lips parted and his tongue slid into my mouth. I was lost in the sensations he was creating. My hands roamed his body, needing to feel every inch of him. I broke the kiss, needing air. We were both breathing hard.

I leaned my forehead against his. "We shouldn't be doing this here," I breathed.

"We aren't," he said against my lips before capturing them again. His hands were at my back, moving to undo the laces on my dress.

"Will I be your first?" he asked. His lips moved to my neck, his one hand cupping my breast as the front of my bodice loosened.

"Yes," I said breathily. I couldn't stop myself from rubbing against him, my need for him suddenly overwhelming me. I broke the kiss, my head falling to his shoulder, trying to catch my breath.

"I am honored and surprised." He sounded breathless.

I gasped as I felt his hands caress skin never touched by another. My hands went up his back, feeling every muscle under his shirt as I slipped them under and dug them into his heated skin.

"Please," I begged.

"You are astonishing, Raina, but not here," he breathed against my neck. His body moving against mine slowly. He gently gripped my hips, lifting me to my feet. He steadied me, taking my hand and leading me away from the table.

Once we were in his rooms, he faced me. "Tell me you want this."

"Yes," I gasped, moving forward. "Otherwise, I wouldn't have married you." I gave him a wry smile. In a flurry of kisses, his hands touching almost every part of me, he moved me to his bed.

In a frenzy my hands swept down to his pants, unbuttoning them with my body humming as we moved against one another. Our eyes locked on to one another, and Lucas's hand shocked me as it slipped down my body, resting between my thighs.

"Please," I begged, gasping when his fingers plunged in my wet folds, massaging in a way that made me moan.

My hands pushed his pants open as he continued attending to my core. Pulling him free, my pleasure pushed closer at his moans when I stroked his hard length. I didn't second-guess my inexperience as we pleasured each other. We removed the rest of our clothing, relishing in the feel of one another.

Lucas moved over me, and I could feel his hardness against the edge of my pulsing center. I ached for him to take me as his hand slipped under my silk undergarments, pushing them aside. I arched my back as his hands gently took hold of me, waiting for me to speak.

"Yes," I said once more. My slickness met him as my legs wrapped around him, gyrating. He filled me slowly, letting out a cry and satisfied groan to match mine. I could feel his hardness stretching me, a little painful at first, and then the sensation was beyond anything I could have imagined. I grabbed his shoulders attempting to get closer to him. My eyes closed, relishing every feeling. I stopped moving, looking into his lidded eyes. He reached up to cup my face with one hand, his fingers entwining into my hair. I started to move and saw the lust in his eyes, the feeling matching my own.

"Don't stop," he demanded, both hands now gripping my waist.

I started to move against him again, matching him thrust for thrust. I squeezed my thighs around him, feeling myself getting closer to the edge. I pulled my head back as I felt my body tense up, moaning out as my insides coiled, every nerve in my body ready to explode. Stars exploded behind my eyes as I fell, pleasure searing into every part of me with wave after wave until I collapsed on the bed, my body limp. His climax followed mine as he shuddered above me. His arms tight around me, holding himself up. My legs around him trembled weakly.

"Are you all right?" he asked softly.

I nodded, kissing his neck while trying to catch my breath. I could still feel the waves of pleasure coursing through me.

My hands gently caressed his chest. "That was beyond anything I've ever felt before."

He kissed down my neck to my shoulder. "Then we must do it again," he said.

"Yes," I replied.

Later, after Lucas had taken me a second time and I lay in his arms, he told me that the vampires had used the cloud cover from the storm to surface and attack during the daylight. Their numbers were more than had been seen before. I hadn't been aware that the reason they attacked at night was because they couldn't survive during the day. I had been curled up in his arms as he stroked my arm.

"Something has changed. These past few weeks…" He paused. "I wish I knew what. Their strength and numbers are growing, and they are attacking with a purpose."

I mulled his words over as I walked down the corridor to my old rooms. My belongings were still being packed up, but Damien's mirror was still in my sitting room. I thought about when the attacks had become more frequent. According to the king it was a few months ago. When he decided he was going to remarry. When Damien first appeared to me.

I scanned my rooms, staring at my belongings, wrapped up and arranged to be moved. I blew out a breath, wiping my face before I entered my sitting room. Smoke curled in the mirror before Damien appeared, not waiting for me to call him.

"How does it feel to be a married woman?" he said, his face blank.

I tried to smile. "Wonderful."

Damien frowned. "Are you okay, Raina? You don't look very happy."

"I am happy, but…" I stared.

"Tell me." Damien's brow creased with concern.

I told him what Lucas had told me, biting my lip before I told him when Lucas said the attacks had started to increase. Damien stilled.

"Are you sure?" he asked, approaching the glass.

"Yes." I nodded. He ran his hand through his hair, pacing the room in the mirror.

"They know I'm here," Damien whispered so quietly I barely heard him.

"What does that mean?" I asked, throwing my hands up. "This all started at the same time. Was it the king wanting to remarry or me summoning you in the mirror?" I huffed in frustration.

Damien stopped, tapping his chin. "The king wanting to remarry..." I waited while Damien looked thoughtful. "There must be a connection, but I think the vampires are trying to get to the mirror."

"Why would they want the mirror?" I shook my head.

"The curse used power from the family line to keep me here. There must be a connection," he repeated.

I opened my mouth but snapped it shut when I heard the doors to my chambers open. I cringed, groaning when my mother's shriek echoed around the rooms.

"What do you mean we can't move into the palace?" My mother's screech pierced my ears, and I had to clench my hands into fists at my sides to stop myself from covering them at the sound of her voice.

I straightened as she entered my sitting room. I was hoping she wouldn't check in here. "Mother, we will be a family, and you constantly remind me how much you must do on Father's estate. I need time to spend with Niv, and I will be busy learning my duties as the queen." I silently prayed she would listen, though the excuses felt weak, even to me. Marrying the king was finally an escape from her daily scrutiny.

"But, darling, we can pass the estate to a steward. Surely you want us close by so we can help you with your duties?" she asked demurely.

I gestured to the door, moving us away from the mirror, not fooled by her change of tone. I was saved answering her by Lucas, who was announced into my rooms by Asher. Niv followed behind. I noticed her gaze fall on my young butler and pink rose into her cheeks.

"Raina. Asher told me you were here." Lucas smiled.

Thoughts of my mother evaporated as his eyes fell on me. My blood started to simmer as his gaze roamed my body. I bit my lip, feeling suddenly lightheaded. Fortunately, my mother had dropped into a curtsey, bowing her head, so she missed our exchange.

"No need for formality," he said to my mother while taking my hand and raising it to his mouth to brush my knuckles with his lips. His eyes dipped to my mouth, and I could smell the sandalwood soap he favored. I fought a smile, feeling my mother's eyes on me. I could imagine the narrowing of her eyes and the jealousy she must be trying to quell.

"Morning, Raina." Niv bobbed her head, strangely reserved.

I scrutinized her face, catching her looks at my mother. The last time my mother had visited, Niv had overheard us arguing. I was taken aback when she asked about it later. I pressed my lips together when Niv's shoulders started to shake, obviously holding in a giggle.

"I wanted to see you before I left. We are expecting another storm." He caught my eye meaningfully.

I glanced at Niv and nodded slightly, my stomach flipping at his grateful smile.

"I hope nothing urgent," my mother said, drawing his attention back to her.

Niv's hands flew to her mouth as she started to shake out of my mother's view. I widened my eyes, giving her a warning look. Which of course, made her silently laugh harder.

"Oh, I wasn't aware," my mother said.

I frowned, having missed what Lucas had said while I was watching Niv.

"Indeed, even my parents moved out when my father

abdicated, and I took over as king." Lucas nodded. "You are welcome to visit. I would rather keep Raina to myself so early in our marriage, though, so not too often." He chuckled.

I saw the twinkle in his eyes and let out the breath I hadn't realized I was holding at his declaration.

My mother's mouth tightened. "Of course."

"Can I borrow Raina for a moment?" Lucas grabbed my hand, and I followed him into my old bed chambers. Before I could speak, he smothered my words with a kiss so full of passion it was an effort to remain on my feet.

My legs trembled as he pulled me close and my hands drifted to his chest. Lucas pushed me against the wall, neither of us speaking when we broke the kiss. Our foreheads touched, and we just existed in the moment.

I jerked at the pounding on my door. "Raina?" my mother shouted. "I need to speak to you."

"Stay safe," I whispered to Lucas. I closed my eyes when his lips met mine, matching his fervor. I was left breathless, leaning against the wall when he left. My mother entered the room with a sneer on her face.

"So that is how you snared him," she said bitterly. "Throwing yourself at him like a common whore. To be young and beautiful again."

My stomach soured at her words.

"That's not what—"

"I didn't help you capture the attention of the king for you to leave us in the gutter," she spat at me, her face turning red.

"You are far from the gutter, Mother." I sighed, brushing past her.

"You were supposed to bring us with you. We will be packing up our things and moving into the palace," she said, following me.

I whirled to face her. "No, Mother. This is my home, my family. It's time I had my independence."

"How dare you?" She glared at me. She inhaled, I'm sure to berate me further, until she caught sight of Niv still standing with Asher. The color drained from her face.

"Would you like me to escort you out, Mrs. Walton?" Asher opened the door for her.

"Please." She sniffed at me as she passed. My shoulders slumped as she left without another word in my direction.

"Are you okay, Raina?" Niv asked.

"I'm fine, Niv." I smiled at her, straightening.

"What shall we do today?" Niv asked, taking my hand.

"Gallery or library?" I suggested, smoothing my skirts.

My father chose that moment to walk into my rooms. "Have you seen your mother?"

"She just left," I answered.

"Not in a good mood, I'm guessing?" He raised an eyebrow at me. "I better catch up with her before she leaves me behind. He approached me slowly, giving me a kiss on the cheek.

"I am glad to see you happy, daughter."

"Thank you." I trembled in his arms for a moment, finding it hard to swallow. "I will miss you."

"I was barely there, Raina. You have become a woman in your own right. It is good to see. It is nice to see you too, Niveus."

"You too, sir." Niv gave a small curtsey and my father smiled at her.

"Look after my Raina."

He turned to leave when Niv nodded, and I let out a breath, my shoulders relaxing.

"I like him," Niv declared. "Your mother, though…"

I giggled. "I know she can be trying. Have you decided yet?"

"Library today," she said. "I am so glad she's not my mother."

I thought of Niv's charming demeanor and cringed inside. She certainly wouldn't have fared well under my mother's care. Niv followed me to my room, where I changed into a simpler dress. Niv chattered away, telling me about some of the gossip in the kitchens. Harold, the palace's head of staff, was caught alone with the cook at one of the staff parties.

"Why can't I go to one of their parties?" Niv asked me. "It would be so much fun to dance with everyone."

"It's their chance to let their guard down. It wouldn't be fair on them for you to intrude," I told her.

She gasped. "Really? I never thought about it like that. As if they would be waiting for me to ask them to do something?"

"Exactly. Are you ready to go?"

Niv nodded, and I followed her through the palace.

CHAPTER 10

RAINA

I joined the king after his council meeting. It had become our routine to dine beneath the night sky together the past few weeks. The wedding seemed like it only happened yesterday, but it had been two whole months. To my surprise my parent hadn't visited.

"How was your ride?" Lucas asked, his eyes didn't leave my face while we ate.

I loved how he always gave me his full attention during our evenings together, and I'd started to miss him during the days when we were apart.

"Wonderful. Niv showed me the orchards and farmland you've been developing within the wall. It is a good idea, more sustainable if we need to prepare for a siege for any reason." I placed my fork down, using a napkin to dab my lips.

"We have never worried about a siege, though it has become more apparent it's possible after these past few months." He frowned, only then looking down at his plate. "I have never known vampires to fight with such organization and ferocity. We used to fight small groups but their numbers have grown further. Something has changed, and I'm still at a loss as to how we can continue to hold them back."

He pinched the bridge of his nose with his thumb and forefinger. We'd had this conversation several times. Damien still hadn't figured out the connection either, and we had been concentrating on growing my powers. I barely needed the grimoire now.

Watching the pained look on Lucas's face saddened me. I rose from my seat, walking behind him to place my hands on his shoulders. The muscles tensed under my palms, so I started to knead them.

"You have faced them for many years and have succeeded against the odds. From what Asher has told me, you've hunted them to near extinction. Something your father started and you've continued to do. The vampire numbers must be dwindling," I whispered, my lips grazing the back of his neck.

"I would like to think that, but their numbers have swelled. I remember a time before my ancestor banished the vampire king…"

My stomach lurched at the mention of his father and the vampire king. I wondered how he had turned out so gentle and honorable considering what had happened with his ancestors.

"I hate ordering people to their deaths," he told me.

"How did your great grandfather banish the vampire king?" I held my breath, waiting for his answer. I frowned when he stilled under my fingers. "What's wrong?"

"It's not something we speak of outside of the family…I've only talked about such things with my father. It is a hard habit to break." He reached up to place his hands on mine. "It is such a lovely evening. Let's save such topics for another time."

I bit my lip, thinking about Damien's words. "Does it involve his brother? Your great uncle?"

Lucas stiffened. "How did you know about the brother?" My insides turned cold at his tight words.

"I'm...not sure," I said lamely. "I must have heard my father talk of him."

Lucas relaxed. "That must be it." He paused. "It broke the family when he was lost, at least that is what my father told me." I leaned down, my arms coming around his chest and my cheek rested against his neck. He spoke softly.

"I love you," I whispered, wishing I could ask him more but sensing I wouldn't hear more tonight. "Thanks for sharing with me. I hope you can trust me with the rest one day."

He leaned against me, his breath tickling my skin. "Let's retire for the night." I smiled at him and pulled away, grabbing his hand as he rose out the chair.

"Let's," I said, unable to pull my eyes away from his.

"Your Majesty." General Brigsten burst through the door leading to the roof as bells started to clang loudly in the distance. Lucas jerked away from me, turning to face his general.

"Be careful, my love," I whispered after him as he strode away. As he opened the door, he turned and threw me a smile.

"I will return."

Then he was gone. My skin felt cold after the loss of his body heat, and I rubbed my arms, closing my eyes and hoping he returned in one piece. He was being called away more often, and I closed my eyes thinking about my power. I wondered if I could use it to help the kingdom, or if I should tell him I could help. Damien had warned me against it, but I felt a pull to go with Lucas. The thought caused a spark of hope within me, and I quickly left to go speak to him.

"You look so beautiful." Kiara put the last pin in my hair, and I watched her put her hands on my shoulders and meet my eyes in the vanity mirror.

I grinned at her. "Thanks." I bit my lip nervously, thinking of the announcement ceremony. We had been married two months, and Lucas had delayed this ceremony to keep me all to himself. I knew he was letting me have the time to adjust to my new position. "I just hope I don't fall flat on my face."

"Raina!" I cringed as my mother called my name sharply. I couldn't help the grimace on my face, and Niv gave me an encouraging smile.

"She has made herself at home in their rooms," she whispered. "I do not think she will leave after your presentation to the kingdom."

"I know. I'm not sure I should have allowed them to stay the night," I groaned. "That is a problem for the future."

I shuddered at the thought of my mother roaming the halls daily, and it made my stomach turn. I turned to Niv, touching her chin and looking into her eyes. "For now, let's celebrate becoming a family."

Niv grinned, smoothing down her beautiful deep blue skirts. The sleeves were full length and the color of black spreading into the bodice. It faded into the deep blue as it cascaded down her small figure in an ombre effect. It looked like a night sky, just before the sun crested the horizon. She twirled for me, and I laughed with her as we approached the doors. Before I took the last step out, I touched Niv's shoulder, meeting my mother's eyes on the other side.

"I will be there in a moment, you go ahead."

Niv frowned, cocking her head to glance at my mother, but she nodded. I watched her skip away along the corridors and couldn't help my smile.

"At least you have her obeying your commands," my mother commented.

"It wasn't a command," I said simply. I drew in a breath and let it out slowly before taking a step forward, past my mother. "Are you coming? Or are you staying here?"

"We need to talk…soon," she said.

"Later," I replied, already dreading the conversation. She didn't follow me out. Niv gave me a sympathetic smile when I joined her at the entrance to the great hall.

This would be my first event as Lucas's wife, and I would officially take my place as queen in the eyes of the people. I tried to squash the jitters within me but they would not settle. My stomach was somersaulting as we walked through to the great hall. Asher waited at the end of the corridor with Harold, ready to announce us to the noble families. I pushed away thoughts of my mother and held my head high.

"Her Royal Majesty, Queen Raina. Wife of his Royal Majesty Lucas Albus. Accompanied by Princess Niveus Albus, daughter, and Heir to King Lucas." Harold raised his voice to be heard over the crowd.

I swallowed hard as all eyes turned to us, each person slowly bowing before us as we walked by.

"You'll do great," Niv muttered as we made our way down a small set of stairs into the large room. The silence was so profound that the air vibrated with anticipation around us. Niv led me to our chairs, and as we seated ourselves, the people rose before us. I endured the open glares and sneers from the women who had attended the lunch to be inter-viewed by the king.

It was an effort to keep my face blank and not shy away from their hostility. My eyes fell on Lucas's throne next to mine, which was of equal size and height. My breath caught when I realized he had put me equal to him in stature in the eyes of his people to bring home how they should see me. Our people. Asher's hand touched my shoulder, and I turned to look at him with a frown.

"His Majesty has not yet returned," Asher told me.

I hoped I imagined the concern. I looked around the room, careful to meet the eyes of every person looking my way before I glanced out the window. Darkness greeted my eyes, the full dark of night. As the summer had given way to autumn, the nights had grown longer and the vampires had been attacking earlier and earlier.

"He wasn't to go out tonight, Asher. What changed?" I spoke quietly, barely moving my lips.

Asher paused. "Watcher third command were cornered near the edge of the forest. From what we could see, they were surrounded but fending them off. King Lucas took his company out to aid them. He didn't want to ruin your day by telling you."

I turned cold at his words. "When was this?"

"A while ago," Harold admitted. I saw no hint of any worry in his position. My head snapped to Niv who had been watching us. Her face was pale and drawn as she listened.

"Will he be okay?" she asked, her blue eyes piercing into me. I didn't answer, rising from my seat. I heard the rustling of clothes behind me as I left the room, our people bowing as I raced back to my rooms that I shared with Lucas.

Determination spread through me as I tore my dress off, not stopping at Kiara's protests. I wasn't sure when she had arrived. I pulled clothes out of my dressing room, ignoring the mirror I'd moved into here. I couldn't remain behind this time, not when I knew I had the power to stop this. I pulled on my riding clothes

"Raina?" Kiara frowned, standing in the doorway. "Where are you going?" she asked me, alarmed.

"Tell Asher to prepare my horse." I pulled the clothes on, pushing Kiara away when she tried to help.

"My lady?" Kiara said, more formal than usual.

"Please," I added, pushing her out the door. I was grateful when she left. I continued to dress, summoning Damien into the mirror without using words and not caring for modesty at this point.

"Raina?" Damien frowned when he appeared. "What is happening?"

"I can't hold back anymore," I told him.

"You're not ready," he cried, his eyes wild as he took in my appearance. "I beg you. Don't do this."

"I must. I'm sorry, Damien," I said, gritting my teeth. "I wanted to tell you I was going. If I don't come back, show yourself to Kiara. She can ask Niv to help you."

"Raina," Damien's shout followed me as I left my dressing room, my feet pounding the ground as I fled the rooms.

The grimoire appeared in my hands, no longer needing words to bring it forth. Quickly, I flipped through the pages to a blank one, willing words to appear with all my strength while trying not to trip over my feet. The passage appeared immediately, unlike when the book fed me each word slowly. I scanned the instructions, taking a deep breath and memorizing the page. This would require more power than I'd ever used before, but I could feel it burning through me, fighting to be released.

"My queen. What are you doing?" Harold appeared, almost stepping into my path as if to stop me.

"What I must to protect my kingdom," I said. I put my hands on his shoulders, gently moving him aside. Kiara appeared at the doors that exited near the stables.

"I hope you know what you're doing?" she said. "I saw what this did to your grandmother. The toll it took on her."

I froze, anger seeping through my panic. "I do not have time for your riddles, Kiara. What would you have me do when I can fight them?"

"I…" her eyes dropped from my face.

I turned, urgency pulling me toward Lucas. "We will have to talk about his later. You should have told me by now." I didn't look back as I left, hurt pulsing within along with disappointment. I heaved a sigh, realizing if I had told her sooner about my powers instead of hiding them, she might have been able to help.

The cold night air washed over me, the breeze whipping my hair across my face. Asher paled when he saw me. He held the reins of Trident, my beautiful stallion, gifted to me by the king during the first week of my visit.

"My lady." Asher tried to pull the reins away from me. "Raina, you can't go out there."

"Asher," I took his hands, prying the reins from him. "Trust me."

"The king's men are being overrun."

I heard running footsteps reach us. I looked toward the wall, trying to remember how to get to the nearest exit. Asher turned to the cry, loosening his grip on the reins. I used the distraction to grab them, pulling Trident forward and mounting midstride.

We raced away from the stables and I was relieved to see the streets were clear. I headed west, knowing the main gates used to send soldiers out wouldn't be far.

"Open the gates," I shouted as they came into view, surprised when they started to rise. I squeezed my legs, urging Trident forward toward the darkness on the other side.

"Raina," I heard Asher calling behind me. I turned to see him following on his own mount, but I ignored him.

Surging forward with each powerful stride, I followed the sound of the fight in the distance toward the trees. I pulled my cloak tightly around me, willing the horse to keep going. As I crested a hill, bile rose at the sight of the battlefield before me. I pulled the horse to a stop, allowing my eyes to adjust to the scene that lay before me. Men ran in every direction, away from the dead scattered across the open space.

The cries of the wounded and dying echoed in my ears, and it took every ounce of strength to turn away from them. My heart stopped when I saw a group in the distance—Lucas and a handful of men holding off a line of twenty vampires. They would be lost if I did not act. I urged the horse into a gallop, his sides heaving beneath me. My heart pounded as I raised my hands, guiding Trident with only my legs. With one final burst of speed, the horse and I flew over the hill.

Lucas whirled at the sound of my approach, a look of horror on his face when he recognized me. I held my breath, holding the passage from the grimoire in my mind. I did not have time to say the words, and I prayed that the hours I'd spent focusing my power with Damien would pay off. I tore past the king's men, hands still raised, and released the energy coiled within me.

A wall of blackfire poured out from me toward the vampires in front of me. I clenched my fists, pulling the power back from Lucas and his men. It spun around them harmlessly as I begged it to follow my will. Trident ground to a halt, nearly throwing me forward, but I held tightly with my legs.

As the fire raged away from me, the vampires instantly exploded into a mist of ash with its touch. I kept my hands up as the energy started to wane, forcing me to dig deeper and draw up more power. The purple hue I was used to seeing pulsed around us all as Trident skittered to the side. This time I didn't have the vigor to remain seated. The ground came up to meet me as I slid sideways, abruptly stopping when strong arms came around me. Cut off from the power, the blackfire melted away, leaving me blinking in the dark.

"Your Majesty," I heard, though my eyes closed and a cold, emptiness overcame me.

"She's well, just tired," Lucas answered. He gave me a gentle shake. "Raina, I have you." I tried to pry my eyes open, not knowing when they had closed.

"Are they safe?" I mumbled.

"Yes. Rest, my love. I will take care of you." My skin tingled as he wrapped his arms around me, and I gave in to the weariness.

"What were you thinking?" Damien chided. I was seated in a chair in the dressing room. It had been an effort to drag myself out of bed.

"I had to do something," I said. I sounded tired, and it was hard to sit up right.

"You should have told me you planned to do it, and I would have warned you against revealing yourself," he said, pacing the width of the mirror.

"I didn't have time to think, the horde was larger than ever. I couldn't lose him," I told Damien.

"His life is not worth endangering yours," Damien said softly. "I don't mean to scold you, but you need to be more careful. He will demand more and more of you, draining you dry. I worry about you." He sounded earnest, abruptly coming to a stop.

"I'm fine, Damien." I tried to push strength into my words, willing them to be true.

"I worry about you," he repeated.

"I'm sorry. I didn't mean to scare you." He had been frantic when I finally came into the dressing room to see him. Kiara told me the king had carried me to our bed and let me sleep for the afternoon. She had left to tell him I was awake; I waited for him to arrive, tightness spreading in my chest. "Do you think this will change how he feels about me?"

Damien looked at me thoughtfully. "Only if he is a fool," he whispered.

I heard the door to our rooms bang open, the king shouting my name and demanding to know where I was.

"In here, Lucas," I called. I tried to stand when he appeared in the doorway, my hands gripping the arms on the chair, but I slumped back down. He rushed forward, reaching up to caress my face with both hands.

"I thought I'd lost you," he said, his voice cracking as he spoke.

"I thought I'd lost *you,*" I answered, reaching up to hold his hands.

"How did you do that?" he asked.

I sighed. "My family has power." I briefly explained what I knew of my family history and my grandmother, leaving out Damien and the link to his family. I was going to tell him, but Damien appeared in the mirror with a warning look. My stomach soured, making me swallow thickly. I didn't have the energy to argue with him if his father had told him a different history to the one Damien had told me.

My hand trembled when he didn't say anything, still kneeling in front of me. He stared at my hands, his brow pinched and his face pale. I closed my eyes, waiting for him to speak. When he didn't, I withdrew my hands from his. As I'd talked, he had lowered his hands to my lap. Before I could pull them away, his grip on them tightened and he turned to face me.

"If it hadn't been for you, my men wouldn't have made it back safely. We lost many last night, but because of you we saved more. Niv would have had to take her place as the queen, and she is so young." He shook his head. "I owe you my life, Raina. This kingdom owes you a great debt of gratitude. Your family must be the one who helped us in the past."

The tension curled within me unfurled at his words. I released a long breath, letting my anxiety over his reaction go.

"You aren't angry?" I asked.

"No, I can understand why you might want to hide it, but you know you can trust me." He reached up to curl a lock of hair behind my ear. "You don't have to hide anything from me. I love you as you are." My heart leaped at his words, and I couldn't stop my lips raising into a smile.

"I love you too, Lucas," I whispered, leaning my forehead against his.

"I have somewhere to be, but can we talk at dinner later? Or do you need more rest?" he asked.

"That would be wonderful," I said. He let go of my hands and paused in the doorway, turning to give me a smile of his own.

"Later, my love." Then he was gone.

"You need to be careful." Damien's voice made me jerk, nearly falling out of the chair.

"Don't do that," I said, holding my hand to my chest over my pounding heart.

"He will woo you into thinking that using your power is your own idea. He's trying to use you," Damien said, shadows whirling around his form in the mirror. I blinked, and they were gone, leaving me wondering if I had imagined them.

"I'm sure he won't," I said tiredly.

"You are being foolish." Damien's eyes narrowed. "Please, Raina, be more careful about how much you tell him. I'm only thinking of you."

I turned away from him, looking out the window at the gray sky. As I watched, droplets of rain started to patter against the glass.

"I will be careful," I agreed.

CHAPTER 11

RAINA

"Can you teach me how to do magic?" Niv asked. She was sitting on a rock near the cave entrance. This was the fifth entrance the king's guard had found for the underground tunnel system leading from the palace.

It had been two months since I revealed myself, and despite Damien's insistence that I limit what I told Lucas and Niv, I had decided to help them as much as I could against the vampire horde. The attacks had become less frequent after I'd blasted them with fire, and we'd had a few weeks of respite. Lucas and I had invited the noble families over and worked together to reassure them we had everything under control.

Lucas and Brigsten had built and fortified a tunnel system over the years, leading from inside the walls to a nearby mountain. It was designed to be used if the vampires ever broke through and overwhelmed the men protecting the kingdom so as many as possible could escape.

The barrier spells had been my idea. I told the king when I managed to get the book to reveal how it could be done. Niv had begged to join me while I made sure each entrance to the tunnels was protected against any vampire attempting to cross through. I had started with the entrance leading from the palace and would continue covering all the exits around the kingdom, including the gates.

"I'm not sure," I said, biting my lip as I drew the runes around the doorway using a paste of sage and rose petals. It was the first time I'd attempted to use a mixture and drawn runes instead of using myself to tether the power. I had no way of knowing this worked unless we captured a vampire and tried to lure them across. "From what I can tell, the power runs in my bloodline."

"Can we at least try?" she said, her eyes sparkling as she swung her feet.

I chuckled. "Let's see what your father says." As I concentrated on the runes and imbuing them with power, Niv started chatting to Asher. I could only see the runes by the faint purple glow of power. This had been a new development since the massive release of power on the battlefield. With one final gesture, I felt power rush out of me and the cave entrance shimmered for a moment before returning to its normal appearance.

"Wow," Niv exclaimed, jumping off her rock. I swayed when she reached me, and she grabbed my arm. "Are you okay?"

"Yes," I replied, holding a hand to my head. A piercing pain lanced behind my eyes. "I don't think I can do more than one at a time.

Niv gripped my arm, helping me stay upright as we made our way back to the palace. It was an effort to keep my feet from dragging along the floor. Asher came up to support my other side, and we slowly made our way through the secret tunnel entrance in the throne room to my chambers.

"Would you like to rest in your bed chambers?" Asher asked.

"No, the orchard room will do," I replied. I had been spending more time there when Lucas was away. It reminded me of our wedding day, which warmed my heart.

"Raina?" Niv spoke softly once I was in my favorite chair.

"Yes, Niv," I said, closing my eyes and relaxing into the soft chair cushions.

"Thank you for doing so much for us and the kingdom. I'm glad you and Father met." She gave me a kiss on the cheek.

"You're very welcome, Niv." I gave her a weak smile. I walked among the trees, which had flourished inside the hall. I touched my fingers to their leaves as I passed, feeling my power coursing through them. I'm not sure when it started, but it might have been why they grew so well. They absorbed my energy when I was near, not enough to leave me drained but enough so that when I was weak I could feel them feeding it back to me as if they were alive. Small apples had started to form even though they would be out of season.

"Raina, you look lovely today." Lucas entered, sweeping me up into his arms when he reached me. I didn't hide my gasp, holding him tightly.

"You look very handsome too." I stared up into his eyes. "Can you get away for a while?"

"Sadly no, I was passing by when I saw you in here." He had dark circles under his eyes, which I reached up to brush with my thumb gently.

"You need to rest too," I told him.

"I have a meeting with my men. I'm going to start Niv's training to fight alongside them," he said.

My eyes widened. "Do you think she is ready?"

"She needs to have their respect, and I started at her age. The sooner she learns to defend herself, the less I will fear for her," he said, sadness entering his eyes.

"You can't mean to take her out with you. She's too

young," I said, pulling away.

He shook his head. "Not yet. How are the defenses going?"

"Tiring, but we are nearly finished."

"It is a wonder what you can do, and I'm very grateful you're helping us. My father spoke of when our family had help from witches in the past, but I never imagined we would have that again. It gives me hope that we can overcome them once and for all."

I frowned. "If they couldn't do it in the past when they had a more knowledgeable witch, what makes you think I can? I came late to my powers." I bit my lip, a thought niggling at the back of my mind. Something to do with when my powers surfaced and the timing of the vampire attacks. Lucas spoke again, chasing the thought away.

"We are blessed. Now I must go. Will you talk to Niv and get a feel for if she would be open to training?" he asked. "She spends more time with you than me these days."

I nodded and he smiled at me, leaning in for a quick kiss.

"See you at dinner, my love."

"I will," I answered, my mouth turning down when he left. My eyes narrowed on a leaf on the nearest tree. It was the only blackened one I could see in the orchard. I reached up to touch it, flinching back as it fell to the ground. I shook my head, crouching to study it and reach for it again. As I did it fell to dust before my eyes. I would have to ask Damien about it.

Wearily I rose, walking slowly back to our rooms and the mirror.

"You can't keep doing this, Raina," Damien chided.

"Shhhh, they will hear you," I said, turning back to see if

Kiara and Asher had heard him in the main rooms.

"Maybe you should try talking to them about their family history more. Find out exactly what spell was put on the mirror," he said, bitterly. "You don't need to let them know I'm here but that you're curious about what happened. You are taking on too much for yourself and need to share the burden."

"I'm sorry, Damien," my insides churned. "I haven't had the time to raise the subject with Lucas again. He's told me parts of the stories, but I'm beginning to wonder if he knows anything about the mirror. He's never mentioned it."

Damien pouted, disappointment on every part of his face. "I think you should concentrate on yourself. You keep draining your power, and you won't have it when you need it," he said, starting to pace across the shiny surface of the mirror. The action pulled at me. When he was frustrated, he had no way to escape to ease his pain. My eyes blurred and the background seemed to curl with dark smoke. I blinked, the image clearing, and Damien looked at me curiously.

"You shouldn't let them use you like this." He pressed his hand against the glass.

"I'm helping them. They aren't using me." I leaned back, closing my eyes.

"Do you need some energy?" he asked.

"No, I don't want to risk you not being able to come to the mirror," I said, giving him a small smile. "Thanks for caring for me. I think I just need to rest. I've been to the apple trees and they've returned a little." I told him about the leaf

"That will be a balance to taking the power back from them," he said, not looking concerned. He reached up to rub the back of his neck. "The king has been in to look at the mirror again."

I inhaled sharply. "I wonder why. He's not asked me about

it since the time he touched it."

Damien shook his head. "He mentioned it was familiar. Maybe he was told about it." A glimmer of emotion played across his face, but I wasn't sure what. I thought it might be hope.

"I will ask him. I'll say Kiara said he was looking at it."

Damien looked resigned. "Just don't be too obvious about it."

"You're looking better, Raina," Niv said. She had decided to join us for dinner this evening.

I glanced at Lucas's empty chair, sighing. He was supposed to be here half an hour ago.

"Thanks, Niv. What have you been doing today?"

As Niv chattered about her day, my mind wandered, thinking about the cave system and how many more exits we needed to seal. One was remaining and then the two main gates into the kingdom were the only weak points on the wall. Three more days and the defenses would be complete.

"Why do you look so sad?" Niv asked, swinging her legs on her chair.

"I miss your father," I said, turning to give her a smile. I didn't think I would ever be so lucky as to have a daughter. She was everything I could have hoped for.

"You won't have to for much longer," she said, tilting her chin toward the door.

I turned, the tension finally leaving my body as Lucas strode into the room. He looked pale and exhausted, but his eyes sparkled as they fell on Niv and then me. His fingers caressed my neck as he leaned in to give Niv a kiss on the cheek. I blushed when his lips met my own, his fingers never leaving my neck.

"How are you?" I asked, frowning at his weariness.

"Well, now that I'm with you both," he said, though his voice didn't have its usual strength.

My brow creased as I watched him lower himself into his seat. He gave me a small shake of his head before turning his attention to Niv. She continued to tell both of us about her day, repeating what she had said earlier about her riding lessons. I watched Lucas listen to Niv, scrutinizing his face. He barely spoke, his skin pale and pasty looking. A sheen of sweat coated his forehead and his eyes were dull, where they had sparkled with joy when he first came in.

I watched Lucas draw in a breath. I reached for his hand, giving it a squeeze. I pushed some of my strength into him, surprised to see some color return to him. He gave me a grateful smile and then looked at Niv.

"We wanted to talk to you, Niv, about starting your training," he said.

The young girl's face broke into a grin. "Really?" She bounced in her seat eagerly.

"Yes, I think it's time you started to learn so you can take over your own guard in a few years and join me on our hunts," he told her and smiled sadly.

I turned to look at him quickly. I'd thought she wouldn't join him on hunts now but, I didn't realize it would be so soon.

"Only if you think you are ready," I cautioned, though I could tell she wouldn't listen.

She nodded eagerly. "When do I start?"

"I've spoken to Brigsten today. He wants to train you himself. You will start tomorrow," Lucas said. He gave my hand a squeeze sensing my unease.

"What about my other lessons?"

"You will attend those in the afternoons, though they

won't be as intense. You will still have to pay attention. They are just as important," he warned his daughter.

Niv threw her arms around Lucas, and he let go of my hand to wrap his arms around her. "Time for bed, Niv," he said softly.

I looked up to the clock in the corner and was shocked to see how late it was.

"Night, Father," Niv said, throwing her arms around me next. "Night, Raina." I sighed contentedly as I watched her race around to my seat and do the same.

"Night, Niv."

I watched her leave and then twisted back in my seat to look at Lucas. "You aren't well."

"I'm fine, my love. Just tired." He put his head in his hands, and I was around behind him in a heartbeat. I reached down, massaging his shoulders.

"You need to think of your health. You can't lead a kingdom if you collapse," I scolded.

"I know. I just need to rest. We scouted the route to the mountains. Brigsten has a plan to try and route out the vampires to weaken them further. He wants you to join us," he asked reluctantly.

I could see in his face. It wasn't something he wanted to ask. "I can tell you don't want to invite me," I told him. "Thank you for asking anyway and giving me a choice." I couldn't love him more for making that difficult decision.

"We will take you in a week. I wanted to make sure you would be safe. I know you can protect yourself." He held his hand up before I could argue. "But I can still worry and not want you to put yourself in danger."

My mouth snapped shut. "I will join you, but spend a day or two with Niv before we go. It will help you rest and she misses you." I continued to massage his shoulders and neck, satisfied at his groan of pleasure.

"Shall we move this elsewhere?" Lucas nodded toward the guards at the entrance to the dining room.

I smiled, leaning down to whisper in his ear, "Yes." I grinned as my longing for him pulsed through me. He took my hand and led me back to our rooms.

It had taken longer than expected, but both the entrances to the caves and the gates were sealed. The week had raced by, and even after a few days of rest before we left to search the mountains, I didn't feel quite at full power. I didn't let Lucas know my worries in case he stopped me from joining them.

"Are you alright, my lady." Asher came into view, his whole body bobbing up and down with the motion of his horse. My body weighed heavily in the saddle, and I gripped the reins so hard my knuckles must have been white in my gloves.

"Yes," I managed to reply through gritted teeth.

"You don't look so good," he commented.

I laughed, but it sounded hollow. "Thanks. I'm just nervous. I've only been outside the walls once." Nausea roiled through me and I swallowed as I tasted bile.

"We are all here to protect you…and you us." He chuckled. "Trust Brigsten. He has never led us wrong before."

"Don't tempt fate," I hissed, my eyes wide.

He nodded solemnly, his lips thin. "You're right."

The horses continued down the route, the trees bearing down on us and blocking the light. I shifted in the saddle, my legs starting to ache from the long ride.

"Something doesn't feel right," I whispered.

I was riding in the middle of the group, Lucas at the front with Brigsten. They planned to find the caves the vampires were hiding in, hoping I could block them using my barrier.

It would be a test to see if the barriers worked, and though it might not hold them long, it might give us a few days respite and time to gather supplies from outside the wall. Our kingdom had been cut off from the others for the last few months since the number of vampires had increased and the days had grown shorter.

Lucas hoped we could send messengers and hire reinforcements from other kingdoms. The idea was that we could hopefully end the vampires' attacks once and for all. The thought made me sit up straighter and stopped me from thinking about what we were doing today. The ride out was taking longer than expected, and at this rate we would have to turn back to ensure we were within the walls by dark.

The horses ahead slowed, and Brigsten put his hand up to halt the hunting party. Trident pulled at the reins, lifting his head. His ears flicked forward, and he shook his head when I didn't loosen my hold. I looked up at the sky, frowning when I saw clouds creep in around us.

"Another storm?" Asher commented. "They've been too frequent to be natural."

"I agree," I said to him. "I will have to do some research when we return." Shadows circled our group as we lost sight of the sun.

"How could they have known?" Asher fidgeted on his horse next to me.

My head shot forward when a cry came from the front of the procession. My heart leaped as I searched for Lucas. Brigsten's signal to retreat rang out around us. I could hear the men behind us turning their horses. I froze in the saddle, hoping for a glimpse of those further forward. When I didn't see Lucas, I urged Trident forward, going around those in front of me. The need for silence gone, the men retreating galloped back through the trees toward home.

"Raina. We need to go," Asher called.

"Not without everyone," I yelled back.

Trident broke into a slow canter as I studied the men going the opposite way. Their faces bore shock and panic as they frantically tried to control their horses. Another cry had ice running through me, and I kicked Trident's side, letting him have his head.

"Lucas!" My shout echoed around us. An animalistic screech followed by a hiss made me flinch, and Trident danced away from the trees on my left. A man who had strayed from the path disappeared ahead of me, his horse left riderless to continue with the others. I breathed out as I finally spotted Lucas and Brigsten, helping men on the ground to remount.

"What happened?" I asked as I reached them.

"Raina, you need to go. We all need to leave," Lucas demanded.

"Then let's go," I noticed the fallen tree blocking the way through and the lone horses following those riding ahead of us. "This was an ambush? A trap?"

"We think so, we need to get as many out as we can," Brigsten said, grimacing. "The tree came down, separating some of us from the rest. We managed to take some of the horses around but not all of us made it through.

A dark shape flew at us and I acted instinctively. Raising my hand, the creature flew back but another followed, lunging for the horses. I pulled hard from my power, creating a barrier around us. Only the three of us remained.

"Let's go," I urged. "We can't do anything for those on the other side."

Lucas cursed, looking back at the fallen tree. The men on the other side no longer shouted or cried out. "You're right. We must return."

CHAPTER 12

RAINA

I squeezed my eyes shut, and they stung, watering when I opened them. My heart leaped in my chest at the view of the palace, the sun setting behind it. I looked around at the silent guards surrounding us on our journey home and then back at the sun as it crept toward the dark horizon. "We need to go faster."

We had galloped until we left the trees behind us. I had sent streams of blackfire out when the vampires had attacked to help us make it out safely. My heart ached at the men we had abandoned in the trap.

"Are you sure, my lady? You're barely sitting upright," Asher whispered.

"The sun," I said, panic lacing my voice. He turned to look at the gate ahead and paled at the sight of the sun, nearly touching the horizon.

"Onward," I heard Lucas call out. Our horses were exhausted, but we pushed them to keep going. I squeezed my legs, and Trident snorted a protest before he sped up. He broke into a trot and then a canter as we moved toward the large gates of the wall.

It was the first entrance I protected with my barrier, though it hadn't been tested by leaving the gates open. The sun sank lower. I glanced behind me to make sure Lucas was still there. He had insisted on taking up the rear of the group, and I hadn't wanted to argue with him in front of his men.

A snapping branch to my left caught my attention. Though we had left the cover of the trees they still surrounded us. I cried out when one of the guards disappeared, pulled from his horse. The animal continued to keep stride with us, its ears flat against its skull. The sound of the guard's cry of pain made my insides turn cold. I twisted in the saddle, nearly pulling on the reins to turn back. I worried Lucas might go after him.

"It's too late," Asher shouted. "Keep going." His horse came alongside mine, so close our legs touched.

Trident veered right but stayed on the path toward the gate. I could see shadows surrounding us on both sides, pale faces pressing in on our group and pushing us closer together. I clenched my teeth and held my breath, urging the horses faster as the gates loomed over us.

I let my breath out as we clattered through the gates, pulling the horses to a stop. I turned to look at the gates, which were still open, holding my breath until Lucas and Brigsten were through. My heart hammered against my ribs. My hand flew to my mouth at the line of vampires crowding the entrance and peering through the narrowing gap as the gates swung slowly.

"Raina."

"Raina."

"Raina."

Their collective voice carried toward me, hisses on the breeze as a tall, dark-haired vampire stepped forward. The voices continued to cry my name, each repetition humming in my ears. I reached up to hold my hands over them, which muffled the noises but didn't mute them.

The tall vampire was dressed completely in black, like the palace uniform. He raised his hand to touch the shield I'd laid over the entrance, pressing it flat and causing the shield to shimmer with purple across the whole gateway. His hand blackened as he pressed harder, and I let out a breath. The vampire caught my gaze and gave me a sardonic grin.

"You can't enter here," I shouted at him, barely hearing my own voice with my hands over my ears.

Lucas steered his horse toward me, concern etched on his face.

"Give it time," a voice, clear as day, made me shiver. I dropped my hands slowly, watching the horde. They appeared to defer to the one dressed in black, and I started to wonder if he was more important than the others.

"Did you hear that?" I turned to Asher and Lucas, both still mounted beside me.

"Hear what?" Lucas asked.

"They're calling my name and..." I stopped speaking when his eyes widened, I looked around to see if anyone else had heard, but no one was listening to us.

"I don't hear anything, Raina." He frowned.

I pressed my lips together and shook my head, turning away from the gates as they closed with a loud thud.

"At least we know the shield works," I whispered.

"You did well. You kept us all safe," he replied.

"Not all." I looked out through the gate, thinking of the men blocked off by the fallen tree. "How did they know?"

"I don't know," Lucas said. He looked defeated, every part of him weighed down by the burden of protecting the kingdom.

Asher dismounted and came around to help me down.

My legs gave out as I landed, putting all my weight on Asher and relying on him to hold me up.

"My lady," Brigsten rushed toward me across the court-yard, soon at my side with Lucas and Asher. His eyes fell on the closed gates. "That was close. I thought they had us." He frowned.

"It felt like they could have but were holding back," Asher told him.

I thought of their hissed whispers of my name, deciding not to let the men know I could hear them speak.

"I'm okay," I said, holding my hand out when Asher reached for me. "Just a little tired." I gave them a stiff smile.

Lucas put his arm around me. "Let me accompany you back to our rooms. You can get some rest."

"Only if you join me," I whispered.

Lucas's eyes met mine, and I gave him a sultry smile. At least I tried to. But my limbs weighed me down and sleep pulled at me.

"I can handle it from here, sire. Both of you should get some rest." Brigsten winked at me and then turned to speak to the guards.

"Asher, take the queen to our rooms. I will follow shortly once I've made arrangements here." Lucas gave my hand a squeeze.

I stumbled toward the palace with Asher taking my weight at times.

Kiara helped me into bed, where I tried to keep my eyes open to wait for Lucas, but they drifted closed of their own accord. I finally gave up fighting the weariness in my body, allowing sleep to take me.

～

I woke with a jolt, unsure of what had pulled me from the depths of exhausted sleep. Reaching across the bed, my hand met a cold pillow. I frowned, reaching up to rub my eyes clear and look around the room. I couldn't see through the darkness of our bed chamber, but my head turned to the direction of my dressing room, where a faint light trickled under a crack in the door. I rose from the bed, shivering when my feet touched the cold carpet, and padded toward my dressing room.

"Lucas," I called when I opened the door.

Lucas's back was too me, and he stared into the mirror. I couldn't see his reflection from here so I moved closer.

"What are you doing?" I yawned as I approached, touching his arm. I pulled gently when he didn't answer, my stomach clenching when he didn't move.

"Lucas?" I said firmly; he still didn't turn. I faced the mirror, confused when I didn't see Lucas's reflection. I didn't see Damien either, just a smoky blackness that appeared to consume all the light, even that from the candle Lucas held. I stood in front of him, blocking his view, and the blood drained from my face when I realized how pale he looked. I pushed against his chest, frustration pulling at me when he didn't move.

"Lucas, you're scaring me," I cried, tears beginning to form and blurring my vision. I turned to the mirror again. "Damien. What is happening?"

Damien didn't appear. The mirror was a dark pit that I didn't recognize. Grabbing Lucas by the shoulders, I pushed him backward, despair clawing at me when he didn't move.

"Lucas, please," I begged.

"Raina?"

I breathed a sigh of relief when his arms came around me. "Lucas?"

"What happened?"

I bit my lip. "I don't know. I just found you staring at my mirror." I clung to him, looking over my shoulder to check the mirror. To my surprise, it looked normal.

"I thought I heard a noise..." he started to say.

I frowned when he didn't finish. "Let's get you to bed. Have you slept at all?" I asked.

"Not yet." He didn't fight me when I took his hand and pulled him through to our bed chambers.

Lucas shook his head, color returning to his face. He fell rather than stepped toward the bed, falling flat fully clothed. I got in beside him, stroking his hair and listening to his breathing. I eyed the door to the dressing room, determined to speak to Damien the next morning.

Lucas had left when I woke up this morning, and the bed next to me was cold. I sighed, disappointed. He had been quiet the last few days, and I hadn't seen much of him. I'd gotten used to him disappearing at all hours the last few weeks, though. I dressed wearily, dreading the day ahead. I had been putting off meeting my mother for weeks since the night I was presented to the kingdom as their queen.

She had attempted to visit nearly every day, but the use of my abilities to protect the kingdom had taken all my time. It didn't help that I was dreading the conversation she wanted to have. Asher had told me she was returning today, and I wanted to put an end to her behavior. We kept going around in circles, and I didn't want to be used for my mother's desire to be moved into the palace. I was acting like a child, but after years of my mother's constant scrutiny, I couldn't have her living here.

I glared at the mirror on the wall. Damien didn't appear, even when I summoned him. I worried that something had happened with the mirror since I first found Lucas staring into it a few days ago. I had found Lucas staring into the mirror every night since. I had no idea why he approached it each night or what was happening to him, and I was desperate for some answers. I sighed, walking through to our receiving rooms and suppressing a groan when I saw Asher waiting for me.

"Your mother is here," Asher said and gave me a wry smile. "Are you going to speak to her this time?"

"I have time this morning, better get it over with," I said, sighing and rubbing my eyes. I checked my appearance and followed Asher to a parlor with doors opening to the gardens. I frequently dined here with Niv and Lucas.

My mother was sitting, tea already poured with a careful look on her face. Her gaze swept over me, her lip curling when she obviously found me lacking. I fought the urge to fidget and bow my head.

"Say your piece," I said to my mother, taking a seat opposite her and helping myself to tea. I glanced out the window at the sunlight streaming through. I blinked against the brightness, taking a sip of tea as I waited for my mother to speak.

She snorted. "At least you could show some respect to your mother," she said, sneering. "You could have chosen an outfit more befitting of the kingdom's queen."

"This pleases me," I said, placing my teacup down on the table so I didn't tighten my grip on it.

I wore a tunic and men's riding pants. It was difficult to ride in a cumbersome gown, and this gave me more ease of movement. My mother had never been practical, and I had never appreciated her taste in elegant clothing.

"It is as plain as you are stupid. You need to show your wealth and power to gain the respect of the nobles. It is the only way your father and I will be able to increase our status."

I turned to face the window again and rolled my eyes out of my mother's sight. I looked out at the palace grounds, and my eyes fell on the wisteria tree. My cheeks heated as I thought of the walk I'd had with Lucas when I first stayed at the palace. I only cared about what he thought of me. I opened my mouth to tell my mother that I didn't care about the nobles, but she spoke before me.

"Now if only you weren't so old, you could bear an heir of your own. If it is a son, you could ask the king to make him the crown prince."

My mouth went dry. "But Niv is the heir. She will make a great queen. And I am not that old," I grumbled.

"What of our family? Our blood on the throne…" Her eyes sparkled at the thought.

"Mother," I scolded and her eyes flashed in anger.

"Don't you dare disobey me, girl. I have worked too hard to increase our status, and my efforts got your father and me into the palace. No thanks to you." Her face suddenly lit up as I saw another idea cross her mind. "Even better if the king were to perish. I heard he had taken ill. Rumors say he has made some foolish decisions. You could take his place until Niv comes of age. By then she will be under your control."

"Mother!" My mouth hung open in shock, and my stomach clenched at the mention of rumors. I would have to talk to Asher and see what was being said. "I do not want him to perish. I love him."

"A foolish notion," she said, coming close to me. "You need to rid yourself of these thoughts and think of your family. I have a concoction you can slip into a drink. No one will suspect."

I gritted my teeth, horror surging through me, so used to

holding back when it came to my mother that my outburst shocked even me.

"Niveus and Lucas are my family. How dare you talk of harming either of them." The sound of my teacup hitting the floor reached me before I realized I had stood. Shoving my chair and the table away from me, I took a step toward my mother as I fought to control the rising heat simmering within me. I slapped her hand away when she reached up to push me backward.

"Don't defy me. I raised you better than this." She reached out and gripped my arm. Her eyes were wide as I stood, looming over her. "You have married the king, taken the first steps. Let us move into the palace with you, and we can take care of you as we always have. We can run this kingdom between us."

I yanked my arm back, watching her eyes widen. "No." Fury welled within me, and a surge of power stirred in my center. Viciousness and darkness spread through me, and my mouth lifted into a malicious smile. My hand raised as if on its own, power uncurling from within me.

I knew I should fight it, but part of me didn't want to. My body wasn't mine to control in that moment as I let something dwelling within me take over. Damien's image appeared in my mind, blocking my sight of the room around me and my mother. I thought I saw a look of triumph on his face, but in the next moment he was gone.

"Raina?" My mother had paled, her chin trembling as she looked at me. She stared at the dark hum of purple power sparking around my hand.

"I have had enough of you," I snapped, feeling the power push out of my raised hand.

My mother was flung backward and crumpled to the floor. She was slumped, not moving as my breathing quickened. I lowered my hand and cocked my head at her form. I knew I should be feeling some emotion at what had just happened, but I felt nothing.

"Raina?" she sobbed, looking up at me. "What have you done?"

The darkness pulsed inside me and then vanished, leaving me blinking and lowering my hand to my side. I could only stare at my mother, a rush of fear finally surfacing.

"What have you done?" Damien's whisper caressed my mind. I shook my head, thinking I had imagined it. "You're a vicious creature, and you will be magnificent."

I shuddered, as the words became my own. I lifted my face, narrowing my eyes at my mother. I gave her a hard look, assessing how badly hurt she was. I felt a pulse of disappointment in me when she rose, which confused me further. The need for her to hurt as much as she had hurt me took over, and I pushed away the guilt.

I held my head high. "You will tell no one of this, and you will stay out of my business." My words were cold and not entirely my own. I paused, watching my mother with a predatory stare as she smoothed down her dress and gave me a small curtsey.

"Yes, my queen," she choked out, fleeing from the room.

The dark presence finally left once she was gone. I looked down at my trembling fingers, blinking away the moisture that made my eyes sting. Had Damien's voice been in my head, or were they my own words I imagined in his voice? My legs wobbled, and I barely caught myself before I stumbled forward. I grabbed the table and slowly lowered into my chair.

"Raina?" Kiara called, gently pushing the door open as I sat with my head in my hands.

I drew in a breath before I raised my head to look at her. She was at my side in a heartbeat.

"What happened? Your mother just left, and she was

white as a sheet," she said, smoothing my hair down. Her arms came around me, and she held me in the way she had when I was a child.

"I need to know more, Kiara. I feel like I'm drowning, and I don't know how to save everyone," I said, sniffling as a tear fell down my cheek. "I need to know what you aren't telling me."

"I wish I could," her voice broke. "But I could make everything so much worse."

"How can it get worse?" I cried.

"It can. You must trust me. Your grandmother was very clear about when I could tell you what you need to know," she replied.

"I don't understand how keeping me in the dark will help," I said, pulling away from her. I wiped my face. "What tests must I pass?"

"I don't know." She sighed, wringing her hands. "Constance said I would know when the time is right. She knew a path must be followed but didn't tell me specifics."

I narrowed my eyes at her. "Why don't I entirely believe you?" I stared at her, raising my eyebrow when she didn't speak.

Kiara raised her hands and then tilted her head when the door opened. Asher took a step into the room, looking between us.

"Sorry to interrupt." He paused, biting his lip. "The king needs you, my queen."

CHAPTER 13

RAINA

I rushed forward to Lucas who lay slouched against a stable door. "What happened?"

"I'm fine," he insisted. "Just lightheaded."

"He fell off his horse," Brigsten told me quietly as I reached them. "He lost consciousness for a few minutes but appears fine now."

"Probably just exhausted. You're doing too much…sire." I bent down to the ground, placing my hand on his head. I flinched back when I touched his ice-cold skin. "You need to rest."

"I am resting. I'm sitting down. Aren't I?" I caught a smile, and my squirming stomach relaxed a little.

"How about an afternoon in bed? I think we both deserve it," I said. I tried to sound playful, but my chest tightened at how weak he appeared.

"I can't rest. I have too much to do. We think there will be another attack with the cloud cover coming through."

My head turned to the clear sky and I frowned.

"You can't see it from here, but clouds are gathering in the west," Brigsten informed me. "We think they will come over in the next hour."

I swallowed hard. "I will stay then and Brigsten is here. You do not need to throw yourself into every battle."

"Ah, my queen, always volunteering to save the day." He smiled at me. "I can't leave you to face them alone."

"If you can stand, you can stay," I challenged, standing in front of him. I looked around, grateful that someone had had the foresight to clear the stables. I caught Brigsten's worried gaze, guessing it was him.

We watched as Lucas pushed his feet under him and used the stable door to pull himself up. I held my breath as he rose from the ground, almost making it halfway to standing before he collapsed again. I reached for him but Brigsten beat me to it.

"Asher," I called. "Help the king to his chambers and send for the physician. We will prepare for an attack." I glanced at Brigsten, relief numbing me for a moment when he nodded. I bit my lip as Asher helped Lucas to his feet, calling another man over whose name I didn't know.

Before he left, Lucas reached for Brigsten, gripping his shoulder. "You know my wishes."

"I do, sire," Brigsten answered. "Rest will help. You'll be back before you know it."

I stood silently as Lucas left, not supporting his own weight. "How long has he been like this?" I turned to face Brigsten when Lucas was no longer in view.

"I suspect longer than I realized." Brigsten lifted a hand to wipe his brow. "This last week he has been visibly worse. He was hiding it well before then."

"He's barely sleeping," I confessed, thinking about Lucas staring into the mirror every night. Was it something to do with the curse? I needed to speak to Damien but hadn't been able to talk to him yet. It wasn't like him to be absent this long. What if the mirror had finally drained the energy from him and had moved on to a blood relative…Lucas? The thought made my stomach clench and my heart ache at the loss of my friend. I couldn't let that happen to Lucas.

"He wants you to take his place. I believe he suspected he would worsen."

"What do you mean?" I said, nearly taking a step back.

"Leading the king's men. He has put you equal in power. That means you lead when he is otherwise detained."

I reeled at the thought of having to lead the men into a battle. "I know nothing of fighting."

"But I do. I can give you the best options, and you make a decision on the advice of those around you."

"I can't," I whispered, taking a step closer to him. I looked sideways, but we appeared to be alone. "I am not ready for this."

"No one ever is." Brigsten smiled at me. "I will be with you."

"I need a moment," I said, striding toward the stables. Trident wasn't in his usual stall but the smell of the straw and his scent gave me comfort.

"Not too long," Brigsten warned. "I will await your orders."

I gulped, leaning against the stable door. I closed my eyes and shook my head as I let his words sink in. Lucas's weak demeanor and pale face flashed through my mind. I needed to get back to the mirror and find out from Damien what was going on. But duty to the kingdom held me back. I braced myself on the stall door, allowing myself to take a deep breath. I blew it out slowly, pushing away from the stables and striding to the gate where I knew Brigsten and the king's men waited.

∾

Trident nudged me as I stumbled back to the stables. I held his reins loosely, barely having to lead him. He had kept me safe and out of danger during the skirmishes, but we had lost more men than we should. Even one lost man was too many. The thought of those we had to leave behind pulled at me, and I scrunched my face up, letting myself feel the pain of their loss.

"You did well," Brigsten said, making my heart jump in my chest at his sudden presence.

"It could have gone better," I admitted.

"It could have been worse. Your powers kept most of us safe. It would have been worse without you there. You kept your head and did what you could," he said, bowing his head in respect. "The king chose well for his queen."

I nodded slowly, too tired to answer. I wordlessly handed the reins to Asher to make sure Trident was taken care of, giving him a small smile.

"I know you're tired, but we need you in your rooms. The king has been waiting there for you with Niveus and..." Asher's voice trailed off.

"What?" I asked, my heart in my throat making it hard to swallow.

"He's worse?" Brigsten asked, slumping when Asher nodded.

"I will go immediately," I told him, pushing away from Asher and stumbling forward. Every step back to our chambers was an effort. Weariness threatened to drag me to the floor as I chose the shortest path through the palace. Despite the short distance, it took me longer than usual.

I froze when I saw Lucas slumped in a chair by the window. His skin was even paler than the last time I'd seen him outside the stables, and his eyes were sunken into his head. Dark smudges under them gave him a skeletal appearance.

"What's wrong with him?" Niv cried as I approached, looking up at me from the floor with tears glistening on her cheeks. She looked up from her position, seated by his chair and gripping his hand.

"I don't know." I turned to Asher. "Help me get him to bed. Then send for the physician."

"He's already been and he hasn't seen anything like it," Asher replied. My arms strained under Lucas's weight, sweat trickling down my back and my legs feeling weaker still.

"What can we do then?" I asked. We laid him on the bed and I collapsed next to him.

Asher coughed awkwardly. "He said the king needs rest."

Niv curled up next to me, and my arm strained as I reached around to hug her. I didn't hear Asher leave as Niv sniffled and we lay on the bed as a family. My heart pounded as I counted the seconds between Lucas's breaths, holding my own when more heartbeats passed than should have.

I gave Niv a squeeze and a kiss on the forehead. "He is strong. He will be well." I closed my eyes and hoped with all my heart that I spoke the truth. Eventually her breathing evened out, and I watched Niv sleep, my eyes wide open despite my body begging me to rest. I gently removed myself from Niv's embrace and padded quietly through to my dressing room.

Damien was waiting for me.

"Where have you been?" I hissed.

"That's no way to greet a friend. The king isn't too dire I hope," Damien said quietly.

"Have you seen what he has been doing every night? I find him here, staring into your mirror. What is going on?" I swallowed thickly. "He seemed fine to me but Brigsten says he's tiring more easily."

"I haven't been able to see him since that first night. It has been a struggle to appear. The curse is preventing me from speaking to him. I watched him today, waiting for you to come back. He didn't come in here," Damien said, scratching his chin. He looked thoughtful but didn't say anything else.

"Why is the mirror doing this?" I asked, hoping Damien would know.

"It keeps me hidden. It could be the curse of the mirror reacting to being so close to one of my bloodline." Damien ran his hand through his hair. "I don't know enough, Raina. I'm sorry."

I blew out a breath, throwing my hands up in frustration and fighting back a cry. "I should have freed you and destroyed that mirror by now," I whispered harshly. "If you would let me tell the king—"

"No, Raina," Damien said, panic entering his eyes. "Especially not now that the king is ill. The mirror might be influencing him. He will blame me for his ailment."

"How can I help you? Kiara won't even talk to me," I told him.

"Kiara?" He gasped, a flash of emotion in his eyes.

"She knows something," I answered. "She knew my grandmother and about our family. She says I must discover it on my own."

"That is unexpected," Damien said, scratching his chin. He looked thoughtfully into the distance. "Don't mention me to her either. We don't know whether she has heard the kingdom's version of history or your grandmother's. Constance was secretive when it came to the mirror and keeping me hidden. She feared my brother would discover me and destroy the mirror with my soul."

"Can we do anything to help Lucas?"

"I'm afraid not, Raina. If it's not a natural sickness…" He trailed off.

"What is the use of having all this power when I can't use it to save someone I love," I said, clenching my fists.

"It's just not the way it works, my dear," Damien said. He breathed a sigh and reached up to touch the glass. "I can feed him my energy from the mirror, but you'll have to move it to your bed chambers. It might also make him worse if the mirror wasn't draining him to begin with."

My heart ached; if Lucas took Damien's energy would Damien fade away? I bit my lip and closed my eyes, holding my hands close to my chest. Would I have to choose between them?

"I don't know what to do," I said. "I can't ask you to sacrifice yourself. I need to save both of you."

"You didn't ask me to." Damien gave me a smile. "I promise I will be fine. I'll make sure you don't have to choose between us."

I reached up and touched my hand to the mirror, the cold of the glass biting into my skin. I pressed my forehead against it and breathed out slowly.

"Raina?" Asher's shout carried through from the other room.

"Here," I replied.

Asher approached me his face drawn and haggard looking. "In the king's absence you're required to direct the warriors."

"I know. Brigsten told me," I said.

He faced me with his hands behind his back. I glanced at the mirror, my stomach clenching at the thought of leading Lucas's men so soon after we'd already fought the vampires.

"Have they attacked again?"

He nodded and my heart sank. I gave him a nod and then gestured at the mirror. "Can you move this into my bed chambers. It has always brought my family luck, and I think the king needs it more than me right now."

Asher frowned but agreed, holding the door open for me.

I quickly changed my rumpled clothes, barely paying any

attention to Asher when he led me to the gate we'd raced through earlier.

"My lady," Brigsten said, approaching us as we entered the courtyard. His jaw was clenched and his eyes tight. "I need to show you something."

I nodded, my tired body dragging as we climbed the steps onto the huge wall surrounding the kingdom. "I've never seen this many," he said as the last of the light of the evening faded away.

He took my arm to steady me when we reached the top. I swayed, suddenly dizzy at the sight before me. Surrounding the entire kingdom as far as we could see, vampires swarmed closer with not an inch between them. They didn't attack. They didn't cry out or snarl as we would have expected.

"What are they doing?" I asked.

"I believe they are forcing us into a siege," Brigsten said, swallowing loudly. "We can't risk leaving to fight them anymore. Is there anything you can do?"

"I'm afraid not," I said, facing him. "I used everything I had earlier. It's like they planned this."

"It can't be a coincidence," he replied, turning away from me. "We could start evacuating the citizens. We just await your order."

"Can't we wait for Lucas for that decision?" I whirled to face him again.

"No, Your Majesty. Niv is too young, and as queen, he gave you the same authority as he has. We discussed this earlier," he told me, his voice holding no scorn as he watched me patiently. "Is there any change with His Majesty?"

"I'm afraid not," I replied, looking out at the vast number of vampires we faced. As I watched, the tall vampire I'd seen earlier approached the wall. He raised his hand, and his claws lengthened as we watched. He reached out, his claws plummeting into the wall in front of him, allowing him to pull himself up. My heart pounded, the sound thrumming in my ears as I watched him slowly climb the wall in front of him.

"Archers," Brigsten shouted.

The men quickly moved forward on the wall, aiming at the vampire. I breathed in sharply as I watched the vampire fall when an arrow struck his shoulder. He slammed into the ground but quickly stood. His gaze met mine as he slowly pulled the arrow from his body. He smirked at me from his spot in the crowd below. Cold washed over me as I saw others lengthen their claws and move toward the wall.

I stood vigilantly with the men through the night as the vampires tried to climb the walls. I threw out blackfire when I could muster the energy and bolstered the men when I could. Passing between them, I watched each man carefully as they strained to stop the horde from breaching the walls.

I heard a man cry out, pointing at a retreating vampire. Slowly the mass trickled away, and my shoulders relaxed as rays from the dawning sun pierced the sky, infusing its warmth into the clouds. Everyone put their hands to their brows, shading their eyes as they watched the shadows shrink, shortening the distance between the trees and the wall.

"They will return tomorrow night," I told Brigsten, knowing in my heart they would not give up.

"I agree. We need a new plan, and you need to rest, my queen. We could have used more of your firepower tonight, and you can't help if you're exhausted."

I nodded my agreement. I would rest ahead of the next long night. "There has to be a way to defeat them."

"Then you will find it."

I blanched at the utter faith in Brigsten's gaze.

~

Niv was still awake when I entered her chambers. Lucas had been sound asleep when I checked on him, and Asher told me Niv had stayed with him while I was gone but left when she heard I was on my way back. I gave her a smile when her eyes looked up to meet mine. Her bed clothes pulled tightly up to her chin, she looked much younger than she was.

"How are you, my dear?" I asked her, padding over to her bed and sitting in the chair next to it.

Her lip trembled. "I am…sad," she said simply.

I reached up to stroke her hair. "I know. Me too." We sat in silence for a moment, my fingers caressing her silky, black locks the only movement.

"Will he get better?" she asked me.

"I hope with all my heart that he does." I blew out a breath. "I only just found you both."

I watched her eyes brim with tears, swallowing thickly and closing my eyes against my own tears.

"I'm glad you're here," she told me. "I couldn't do this without you."

"I'm glad I'm here too. I just wish we knew how to help your father," I said.

"Is there anything you can do to help? Maybe with your magic." Her voice held a note of hope.

My heart squeezed as I prepared to tell her I didn't know.

She reached out to touch my arm. "It's okay. I know you would do something if you could."

I shook my head, closing my eyes. "I have searched my grimoire, but nothing is coming to me." I had searched every night until my head ached. "Maybe I'm not asking the right questions."

"We can find answers," Niv said. Her certainty gave me pause. "We can do this together, Raina. I know we can."

I gave her a smile, taking a deep breath and wishing with all my strength that she was right. I knew better than to make a promise I wasn't sure I could keep. Holding out my other hand, I focused on the love I felt for Niv, wanting to create something that would give her comfort. Golden light danced around my palm for a moment before settling into the shape of a small mirror. I smiled at it, placing the small replica of the mirror on my wall in her hand.

"I will do everything within my power," I told her, leaning forward to give her a kiss on the forehead. "This is for you. Whenever you're scared, look at the wonderful person you are and think of me."

"I love it," she whispered, clasping the mirror in her hand. "Will you stay here until I fall asleep?"

"Of course, I will."

"And then will you make sure father is…" her words trailed off.

"I will. I won't leave his side unless I must."

"Thank you, Raina," she said, closing her eyes. I watched her dark eyelashes flutter for a moment and stroked her hair until her breathing slowed. Her hair was strewn over the pillow, surrounding her beautiful face. She would be a stunning young woman one day with pure strength and compassion I had never seen before. I hoped I would still be here to see that. With Lucas by my side.

CHAPTER 14

RAINA

"Seven nights now," I said. "They are relentless."

Lucas watched me pacing from the bed. He had been unable to gather enough energy to leave it since he collapsed by the stables. I tried to push away my worry, but he looked thinner than yesterday. At least in bed he hadn't been waking in the night to stare at the mirror. I eyed it as I paced the room, wondering if I'd made a mistake moving it in here with him. But Damien had assured me he could help Lucas with its proximity.

"I don't understand where they are coming from," Lucas said. "We drove them to extinction. We were being attacked by small groups, twenty at the most. Now there are hundreds."

Wearily he reached up to rub his face. I'd had the same conversations with Lucas and Brigsten over the last week. The numbers were growing, and we didn't know how that was possible. They'd both told me that creating vampires was an ability that only the vampire king had. We were discussing the possibility that he had returned and was hiding in the mountains with the vampires. But why now?

We hadn't been able to leave the kingdom to check, and after the last journey to the mountains where we had been ambushed, we were loath to send more men out. The sky had darkened to the point where daylight was rare. Unable to trade with neighboring kingdoms, we were relying heavily on our stores for winter.

"We should start moving those who live close to the wall," I said, turning to see a pained look on Lucas's face.

"I know you're right…" he paused. "We haven't had to consider that in many years. We were winning."

"I know." I approached him, perching on the edge of the bed. I leaned over to cup his face with my hand. "We must think of the people first. They will be safer nearer the palace, especially those in the east. What if the vampires start to circle around the kingdom instead of concentrating on the palace wall?"

"Do you think we could send any away through the east gates during an attack?" he said. "You have more knowledge of their actions."

I thought it over. Despite our efforts, the vampires had been circling around. They no longer retreated to the mountains, preferring to shelter in the trees when the sun appeared. I was grateful that they had at least that weakness, even if the appearance of the sun had lessened in the last few days.

"I should have cleared a path through the trees to the neighboring kingdoms," Lucas grumbled. "That way we could risk sending out people during those hours of sunlight."

"We couldn't have foreseen this," I soothed. "The vampires would just wait on the edges of the trees and then ambush any group we sent when the sun disappeared." I chewed on my lip.

"What about the escape tunnels?" he asked.

"I've secured them with barriers, but they aren't large enough for masses of people. Once they start trickling through, the vampires will know where the exits are. I'm waiting for them to breach the walls so they are distracted."

"Many won't escape," Lucas commented. "We won't have the time." He looked pained.

"I know," I whispered. "We are in an impossible situation."

"I wish I knew the cause of this," he said. "Why now?"

I leaned in, embracing him to comfort him as much as myself. "I don't know." I longed to say more and tell him it would be well and we would all be safe. A knock on the door broke through the moment, and I quickly stood. Lucas scowled, looking down at himself, but didn't comment. I would be frustrated in his place, so I could understand his ire.

"Be well," I said, rising to leave and trying to settle the churning guilt at having to leave him. I gave him a soft kiss on the mouth. "I love you."

"Your plan to use oil and set them on fire as they climb has worked for now," Brigsten said, running a hand through his hair. "It won't hold them for long, though."

"It doesn't need to be long," I told him. "It just needs to buy us time."

"You're right, my queen," Brigsten agreed, nodding his respect as two familiar figures approached us.

I suppressed a groan when I saw who it was. "Father, Mother?" I said with a frown.

"My dear, we were so worried," my mother said, rushing forward to embrace me.

My frown deepened as she gave me a squeeze. I saw no trace of fear in her eyes, though she trembled when she touched me. I was sure this was the first time in my life she had willingly hugged me. Her next words made my back stiffen. "Let's find somewhere to talk, dearest."

"Asher, Brigsten. I won't be long," I told them, leading my parents into a nearby receiving room.

"No refreshments," my mother sneered as I closed the door behind us.

"If you haven't noticed, Mother, we are in the middle of a siege. We have other priorities," I said, clenching my jaw. I noticed she stood closer to my father, using him to bolster her bravery.

"More important than your own parents?" My mother huffed.

"Now, dear, give Raina a break," my father said, looking around the room, unaware of my mother's demeanor toward me. "It seems like the palace is in a bit of a crisis here."

"If our daughter had let us come and live here when she became queen, we would have been able to help," she replied with narrowed eyes at me.

I sighed. "I'm afraid it's worse than it appears."

"I imagine so if the king doesn't have time to welcome us. After all, we are his family as well," my mother sneered.

My heart squeezed when I thought of Lucas up in our bed chamber. "The king is a busy man," I said. We hadn't made it public knowledge that Lucas was unwell.

"You seem to have a lot of authority around here." My mother took small paces around the room. "I feel like you could have put a good word in for us so we could join you in your lavish lifestyle. I put you in this position, Raina, so all of us could benefit."

I gritted my teeth, turning away from her to look out the window at the gardens so I wouldn't snap at her. My father reached out to touch my shoulder.

"You seem tense. Has something happened?" he asked.

I fought back the sting of tears. "I'm afraid so. You'll have to join with the rest of the kingdom and move closer to the palace." I turned to face my parents, and my mother took a step back, the color draining from her face.

"What do you mean?" My father frowned.

"The vampires are about to breach the wall. I—we have called for an evacuation to the safety of the tunnels leading out of the kingdom. We plan to send as many as we can to the neighboring towns when the vampires breach the wall. They have never had trouble from the vampires, so let's pray they don't follow us." I took my father's hands. "You must be quick; we don't know how much longer we can hold them off, and we aren't sure how many will make it through."

"This is a disgrace. With you in charge we have had to abandon the kingdom. What did you do? Surely with your talents you could have prevented this," my mother said with a sneer.

I gave her a cold look, and she gasped, rushing to grip my father's arm.

"Why do you think it is my fault?" I finally snapped, looking her in the eyes. "I am happier here than I've ever been. What could I have possibly done to bring a horde of vampires—vampires who have been trying to breach the walls for generations, I might add—to our doors?" I folded my arms and waited for a reply, watching my mother's face redden and her lips thin.

"You were always a waste of my time," she scowled as she spoke. "Away with the fairies in your books and never searching for a suitable husband. When you do find one, you ruin it."

"Now, dearest—"

"Do not try to placate me." She turned on my father. "This is your fault too, allowing her so much independence and freedom. She has been the downfall of our family and selfish." Despite my mother's genuine fear of me, she managed to make her point.

"You have done nothing but berate me. When I did find suitors, you drove them away," I seethed, clenching my fists.

A door nearby opened, and it was an effort to compose my face.

"Everything alright, my lady?" Asher's head appeared behind the door.

"Yes, Asher, my parents were just leaving," I told him. I turned to embrace my father and gave him an apologetic look as he pulled me close.

"Stay safe," he whispered.

"You too," I replied, swallowing the lump in my throat.

My mother strode away without looking at me, and I couldn't help the relieved sigh as she left. My father gave me a small smile before following her.

"Your mother seems like a character," Asher said, approaching me as I sat heavily in the nearest chair.

"That's one way of looking at it," I said wearily, dread coiling within me. "How long does Brigsten think they can hold off the vampires?"

"Taking shifts and using the resources we have left...two days," Asher stopped in front of me. "You need to rest."

I closed my eyes and shook my head. "Two days? I'd hoped for longer to allow the rest of the kingdom to make it to the palace and through the tunnels."

"We will do our best. You should go and be with the king," he said, helping me rise out of the chair.

I nodded, my heart sinking at the way Lucas had looked, but I shook my head. "I'm needed at the wall."

Asher didn't comment as he followed me to meet Brigsten. I was grateful for his support and advice. I didn't think the men would have followed me in Lucas's place without him.

LIZ CAIN & ANNE K. WHELAN

"My queen," Brigsten greeted me as I approached.

"Any developments?" I asked him, nodding in greeting. He shook his head, looking out over the horde before us. Unbelievably there looked to be even more vampires.

"Where are they all coming from?" I exclaimed, sighing when Brigsten shrugged.

"I do not know."

I eyed the dark-haired vampire that seemed to appear at the front when I came to the wall. He had grinned at me when we had ridden through the gates, and I shivered at the memory.

"I wonder," I muttered.

"What was that, my lady?" Asher asked.

"He appears to be some sort of leader. He's the one that started climbing the walls," I answered. I leaned forward, bracing myself on the wall with my hands. A shock jolted through me when the vampire's eyes met mine.

"Raina," I jerked away from the wall at the monstrous whisper.

"What—" I whirled to Brigsten and Asher. "Did you hear that?" It was the same voice that had echoed through me all those weeks ago.

"I didn't hear anything," Brigsten sounded uncertain. "Are you okay, my lady?"

I opened my mouth to speak, snapping it shut and shaking my head at his concerned look. "I'm fine." I turned to look at the vampire again, a queasy sensation in my middle. Was he speaking directly to me.

"Could he be the vampire king?" I nodded toward the vampires still staring at me. "He appears more intelligent than the others. Isn't he the one that started them climbing the walls?" I looked along the wall, grateful to see that none had attempted to do that this night. They all stood, eerily still, watching the wall.

Brigsten came up alongside me. "I am unable to tell you. I have never seen the images of him. His Majesty's father kept them locked up. He does seem more capable than the others." Brigsten frowned. "What are they waiting for? I hate when they stand around. I'd rather they attack."

"I'm grateful for the reprieve," Asher interjected. "At least this way some of the men can get some rest."

"True," I said. "Fewer injuries this way."

Brigsten snorted, looking out and watching as more vampires joined the back of the large crowd from the trees. They streamed in each day, swelling their numbers. "We need to be prepared for a large attack. I can feel it."

I nodded my agreement, pushing away the bile rising in my throat. "Let us hope we can help the people escape."

Neither of the men commented further as we stood there, watching the dark skies shadow further as the evening drew to a close.

Lucas looked even more gaunt than he had when I left, his skin taking on a grey tinge, and he didn't stir when I lay next to him. Kiara waited for me in the doorway as I brushed the hair back from his face.

"Where is Niv?" I asked her.

"I sent her to get some food. Poor dear hasn't been eating enough," Kiara said. She tilted her head and gestured back out the room, giving me an apologetic smile when I rose slowly from the bed.

"You look tired," she said to me, pulling me into a hug.

"My mother…" I shook my head, not having to say more.

Kiara chuckled. "I wondered when she would appear again. Do you think she will follow you when we are all forced to leave?" I groaned, not having thought of that. "Can

I get you anything?" she asked, hesitantly reaching up to touch my shoulder.

"No, I just want to rest and spend some time with Lucas," I said, squeezing her arms. "Although…Kiara, now is the time to tell me what my grandmother passed on."

"I cannot, my sweet girl. Your grandmother was very specific about what and when I could tell you anything." She frowned, her lips thinning.

My shoulders sagged and I looked at the floor. "You should get ready to leave. Thank you for being there for me when you could. I don't know how I would have survived that house without you," I told her, reaching to give her hand a final squeeze.

Kiara nodded. "I am proud to know you, Raina." She left my chambers, surreptitiously wiping at her face. I turned back to enter my room and gasped when I saw Lucas's eyes were open. He moved his arms weakly, trying to turn but failing to move.

"Wait," I called. "You need to rest, Lucas."

"What's happening?" he groaned and didn't fight me when I pushed him back down. I knelt on the floor next to him, holding his hand in mine.

"The vampires…they." I closed my eyes and braced myself, and then I told him about the horde outside the walls still growing.

"But the palace is secured?" he asked.

"Not for much longer. I'm sorry, Lucas. The men are holding them back, but there are too many. I ordered the men to prepare for evacuation. Our people are coming to the palace."

"You did the right thing," he said, weakly squeezing my fingers. He closed his eyes, letting out a weary breath. "Why do I feel so drained?"

"I don't know," I told him. "The physician says he can't

find anything wrong with you." I glanced at the mirror, catching a glimpse of Damien flash out of view. I could feel a hum of power linking the mirror to Lucas, Damien giving him energy. I held on to Lucas tightly and hoped I wouldn't lose either of them.

"Come and lie with me," he said.

I walked around to the other side and curled into him, his body like ice next to mine. I wrapped my arms around him, pressing the warmth of my body into his.

When he finally settled into a deep sleep, I untwined our bodies and approached the mirror. Damien appeared instantly.

"He won't last much longer," he said somberly.

I closed my eyes, my hands coming up to my chest as pain threatened to stop my breath. Anguish clawed my insides and I struggled to pull air into me.

"I can't—" a sob broke free.

"Oh, Raina, I hate to see you in so much pain," Damien said, his voice soothing and almost mesmerizing.

I looked up, my eyes wide. His eyes held concern, and his hand was on the surface of the mirror. I slowly lifted mine to press it against his, a trickle of my power streaming through to meet him. I saw color return to the mirror as some of my energy pushed through.

"Save your strength," Damien said, though he didn't move his hand away.

"I need to help in some way. With the vampires overpowering us and Lucas…I feel so helpless," I let out a shuddering breath. "I can't do nothing. I can't lose either of you. I have already let you down."

"The grimoire still not forthcoming?" he asked.

I shook my head. "It's been so quiet since I stopped having to use words for my power."

"It is because you're growing out of it. You will be able to will what you want soon. Then you can help me," he smiled at me reassuringly. "I have faith that you will overcome this and all will be well."

"It is hard to see." Despite my misgivings, I took some comfort from his words.

"Rest, Raina." He dropped his hand. "Tomorrow will be an important day."

CHAPTER 15

RAINA

"Asher," I begged. "You need to take her away from here." A huge explosion rocked the palace. We'd held the vampires off for four days, but somehow they had managed to get hold of some explosives and started blowing holes in the wall instead of attempting to climb over. It wouldn't be long until they managed to get through. "Keep her away."

Asher gave me a hard look. "I can't make her do anything, Raina. She's stubborn and you know it. How are there so many?" he asked. "We hunted them to extinction, first the horde and now more showing up every day."

"The king's illness… It's like his presence held them off, but now…" I shook my head. Lucas had weakened further and hadn't woken in days. "We have no match for their ferocity."

I saw Brigsten ahead, his armor dented in places and his hair disheveled. He looked tired, as did many of the men I'd just left on the walls.

"They have breached the wall," he cried, running toward me. "It won't be long now, my lady. We got the people to the palace but they need to be led out. You need to escape with the council and Princess Niveus."

"I won't leave him," I told him, turning to Asher again. "You need to find the princess and make sure she leaves with the others. She at all costs needs to be kept safe."

"What about you, my lady?" Asher looked pained, stopping to turn me to face him. "Raina, you cannot stay here."

"The king cannot be moved and I won't leave him to die alone. If I make it out, I know where to meet you," I said. I had no intention of making it out if Lucas perished. I would fight until my last breath to keep him safe. I wondered if I had enough energy to create a barrier around us both and how long it would hold. "Take the princess away from here."

"I can't make her do anything," he grumbled, finally turning away from me.

I waved at him. "Try," I yelled over my shoulder, heading toward the royal chambers. The king's men had never faced so many vampire attacks in such a short span of time.

"Where did they get the explosives," I muttered to myself as I continued my way through the palace. Their intelligence, which had once been nonexistent, according to Brigsten, appeared to have increased since I came to the palace. What was left of the army was devastated by the battle this morning. We had nothing left to hold them off. My heart broke when I thought of the men who had sacrificed themselves to buy the rest of the kingdom time to escape. Their homes would be overrun. I had to make sure their families would escape.

I walked through halls and passed rooms that held joyful memories. I had been happy here. Not speaking to my parents since I told them to evacuate and having a short time away from my mother had been a gift, despite her months of trying to petition for a home in the palace. Guilt ate at me when I thought of my father, but I hoped they had escaped.

My chambers appeared up ahead, and I quickened my pace. I braced myself before I entered as I looked down the deserted corridor, willing the staff and our people to make it to safety.

Pushing open the door, my heart trembled when I saw the king still unconscious on our bed. His face held a glean of sweat; eyes and cheeks sunken, he looked like a desiccated corpse. If not for the small movement of his chest as he breathed, I would have thought him long dead. As I reached him, I clasped his hand and his eyes flew open for the first time in days. Panic flashed in them as he saw me.

"Whe—" he coughed. "Where is…"

"I told her to stay away. She's safe," I said. A large boom broke in the air and I winced. Lucas reached up, his hand caressing my cheek.

"We did everything we could. You need to keep fighting without me," he spluttered, coughing again.

"Don't say that!" I cried, anguish building in my chest and robbing me of the ability to take a deep breath.

"Tell Niv I love her," he asked, his hand going limp and dropping from my face.

My eyes stung as they filled with tears, dampening my cheeks as they spilled.

"Damien," I turned to the mirror on our chamber wall. Panic gripped me. "Damien," I all but screamed at the mirror.

"Yes, Raina," he appeared, speaking softly.

"Save him," I shouted, still gripping the king's hand.

"I told you, Raina. I can't. This illness has been cruel but I cannot take it from him," he said, sorrow evident in his eyes.

"There must be a way," I said. I leaped up and strode to the mirror. "I will do anything."

"Well." Damien looked over my shoulder at the king on the bed. "It is dangerous and may rob the last of my energy. I will be gone forever if that happens, Raina. Are you willing to sacrifice me?"

"Please try," I begged. "I can give you all of my energy." Hurt flashed in Damien's eyes. I squashed my guilt as I asked this of him.

"Very well. I won't drain you too, Raina. I have had long enough in this world. Place my mirror next to the king on the bed. Then put his hand on the surface. I will do what I can."

Frantically I ripped the mirror from the wall, plaster scattering when I turned to place it on the bed next to the king. My heart squeezed at the thought of losing Damien. He had been a friend to me, teaching me how to use my power. I felt a twinge of guilt that I had never discovered how to free him. I never even tried to talk to Lucas about him, so I would do my best to make sure he stayed.

"Thank you," I whispered, reaching for Lucas's hand. "What can I do to help, so you don't lose all your energy?"

"Place your hand on the mirror too," Damien responded.

I intertwined the king's fingers with mine, gently placing my hand on his chest. It still rose and fell but weakly.

"Stay strong, my love," I said.

The surface of the mirror felt cold when I touched our hands to it. I gasped as sparks of pain jolted up my arm into my body. It was an effort to hold our hands against the mirror. A strong wind lifted around us, whipping my hair around my face and gaining speed. My teeth clenched so tightly my body shook, stealing my ability to pull away or turn when the door to our chambers burst open.

"*Father!*" Niv screamed, the cry wrought with pain as she burst into the room.

"Stay back, Niv," I yelled, willing a barrier into place around us. It sprang up instantly, surprising me with how easy my powers came to me now.

The surface of the mirror turned to liquid, and horror

welled within me as I watched it ripple and break, a hand appearing and slowly rising from the surface.

"Is this part of the spell?" I called to Damien. I still could not move, paralyzed by the magic. "Damien?"

Cold washed over me as a dark figure rose out of the mirror, his familiar form shrouded in shadows and darkness. I felt someone briefly touch my barrier before a powerful force lurched through me, throwing Niv away from me. The air howled, the force lifting furniture and swirling papers through the room.

"Raina!" Niv shouted behind me. Fear clenched at me when she called again. "What are you doing?"

I fought to answer, my body still frozen and my mouth clamped shut. When Damien stepped from the mirror off the bed and turned to face us, I could barely breathe. My eyes followed his movements as I pushed to move any part of my body. The hand I still had on the king's chest heaved when he took in a rattling breath. I saw Lucas tense in front of me, his back arching.

When he dropped back to the bed, my heart broke as he let out one final breath and fell still. The magic finally released me and I threw myself on him.

"Lucas," the word tore from me as I sobbed.

"Thank you, Raina, for keeping your promise," Damien said, his voice rich and sultry. "Our work has finally paid off."

Cold spread through me as I looked up into his eyes, completely black and devoid of any feeling. Every muscle in my body ached, and I couldn't speak as I realized what I'd done. I'd believed him. Every word he had told me I had stupidly taken as truth. Distracted by the discovery of my power, I never questioned that grandmother would have kept the mirror so she could help him. He had used me and guided me for his own gain.

He stood before me, free from the mirror. His long hair

lay slicked back from his face, and his smile turned to a grin when I tried to reel away from the fangs protruding from his mouth.

"Raina?" Niv asked behind me, panic lacing her words. "How could you? I thought you loved us." The pain in her voice vibrated through me, my body finally free from the spell.

I whirled to face Niv. "I—" The anguish on her face pierced through me. I didn't know what to say. Paralyzed now by the look on her face and no longer the magic from the mirror, I looked down at my hands. Purple magic whipped around them. I had done this.

"Now, now, dearest." Damien's hands dropped on to my shoulders from behind, making my stomach jolt. "It is time for your reward."

"No," I managed the small cry before pain exploded through me, starting from two points at the base of my neck. I lifted my head and gasped, closing my eyes to shut out the sight of Niv watching as Damien's hands stroked downward, exploring my body. His touch caressed my power, causing an unnerving pleasure to course through me. I wanted to hate him for what he had done, but my body's reaction to him pushed away any reluctance. I leaned into him, desperate to get closer.

Ice seeped into me from my shoulder, pushing everything I knew was warm and feeling away from my heart. Blackness surrounded my vision with a pressure pushing into me. My teeth started to ache and tingle, a dry burn overcoming me. Leaning into Damien as his mouth released me, his nose trailed up my neck and his breath tickled near my ear.

"You are magnificent," he whispered, his fingers trailing up my arms. I looked down, my eyes falling on Niv. I cocked my head at her eyes wide and the pulsing vein on her neck.

I licked my lips.

"What is happening here?" Kiara shrieked as she appeared behind Niv. The blood drained from her face when she looked at me, her hand flying to her mouth as a heart-wrenching cry tore from her.

"No," she wailed. "It wasn't supposed to be this way. Constance—"

Damien took a step forward and in one quick motion snapped her neck. Her body crumpled to the floor and Niv screamed, scrambling away from us.

I felt nothing. Nothing for the woman who had raised me, sheltered me from my mother's ire, and treated me like her own daughter. I barely registered that she had been speaking of my grandmother. Damien turned to me, prowling forward as I admired his lithe body.

He reached up, putting a finger under my chin and tilting my head to look into his eyes. "Now kill his heir and the last of my brother's weak bloodline."

"Yes," I hissed quietly. Once again, my gaze fell toward the girl cowering near the door. Niv's eyes rose to meet mine, and she whimpered when I reached for her. Grabbing the slim pale neck of the child I had come to think of as my own, my lips twitched into a smile. My heart stuttered as I looked into her eyes, her father's eyes. A presence within me threatened to push forward at her gaze.

"Run for your life, little girl." I pushed her through the doorway, watching her stumble. Briefly, I glanced at Damien over my shoulder. Looking to his left, I could see the mirror of my vanity that I'd brought from my parents' house. Slowly I approached the mirror, seating myself before it.

"Don't give her too much of a head start." Damien came up behind me. "I can understand the thrill of the hunt, dear, but you must end her." His hands rested on my shoulders.

My skin matched his pale, translucent coloring. My hair was darker and the blackness in my eyes seemed endless, matching the black of my gown. All the color had seeped away from my face. I reached to touch my image, a flash of memory from when I had seen myself in the mirror the day I met Damien all those months ago. When I first touched the mirror he had started to gain power.

I rose, turning to face him. "I won't," I said simply. His hand reached for me, stroking my neck before his fingers entwined in my hair, forcing my head back.

"How I have looked forward to this day," he said, leaning forward. Heat rose within me as his lips met mine. The kiss was rough and left me tingling, hungry for more, to feel more of him. I reached forward, placing my hands on his chest. I had imagined this moment, pleasing him and him pleasing me in return, until he had rejected me. Hadn't I wanted this? Or had I craved another? I pushed away the thought, looking at the doorway when our lips parted.

"Ready or not, here I come, Princess. Time for my hunt," I said, my voice sounding more like a song. I leaped forward with a speed and grace I never could have imagined. Niv's scent lingered in the air along the corridor, making this far too easy. A thrill ran through me as it grew in strength, heating my blood. I could smell her fear as I rounded a corner, and my lips curled into a snarl. I was close now. It wouldn't be long until she joined her father.

From the mirror I watched the vampire in my body, I could feel the cord between us and for a moment could watch through my eyes but I couldn't take control no matter how hard I fought.

"Well, well, dear Raina." Damien turned, catching sight of me in the mirror. I clenched my fists as he approached, prowling closer.

"What did you do?" I spat. "Wh—"

"No need for such venom, my love. I have made you into a creature fit for your potential."

"That creature is not me."

"On the contrary, all that darkness and anger in you has been unleashed. You are what you were meant to be." He paused. "It is curious, though. I am unsure how you ended up in the mirror as well."

I watched him reach up and run a hand through his hair. "How am I here?"

"It appears the goodness in you resisted and has taken up residence in my old location." He chuckled. "I hope you like it better than I did." Bile rose in me and I choked back the urge to throw up.

"What are you going to do?" I flinched when his fangs appeared in a toothy grin.

"What I always intended to do. Use the power as the rightful heir of this kingdom to increase my power further. I will show this world what happens to traitors, those who don't join me will be no less than cattle," he told me. I blanched, watching him as he spoke. I couldn't fathom how I ever found him attractive.

I swallowed hard. "I will stop you."

He laughed. "How? You were weak, Raina. Now your body is strong and you are mine."

I stumbled as images came to me. Suddenly in my own body I looked down at my blood-soaked hands. Vampires surrounded me and a spike of fear at their closeness shot through me. I felt my body grin, warm coppery blood soaking my tongue. I gave in to the draw of my vampire self, vertigo threatening to overcome me as I wholly looked through *her* eyes.

The vampires bowed as I passed, stepping over bodies of the palace staff as I looked around the once beautiful orchard room Lucas and Niv had created for me. The leaves were now pure black and the red skin of the apples gleamed. I brushed my hands along the leaves as I approached the doors. I caught sight of Niv ahead of me, stumbling toward Asher and Brigsten. I clawed at the control on my body, and it jerked once before halting. Breathing heavily, I looked at my closest friends and Niv.

"Run," I screamed at them, trembling at the effort it took to hold the vampire body in place. "Before she takes control again." I shook harder as I watched them stare at me. I let out a piercing shriek as my control broke and I was thrown backward, falling onto the floor of the reflected room in the mirror.

I cried out in frustration, leaping forward to pound against the glass.

It did not move.

Tears streamed down my face as I continued to push the glass. Damien was nowhere to be seen, leaving me alone in the reflection. I sobbed, clutching at my chest and dropping to my knees.

The thought of the grimoire came to me and I called it to me, relieved when it appeared in my hands. I opened it in the center to a blank page and struggled to concentrate. It took many attempts before a spell appeared.

I wiped my eyes, surprised to see words on the page. It had been weeks since the book gave me a spell in words. I was grateful that anything appeared.

I said the words quickly. "One as one, she is me. From me to her, let me see." I gasped as my vision tilted and I was back in my body.

I faced Damien on the highest point, a tower once built to watch the advance of invading armies. It was used to warn the king of the approach of the vampires the last few generations.

"Is it done?" he demanded without turning to look at me.

"Yes, my love. She is dead," I answered, coming to his side. Pleasure and horror warred within me. He turned to face me, pulling me close to him, his hands around my waist.

"I have waited years for this since your grandmother trapped me in that forsaken mirror. I knew the moment you touched it that you would be the one to free me." As he spoke, his lips traced along my jaw. I closed my eyes, relishing the feel of him pressed against me. Heat seared through me, making my core tingle.

"My brother was a fool to think he could destroy my vampires. I could feel every single one fighting to reach me. His descendant was more of a fool for taking what was rightfully mine." I saw anger in his eyes as he smirked at me. They started to pulse with a tinge of red at their center when they met mine. I swallowed thickly, biting my lip as he stared at me, a deep hunger awakening at the want in his expression.

"Now the kingdom is mine, I shall take my place as the king of all—vampires and humans alike—with you as my beautiful queen." He tilted my head, exposing my neck to him.

My eyes fluttered when he kissed a fiery trail down my neck, the touch pure bliss as he reached down to pull my skirts up. A moan escaped me as he gripped my thigh, pulling our bodies closer. I couldn't help my satisfied smile when I opened my eyes to look at the view of our kingdom.

"I need to be inside of you," he whispered in my ear, his hands caressing my breasts and my nipples hardening under the thin layer of material.

I gasped at the thought, and my body quivered, the ache between my legs almost unbearable. I moved my hands over his chest, trailing down to the top of his breeches, the lust in my eyes apparent. I moved my hand to his, his fingers entwined with mine. I felt him hardening at my touch, the animalistic feeling of power coming over me. I reached down and freed him, letting out a moan as he moved between my legs. He pushed me back against the wall, lifting me to sit atop it. The open air behind me added to the heady feelings of this moment.

He groaned and closed his eyes for a moment as I explored him, running my hand over him as he pushed my legs further apart.

"This feels so good," he groaned, his hands tearing the lace on my dress and freeing my breast. The shock of cold air made me shiver as my body responded to him.

He leaned down and kissed me once more, his tongue plunging into my mouth. I gasped when he entered me in a single thrust and moaned at the feel of him filling me, sensations threatening to overcome me. I wrapped my legs around his waist as he moved, a cry escaping from my lips. I arched my back, pushing against him.

I pulled him closer, my hands tangled in his hair as he pushed in and out of me with strong movements. I writhed against him, holding on to him with a ferocious grip. My hands clawed down his back, making him growl and thrust harder.

I let out a cry as I reached my climax, my body shaking in the aftermath. He soon followed me, moaning his triumph. I felt his hands wrap around my waist, gripping me hard, and as I opened my eyes he gazed at me with a possessive gleam in his eyes.

"You are mine," he growled. "Forever."

PART II
TRUE LOVE'S KISS

CHAPTER 16

RAINA - EIGHT YEARS LATER

"*I* don't know what else to tell you without saying too much, Raina," Niv explained, her jaw clenching. "How much longer can we keep this up?"

"I can keep myself separate, but all it will take is one slip-up, Niv," I answered. "You can't trust me. No specifics, no locations. Since I said that first spell, I often slip into her... my mind. It is enough to know you are well." I gave her a pained look as I watched her through the mirror's surface. She had a dark curtain behind her and nothing else in view, I made sure she kept the mirror covered unless she needed to speak to me.

She narrowed her eyes on me. "What about you? Any luck?" We rarely spoke about my attempts to take control back of my body. I was thrown into it often enough, forced to watch the horrific actions my vampire counterpart performed. I gave my head a quick shake, not voicing my disappointment. "It was enough that I could save you."

Niv's lips thinned, but she didn't say anything.

It shocked us both when the small mirror I had gifted her

let us speak to each other through the mirror on my bedroom wall. Niv had destroyed the gift when she realized who was on the other end. But no matter what she did with it, it always appeared next to her bed the following day. An object created from my love for her, it kept that connection for us.

"What about what Kiara said?"

I shook my head again. "I'm still able to call the grimoire, but it is getting harder. I don't know what she was trying to tell me. She kept telling me I needed to learn it myself. I was hoping the grimoire would let me learn it by now."

Damien had killed Kiara before she could tell me what my grandmother had passed on to her—the knowledge that would help me. My heart squeezed, and I flinched when the sound of her neck cracking echoed through my mind.

I had been grateful for the book in the early years of my imprisonment, and I'd been passing the knowledge on to Niv. We risked my other self finding out, but it was a risk we had to take. I had been pushing my power into Niv for years through the mirrors, teaching her what I could with the grimoire's knowledge. She mostly figured it out on her own after I warned her of the dangers of being guided by another. I closed my eyes, pushing away my hatred of Damien after his manipulation. How my power had been corrupted by his influence.

Months passed before Niv had trusted me. I couldn't blame her, and I still wasn't sure she would ever fully trust me, but she needed me for now. I knew she argued with Asher about it, words from their arguments sometimes drifting to me through the mirror. I tried to ignore it when it happened, not wishing to pass any information on to my other self. She couldn't trust me. When I was snapped into my body, I worried that my vampire presence would be able to read my memories.

"Keep trying, Raina," Niv told me. "We need to stop him. I feel helpless, like I've abandoned my people." I was surprised she admitted that to me.

"I know. We need to keep you safe so you can fight back," I said wearily. I turned at the sound of a door closing in the distance, panic gripping me. "Someone's here, Niv. You need to go."

Niv's eyes widened and she nodded. The mirror went black as she dropped it into the bag she kept it in. The glass of the mirror shimmered before the reflection of the bed chamber I'd shared with Lucas appeared.

Rumpled sheets greeted me, and I braced myself as the bedroom door opened. I sagged when I saw my body appear, inhabited by everything I hated about myself. The Raina in the real world was immature and thought of very little but her hunger.

"How is our dear little Niv?" she said to me, giving me a wicked grin. I sighed. I should have known she felt me talking to her.

"Don't you already know?" I asked.

She cocked her head and raised an eyebrow. "I can feel when you speak to her, not what you say. It amuses me that you still think I can."

I didn't believe her, of course. We were the same person… in a manner, and I could never relax my guard in case she gleaned my thoughts. We were still connected. She waved a hand, twirling and stretching before she finally came to stand before the mirror. She raised her hands to smooth her hair, coming very close to the glass but not touching it. Another game she often played, pretending to change my appearance.

"What do you want?" I snapped at her, drawing her attention back to me.

"Wanted to make sure you were okay." She shrugged. "It must be boring up here by yourself all day."

"What is the real reason?" I asked, crossing my arms over my chest.

"Fine," she huffed. "I need you to look something up in that dreaded book for me."

"Do it yourself," I spat the words.

"You know I would if I could, but it stayed with you." She smirked at me. "It should consider its loyalty. The book is the only useful quality about you. I don't know how you survived for so long without me, let alone had the strength to release my beloved."

I shivered, trying not to gag. "You sound like Mother."

"That old crone." She cackled. "She wailed when I finally killed her. It was a *delicious* end for the bitter old bat. *'Raina, don't please. I always loved you. I was only trying to do what's best for you.'*" Her voice turned nasally and high-pitched in her imitation.

I rolled my eyes. She often gave me stories of how she had killed one person or another. They were all so different, so I wasn't sure to believe who was alive and who wasn't. At first I had refused to give her information from the book. She whined and moaned like a child, eventually bringing people from the kingdom into our room and torturing them until I complied. Her actions tore at my heart; it was bad enough I had no control over what I saw when I shared my body with her but for her to drag humans up to torture them in front of me…I couldn't bear it.

I watched the creature pivot and throw herself onto the bed, very much how I used to as a young girl. She stretched out her arms.

"It's just one little spell," she moaned. "You know I have all the power here; I could shatter that mirror and be done with you." She had used that threat often, but I realized it couldn't be that simple. Otherwise the mirror would have been destroyed when Damien was trapped in it.

"Who would entertain you then?" I replied. "Or help you when you can't do magic." She was a blunt instrument for Damien, able to kill at will, but she always got bored, wanting more of a challenge or more inventive ways to kill. I never gave her anything too dangerous, but she was more malleable when she had something intricate to work on.

The last spell I taught her was how to create sunlight at will. She had then used it to torture some of Damien's men. The kingdom was blanketed with an everlasting night since Damien was released. I was unsure whether I had somehow created the spell when I freed him or whether he influenced the darkness. I had laughed at his image in the mirror when he stormed into the room, cursing my name and demanding I didn't teach her anything that could harm his creatures. It was worth the time teaching her that one just to annoy him.

The vampire sat up quickly, sniffing the air and scowling at the door. I groaned when I realized whose footsteps approached. I turned away from the mirror and slumped down the wall until I sat on the floor. I put my hands over my ears, not wanting to hear Damien and my vampire self. He'd laughed when I asked him to move the mirror into the dressing room, and I immediately regretted the request when their sexual activities increased. I cringed at their cries of pleasure and squeezed my eyes shut, wondering what awful spell I could teach my other self to pay Damien back.

"Oh, Raina."

I squeezed my eyes shut and sat on the floor below the mirror. I couldn't hide from Damien, and he knew that, but I hoped he would leave me alone.

"Come now, dear, I miss you," Damien crooned. I groaned as I got to my feet, reaching for the wall when I stumbled. "Ah, there you are. Did you enjoy that? I know you like to watch."

I cringed. "Surely you have better things to do than worry about my entertainment. You have *her,* so you shouldn't miss me."

"Are you jealous? What could possibly take precedence over spending time with my savior. After all you did for me," he said, smirking at me.

I studied his face, my stomach fluttering when his smile widened. "We all know you're the brains and the soul. She is but a shell of your magnificence."

I gritted my teeth, as I couldn't help admiring his face. I was frustrated that he still had that effect on me. Unbidden, images of him using my body caused me to shiver. I hated him, but even after years, I still reacted to him physically. I scowled at him when he chuckled, clenching my jaw so I didn't say anything.

"I can see how you react to me. It's curious, though. Is that still your own attraction to me or is your vampire self influencing you?" he raised an eyebrow when he finished speaking.

It was an effort to turn my back on him, but I did so, walking to the other side of the room. It was better not to engage in conversation as the arguments would last hours, and they didn't make me feel any better.

"Come now, Raina. You've proved very useful with her training. It was a surprise that you could keep hold of the book, but I've come to realize it's better this way."

I counted to ten, very slowly staring at the wall. As I reached nine, my body convulsed. "Not again," I groaned before my body crumpled, throwing my consciousness to the other side of the castle. It was almost a relief to escape Damien.

I blinked, stumbling to a halt, my vision blurring for a moment as I reorientated myself. My hands reached out to the wall of their own accord, and I groaned internally when I realized I did not have control.

"Nice of you to join me." It was my voice but not my voice.

As I started to stride forward, I reached with my mind to try and grasp at control of my own body, and for a moment I could feel myself instead of the feeling of floating in nothing. A growl escaped my lips, and once again I was unable to do anything but watch. My pace quickened as I left the palace and strode through the garden. I couldn't see anyone around and wondered why my vampire self was leading us out here.

"Too many eyes inside," she whispered, answering my unspoken question. "And we need to talk." Despite my lack of control over my body, my chest twinged as we approached the wisteria tree. I could sense the creature's nervousness within me and mentally sighed. How could we talk when I was only a passenger?

I approached the trunk of the tree, giving it a light caress before I slowly dropped to the ground, seating myself with my back to the trunk.

"This will have to be quiet. I don't want the others to hear," she said to me before letting out a breath. "I need you. More than I realized when we were first fractured. I feel more real when we are together, and I wasn't able to make it permanent."

"What do you mean fractured?" My response was instinctive, nevertheless words left my own lips and euphoria surged through me at being able to speak in the real world.

"Quiet," she hissed back at me, looking around to see if anyone was nearby. Her... my leg jiggled restlessly. "When you freed Damien, I think it broke you. Killing your king fractured our soul, and you somehow used magic to separate from the darkness. Whatever Damien infected us with was too strong, and you ended up in the mirror. We are split, but we aren't meant to be. It feels wrong."

I hesitated as I thought about that day. "Had I known what would happen, I never—"

"Of course, you wouldn't have, even though you would have been capable of it. I am you. You had love for your king," she said mockingly. "However... I know how you feel about Damien. I am you..." she paused. "Just the darker parts of you. The parts that wanted to lash out at dear old mother when she pushed us too far. I can feel your attraction to him, same as mine."

She bit our lip and heat rose in me. I tried to push it down, but denying my attraction to Damien would be impossible. If what she said was true.

"Why should I believe you?"

"Why shouldn't you?"

"Why now then?"

"I tire of being trapped here." My hands slapped down on my legs. "Never leaving the kingdom and...I miss Niv...and Lucas. Despite the darkness, your love for them is stronger. It makes me weak."

I recoiled at her words, stunned by her admission. I could feel the truth in her words. Unless...

"Is this a trick?"

"No," she answered, wearily. "I can feel the wrongness of what I am, and without the other half of me, I feel empty. Numb. I tried to feel something, use the power, but I grow tired of this existence. I need you back in me. Better than what I am now, even if it means being polluted by your goodness."

"Why would I do that? Why would I help you? Why would you help me escape the mirror?"

"I know Niv is planning something. You can feel she is. It won't be long before he realizes she is still alive."

"Why did you tell him she was dead?" I asked her. I had always wondered but she never gave me an answer.

"To protect her. You really are an imbecile."

I huffed, not replying. If I could have some control over my body, maybe I could help Niv if she did attack the palace.

"Won't work," she said, singing the words to me. "We have to become one for you to be in control, which means accepting the dark parts of you as well."

"And if I do, what happens to you?"

"The same thing that happens to you. We will become whole, and neither of us will be the same. Darkness and light, we will be capable of so much more. Imagine the power." I could feel her hunger for power growing, but if I could have control and fight the darkness, maybe I could do more.

As she finished speaking, I could feel myself slipping away from her. I struggled to hold the connection, but my vision darkened.

"Don't wait too long to give me an answer. This is the first time I've managed to summon you to me when I was alone. When you're ready I'll come to you."

My eyes fluttered, finally opening to stare at the ceiling of the bed chamber within the mirror. I propped myself up on my elbows and looked toward the mirror on the wall. Damien was no longer there and my shoulders relaxed. I lay back down, too tired to get up, and repeated the conversation in my head. There must be a way for me to find out if it was a trick. Calling the grimoire to me, I sat up slowly, staring at the cursed book.

"Let's see if you can finally help me."

I never got tired in the mirror, which was now a blessing after the years of never-ending boredom as the grimoire was finally "speaking" to me. I scanned another page, which outlined more of my family history. I had read this years ago when I first summoned the large tome, but now it had extra information. What Kiara had said about learning the power myself was true. Damien must have known this, and by guiding me in how I learned my magic, he managed to shape the power into a tool. I grimaced as I read, realizing how easily I had fallen for his manipulation.

The words on the page blurred as tears welled up. I wiped them away furiously, finally stepping away from the book and laying it on my bed. I clutched at the ache in my chest, wishing with all my heart that I could have spoken to my grandmother about this.

"Well, it's about time you called me."

I took a step back, my eyes wide as my grandmother appeared before me. My eyes trailed over her, the same as the last time I had seen her. Her gray curly hair was held off her face by a purple headband, matching the color of the purple gown she wore. The simple style was much like my own. I took another step back when she walked toward me, bumping into the bed behind me.

"Let's look at you," she said, reaching for me and holding my shoulders.

"How—"

"Magic, my dear child. You've got yourself in a fine mess, but as I told Kiara, it had to happen this way." She reached up to cup my cheek. "I am sorry you had to watch her die and that she couldn't help you. It was the only way."

"You knew it would happen?" Anger surged through me and I had to stop myself from pushing her away.

"The book showed me before I passed. Didn't warn me about that, though. Did it?"

Her eyes narrowed as she spotted the book on the bed. I bit my lip, but it twitched as she glared at it. When her eyes met mine, I let the laugh out. And I laughed, until my stomach hurt and tears continued to stream down my face.

"Let it all out, dear."

"I'm sorry. This is ridiculous. I'm trapped in a mirror with my dead grandmother while a vampire inhabits my body and…" I struggled to suck in a breath.

"Gets dirty with a lost vampire king?" Grandmother continued for me, raising her eyebrow.

I cringed at her words. "Grandmother!"

"Well, it's true."

My amusement drifted away as she watched me. "You know everything that happened?" I closed my eyes as the guilt and shame gnawed at me. Taking a seat on the bed, I moved over when my grandmother approached. She sat down next to me, raising her arm to put it around my shoulders.

"You weren't to know. Damien is charming and very handsome. He even managed to sway me in my youth."

"Really?" I said, turning to face her.

"Yes, I used to aid the king in his fight against the vampires. I eventually managed to trap Damien in the mirror but never managed to fully destroy his creations."

"It was you!" I exclaimed. "You trapped Damien in here."

Grandmother smiled. "It was the only way to stop him. I didn't manage to discover blackfire as you did. I don't think I was powerful enough to trap him. You should have seen his face when he realized what I had done. Trapped with no one to corrupt."

"And I set him free," I said, putting my head in my hands. "You fought against him and I gave him what he wanted. If you knew this would happen, why didn't you stop me somehow?"

"I am sorry, my child. The book only showed me so much. I didn't know how this would turn out. I would never have put you in this position if I'd known." She embraced me and we stayed there for several moments. "Now it is time for us both to put things right."

CHAPTER 17

RAINA

It took her many hours to tell me the whole story. I insisted on hearing it from the beginning when she started working for the king. Lucas and Damien's bloodline held power, not like that in our family but an inactive one. They aged slowly, able to look young for years beyond that of a normal human. They had a charisma that allowed them to influence others, rally people to their cause if necessary. The bloodline was also more resilient, strong, and not prone to illness. I swallowed when I thought of the strange illness Lucas had, realizing only after I'd freed Damien that the vampire must have used the mirror to drain the life from Lucas, and then I was the catalyst that freed him.

"Chin up, Raina." I looked up to see Grandma smiling at me. "You did the best you could with what you knew. This is not your fault."

Heat surged through me, and hot anger that boiled within me broke free. "I knew nothing. You think I would have freed him or even spoken to him if I'd known what he was?" I clenched my fists at my sides, my nails digging into my palms. "Why didn't you tell me?"

"Believe me when I say—"

"Why should I believe anything you say? You could have warned me. All that time we spent together when I was a child…" I threw my hands up in exasperation. "Why couldn't you have just told me? Why leave the mirror in a position where it could be taken and given to me."

"I don't know, child." My grandmother stood before me, dropping her head into her hands. "I should have been able to destroy him, but I wasn't powerful enough. I ran out of time."

As quickly as it had come, my anger drained away. I took a step toward her, "So that's why you trapped Damien, a problem to deal with later when you were strong enough?"

"I trapped him at the behest of his brother, and I made him a promise that I would try to save him. It was the only way to stop him. Being stronger and living longer wasn't enough for Damien. He wanted more power, to live forever, and he seduced a witch to help him…my sister." Grandmother's lip trembled before she continued. "The power they unleashed was never supposed to exist. It perverted Damien's bloodline, twisted his soul. He became more violent, started to crave blood, and gained the ability to pass on his curse."

"I didn't know you had a sister," I said.

"She was the first to perish, becoming one of his creatures. He used her and her power until he grew bored of her. I had to destroy her in the end."

"I don't want to know." I thought about the vampire in my body, how he was using her now.

"It won't be the same for you, Raina. You are so much stronger than you know, and he could never hurt you."

I bit my lip, taking her offered hand. "Why did I have to do this alone? Why didn't you leave me better instruction."

"Our line is powerful, but we have to come by the power

within ourselves without outside influence." She gave me a sympathetic look. "We have to develop ourselves naturally."

"Kiara mentioned that." I swallowed thickly, shivering when I recalled her final moments. "She was trying to tell me something when Damien…"

"I know, my dear," she sighed. "She was trying to warn you about Damien and what happened. Now you know."

"Why couldn't she tell me?"

"That was my mistake. This never should have happened. I told her that she couldn't tell you anything until you passed the tests. I don't know how you ended up with the mirror. It should never have been able to leave my house. Damien must have somehow disabled my wards."

"I had that mirror for years after you died. Why now?"

"It took time for him to gain the strength to appear to you after my death. My life energy kept him contained all these years. Once he was strong enough, he could influence you."

"That would make you hundreds of years old, Grandmother."

She gave me a wink. "And I don't look a day over one hundred and fifty."

I shook my head, exasperated. "Take this seriously, please. I am stuck in a mirror." I pointed at the mirror. "And some evil vampire is running around in my body." I raised my eyes to the ceiling and screamed until I ran out of breath.

"Feel better?" my grandmother asked, crossing her arms, and raising her eyebrow at me.

"Actually…" I paused to smooth my dress. "Yes, I do."

"Good. This shouldn't be happening to you, but you can't change what has happened. Only what comes next. Raina, my dear, you know what I'm going to say."

"I need to do what the vampire in my body says." I turned to look at the mirror. "She's so evil, so dark."

"She's still a part of you, Raina, just the parts with no

inhibitions. You're not whole, and I agree with her, sadly." She grimaced. "What has happened is not natural, and one way or another it will have to be put right. You need to join with her and hope the good outweighs the bad."

"And Damien is the part of him with no inhibitions?" I scoffed. "You're going to tell me that I need to put the good from him back in him?"

"No, he's the original. His own corruption led him to the darkness. He wanted this. You didn't and you are strong. You can overcome that part of you once you're whole. You are so good." She gave me a hard look. "Search within yourself. You can feel a part missing."

I didn't want to believe. I tried to push her words away, but I knew. The vampire in my body had said the same, that she didn't feel complete, and deep down, I could feel something missing.

"You fractured your soul to protect yourself when Lucas died, and it is time, dear. You need to face this, and you need to finish it." She put a hand up when I started to speak. "This was my doing, and you will never understand how sorry I am that you that must finish this."

"What if I can't overcome her? What if she is me?"

"Please..." Grandmother chuckled. "You are not your mother. She was always a spiteful and cruel person. I am so glad she never discovered the power."

"Is that why you never..." I bit my lip, not sure how to continue.

"Treated her nicely? I just gave as good as I got while she was growing up. I did try with her." She looked at me, begging me to believe her. Her shoulders slumped. "I could have done better." She looked out the mirror to the real world.

"How do I even make myself whole?" I whispered, sitting down on the bed.

"You will have to figure that out for yourself, dear. I can't stay much longer, and the power is purer when you discover it yourself." She reached down to cup my cheek. "It has been wonderful being able to see you one last time. I know you can do this, Raina. Have faith in yourself."

She sat next to me and pulled me into her arms. I rested my head on her shoulder and breathed in the scent of sage and roses. When I released her, wanting to look into her face one last time, she had vanished.

"Raina, you can't." Niv's cry chilled my blood, and I gave her a small smile. It was the first time I had seen concern from her since her father's death, and it warmed my heart. "You don't know what it will do to you. You could end up entirely evil."

"My grandmother wouldn't lead me wrong," I reassured her. "I don't know how I will do it. Only that I must. She is me and I am her."

"You will make her stronger," Niv exclaimed, and the mirror shook in her grip, causing the image of her to blur. "She is a monster. She killed my father, and if you help her, what I thought about you being evil is true."

"It was me, all of me," I said sadly. "My actions caused your father's death. Maybe when I am whole, I can at least help you."

Niv huffed, her lips thinning. I knew she hadn't forgiven me for that day, and I never expected her to. I looked down, smoothing my dress.

"I can never make up for what has happened, Niv, but I will do everything in my power to ensure the safety of the people in this kingdom. Even if I must lose myself."

Niv nodded. "Then I will do what I must to ensure the safety of this kingdom. I will end you, if I must."

The mirror went dark and I sighed. I worried my lip with my teeth. "I hope you stay safe," I whispered, knowing she wouldn't hear me. I didn't know if I would ever see her again, and the thought made my heart ache.

I took in a deep breath and released it slowly through my nose, closing my eyes. I pictured the wisteria, instinctively knowing I would find my body there.

"Well, it's about time," I heard my voice say.

"I wasn't sure I would be able to find you," I said softly, the words coming from her mouth. We were sitting cross-legged at the base of the wisteria, surrounded by the thick canopy.

"You have made a decision." It wasn't a question.

"What must I do?" I asked.

"Will it."

"That's all?"

"That is all."

"And what will become of you?"

"We've been over this!" she snapped.

"Very well. I will see you soon."

I paced the mirror as I waited for her to appear. The seconds ticked by slowly before she finally entered the room and approached the mirror. She gave me a smirk before I saw my eyes close on her face, and I braced myself as she reached up to touch the mirror.

I let go, closing my eyes in the mirror and reaching up to touch the glass. I released all of it: the hurt and the pain of Lucas's death, the fear I could never correct my mistakes, the guilt and shame of my actions, and the worry that I wouldn't be able to resist Damien.

A force of darkness pulled at me as a purple haze crept in on me. Pain lanced through my consciousness and I tried to scream, but only silence greeted me as the force seeped into me slowly. I had never known pain like it as I tried to pry my eyes open to no avail.

Let me in, her voice, my voice echoed, a whispering caress within myself. I forced myself to relax until the pain eased. I became aware of my hands in my lap, my fingers twitching. Then my feet crossed beneath me. I gasped in a deep breath opening my eyes, knowing one moment of peace before I convulsed. I threw my head back in a silent cry, struggling to release the air from my lungs. The power I held pressed in on me, forcing its way in.

Finally, the pressure released me, and I stumbled backward until I sat heavily on the edge of the bed... breathing deeply, finally able to expel air.

"Raina?" I croaked, coughing, and putting a hand down to steady myself. "Raina?"

There was no answer. I couldn't feel her presence within me, but I felt different than I had for the years after Lucas's death. I reached up to touch my face, the skin cool and firm, more real than I had felt in years. A breathy laugh left my lips, and I grinned wickedly, feeling the influence of my darker self. Once more whole, a thrill ran through me, and I leaped to my feet with a fluid grace.

I rolled my shoulders, letting out a breath. I thought about what I needed to do, wondering why I cared what happened to Niv. But the thought of letting her down pulled at something, deep in my heart.

I bit my lip as I thought of Damien. His beautiful face came to mind, and I wondered what it would be like to be present while he used my body. I imagined his hands on me and smiled. I shook my head, trying to shake off the impulses. I needed to remind myself that helping Niv came first.

"Time to find Damien," I said to the empty room around me. "He will not see me coming."

My skirts billowed behind me as I strode through the palace until I reached a door to the gardens. I waved my hand, satisfied to see tendrils of purple curl through the fabric of my dress, the only color I had seen on myself in eight long years. I turned to spin, letting the euphoria of freedom consume me as I exited onto a patio. The air felt warm to my cold skin, caressing my hands as I reached out and looked up to the midnight sky. My senses felt more heightened than before I had been trapped in the mirror. My sight was clear, despite the blackness of the night around me. The permanent bleakness had settled over the kingdom.

"That's the first of the many ways I can put this right." I couldn't help but say aloud letting the euphoria of my release guide me. I raised both hands before me, palms up, and reached with my power. I could feel my connection to the darkness and the strands reaching down toward the palace. They must be connected to Damien. I laughed at how easy this would be.

With a vicious thought, I sliced my hands through the air, and the power ripped out of me toward the sky. It resisted my will at first, the need for night around the vampires trying to stop my will as I pushed. The clouds of malice raced away, fleeing from my power, and I smiled with satisfaction as the sky cleared to show a blanket of stars. The moon, high and proud, pulsed with light as it streamed down covering the kingdom in the first true night it had seen in many years. I bathed in the starlight, my arms wide and head facing the heavens.

≈

"My love," I purred as I entered our bed chambers—the ones I had first used when I arrived at the palace. I had spent several hours staring at the night sky and letting the breeze caress my skin.

Damien lay on the bed with a book in his hand, and I reached out, running my fingertips against the wall as I prowled closer. It was strange, feeling myself but not myself, an effort to stay on track and not be distracted. I had only known to come here because I could feel my draw to Damien tugging at me, but I still wanted to explore the palace. My posture and behavior seemed natural to me, but I had never acted this way until now. I was her and she was me.

Damien watched me as I stalked closer. I wasn't sure what I would do when I got close to him but his proximity made my insides quiver. Part of me wanted to destroy him. The other devoured his form hungrily, my fingers itching to caress his muscular chest. My stomach fluttered, and I damned the attraction I still felt while trying to hold on to the pleasant feeling. I hated him, but he was delicious to look at, his body large and toned. I could feel the power pulsing from him as his eyes roamed over my own body, the temptation almost too much.

"Where have you been?" he asked, rising from the bed to meet me before I reached him.

I swallowed thickly, his scent taunting me as I inhaled. "In the gardens," I answered, my voice sounding breathy.

"You have been spending too much time there recently," he commented.

I shrugged, my fingers leaving the wall to trail up his chest. "I like the colors." My eyes met his, and electricity sparked in the air around us. My skin began to tingle and I shivered.

Loud footsteps approached us from the corridor. "My masssterr," the vampire, one of Damien's minions, hissed as it entered. I was both relieved and furious at the interruption.

I recognized the tall vampire I had seen those years ago, leading the horde to attack the castle. I smiled when he edged around me warily. His hissing voice raked across my senses, disorientating me for a moment. Damien caught my arm to steady me, frowning as I leaned into him.

"What, Lewis?" Damien snapped.

"The ssssskyyy," the vampire hissed.

I was suddenly alone, Damien across the room before I could blink. He stared out the large window, his hands resting on the pane of glass.

"Impossible!" he exclaimed.

I bit my lip as he slowly turned, keeping the rest of my face blank.

"What did you do?"

"Me?" I answered, innocently, lifting my hand up to examine my nails. "You'll have to be more specific."

"Raina," he spat, rushing from the room.

I followed him to the royal chambers and laughed to see him approaching the mirror.

His fist pounded the wall next to it. "What have you taught her now?"

I grinned as he searched the mirror for me, taking a step toward the door. I didn't want to miss his reaction, but I knew I might need a route of escape.

"Massssster," Lewis interrupted Damien's cursing at the mirror. He must have followed us up here. "There'ssss more."

"Well?" Damien glared at the vampire before looking back and peering into the mirror.

"We are unnnder attack."

Damien roared, his cry animalistic and snarling. "What? Who?"

"The rebelssss, my massster." The vampire shrank back as Damien charged from the room.

I swayed as his motion disturbed the air around me and pressed my lips together, failing to hide my smile as Lewis followed him. Glee bubbled up and I raced out the room after them. The speed at which my body moved and the strength I could feel in it didn't surprise me, but it was strange to experience it for myself.

I felt different, as if the missing part of me was finally present. I had been right to give in and join with this creature. I could sense the evil presence within me, the one that had pushed me away when Damien first turned me. I must never let it take me completely, but it was an intoxicating feeling.

I made it to the walls overlooking the kingdom, used as lookouts for the vampires when Lucas had been alive. Within the kingdom I could see flares of fire, blackfire, surging high toward the east. Damien turned from his position ahead of me, glaring.

I shrugged. "I am standing right here. It's not me."

He scowled, raising his arms, and I watched the vampires swarm toward him. I grinned, letting a chuckle pass my lips at his confused expression. I turned back to watch the path of the fire approach us. Each one signified the death of one of Damien's vampires.

I watched as the blackfire got nearer, hoping Niv would hear the gentle plea in my mind. I hoped the breeze would carry my mental plea and see her safe. When she realized what I was about to do, she must have put her plans in motion to attack the palace. Another part of me relished in the massacre taking place and looked forward to seeing how this would play out.

CHAPTER 18

NIVEUS

"Flank them," Niv cried, thrusting her arms forward to blast fire at another vampire. She had used the tunnels her father had designed within the city to travel undetected. Unfortunately, one of the creatures had seen them sneaking through the streets, so stealth was no longer possible. Niv had hoped to avoid any fighting among the residential areas of the kingdom but hadn't seen any of the citizens in the area. At least they weren't out in the open where the number of their enemy would overcome them.

"On it," Asher replied, twisting his blade as he plunged it into a vampire's chest. Niv turned to glance at the men with her—a small group she trusted implicitly. Asher had Mal, Paxon and Keres at his back while Galen, Som, and Gunvor trailed her.

"Forward," Niv cried. She surged ahead with Galen on her right, slashing with her sword in her right hand and flames in her left—a deadly weapon, honed from the tragedy that had fallen on her kingdom. With another slash and blast of heat she could see the palace steps in front of her. Keres stepped up to her left, and she assumed Gunvor watched their back.

Before long, the palace loomed above them. Niv took a moment to stare at what was once her home. Asher's group joined them, making their way toward the large arch in front of the group.

"Are you ready?" she called, and the seven men shouted their agreement. "I know you'll see me safely from here. Make sure you wait until it's safe to enter. She waited for each of them to look her in the eye and nod. Turning, she didn't hesitate this time before she strode away.

Niv approached the court entrance, which allowed carriages to reach the main doors to the palace. She looked around the area, her heart falling at its state of disrepair with broken walls and carriages surrounded by scattered bricks. She gritted her teeth, pushing past the ghosts of her home and reaching the gate to the main courtyard. She made it to the center, seeing the shadows of figures start to close in around her. This would be the risky part of the plan; she was surprised she had managed to persuade the others to agree, but after years of inactivity, they craved action and knew it was time.

As Niv stood waiting, she glanced up to the wall facing the west on the other side the expanse of land, leading up the mountains from which the creatures had emerged. Her father used to stand there and direct the men before the invasion. Her breath caught when she saw the man, the vampire, looming over her and staring down into the court-yard. He hadn't aged a day since he had stepped out of the mirror and embraced Raina.

His face looked down with such fury she thought he might burst into flames. Behind him, her heart stuttered when she caught sight of Raina. Her skin was pale and eyes hollow, an aura of darkness curling around her. Niv swallowed, pain lancing through her heart at the sight of the woman who had killed her father.

Time stood still when Raina's eyes met hers. Niv examined the woman who had loved her and broken her. She shook her head, her heart aching. Looking around, she watched as the shadows approached her lone figure in the courtyard.

"Hello, little moussse," a vampire to her left hissed, slowly stalking toward her and pulling her attention to it. At the sight of him and his fellow vampires surrounding her, she smiled, gripping her sword tighter. She could never take them all in combat, and she wouldn't have to.

"Sssssillly to come alone," another said to her left.

Niv glanced up, looking Raina in the eyes.

"I am never alone," she spoke softly, turning to Damien and blowing a kiss at him.

His fury changed to confusion, and she stifled a laugh at his frowning face. Niv looked around at the vampires in the courtyard, and satisfaction enveloped her at Damien's roar.

"*Nooooo!*" he cried, and she caught sight of him rushing forward.

She opened her arms, hoping he would be caught in the blast as she released the power coiled within her and bathed the courtyard in blackfire. Its heat and hunger consumed all those surrounding her, a large portion of Damien's forces. She turned as the red flames pulsed around her, taking in all the destruction she'd brought on them. Too soon, the energy within her ebbed and the flames sputtered. She dug deeper and pushed harder, willing the fire to keep burning, but it started to draw closer to her, no longer able to make the distance. Niv fell to her knees, wincing at the impact. Her palms hit the floor as she panted and stared at the ground.

Slowly she looked up at the charred bodies around her and swallowed bile as the smell of burned flesh reached her nose. Even knowing they were monsters couldn't settle her stomach. Niv stumbled as she rose, her stomach roiling as she picked up her sword and got to her feet. She looked around, her vision blackening at the edges as consciousness threatened to leave her. She blinked a few times, relieved to see the seven figures approaching her from the direction of the main gate. As Asher came into focus, she lurched toward him, trusting him and the others to keep her safe as they retreated.

"That was certainly a statement," Asher said, looking around the courtyard. He wrapped Niv's arm around his shoulders and helped her stagger away. The rest of the seven surrounded her, Mal and Galen leading them back toward the streets. She looked over her shoulder one last time at Damien, wishing she'd been able to reach him at the top of the wall. She grinned at his scowl, only kept back by flames still licking up the wall toward him. The red fire started to shimmer with gold intertwined within its heat. Niv shuddered, glancing behind him and gasping at Raina's smiling face. Shock jolted through her as Raina gave her a wink and a nod.

Niv barely stayed awake as her men led her through the houses; they hadn't seen many people on the way in, which had concerned her. She was overjoyed when she caught the sight of eyes watching them from some of the homes. This boosted her hope that they survived under Damien's tyranny.

"I wish we could take them with us," she rasped.

"Not this time. We need to get you to safety."

"We could start smuggling them out one by one," Keres suggested. They'd had this argument repeatedly.

"We can't risk the tunnel being discovered. The more people who know, the more likely they will be sealed," Mal snapped at Keres impatiently.

Niv stumbled, nearly slipping out of Asher's grasp.

"Not far now," she heard Asher say. She was losing strength in her legs, and her feet started to drag as they continued. She could see the entrance to the tunnel up ahead that would lead them to the other side of the wall and relative safety.

Niv slumped against the wall next to the entrance when they reached it. No one would be able to tell the difference in the rock unless they knew to look for it since the cracks were too perfectly in line. She watched as Asher pushed a smaller brick, and a section of the wall slowly separated. The men braced themselves to shift the large section covering the entrance aside. A small cemetery and the entrance were hidden between a large crypt and the trees in the wall surrounding the kingdom.

"Why didn't he follow?" Paxon asked, grunting as the rock shifted.

"Too much fire still there," Mal answered, brushing his hands together as he released the rock. "Niv got them good."

"Who cares? Let us depart from here before they do follow us," Galen scolded. He was the first to enter the tunnel.

"No," Niv said softly. "Look." She tilted her head looking east.

The men beside her fell still as they spotted the haze of light. They looked up at the sky, only then noticing the lack of storm clouds that had blanketed the sky since Damien was released.

"This kingdom is about to see its first sunrise in eight years," Asher said, in awe of his words. "But how?"

"Raina," Niv said, one side of her mouth lifting into a half smile. "She took control back."

Asher scoffed. "You can't trust her."

Torn, Niv shook her head. In her heart, she felt as if Raina was two different people—the woman she loved as a mother and the monster. "I know. Come on. Let's go." Niv refused to move until only Asher remained, and she let him help her through.

"Come on, Princess. You don't really need my protection here. You just didn't want to be alone," he joked as they entered the gloom, pausing to make sure the others covered the entryway before they all breathed a sigh of relief.

"We aren't safe yet," Galen commented. He approached Niv to put the back of his hand to her forehead. "Your temperature isn't too high. Better than the last time you expelled that much power. We need to keep moving." He gave her an apologetic look and she nodded.

"Aye but we can rest here for a moment," Som joined her leaning against the wall. "We've been up nearly a full day and night. We all deserve a rest."

"Better to rest at home," Mal said, giving Som a push.

"A couple of minutes," Asher said firmly as he studied Niv as she leaned against the wall. She shook her head at his questioning gaze.

"Let's go," she announced, pushing off the wall with effort and starting down the path that would lead them under the wall and come out near a river several miles away. "If we get back to the horses, we can rest while we ride."

"Some rest," Som complained but followed Niv down the tunnel. Gunvor held back, taking her other arm to help her down the tunnel. He blushed furiously when he touched her but didn't say anything. The only sound for some times was their steps as they traveled away from the kingdom, moving farther from Niv's home.

Eventually light appeared before them, shrouded in a light mist near the tunnel exit. Niv took a deep breath, trying to ease the ache in her heart at once again leaving the kingdom and her people behind. Silently she promised she would return soon.

The group froze when a shadow passed over the light in front of them. Niv turned and nodded to her men, each drawing their sword slowly as they silently moved forward, creeping closer to their exit and the foe ahead.

Asher held out a hand, walking alone until he reached the end of the tunnel wall. He put his back to it, glancing over at the group before he looked around the rock with a large grin on his face. Niv gave him a quizzical look and he laughed.

"It's the horses. No one is there. It's safe," Asher said, still smiling.

"Oh, thank the gods," Galen huffed, reaching to help Niv as they left the tunnel. One of the eight horses was loose and Niv wasn't surprised to see it was hers.

"It's always Trouble," she said fondly, reaching for his reins when he approached her. "Good thing he knew to stay with the others. Otherwise I'd be taking your horse, Mal, and leaving you to walk."

The group laughed when Mal scowled at her. The tension that had hovered over them drifted away as they mounted and set off, putting more distance between them and the kingdom of vampires. They pushed the horses hard until they reached the border of Avilar, the neighboring kingdom Niv had fled to when she escaped.

"You knew. Didn't you? That Raina would take back control today," Asher said, drawing his horse up beside hers. It wasn't a question.

"Yes," Niv answered anyway.

"Why didn't you tell me?"

"It wasn't a guarantee."

"This is why you wanted to attack tonight."

"Yes," Niv replied simply.

"While they would be distracted? Or so you didn't have to destroy her? You waited until she was safe."

"Don't be ridiculous. Now was the right time. This way we won't have to face both. Raina might help us."

"I can't believe you still care for her after what she did."

"Don't be ridiculous." Niv frowned at him. "She murdered my father, but we need her to defeat Damien."

"I think you need to remember that more than I," Asher said, kicking his horse forward and trotting away from her.

Niv scowled at his back. Raina was a means to an end. Having her with them rather than against them was always the best way to defeat Damien. There was no guarantee. She was still a vampire, and when this was all over, she would die like the rest of them.

They had all discussed this, over and over. They needed the years to prepare and build an army. Niv was too young when she and Asher first escaped, only now after years had they recruited enough strong men to help them take back her kingdom.

Niv sighed, giving Trouble a nudge with her heels. They gained speed, catching up to the others as they approached Avilar. They had needed a larger army, but no one wanted to risk their kingdom against an undefeatable foe. Only the seven men with her were crazy enough to follow her into battle. She looked up as the sun shone on the neighboring kingdom. She was ready to rest and then continue to plan their next attack.

Niv stumbled down the corridor, tears blurring her vision and making it hard to see where she was going. She gasped for breath, struggling through her sobs as she fled the chamber where Raina

had just killed her father. Her legs wouldn't move underneath her, and she fell, her palms slapping against the floor.

"Niv, what happened?" Asher ran toward her, helping her to her feet.

"Raina, she—" Niv sobbed.

"Raina, what? Is she hurt?"

"She...killed...my father." Her lip trembled as she choked out the words.

"No." Asher shook his head. "You must be wrong. She would never hurt him. Or you."

"We need to go." Niv pulled on his arm, tugging harder when he didn't move.

"I don't understand." Asher paled, looking back the way Niv had been running.

She pulled him harder until he followed her. "Come on," she cried, relieved when he followed her. "We need to get out of here. She's one of them and she's coming."

They ran, gripping each other's hands as they raced through the palace. Niv didn't know where would be safe but aimed for the main entrance hall, the one used for grand balls and receiving important guests.

"Princess," Brigsten called. "They've broken through the wall. Where is the queen?"

"She's one of them," Niv said, sniffling. "She killed my father, and a vampire came out of the mirror."

"The mirror? What mirror?" Brigsten frowned.

"No time now," Asher said, taking a deep breath and looking at Niv. "We need to get her out of here. Raina is coming for her."

"This way." Brigsten led them toward the kitchens. "An escape has been prepared in the graveyard. Asher knows the way."

"Now I know why you told me," Asher said giving Brigsten a meaningful look. Niv stumbled after them, not following the conversation.

Brigsten nodded his eyes widening as the door to the orchard *crashed open. Raina stumbled through the door, her eyes wild and darting between them. Niv's heart pounded as Raina tripped, righting herself by holding on to the door.*

"Run," Raina hissed before letting out an ear-piercing scream.

Niv took a step backward, Brigsten moving to stand in front of her.

"Asher, take the princess," Brigsten ordered.

"What about you?" Niv called as Asher caught her around the waist and pulled her with him.

"I'll be fine."

Niv reached for him as Asher continued to drag her away, shrieking when Raina calmly stalked forward and grabbed him by the throat.

Jerking awake, Niv panted as she woke from the memory. She frantically searched the room for danger, gripping the knife she kept under her pillow in her hand. When nothing attacked, she forced her body to relax, keeping the knife in her hand as a comfort. Her muscles protested as she swung her legs around and rose from the bed, walking across the modest room to where she kept a basin. Only then did she release the knife and splash water on her face.

It had been years since she had woken from this nightmare. Returning to the palace must have stirred up these memories. She squeezed her eyes shut, pushing away the sorrow of losing her father and Brigsten in the space of a few minutes. Raina's choices had torn her world apart. Shaking herself, she walked to her bedroom door, needing to escape the lingering dream.

Niv emerged from her room to the sound of bickering in the common room. She smiled at the familiarity of waking to the brothers arguing. The group lived in a deserted tavern, large enough for them to each have their privacy and a common room where they all ate together. Asher and Niv had met the six brothers a few years earlier, and the group had become inseparable.

Asher and Niv had traveled to Avilar in the hope of securing help, an army, anything to dethrone Damien and avenge her father. As far as Niv knew, no one had escaped other than her and Asher. Brigsten had been struck down, giving them the time needed to find the tunnel out of the kingdom and escape.

They hadn't even been able to gain an audience with King Aaron. They petitioned each month but had never been accepted. A general in the king's army had taken pity on them and let them train in the Avilar army while they waited, knowing they would need to be prepared to fight.

Niv stepped into the common room of the tavern. Mal and Keres sat at the table in the center of the room, their loud voices ceasing at the sight of her. Mal gave Keres one last scowl, and Niv laughed. The two mercilessly teased each other until Mal took it too seriously. The bickering often came to blows between the two, but Niv wouldn't have them any other way. Most would find it aggravating, but Niv found it endearing. Having never had a sibling, she relished the chance to be part of the large family.

Keres seemed to have terrible luck and always suffered with one illness or another. He was particularly bad during the summer months when the trees started to bloom. Mal had an ill-tempered disposition causing the pair to clash. Niv had seen how he treated those he cared about, though, and despite his prickly demeanor, he would protect those he loved fiercely. Galen had been training as a physician when the brothers decided to leave their village, searching for a grand adventure. He now cured the group of any ailments, and Niv was sure he harbored a crush on Asher.

Niv smiled when Som entered, yawning. His name was short for Somnus, and he had a reputation for sleeping through anything if you didn't give him a whack to wake him. Galen followed him, guiding Paxon slowly through the door. Paxon had made it all the way back to Avilar before falling from his horse as they got back to the tavern. He was the best swordsman Niv had ever met, even better than Brigsten had been. She had learned a lot from him over the years, but he was extremely prone to injury when he wasn't fighting for his life.

"Where's Asher?" Gunvor asked from the door to the tavern.

Niv hadn't heard him enter. She shook her head and ignored Gunvor's blush as she answered him. She never teased Asher about Galen's crush because she knew he would answer with teasing of his own about Gunvor. She gave Gunvor a smile, holding back a chuckle when he avoided her eyes and sat next to his brothers. He was the youngest of them by fifteen years and had been a shock for his parents. It had been a surprise when he followed his brothers as he was barely old enough to be considered a man.

"He will be back soon," Galen answered Gunvor. "He was going to visit the barracks to see if he could petition for an audience with the king again. I don't know why either of you bother. You haven't had an answer in eight years."

Niv sighed. When they had arrived seeking help, she was sure she was going to return to her home and rid it of the vampires within a month. Without an audience with the king, they could do nothing to gain support. If she tried to raise an army from the people of Avilar, they would have been arrested. Avilar was too far away for the vampires to travel in one night, the fear of the sun preventing them from coming this far. The Avilar general had explained there was no reason for the king to draw Damien's attention, especially after the rumors about the powerful sorceress the vampires had with them.

Niv had been shocked when Raina had contacted her through the mirror. Even after it had been destroyed several times and reappeared, she hadn't been able to avoid her. Asher had argued with Niv when she started listening to Raina, but she could feel the woman's regret.

Raina wasn't the monster that had chased her from the palace. She was the same woman Niv had grown to love. Niv wasn't sure she had believed Raina was that naive as to be tricked into killing her father; and it wasn't forgivable. But when Niv had felt the draw of the power, when Riana had started sending it to her through the mirror, she couldn't deny that Raina wanted to help.

"We need to plan," Mal said with a huff. "We've surprised them, and while they are still in shock, we need to act."

"I agree," Paxon said, hobbling to the table and taking a seat. "Now is the time. We've shown our hand and revealed ourselves. We can't sit back anymore."

Niv seated herself next to Paxon, smiling gratefully at the men before her. They followed her and Asher, supporting their belief that they could take back the kingdom, despite their small group. Niv frowned. She guessed Asher no longer believed that if he went to recruit soldiers from the barracks. She sighed, looking at the windows and the pitch-black night. She couldn't wait until the longer days of the summer when the sky didn't darken in the early afternoon. She could feel the restless energy in the room.

"Here." She rose from her seat and pulled the pieces of parchment they had piled in one corner. "Let's go over the maps and tactics we've already put together."

It was hours later, Som still yawning every few minutes, when the door to the tavern opened and Asher entered carrying a crate in his hands. He must have had to wait into the evening to submit their request.

"Found this outside. Looks like supplies," Asher said, placing the crate on the table near the window. He glanced at the pages on the table and rolled his eyes. "No rest for tonight then."

"You know I can't sleep at night," Niv answered, not looking up from the map she was studying. She hadn't been able to sleep since the vampires had taken her home. Knowing they were active only at night, she didn't want to be caught unaware. Even if it was suicide for any of the creatures to come to Avilar since they would never make it back to Lestoria.

"You know what I think about that," Asher grunted. "They wouldn't survive the trip back if they made it this far. We are safe here."

"We are never safe," Niv said simply.

"Any new ideas?" Asher asked.

Niv paused. "That depends on Raina."

Asher's face reddened. "We can't rely on her, Niv. It could all be a trick."

Niv shook her head. "This is different. I told you she had found a way to take her body back."

"Her vampire body."

"Yes, but she thought she could control it."

Niv looked around, none of the men at the table looking at her as she argued with Asher. Gunvor rose, strolling over to the crate in the corner.

"Don't any of you believe me?"

Paxon coughed next to her. "We do believe you. We just don't want to rely on the person who killed your father and destroyed your kingdom. We can do this ourselves."

Asher's eyes flashed with anger. "Don't you remember what she did to Brigsten?"

Niv swallowed. She did remember, and she shuddered when memories of the dream she'd had earlier threatened to surface. Gunvor took the lid off the crate and rummaged through it.

"Damien might kill her if he realizes she's back in control," he said, lifting a bright red apple from the crate. He curled his lip and placed it on the table, rummaging through the box further.

"Fruit is good for you," Galen told him.

"They could have delivered some meat. This box is mostly fruit," Gunvor said, abandoning the crate and seating himself at the table again.

"You are a fool, Niv," Asher exclaimed, throwing his hands up. "She will kill you. All she wants is to see you dead."

"You don't know that," Niv insisted. "Why would she give me her power and help us this far. Did you see Damien's face. He had no clue I was still alive."

Asher scoffed, crossing his arms. "You are not a girl anymore, Niv, and you need to make the tough decisions. Our plan should not involve her. For all we know she's been corrupting you with the power she's sending."

"Come on, lads," Mal said, his chair grating along the floor as he rose from the table. "Let's give these two a moment." Niv remained quiet while they left the room, their awkward glances pulling at her.

"It's not your decision, Asher. I'm the princess here."

"Princess of nothing, Niv. Your kingdom fell."

Niv recoiled as if he'd slapped her.

"I'm sorry. I didn't mean that." Asher ran a hand through his hair. "I just don't want you to be betrayed again. I saw you after we fled. You were inconsolable. I know you loved her, but she did this. Through her actions your father died."

"I know," Niv whispered. She rose from her chair to pace the room, picking up the apple Gunvor had left out and throwing it between two hands. "I just feel it. I know she hurts. You don't see her like I do."

Asher approached, taking the apple from Niv's hand and placing it on the table. "I know how hard this is for you." He took her hands, staring into her eyes, and Niv bit her lip.

"I just want this to be over."

"I know, Niv. I know." Asher was quiet for a moment. "We could leave. The vampires can't leave the kingdom. They are isolated here, and no one trades with them."

Niv took a step back, dropping his hands. "I can't abandon my people."

Asher's shoulders slumped. "I know. I do understand. I just couldn't bear it if anything happened to you." He picked up the apple, handing it back to her. "Get something to eat, and then I need to go and rest."

Niv took the apple, rolling it between her palms. "Thanks, they always were my favorites." She grinned at him. Lifting the apple to her mouth and taking a bite.

CHAPTER 19

RAINA

The apples gleamed, a bright unnatural red in the room where Lucas and I had married, almost pulsing in the darkness. I examined them as I passed each tree, the trunks rotten and the leaves blackened.

I had slipped away while Damien was distracted by Niv's display, knowing he would turn his wrath on me. I wasn't quite ready for him to discover that I had escaped the mirror. I bit my lip, smiling at the power Niv had shown. I could never have imagined her control or the destruction she could cause to the vampires. She had announced her return and made her intention clear. She would not settle for less than the total eradication of Damien and his creatures.

My smile widened as I felt him approach, his dark presence spreading into the room. I didn't turn as he came into the room, his power pulsing toward me as I continued to stroll through the trees.

"My lord," I said, daring to reach toward the trees and trailing my fingers through the air near the foliage.

"Raina," he replied.

I turned to look at him, amused at a muscle in his jaw

twitching. "How is it that Niv is still alive when you killed her yourself years ago?"

I gave him a careless shrug, how I had seen myself do in the mirror when I had been trapped. It felt natural to me in my body. "She wasn't moving when I left her."

"You're not that stupid," Damien growled. "Tell me, my sweet." His voice was like syrup and despite myself, I shivered at the sound.

"I was young, newly made," I commented, giving him a saccharine smile. "What do you expect?"

"Do not play with me, Raina." Damien stopped before me. Barely inches away, I could feel his breath on my face. I had to resist taking a step back, aware that I had reached the wall and had nowhere to retreat, even if I had wanted to. I held my head high, staring into his eyes.

Raising my eyebrow, I cocked my head. "I can play a game if you'd like." I half hoped he would take me up on the offer.

He watched me slowly, looking deep into my eyes. I gasped when his hand gripped my throat, my back screaming in agony as he pushed me hard against the wall. "I knew it," he growled.

His grip tightened, though I didn't move, welcoming the pain and welcoming the pressure of the wall behind me. Free from the mirror, I finally had control, and with his body this close, I couldn't help it when I moved my own against his. I laughed at the surprise on his face.

"How did you escape?" He narrowed his eyes, his lips nearly touching mine. "Why now after all these years?"

I looked up at him through lowered lashes and licked my lips before I spoke. His hand did not move, keeping a light pressure on my neck and holding me in place.

"You're clever, Damien," I purred. "I'm sure you can figure it out."

"If only I could control you as easily as I could your body," he said, reaching up with his other hand and stroking a finger down my cheek. I was surprised to see awe and admiration in his gaze. "You are remarkable, Raina. I always thought so."

I couldn't hide my gasp or ignore the heat spreading to my cold cheeks as his finger trailed down to my collar bone. I had to bite back a moan as my body responded to his closeness when he pressed against me. With my back to the wall, I could not escape. I hated him, but I couldn't resist him. When his lips met mine, I kissed him back with a desperation I couldn't control nor wanted to control. I moaned when he pressed into me harder, his desire evident against me. His hand never left my throat, holding me in place.

"Massssster."

We both growled at the interruption, but the sudden space between us cleared my head, and I closed my eyes, fighting my desire for him.

"Get out," Damien spat, approaching the creature menacingly.

"Massssster, the ssssssky. The attackssss. What will we do?" The vampire cowered, pointing out the windows. The windows now tinged with rouge along the horizon in the east.

Damien growled, taking a step back from me. I bit my tongue to stop the laughter threatening to escape, but I couldn't hide my amusement when Damien turned on me. In two strides he was on me, and I lifted my chin daring him with my eyes to hurt me.

"Go on, do it!" I growled, all passion erased by my fury.

"You defy me, Raina. You have gone too far." He flung his hand toward the window. "How did you escape?"

"You cannot make me obey you, Damien." I smirked. "I am too powerful for you, and you made me this way. Go on. Try it."

His lips thinned while I taunted him. Finally, he turned to the door.

"Where are you going?" I sang at his retreating back. "We were just getting started."

"To protect my creatures. I may not be able to make you obey, Raina, but I can still hurt you. You don't want to anger me further," he called over his shoulder.

I shook off his words as he left. What could he do that he hadn't already done?

I lay in my old chambers, not wanting to go back to the rooms I shared with Lucas. After my response to Damien, I didn't want to be near him in case I lost myself again. I had wandered the palace for several hours while it was light outside. I regretted my decision to rid the sky of its protective cover, but I knew it had been the right thing to do. It might trap me, but it also trapped Damien and his vile creations. I lay on the bed, knowing that darkness had fallen but not caring to go outside. The hours slipped by as I thought about what I would do next.

I sighed, no longer able to bask in the warmth of the sun and fight what I had become. I had seen no humans, only Damien's wretched creatures. I learned that the humans were kept within their homes or the dungeon, near starving with so little food available. The vampires brought them supplies but not as often as they should from what I could tell. I raised my hand, staring at the purple flames dancing across my fingers.

"Should I be worried?" Damien said coolly from my doorway.

I leaped off the bed, instantly ready to face him. It

worried me that I hadn't heard him approach, lost in my own thoughts.

"I don't know," I replied coyly. "Should you be?"

"I was hoping I could join you." He raised his eyebrow with his eyes on the bed.

I sucked my teeth, watching him in the doorway. I damned his good looks and my reaction to his presence. I longed to give in, and I briefly wondered if this attraction to him stemmed from the vampire inside of me—the evil that had inhabited my body, a left-over residue still present now I was whole. Deep down, I knew it had always been there. His darkness now excited me because it spoke to my own.

"You may not," I told him reluctantly, my mouth watering at his broad shoulders. I argued with myself. Who would know if I gave in to my desire? Damien's brow pinched, lines appearing between his eyes as he watched me. I gasped when he charged into the room, at once pinning me to the bed. His weight on top of me was a thrill, which caused me to lose my resistance for a moment. I leaned into him, watching his lips.

"All those years ago, you told me you killed Niv. How is she now alive and attacking my court, Raina?" Damien growled.

I shivered as he ran his lips along my jaw, his scent intoxicating.

I tried not to moan, giving him a shrug, but our nearness made it more of a writhe beneath him. "I don't know," I said softly.

"You let her go."

I didn't answer, his lips now near my ear. I needed to push him away. I didn't want to.

"How did you manage it? Why would you betray me?"

"Betray you!" I exclaimed. His words drenched me in the cold shock I needed to push him off me. The anger at his words was sudden and hot, making my skin prickle. It didn't take much effort, and I barely registered his shock. "Betray *you!*"

With a flick of my hand, I threw him against the wall, his feet hovering above the ground. Damien went stiff, his entire body convulsing and jaw tense when I twisted my hand. I made sure an intense pain radiated through his body. A flash of fear crossed his face.

"You *used* me. Tricked me into killing the man I loved and betraying everyone in this kingdom." I held my hand in a fist, squeezing him harder.

My voice deepened and didn't sound like me. A thrill surged through me, and I remembered my love for Lucas as if it was a dream, but the pain from his loss was seared into me. The anger at my own actions was very real. My rage at Damien was palpable. Could I kill him? Could I succeed where my grandmother had failed?

As I thought it, the energy seeped away from me, even as I clawed at it harder. I started to panic as it slipped through my fingers. Damien started to smile, broadening into a grin as the power I held dissipated. He dropped down gracefully, prowling toward me. Frustration warred with shock as he came closer.

"Very impressive, Raina. I'm surprised you managed to do that much. But you forget that I made you. You are my creature, and your power is mine to do with as I will. You have your moments of freedom, but you can't harm me."

I blanched. "I will break free from you, Damien. You can't hold me off forever." I hoped this was true. "You gave me time to figure out a way to end you."

"Indeed. I can, however, still hurt you," he said, repeating his words from earlier with a gleam in his eyes. "In fact, I may already have. Finishing what you should have."

The blood drained from my face at his words and I

swayed on my feet, thoughts of Niv and the attack penetrating my anger. "What did you do?"

"You'll find out soon enough." He smirked.

I gritted my teeth and launched myself at him, clawing at his eyes. I managed to rake my nails across his face before he grabbed my wrists. He threw me to the ground, laughing. His amusement stoked my anger, and I was on my feet in an instant, ready to charge forward again.

He held up his hand, and I watched in fascination as the slice of red across his face healed.

"That is useless, Raina. I tire of this game. I shall leave you to think about the consequences of your actions. You should consider truly joining me. I am on the winning side, after all." With that, he turned and strode from the room, leaving me standing there staring at the empty doorway. It took a heartbeat before I followed him.

Damien moved through the castle quickly and ignored me when I called after him. He only halted when we were in the apple orchard inside the hall. All the curtains had been pulled closed, and the hall lined with candles to light the trees. When he turned to face me, I glared at his malicious grin.

"Beautiful trees aren't they? They turned this color after I turned you. It's fascinating what you can do with your power, Raina. I've never seen its likeness. I knew when I saw you staring into my mirror that you would grow to be an incredible woman."

"What is this about, Damien? What did you do?" My panic at what he might have done to Niv had driven away the darkness possessing my body. It had abandoned me, and I felt more like my old self.

"I told you. You'll know soon enough." He smirked at me. I whirled to face the entrance to the small hall and a commotion behind me and two vampires dragging a human through into the hall. I gasped when I recognized him as Harold, the palace head of staff. I took a step forward, blanching when he flinched away from me.

"Get away from me, you monster," he said, spitting at my feet.

I stepped back. I knew I deserved worse after what I had done to Lucas. My shoulders slumped, and I didn't move as Harold was dragged toward Damien. Then I realized Damien held an apple in his hand. The red skin looked unnatural, but the way it caught the candlelight was mesmerizing. I watched Damien throw the apple up and catch it, my gaze never leaving the red fruit. Harold was dropped unceremoniously at Damien's feet. He struggled to stand and was forced back down, his knees hitting the floor with a crack. I crossed my arms, biting my lip and curious as to what Damien planned.

"Now, human. I want you to eat this fruit." Damien offered the apple to Harold, who scowled at him.

"Vile creature," Harold spat at him, all proper behavior left behind. I had never seen the man anything but quiet, concise, and perfectly put together. It was unnerving watching his disheveled form, cowering before Damien.

"Damien, leave him be," I said, trying to sound bored while taking a step toward the group.

Damien raised his hand. "A moment, my dear. Take this, Harold, or I'll bring that pretty daughter of yours here from her home. You wouldn't want that."

I walked to Damien's side, looking down at Harold, who avoided my gaze. Reluctantly he reached forward, taking the apple from Damien. He turned it in his hand, the red skin shining in the candlelight surrounding us.

"We don't have all night," Damien gave Harold a hard look. Harold sighed, the apple rising to his lips. He took a bite, the crunch of the flesh the only sound in the room.

Slowly he chewed, staring at the fruit in his hand. One moment he was perfectly fine, the next he crumpled to the floor. The apple hit the ground and rolled away from us. I watched in horror as Harold's body shriveled in front of my eyes, his skin tightening over his bones and body unmoving.

"What happened?" I demanded, my eyes wide.

"The same fate as your dear Niv," Damien said, smiling cruelly.

"You lie," I exclaimed, turning to face him.

"Last night, I sent my creature out with a gift for the group that invaded our sanctuary. They were very brave, truly devoted, knowing they wouldn't make it back by nightfall and sacrificing themselves in the daylight to ensure our future safety," Damien told me. While I had been wandering around the castle, lounging in my old rooms, he had been planning. "They followed the trail from where our enemy emerged from a tunnel and then traveled to a tavern in Avilar."

My blood turned to ice in my veins, and my already cold body stiffened as he explained the gift he'd sent.

"Each of them will have taken one of your apples, Raina, the ones turned when you were, and they will have been defeated with little effort from us."

I swallowed hard. "When?"

"Any moment now," Damien's hand swept toward the window.

I didn't know how I knew, but I could feel the rise of the sun. It was about to crest the wall, the light streaming onto the palace grounds. He'd timed it perfectly. If I escaped and tried to find Niv, I would perish in the daylight. I had wasted the night when I could have escaped and found her.

Damien expected my attack, but this time I attacked with my power and the claws that grew from my fingertips at the same time. I mauled his face as the power bombarded him.

He held me back, the power ricocheting off a shield that formed around him. Anger surged up within me, as he held me back. I closed my eyes and let it, the power building at my center.

"I love it when you're angry," Damien said silkily as he struggled to hold me off him. I could feel his amusement and pleasure. I relaxed, eyes still closed, and waited as the power still pulsed inside me, invisible flames licking at my skin. I let them, relishing in the heat. I didn't stop, even when Damien's lips met mine. I didn't kiss him back as he nibbled my lip, and for the first time, my body didn't react to his proximity.

"Come on, Raina," he purred. He twisted and rolled until he was on top of me in the middle of the hall. Still my eyes remained closed as I let the power build, flinching when he kissed my cheek. "We could do so much together."

I opened my eyes, feeling more in control than I had so far. "Never."

I let go of my hold on the power and let it roll out from me as Niv had in the courtyard. Damien's face was an inch from mine, and it scrunched up as the purple blackfire shot out from me. I heard a roaring in my ears and breathed hard as it poured from me. I tried to direct it to Damien, but the flames curled around him, leaving him unharmed.

I pushed harder, willing it to penetrate his protection, but tiredness pulled at me. I could feel myself slipping away from consciousness, and I welcomed the oblivion. I forced more of myself into the magic and hoped some of it would scorch Damien. My head fell back as I could no longer hold myself up, and I let my body relax. I let exhaustion take me, barely aware of Damien's hands on me when he lifted me from the ground.

"What am I going to do with you, Raina?" Damien whispered.

I managed to open my eyes, and a thrill of satisfaction

shot through me when I saw the room, blackened by the flames with the curtains still alight. I smiled at the piles of ash where the apple trees had been, each one destroyed by my blackfire. Damien would be unable to hurt another human with the apples.

∼

I woke to a shooting pain in my head and a burning thirst in my throat and stomach. I rose from the bed, doubling over with the agony. I had never known such pain.

"You need to feed," Damien said sharply from a chair in the corner.

I looked around, surprised to see that Damien had taken me to the rooms with the mirror. The curtains were drawn, and it was softly lit with a single candle. The mirror caught my eye and I scowled at it. Turning to Damien, I continued to scowl at him as I rose and tried to walk past him.

He clutched at my hand before I could get out of his reach. "I mean it, Raina. You're weak, and you need to feed."

"Why do you care?" I snapped, only the anger remaining, boiling beneath my skin.

"You know why." Damien looked lost. "You know I care for you greatly. I love you."

"You care so much you turned me into a monster and destroyed my family. You destroyed this kingdom and now —" my voice cracked. "If any harm has come to her, I will find a way to end you."

Damien frowned, a confused look on his face. "I don't understand how you can withstand it. You're obviously in pain from hunger, but you're not racing out of here to find the nearest human. Raina, my actions may seem uncaring, but I love you. I have done all of this for you."

"You have not," I said cruelly. "You only think about yourself, your power. You nearly destroyed your own family to become what you are, and now you've destroyed mine. You don't know what love is."

"And you do?"

"I loved Lucas with all my heart."

"Loved. Past tense." He smiled. "You love me now. I've seen how you respond to me. Even since you left the mirror you can't resist me for long." I ignored the smug look on his face, trying to leave again.

"Never," I whispered.

"You will come around. Now it is time for you to feed. You need blood."

Bile rose in my throat as I thought about drinking blood from a human. Yet my mouth watered and my teeth started to ache. I'd seen Damien do such things while I was trapped in the mirror. I shuddered at the memory of him feeding on the bed, my other self with him, sharing the meal. I swallowed thickly, trying to pull away from him.

"Let me starve. Then you'll finally be rid of me," I said, taking a step away from him and folding my arms around my chest.

"I don't want to be rid of you. I want you to submit, as you already have. Be queen and share my throne. You are mine, Raina. Nothing will change that."

"Your death will change that. I am my own person, Damien." I scoffed. "I belong to no one."

He chuckled. "If only your mother could see you now. Maybe I will bring her out to play if you behave. I know you'd love to torture her."

I felt a flutter of air touch my face as he disappeared, leaving me alone in the room. Stunned that he had left me alone, it took me a moment before I could think about how I could leave. If only I had a way to contact Niv and find out if she was okay. My eyes fell on the mirror. Slowly I approached it, my hand clutching at my stomach at a new sensation of pain as I tried to ignore the gnawing hunger.

As soon as I touched the mirror, the surface shimmered. Blackness appeared in the reflection, the inside of the bag Niv kept the mirror in, ensuring it was covered when it wasn't in use.

"Niv," I cried, my heart beating faster as I waited. Looking over my shoulder before I called her name again. I would have to be quick. "Niv."

I could hear a faint scuffle through the mirror, and my heart leaped when light appeared. I tapped the mirror, impatiently waiting for Niv to appear. Hoping, against hope, that she was safe.

My heart sank when Asher's face came into view. "Asher? Where is she? Tell me she's okay."

"Traitor," Asher said, acid in his voice. He had dark shadows under his eyes and I could see the pain behind his stare. "What do you want? Haven't you done enough damage?"

"Tell me she is safe. Tell me she is well," I demanded. I looked over my shoulder again, straining to hear if anyone approached.

"I can't."

"No," I whispered. "She can't be. She can't." Anger rose in me, and I bit back another cry as I squeezed my eyes shut. The hunger was finally quiet inside me, replaced with a profound loss and despair.

"You finally killed her. I told her not to trust you."

"It wasn't me. I swear," I insisted. "Damien, he—"

"Your lover, then. It's all the same. You are both as evil as each other."

"I can help. I can—" my mind raced as I thought of any way to fix this.

"Even you can't raise the dead," he spat.

I thought of Harold and his reaction to the apple. I had to try. "Don't bury her or burn her. Give me a day, and I'll have a cure." I would do anything to save her, no matter the cost. She meant more to me than anything left in this world.

Asher stilled. He seemed to finally be looking at me. "Why should I? You tricked her into working with you. She should never have trusted you. She thought you'd managed to take control. She believed you'd help us when we attacked and you just stood there."

He was right. I stood back and watched, proud of Niv's actions. They didn't need my help, but I hadn't shown that I supported them.

"You didn't need me," I said firmly. "I will bring her back, and we will kill him if it's the last thing I do," I said with such venom that Asher's eyes widened.

"Give me a day," I begged him. "I will find you and let you know what must be done." Determination swelled in me, and I knew I would find a way. I had to.

"One day. Then we put her to rest," he said reluctantly, narrowing his eyes. "Don't betray us, or I promise you, Raina, you will die." With that he stuffed the mirror back in its bag without another word.

CHAPTER 20

RAINA

$\mathcal{I}$ stared at my reflection in the mirror as the connection severed. It was the same image I had seen, all those years ago. Darkness surrounded me and had seeped into my soul. I needed to keep it at bay until I could help Niv and end Damien. I lowered my eyes from the haunting image and turned at the sound of the door behind me as Damien entered the room, dragging a bedraggled man and woman behind him.

I froze when I saw my mother, cowering at Damien's feet. Expectantly I turned to the man, disappointed when I realized it wasn't my father. He looked familiar as he stumbled toward me, pushed by Damien. "Brigsten," I murmured, shocked at his dirt-ridden face, a beard now on his once smooth face and his uniform tattered.

"Gifts, my dear." Damien raised his eyebrow and hauled Brigsten toward me. "You need to feed."

I narrowed my eyes at him as he left, closing the door loudly behind him. I shook my head, wondering why he had left me alone again. My gaze fell on Brigsten, and I swal-

ROTTEN TO THE CORE

lowed, taking a cautious step forward and reaching out to help him up.

"Are you okay?" I asked, pulling my hand back when he held up his own. I ignored my mother, unable to face her, expecting her usual disappointment and scorn.

Brigsten rolled and pushed himself to a seated position. "Just great."

I watched him carefully, waiting for him to get his bearings. Slowly, he made his way to his feet and surveyed the room.

"Have you been trapped in here since…" His voice trailed off, watching me carefully.

"In a way," I told him. I seated myself in a chair in the corner, waving toward the mirror. "I was in there until recently." Another wave of agony swept through me and I bent forward, holding my stomach.

Brigsten frowned, staring at me warily. "I saw you that first day, when Niv… It was like you were possessed and then took control for a moment. You told us to run and then you attacked me."

I shook my head. "I don't have any memory of this."

"They say you killed Lucas. That you took his place and became the vampire queen."

I closed my eyes, not saying anything for a moment. I didn't know what my vampire body had done over the years, but I could imagine. "It's a long story."

Brigsten looked at me doubtfully. "You look like them."

"I am one of them. Damien turned me the day Lucas…the day I failed him. This is my doing, but I will put it right," I told him.

Demented cackling had us both turning to face my mother—the one I thought was dead. My vampire-self had taunted me with the death of my parents more than once. Told me they were dead but here she was. Acid crept through my gut, and my eyes widened at the filth on her once-plump cheeks. Now a gaunt shadow of my mother, she laughed at me.

"Another trick, my dear daughter. Escaped from the mirror?" she scoffed. "Don't fall for it, you fool. She will kill you like she has killed so many others. She is a selfish, evil creature...always has been."

I frowned, choosing to ignore her words. "Where is Father?" Hope surged in my chest that he was alive too.

"Dead," she spat. "Killed by that demon when he tried to escape and find you. They dragged him back and killed him right in front of me. You should have listened to *me*!"

My heart sank, heavy in my chest. "Mother, I..." I swallowed. Falling back into old habits, I hunched my shoulders.

"Pathetic, now if you'd killed both off and not let this demon take control. How come when I suggested it you objected?"

"Madam." Brigsten took a step forward scowling. "Did you have a hand in this?"

"No." My mother grimaced. "Turns out my whore of a daughter did this all on her own. Ruined this kingdom and our family."

I couldn't take it anymore. A red haze tinged my vision, and something snapped within me. I sprang forward, wrenching her head back and sinking my teeth into her neck. All those years of taking her harsh words, the resentment she felt for me made me believe I was worthless. I drank until I could pull no more from her, dropping her lifeless body to the ground. I felt no horror at what I'd done.

"Raina." Brigsten's voice quivered behind me. I turned to see his hands raised in a calming gesture. "Just take a breath."

"You have nothing to fear from me," I said, reaching up to wipe my mouth. He took a step back, crossing his arms over his chest.

"So, it's true? You did this?"

I nodded slowly. "I will put it right," I said again. I curled in on myself as I caught the scent of his blood in the air.

Brigsten shook his head. "I don't understand."

With no emotion I told him what had happened and how I had freed myself from the mirror. Brigsten listened carefully, never relaxing, so I kept my distance.

"What about her?" He gestured to my mother.

"She deserved it. If I wanted to kill you, you'd be dead already," I said, my tone hard. "What about you? Last I saw you were escaping with Niv."

Brigsten nodded. "I stayed to hold them off, so they could escape. I thought they would turn me but they didn't turn many at the start, though something has changed in the last day. They've been pulling us from the cells and turning as many as they can. When I was taken by *him*, I thought I was next." He shuddered.

"It was Niv."

"The princess? She made it out?" he said sharply.

"Yes."

"Is she safe?"

I put one hand to my face. "She was incredible when I saw her yesterday. She destroyed a substantial portion of Damien's creatures."

Brigsten looked at me expectantly. "And?"

"Damien, he sent her an enchanted apple. Asher said she's dead, but she can't be. I'd feel it." Dread curled in my center. I was sure I would have felt if she was gone. "I will do what I must to save her."

Brigsten's face crumpled, and he squeezed his eyes closed. I watched him, wondering if I could make him trust me enough for us both to escape. When he opened his eyes, he still looked wary, and I didn't blame him. "What can I do?"

I looked up, my eyes wide. "You'd trust me?"

"I will do what I must," he echoed my words, though his eyes caught on my dead mother. "We must find Niv and Asher. Save her and help her kill them all."

"I agree," I said. Something in me tried to resist the words but I ignored it. "Tell me everything you can about Damien's activities."

"You would know more. You barely leave his side according to the others kept here." He sniffed. "What can I tell you that I don't already know?"

"I only recently escaped the mirror." I gestured to the wall. "I only remember being in here the last eight years."

"Then I will tell you what I can."

"The book taught you everything?" Brigsten asked as he watched me. I'd turned to a blank page. I quickly told him it was hard to read, but I could tell he didn't trust me. That was probably better for his health. I glanced at my mother's mangled body, much better for his health.

"Sadly, not just the book. Damien was in the mirror before I freed him." I nodded toward the mirror on the wall. "I inherited it from my grandmother, who was the enchantress for Damien's brother." I frowned. "I never did figure out how many generations ago, but he's some great uncle to Lucas. He was imprisoned by his brother and my grandmother in the mirror. Damien used to speak to me," I explained.

"That's creepy." Brigsten paced the room while I checked the book. I glanced at the door, wondering why Damien hadn't barged in yet.

My cheeks heated. "I was a fool. It's no excuse, and I wish more than anything that I hadn't been tricked by him.

Lucas…" I swallowed, realizing that with Damien gone the dark urges I'd been having had lessened.

"I won't pretend to understand," Brigsten said, pulling the curtain back and looking out the window. "I failed him too. I should have thought about enchantment when he fell ill. In all the years I'd known him, no ailment ever affected him."

"That's his bloodline," I told him. "They aren't entirely human. Damien is a perversion of that magic in them. The family could already heal fast, live longer, and never fall ill. He wanted more."

Brigsten shook his head. "I will never understand any of this."

I gave him a sympathetic smile. "I know. I feel the same sometimes."

"You understand more than I do."

"But not enough to have saved Lucas," I murmured, staring at the blank page. Would the book even work for me now that I was in a vampire's body? I caressed the page, leaning on my other hand as I looked at the book. Instantly words scrawled across the page.

> *Give him hell, my dear child.*
> *Niv can be cured. Damien can be defeated.*
> *True love's kiss and your power untainted.*
> *You'll need to think this one through, darling.*
> *I know you can do this.*

I smiled at the page, my grandmother still helping from another world. "True love's kiss and power untainted."

Brigsten looked over my shoulder. "What language is that?"

I frowned. "Can't you read it?"

"No."

"Good to know." I flicked my wrist and the book disappeared. I chuckled at Brigsten's shocked gaze. "I wonder if Niv had a love, someone to kiss her. She's close with Asher. I always wondered if there was more there than friendship." I stopped pacing, not realizing I'd moved until then. "That doesn't feel right. Not *a* true love. A kiss?"

"There's a flower called true love's kiss," Brigsten said. I turned to him and he shrugged. "My father liked exotic plants, so I picked up a few things."

"Will there be any of that in the grounds?" I asked. My heart fluttered as I wondered if it would be that easy.

Brigsten shook his head. "No, it grows on the west side of the mountains. My father wanted to venture that way to see if he could discover it, but the king denied his request since the vampires were known to shelter there."

I nodded, slowly. "It makes sense if it's a powerful plant. We don't know much about the lands to the west, but history tells us that creatures from myths may still live there."

"I don't think it's powerful. Just rare," Brigsten continued, rolling his eyes. "I've never heard of it having healing properties, and those are still myths."

"I'm a powerful charmarutha from a long line of charmarutha. We are known to be myths. You don't know what might still be out there. Lucas's family are from a powerful bloodline—one that is strong and resilient. Who knows what is still out there. We need to get to that flower, one way or another. First we will need to get out of here." I looked around the room. "We need to get out of here." I looked at my mother's body.

"I will need supplies. I haven't eaten in days, and I won't get far."

I glanced at the mirror. "I need to tell Asher our plan. It's not morning, but I don't want to waste time waiting. I wish I could go to Niv first, but it's in the opposite direction."

I touched the cool glass, not surprised when it connected to the smaller mirror. "Asher."

It was some time before I received an answer from him, the light behind him barely showing his face. "Raina?"

Asher looked haggard, as if he hadn't slept in days. "I wasn't expecting to hear from you so soon. Do you have news?"

My heart cracked at the hope in his voice. I bit my lip. "I think so."

Asher scowled at me, and then his eyes widened when he looked over my shoulder. "Brigsten? I thought you were dead."

"Still here." Brigsten gave Asher a smile. "It is good to see you, boy."

"Not a boy anymore," Asher grumbled.

Brigsten sobered. "How is she?"

"She looks like she's sleeping, but she's not breathing."

I frowned. "She hasn't shriveled up?"

Brigsten gave me a questioning look, but I shook my head, I couldn't think how else to describe it.

"No, she looks the same. Just as if she's in a deep sleep."

"I wonder why she's different from Harold." I thought about his withered body. "It must be the power I gave her. That would make sense. From what Damien said, the apples were born from my power when I was turned. Tainted as I became a vampire." As I said the words, something settled in my stomach—a rightness to it.

"When my power was tainted," I said simply. "Niv's power has never touched that evil."

"Hmmmm." Brigsten nodded slowly. "Niv has an untainted version of your power. If you protected the good in you in the mirror, that part of you wasn't touched by Damien's curse until you joined with your body again."

"What are you both talking about?" Asher yelled. I looked

over my shoulder at the closed door and then gave Asher a warning look.

"We know how we can cure her, and if we can, she can defeat Damien," I told him, the words coming in a rush. "We need to escape here, find a flower, bring it to you, and then come back to defeat Damien."

"Is that all?" Asher huffed. "How are you going to do all of that when you can't survive in daylight?"

"I can conjure darkness. I just need enough to cloak myself until I find shelter if we are caught out in the daylight."

Brigsten looked dubious at my words but didn't comment. I couldn't admit that I felt the same.

"When will you leave?" Asher said.

"As soon as we can leave this room," I said confidently.

Asher nodded slowly, looking past the mirror.

"She will be well," I told him softly. "I promise."

"Don't make promises you can't keep, Raina," Asher said, his lips thinning.

I shook my head as the mirror went black.

"Clever trick," Brigsten said. "Have you been in touch with Niv all this time?"

"Often," I confirmed. "Though I don't blame her or Asher for not trusting me. It took time for Niv to believe me. At least I thought she might."

"We are leaving now?" he asked.

"Yes, though I will go first, and you should follow in a few minutes. Head to the kitchens, and I'll meet you there once you've finished gathering what you need. You're not going to like the next part of the plan."

I took a deep breath before I tried the door. It opened easily. I was surprised it wasn't locked; not that a locked door would prevent me from leaving.

"You look better," Damien commented, emerging from the shadows near the doors to the main halls. I cocked my head, watching him approach. "Did you kill them?"

I opened the door, showing him my mother and Brigsten's bodies, blood smeared over their necks. I smiled at him, running my hand along the wall as I approached.

"I'm surprised you didn't have more control. You were on the edge of starvation, though. That'll teach you to drain yourself." He studied me. "You look much better."

I watched him, frowning at his soft demeanor. He spoke almost gently and with genuine concern. He leaned casually against the wall, blocking my escape. I stalked closer, forcing my hips to sway and making my dress swish around me. I reached up with my hand to cup his cheek.

"You are in my way," I said coolly and pushed his face awkwardly.

He scowled. "I'll give you space for now, Raina. Please consider what you're doing. We could be great together. You should take my offer."

I watched Damien stride away, unable to move as I bit my lip. I had never seen him act this way, as if he would do anything for me. I shook my head to clear it and started walking in the opposite direction to the one he had taken. "You destroyed someone I care about, Damien. I'm going to destroy everything you care about," I said quietly.

I quickly thought about my best route through the palace. I needed to lead as many vampires as I could away from the kitchens.

I headed to the opposite side of the palace, searching for any of Damien's creatures. I smiled with satisfaction when I saw a group in the next corridor.

"Hello," I said sweetly, holding my hands up draped in blackfire. "You will do nicely."

The flames shot from my hands and the group disintegrated into piles of ash. I cursed, not intending to kill them all so quickly. Fortunately, another vampire flew around the corner at the commotion.

"Missssstressss?" He gave me a quizzical look before turning to flee. I smiled widely and followed him down the corridor, only just avoiding a vampire as he grabbed for me. I smiled when I saw another group.

"Raina! Stop!" Damien called. I turned, grinning when I saw him.

My eyes fell on the ceiling above him and I raised my hands. Damien's hands flew up to protect his head. It didn't take much energy for the ceiling to collapse under my barrage of fire. Chunks of the ceiling fell, and I watched in satisfaction as it continued to crumble, burying Damien beneath a pile of rubble. I knew it wouldn't hold him long, so I acted quickly.

As if cleansing each part, I ran through the palace, destroying every beast I could see. Word spread of my massacre, and the vampires thinned. Each one I saw ran in the opposite direction to my path. As I planned, there were no vampires once I reached the kitchens, and I was alone when I pushed my way into the large area.

The room was empty when I entered. I rarely visited the kitchens when Lucas was alive, but when I had, it had been full of staff and noise.

"Brigsten," I whispered loudly, hoping I didn't attract any stray vampires. They should have fled to the other side of the castle after my assault. I heard a rattle to my right and turned quickly in that direction.

Brigsten entered the room from a larder, and my shoulders relaxed. I lowered the hand I'd unknowingly raised in his direction.

He narrowed his eyes on me. "Any trouble?"

I shrugged. "Nothing I couldn't handle." I nodded at his pack. "Are you ready to go?"

"I had no trouble either," he said stiffly.

I frowned at him. "I assumed you wouldn't want any trouble. Did you have any problems?" I asked as an afterthought. I took a deep breath, opening my eyes to meet his gaze. "What is the issue?"

He huffed. "Let's leave this cursed place." I nodded, gesturing to the door without another word. Brigsten led us out a small door and down a narrow passage, the magical night enveloping the kingdom in darkness and hiding us from anyone looking out from the palace.

Sooner than I expected, we were on the streets of the kingdom—a place I had never been. I wrinkled my nose at the distinct smell. Brigsten strode ahead, further away from the palace. I nervously looked at the darkened sky, knowing we wouldn't have long until the sun rose once we left the kingdom. I hurried after him, lifting my skirts and trying not to think about what I was walking in.

"Where are we going?" I whispered, almost a command.

"You'll see."

Time raced as we navigated the streets, the seconds draining away. I was surprised to see no one around. Even during the early hours of the morning, people should have been preparing for their day.

I opened my mouth to ask Brigsten when he flung his hand out, flattening us both against a wall. I bit my lip, not daring to breathe as a figure walked past another alley across the street. I squashed the urge to retaliate at Brigsten pushing me. Warmth from Brigsten's arm saturated the air around us. The aroma from his skin made my mouth water, and my jaw started to ache. I inhaled deeply through my mouth. Brigsten jerked his hand back, a furrow appearing on his brow as he shook his head.

I took a step back, ripping my eyes away from his exposed neck and catching sight of the figure disappearing around a corner. I swallowed thickly and nodded ahead of us at our path. Brigsten's gaze hardened, and he turned, darting away in the opposite direction to the figure. We walked in silence, making sure to carefully pick our way through the streets until we reached a cemetery.

I pushed back a shiver as the breeze lifted my hair, the loose strands tickling the back of my neck. I reached up and rubbed my hand across my bare skin, which felt cool to the touch in further contrast to the heat I could still feel coming from Brigsten as we passed gravestones. I avoided looking at the fresh graves only a few feet away.

"Why are we here?" I asked quietly, wrapping my arms around myself. I rubbed my arms.

"An exit in here will take us outside the wall." Brigsten looked around, frowning. "I can't quite remember where, though."

"Did Niveus know this was here?"

Brigsten nodded. "It was one of a few escape tunnels the king kept clear. A few were built centuries ago to enter the kingdom secretly. We never knew why they existed but figured they would be useful one day."

He ran his hand along a wall, coming to a large crypt. He paused, peering at a section of the wall under his hand. "It must be here," he murmured.

I glanced at the sky, dismayed to see light begin to glow above the wall. "Hurry," I exclaimed.

"Almost there," Brigsten said, glancing at me. He moved his hands across the wall until he found a smaller brick, giving it a push. "Got it."

I jumped back as a large section of the wall pulled away. I stared as Brigsten heaved his shoulder against it, grunting as the section slid sideways an inch. I looked up to the sky again and back at Brigsten struggling to push the section of wall across.

I waved my hand, using my will to help him. "Allow me."

Brigsten slid on the mud-covered ground, only stopping himself from falling by gripping the section of the wall, which I moved easily with my power to reveal the tunnel entrance. I darted forward, looking over my shoulder to see Brigsten retrieve his pack and follow me into the gloom.

"Now what?" I asked.

"We need to cover the entrance," he replied.

I waved my hand again, moving the slab back in place. Brigsten scrambled at the wall of the cave we now stood in before finding a lever and pulling it once the stone covered the doorway. The wall grinded as it snapped back into place, leaving us in complete darkness. At least Brigsten would be in darkness.

I blinked my eyes and they easily adjusted to the lack of light. "Do we follow this out?"

"Yes," Brigsten said, waving his arms around until he touched the wall. "I should have thought to bring a torch.

"I can lead you." With my improved vision, I saw the doubt and suspicion on his face. I didn't blame him. I had caused the death of the king and the fall of the kingdom. My shoulders slumped and I sighed. Reaching forward, I tried to ignore his flinch as I took his arm and led him away from the tunnel entrance. Brigsten stumbled as the tunnel sloped down, and we made our way deeper into the darkness.

My ears strained the entire journey along the tunnel, waiting for the sound of pursuers. Brigsten's arm was steady in mine, and I tried to quell my nervousness as butterflies rolled through my stomach. The darkness loomed before us, seemingly never ending.

Brigsten relaxed against me as a haze of light finally appeared ahead. It hadn't taken us long to travel through the tunnel, but it felt like an eternity. He quickly pulled his arm from my grasp. I stayed back as he lengthened his stride, moving swiftly toward the exit. I stood frozen, watching him leave the cave and the sunlight fall over him. I swallowed, watching the light dance as it reflected off the metal buckles on his pack and glint off a weapon I only now realized he carried at his hip. I wondered when he had found a sword during our escape.

I closed my eyes, mourning my loss of daylight. I had been trapped in the mirror for eight long years, and even now I was a prisoner. I let out a heavy breath, leaning against the wall. The sound of footsteps jarred me from my self-pity, and I looked up to see Brigsten at the cave entrance. He still stood in the daylight, right on the edge of the shadowy entrance.

"You can't leave." It wasn't a question.

I shook my head, staring longingly at the sun. I approached slowly, reaching forward with my hand, and I flinched as I expected it to burst into blisters as the light touched it.

Nothing happened.

"How is this possible?" I had seen the vampires destroyed by daylight when the castle had been under siege. Hadn't I?

"I've never seen the creatures survive in the daylight. They always feared it." Brigsten took a step forward.

"Cursed disease," I spat. I looked up to see Brigsten watching me. "It's not killing me, but I feel weaker."

"I will find the princess. You can head west to find the cure," Brigsten said, turning to leave.

"Wait," I called after him. "I'll need you to identify the flower I need."

He looked at me doubtfully. "You truly want to cure her?" he asked.

"Yes, she is everything." I could hear the lack of emotion in my voice. Even I wasn't sure I believed myself. "I know what I am. I know what I must do," I said, resigned.

A war was taking place, not just between Damien and Niv but within me.

"How can I trust you?" he replied angrily, taking a step forward. Anger surged unbidden within me, and with a speed I'd never known I had, I burst forward. I grabbed Brigsten around the throat and dragged him into the cave, slamming him against the wall. I hissed, my face so close to him our noses nearly touched.

"You shouldn't," I said harshly.

The darkness of the creature I had become pulsed within me, and for a moment I didn't care. Brigsten's eyes were wide, and the color had drained from his face. It was freeing, this feeling. It would be so easy to snap his neck. I didn't care that I could feel his contempt for me or his judgment. Flashes of the treatment my mother had given me pushed into my mind. Her derisive and condescending words came to me easily. Years of my worth being questioned weighed on me, threatening to tear me apart. It would have been so easy to let go, to let the creature take full control. It was an effort not to give in.

Why was I even resisting? I couldn't stop what was within me. Nothing was worth fighting the hunger and the darkness. I caught a glimpse of Niv's smiling face in my mind, for just a second. Her smile and sweetness outshined the harsh words of my mother, and that's all it took for me to loosen my grip. I took a step back from Brigsten, narrowing my eyes. "We rest for now, very briefly. We find the flower. We cure Niveus, and we end Damien. After that…" I paused. "After that you can have your revenge on me, if you can."

I turned, walking deeper into the darkness of the tunnel. I looked in the direction I expected any enemy that dared follow us would come. It would be their end if they had. I hoped they would despite the daylight.

CHAPTER 21

RAINA

To my surprise, Brigsten didn't leave after I'd left him at the entrance to the tunnel. He had moved into the daylight and started a fire, cooking himself a humble meal while we rested. It was pure torture waiting for the sun to inch closer to the distant trees, but I knew I'd need my full strength for what was to come. I could sense where the sun was in the sky, and I waited for it to crawl to the horizon.

As the final hours of the day waned, I heard the thundering of a horse's hooves causing my breath to catch. Listening closely, I realized it was more than one, and we would soon have company. I took small steps closer to the tunnel entrance.

I knew it couldn't be Damien or his creatures as the daylight still held them prisoner. At least I hoped that Damien was still trapped inside the palace by the sun. I saw Brigsten give me a quizzical look, and I nodded to the east, wondering when he would hear our visitors approach.

"Company," I told him when he didn't react. "Three riders from what I can hear."

"Your hearing might come in useful," he said begrudgingly, hurrying to pack up his meager belongings before reluctantly entering the cave to stand beside me. I wished I had thought to get a better view of what the cave looked like from the outside to know if it would be noticeable by the people approaching. I stood perfectly still, even holding my breath as the thundering got louder.

I heard the horses skid to a stop, and men's voices carried toward us. The sound of Brigsten slowly drawing his weapon rang softly through the cave. I clenched my fists, waiting to see if the men would find the cave entrance. Hope of them overlooking it disappeared as I saw the outline of a large man blocking the entrance to the tunnel, his shadow stretching along the floor.

"Raina?" A thrill of fear shot through me at the sound of my name, and it took me a moment to recognize Asher's voice.

"Asher?" Brigsten called.

"Brigsten? I thought you were dead. When I saw you in the mirror, I thought it was a trick," Asher's face came into view and Brigsten strode forward to embrace him.

I stared at Asher, no longer the young butler I'd called a friend. Before me was a man with broad shoulders and a confidence that came from a hard life and maturity. I studied his handsome face, my eyes trailing along his broad shoulders and chest. Desire curled within me, and I shook my head to clear it. Disgust with the direction my thoughts had taken warred with my attraction to him. I swallowed, taking a step out of the shadows of the wall. The two men turned to me, both watching me as I approached slowly. The wariness on their faces was deserved, so I tried not to let it irritate me.

"Can you save her?" Asher pleaded, his gaze catching mine with an intensity that made my heart stutter.

I pushed away my increasing desire for him, hoping it

was the vampiric influence on me. I kept my answer short. "With Brigsten's help."

Asher took a step forward, halting when Brigsten grabbed his arm. "She's not Raina," he warned Asher. Despite knowing he was right, the comment still riled me. "Not the Raina you knew."

Asher turned to look at me, frowning. "Raina? Can we trust you?"

"I can't be trusted," I snapped, venom in my voice as the anger in me tried to push forward. It would be better if I didn't let them get too close to me. I looked outside as the last ray of the sun finally disappeared. "But I can help you, and that's all that matters right now. Stop asking if you can trust me and hoping for a different answer."

Brigsten gave me a nod. He would likely try to end me with Damien. Until then, I needed to keep my vampire side at bay and control the anger weighing on me. I walked slowly, so as not to startle them as I passed them and walked outside into the evening air. "We need to move."

I jerked to a stop when I saw two strangers holding three horses. They dropped the reins and drew their weapons when they saw me.

"You were at the palace," the man on the left exclaimed, pointing his blade at me. The end was inches from my face.

"Vampire," called the other man. His eyes darted to look over my shoulder to where Brigsten and Asher must have come up behind me.

"Keres, Mal," Asher said. "Meet Raina."

"Raina?" the man on the left said. "Did you hear that, Mal? It's Niv's friend."

"She's a vampire, Keres. I don't see how she can be Niv's friend," Mal scoffed. Both men still held their blades on me. I narrowed my eyes at them, baring my teeth. I chuckled when they both took a step back.

"Don't worry, boys. I won't bite. Much." I snapped my teeth in their direction.

"Behave, Raina," Asher said, frowning as he walked toward the horses, which had bolted when Keres and Mal drew their weapons.

"That's who we were coming to meet?" Mal asked, gesturing with his sword. "Why didn't you tell us, Ash."

"Because you would have talked me out of it. We need her to help Niv."

I turned to face Asher. "Why did you come? And how did you know we would be here."

"It's the only tunnel through the wall we knew of. I couldn't sit there with her anymore. I needed to do something. I hoped you'd be here." He eyed me. "Why are you doing this, Raina? You've terrorized the kingdom for years. Why are you helping us now?"

Brigsten shook his head. "I've been wondering the same thing."

"I know you argued with Niv about this, Asher. I could hear you on the other side of the mirror," I snarled. "She's all that matters. Let's move. We need to head to the other side of the mountain before Damien realizes where we're going."

"Raina, wait." I turned to Asher, raising an eyebrow. He bit his lip. "This will help Niv?"

"Yes, I've already said that," I replied softly and turned again to walk. Before long I heard the horses following me. I looked over my shoulder to see Brigsten sharing with Asher. Keres and Mal were also mounted. The sun had finally set, and even though I could survive in sunlight, I wanted to make sure I was at full strength if we were attacked. The power of the night called to me, urging me forward.

"I hope you can keep up," I called, breaking into a run and then a sprint. The horses surged behind me, the sounds of hooves chasing me into the trees and toward the base of the mountain. I let the thrill of running fast on my own two legs take over for now, heading west toward the mountain.

～

"We need to rest, Raina," Asher called, his horse coming alongside me as I ran through the trees. I slowed to a walk. The horses were breathing heavily, their nostrils flaring. I scowled at the useless creatures and their riders.

I huffed. "Weak humans." I grimaced as the words escaped my lips.

"It's getting stronger. Isn't it?" Brigsten whispered while the others cared for the horses.

"I don't know what you mean," I answered.

"Hold on to your humanity, Raina. You need to hold on enough to help Niv. I didn't believe you when I first saw you, but I can see you fighting what you are. You're not the same as the vampires in the palace."

I sneered. "You do not know what you speak. Annoying me is not helping." I turned away, hearing his footsteps retreat. I looked over my shoulder and tried not to scowl at his back. I walked in the other direction toward the edge of the trees and sat down at the base of a tree. Watching the men, I got lost in their movements. I admired their muscles as I they strained to unsaddle the horses to give them a rub down.

Instinctively I knew we had a few hours of night left. "We can't stay here long," I called to the group, trying to drag my mind away from thinking about them inappropriately.

"We can't keep this pace up. We will kill the horses, and we need them if we are going to travel fast," Asher told me.

"Damien will send a hunting group out for us," I told them. "We have moved quickly, but we need to keep going while they still have the night to follow us."

"Shelter them, you mean," grumbled Mal.

"Give us fifteen minutes," Asher said, I could hear the weariness in his voice. "We haven't slept the last two nights."

I snorted, cocking my head and listening. I could hear animals around us, quiet along the trail we had taken, but I could hear them starting to rustle back into the areas we had ridden through. I expected to hear Damien's creatures pursuing us and was surprised we hadn't seen any yet. Maybe I had taken out more than I realized at the palace.

Once the men were settled, Brigsten leaning against a tree with his eyes closed, I caught Asher watching me.

He got up and walked over. "Are you okay?"

I snorted. "What happened to you not trusting me?"

"Old habits die hard. I cared for you, Raina, for years," Asher said. "I'll never understand why you did what you did, but I can see you're struggling, and Niv always insisted you were helping us. I guess part of me wants to believe you're still good."

"I'm not." I stared into the forest, looking away from him. "Yet you're still asking me if I'm okay."

"Crazy, I know."

I smiled at him, so different from the young man I knew. "It is good to see you," I said truthfully, my mouth twitching into a half smile. "But you know what I'm capable of."

"Why, Raina? Why did you do it?" He sounded desperate. I didn't know whether he was talking about Niv or Lucas. Or both.

"I…" My words trailed off uselessly. I couldn't explain it. I had no excuses. I was a naive fool, who had taken my mother's abuse for years and trusted the wrong person. "I'm rotten inside, Asher, and you should never forget that."

I stood quickly, walking away from him and into the trees. I looked up at the sky, realizing we had already stopped for longer than the fifteen minutes Asher had said we would stop for. But I was finding it hard to care. Let Damien catch up and bring as many of his creatures as he wanted. He couldn't kill me. I was too strong...but he could kill the others. I sighed, my mind fighting a war with myself as I continued to walk.

I walked through the trees, welcoming the darkness and silence around me. A moment of peace, away from the palace. I had the urge to run, head west and never return. I looked within myself, searching for the creature, the darker side of me. I was me, whole once more, but with a darkness within me thanks to Damien's curse—one I could feel seeping into every part of me.

As I thought of Damien, I realized we didn't have much night left, and the men could rest during the day if I could find shelter. I whirled, striding back toward the clearing. As I drew closer I listened, realizing I hadn't been paying attention to my surroundings. I quickened my pace as I heard rustling in the clearing ahead. A loud clang propelled me forward as I realized men were fighting.

As I burst through the trees, I dodged a vampire flying at me, blackfire at once licking flames around my palms. I touched the vampire, and with a *whoosh,* he disintegrated into ash. I stepped forward studying the scene in the clearing.

Each of the men fought creatures, surrounded by a circle of them standing. They were watching the fighting, playing and taunting with them. I smiled wickedly, ready for a fight.

"What do we have here?" I stalked forward, letting the fire spread up my arms. I peered over the row of vampires in front of me, admiring the vicious movements of the men fighting them off. It would be a shame to end it.

"Raina!" Asher's shout brought me back to myself. "A little help?"

I sighed, approaching the snarling creatures as they

LIZ CAIN & ANNE K. WHELAN

charged me. I let them, none of them surviving my touch as they came at me. I stood there, unmoved until the only vampires left were those fighting Asher, Brigsten, Mal, and Keres.

I watched them working together to kill the last few creatures. I clenched my fists so I wouldn't touch the men when I reached them. The scent of blood in the air was intoxicating. One of them had been cut. I needed to resist.

Keres bent over the body of a beheaded vampire, panting. "Thanks," he said grudgingly.

"Thanks? She just stood and watched at the end," Mal said, scowling at me.

"You didn't need my help." I shrugged, licking my lips. "You were doing magnificently without me."

"At least we didn't have to fight them all," Brigsten conceded, wiping his brow.

"We need to move. More will come. You can rest on the horses," I said cheerily, my voice sounding husky and out of place after what just happened.

I clenched my fists again, watching the men saddle their horses. I was surprised the animals hadn't bolted when the vampires arrived. Once ready, I scanned the trees behind us, listening as I had been doing since the attack to make sure we weren't surprised again.

"Let's go," Asher said.

I nodded and set off into the trees, heading west once again.

"We only have an hour, two at most, before the sun will stop us traveling," I yelled over my shoulder. "You can rest more then."

～

I watched out from the canopy of the trees as the rain poured down in sheets. The sun had risen two hours ago. The men slept under the cover while the horses rested. I resisted the urge to pace as the seconds slipped by, sheltered in the shadows of the trees. The sun didn't burn me, but I could feel my power draining away the longer I stayed in the light.

I chewed on my lip, hating waiting around so much. I needed to be moving. All I seemed to do the last few days was wait for the sun to set so I could move in the open. I wondered if Damien had sent more of his minions after us or whether they didn't dare venture this far from the safety of the palace. I blew a breath out my nose, narrowing my eyes at the rain.

"It's bad enough that we are stuck here until there's enough cloud cover without being soaked to the bone," I muttered, glaring at the clouds. The sun taunted me as the trees around us sparkled with the dappled light. At least it meant the vampires couldn't follow us easily. I didn't turn at the footsteps behind me, recognizing their gait.

"It is frustrating," Brigsten commented.

"It can't last forever." I sighed, not feeling the calm my appearance belied to Brigsten. I dropped my hand when I realized I was chewing on my nail. I looked back in the direction of the castle, biting my lip. The area where we hid still had patches of sunlight, but the path back to the castle was draped in darkness. So much for them not being able to follow us.

Brigsten's gaze followed mine. "Are you sure about that? This doesn't feel natural. How is he doing this?"

"Damien?" I asked. "I don't know.

"But he is doing it?"

I nodded.

Brigsten sighed. "I'll get the men ready to leave." He roused the men, who reluctantly readied the horses.

Asher gave the reins of his horse a tug, leading them both over to stand in front of me. "Ready?"

I sighed. "Yes."

As he walked away, I could hear his heart and imagined the taste of his blood. Swallowing I gritted my teeth and continued forward with Asher, Keres, Mal, and Brigsten close behind on their horses.

I tired slowly at first, but as the ground beneath our feet sloped upward and the day wore on, my energy drained as I was forced to travel in patches of sunlight. I tried to bring darkness around me to protect me from the sun, but this was also draining as the day wore on. The horses were keeping pace with me easily, no one speaking as the weight of our task pressed down.

"We should rest," I heard Asher call behind me.

I clenched my fists. "No, we should keep moving."

"Raina, we are all exhausted. We've only had a few hours' sleep in…I can't remember how many days. I want to push hard to save her too, but we need to be smart."

"We don't have time for this," I snapped, pushing myself harder.

"Raina…" Asher's voice trailed away as I pushed myself.

Darkness had followed just behind us, and the feeling of being chased had risen as the day wore on. I knew Damien was on our heels, and we needed to beat him to our destination. I pushed away the thought of what we would do when we had to turn around and journey back to Niv. Damien would be between us and Avilar, where Asher had told me she lay.

I remembered Harold's body and forced the image of her shriveled corpse from my mind. Asher had told me that she looked as if she slept. We still had time to save her if we could make it to the other side of the mountain. As the day wore on, and for the first time since I'd joined with my vampire body, I was beyond weary. I glanced at the men beside me and slowed to a halt, my shoulders slumping. Everyone was pale and exhausted. If we were attacked now, we would not survive. I was relieved that I was still able to feel concern for the men, despite also wanting to tear out their throats.

No one spoke as I led them to a sheltered area in a rock face. I watched, the silence stretching as the horses were taken care of and a small cold meal eaten by my companions. I sat picking at the pants I wore, waiting for the day to pass. Hunger gnawed at my middle, and I knew I needed to feed before long. I cursed our predicament and sighed, closing my eyes and wishing I could sleep.

CHAPTER 22

RAINA

"What are we looking for?" Asher asked Brigsten.

"My father described it as deep purple petals and unusually green roots," Brigsten said, shrugging. "He said it supposedly looks like it's glowing."

"This is useless," Asher's outburst had birds taking flight in a nearby tree. "Why are we here?"

"To find the cure for Niv," I said with a confidence I didn't feel.

"You have brought us on a wild chase." Asher whirled to face me with the full attention of his fury. "None of this would have happened if you hadn't married the king."

A growl from me surprised us both. My hunger had been growing and with it my patience waning.

"Raina," Brigsten warned. Asher took a step back, suddenly pale.

"You know nothing," I snapped, baring my teeth at Asher. I took a step toward him and found myself face to face with the tips of two swords. Keres and Mal had stepped in front of him, blocking my path.

I snarled at them, only pausing when Brigsten spoke. "Everyone, back off." I didn't take my eyes off the swords, but I did take a step away. "Fighting each other won't help, and we are wasting time."

I licked my lips and laughed, my eyes trailing down the arms of the men before me and settling on their throats. It would be so easy. I was faster and stronger than them. One step to the side and one forward. I could kill them both. Asher would be next and Brigsten last. It would all be over with no one left to compound the guilt I felt, the pain of betraying those I love. It wouldn't matter anymore.

I turned my back on the group, walking until I could take a deep breath of fresh air. No scent of them, just the rain to clear my head. It would matter. It would matter to Niv.

"Raina? Are you under control?" Brigsten called.

I didn't turn to face him. "Let's find this flower and get moving."

"She's going to need blood, or this will get worse," I heard Brigsten whisper. I took a step away from them and then another as my eyes searched the foliage surrounding us. Asher was right. What chance did we have of finding the plant we needed?

Cursing myself for not thinking to check the grimoire, I called it to me. It was harder than it had been in the past, like I was having to pull it through thick mud to retrieve it from where I kept it hidden in the "unknown." I shuddered when the book appeared in my hand, my breaths coming fast.

"Raina?" Brigsten came to stand beside me, watching me warily.

"I'm fine." I opened the book, dismayed to find the writing was fading on the pages.

"Is that supposed to happen?"

"I don't know," I replied softly. I quickly flicked to a blank page, hoping with my entire being and willing the book to help us locate the flower we needed and tell me what we needed to do with it. For Niv.

Words flickered on the blank page, finally settling in a short message.

Found at the root of the tallest tree.
The petals must be steeped in boiled water for three minutes.
Allow to cool. When the liquid turns gold, administer.

"Anything?" I jerked at Brigsten's question.

"Yes," I said, my words barely above a whisper.

As I told him what the passage said, the book in my trembling hands shook. I closed it, stroking the spine. I handed the book to Brigsten, a line formed on his brow and he cocked his head as he took it. When he opened it, the ache in my chest spread at the blank pages.

"What is this?" He frowned.

"Give it to Niv. If she is meant to have it, the words will appear. I am the last of my grandmother's blood, and I am no longer its keeper." As Brigsten scratched his head, staring at the blank pages, I looked up to the tops of the trees. "We need to find the tallest tree," I called to Asher and his guard dogs.

They had sheathed their swords but all watched me with wary expressions. I ignored their faces, pointing to the sky. "The roots of the tallest tree."

"It can't be that simple." Asher crossed his arms across his chest.

I shrugged. "It hasn't been simple so far."

"Some magic book told you that," Mal scoffed. He elbowed Keres and chuckled. "She's nuts."

I growled at him and his smile vanished. "Trust me."

"So, we blindly follow you?" Asher asked, his hands clenched into fists. Despite his words, he looked up and followed my example, searching the skies for the tallest tree.

I ignored him and looked around, unable to see above the trees around us.

"How do we know we are in the right area?" I muttered, making sure the others couldn't hear me. I followed the path of a trail up the mountain in front of us, groaning when I realized the tallest tree could be a long hike.

"Isn't there a tall tree that towers over the others further west of here?" Keres spoke into the quiet of our group. I turned to see him whispering to Mal.

"Don't be daft. That's a myth," Mal snapped at him.

"What tree?" I asked Keres. His eyes widened when I spoke to him, and he looked at the ground.

He shrugged, composing himself. "Just further west. I heard that you follow the mountain trail away from here and head toward the sea. It's not far from the mountain, you just can't see it because…well, we are in the trees." He shrugged again.

I looked at Brigsten, who nodded. "Better than searching aimlessly."

I nodded my agreement and looked at Asher. He hesitated before nodding. "One more day, and then I'm going back to lay her to rest. She deserves peace."

I grimaced. "We will find it and I will cure her."

No one answered as they mounted their horses.

It didn't take a day. We were all shocked to find Keres had been right. No one more so than Mal, who grumbled about a broken clock being right twice a day. I shook my head at the brothers as they bickered. Just as much to clear my head as at their arguments.

The tree had appeared when we entered a clearing. Its trunk was so large that we could all hold hands and only cover half the circumference, even stretching as far as we could. The branches were so thick and intertwined, it was hard to tell where each came from in the tree. Thick leaves covered the canopy, blocking out the moon entirely. Night had fallen as we traveled from the mountain to my relief and annoyance. I would not weaken but Damien and his creatures could travel freely.

"Here," Brigsten offered me a cup of dark liquid.

I flinched back as the rich smell of blood hit my senses. I covered my mouth and shook my head hard while trying not to snatch at it. "You need your strength. We will encounter opposition on our return, and we need you at your strongest," he told me.

I shook my head again, though with less vigor. "I can't," I hissed, my mouth watering. "I might not be able to stop," I said, surprising us both by my honesty.

"You can. It's already done so don't let it go to waste. Now quickly, the others don't need to see this."

I swallowed thickly, still reluctant but taking the cup and turning away from the others. I walked into the trees further away from them and gripped on to a young tree. The moment the sweetness touched my tongue, I moaned, tilting the cup back to drink faster. I guzzled until no more would pour out and eagerly licked the rim of the cup, trying to take in every drop. My grip on the tree tightened as I thought about the warm bodies behind me, their heartbeats faintly echoing in my head.

"You good?" Brigsten called.

I nodded, not daring to speak or turn around, and willed it to be true. I gulped in a lungful of fresh air, to rid myself of the scent of blood.

"You're welcome," I heard him say quietly.

"We need to get moving," Asher yelled. I breathed for a few more moments before I trusted myself to turn and follow them toward the tallest tree I'd ever seen. Asher, Keres, and Mal were all searching around the roots of the tree. A cry from Asher drew our attention, and we turned to see the three men crouched over the roots. Relief surged through me at their jubilance. Slowly, still wary of their proximity, I stepped toward the area they had been searching.

The flower was the most beautiful I had ever seen. The color was so deep and rich, but with an almost translucent shimmer making the plant hard to see at first. If we hadn't been looking, I doubt we would have seen it.

"It's beautiful," Mal said, his eyes wide and mesmerized by the flower. I walked past them all, reaching for the plant.

"Wait," Asher said, slapping my hand away. I unintentionally released a low growl at him. He held his hands up. "We can't just take this. It doesn't feel right."

"You might not be able to, but I will. For her I will." He didn't stop my second attempt to pick the flower. As the stem broke, I ignored the pang in my heart at having to sacrifice something so beautiful for the life of someone I loved while the monster in me relished the destruction of something precious. I turned to Brigsten, who handed me a handkerchief to wrap the flower. Reluctantly, I handed the delicate beauty toward him.

"It is our only chance," I said, scanning the ground to see there were no others. I hated the idea of picking a second flower to be sure, but I would have if I'd seen one. The horses moved restlessly next to the tree.

"Are we done here?" Asher asked. I opened my mouth and froze when cold words cut through the group.

"That depends on what you are doing at the sacred tree," Damien drawled, stepping into view only a few feet away. Instinctively I stepped between him and the group of humans. The sound of ringing metal followed as swords were drawn. Power flickered to my fingertips as shadows stepped out from the trees surrounding us.

"Damien, welcome" I said sweetly. "Can we help you with anything?"

"Beautiful and powerful as ever, my love," Damien said, stalking closer. When my eyes met his, my insides quivered. Part of me revolted by my reaction, and the other anticipated his touch, longing for him. Brigsten came to stand beside me, an unwelcome intrusion. I turned to look at him and saw the unspoken understanding pass between us in a brief glance. "Another you claimed to have killed yet lives," Damien commented when he noticed Brigsten.

"I'll try to make a habit of it," I answered, turning to face Damien again. I heard Brigsten step back and hoped they would be ready. I silently counted the creatures around us, too many for the men to fight. It would be up to me to clear a path. I grinned at finally being able to let go of my control once the men left.

My hand twitched, and I caught Damien smiling at me. "I can see what you're thinking, Raina. It won't work. Even if those pitiful humans escape, I will catch them. What have you achieved by coming here?" He gestured toward the tree. "This won't help you defeat me."

I straightened, lifting my chin. "What will defeat you?"

He laughed, the rich sound echoing through me, making it hard to think. "Nothing will."

He gestured and I reacted quickly as the creatures surged toward us. Blackfire shot from my fingertips as they swarmed toward us. I poured as much power into it as I could, creating a barrier between the vampires and the men; satisfied to see the creatures devoured by the flames. I heard the horses flee, Brigsten, Asher and the brothers racing away into the night through a gap I had created in the circle of enemies. Once they were safely away, I let the blackfire spread further, where it continued to destroy the creatures around us. I laughed as I poured more power into the attack, maniacally letting the feeling take over until a force slammed into me.

Smoke and ash floated around my vision as I lay on my back staring up at the large tree, which was miraculously undamaged. Blinking, I tried to clear the haze over my vision, annoyance making me frown when I couldn't move. The weight on me shifted and my body started to hum.

"What am I going to do with you?" Damien growled, pinning my arms above my head, his voice making me shiver.

"Stop underestimating me," I said through gritted teeth. I closed my eyes to shut out his handsome face.

I was surprised at his chuckle, my eyes snapping open. "I love how you impress me each time I do." His breath caressed my face, his words affecting me more than I would have liked.

"Get off me," I said, my voice sultry when I had been hoping for irritation. I jerked, trying to throw him off.

"Are you sure you want me to?" Damien raised his eyebrow, his lips only a breath away from mine.

I couldn't help my moan when his mouth captured mine. The kiss was aggressive and hungry. My resolve slipped away as he explored my mouth, and I kissed him back, matching his passion. A fleeting thought about distracting him and allowing more time for the men to escape passed through me. Though it was only an afterthought to the delicious waves of pleasure as Damien deepened the kiss and his hands roamed my body.

Damien's mouth crashed again on mine, and his hands moved to push aside my tunic cupping my breast. I could feel every inch of him, his body a hard wall of muscle. He was pressed against me, completely trapping me. His hands didn't stop moving over my body, resting on my hips. He broke the kiss and his mouth began to trace the column of my throat, his eyes smoldering and his breathing heavy. My mind raced, unable to form a coherent thought. My entire being was a mass of confusion as my traitorous body moved against his. His lips continued to trail kisses down my neck, each one sending shivers down my spine, and my body relaxed into him as I gave in to the temptation of his touch.

Disgust at myself was all I felt as I pulled my clothes back on. I hadn't been able to resist as Damien had taken me. Not that I didn't enjoy it, but the conflict inside me was tearing me to pieces. I could barely understand my own actions, drawn to Damien but loving Niv so much it hurt. I trembled as Damien's lips touched the back of my neck, trailing kisses around to my jaw. His hands roamed over my body, pushing my shirt higher until I pushed them away with effort.

"You can't resist me," Damien said, smiling. I bit my lip at the sight of his bare chest, slick with sweat. He'd dress in pants as I had put my clothes on, and they hugged his hips in a way that made my heart flutter. I closed my eyes and turned away, tugging my shirt down harder than necessary. When I opened my eyes, I wasn't shocked to see that none of his creatures remained. Any that had escaped would have chased after Brigsten and Asher. I hoped they were able to deal with the number I hadn't destroyed.

Damien's hands reached for me again, and I danced away, stumbling on a root of the huge tree. "No," I said firmly, huffing at the amused smile Damien gave me.

"Join me, Raina. Be by my side and rule the kingdoms with me. Your powers will only grow, and with darkness spreading through the land, we can take more than just

Lestoria. We could rule all the known land, and the humans would be powerless against us."

"No," I said, trying to be firm, though the idea was very tempting. "If you really cared about that, you wouldn't have turned me against my will." I turned to jab him in his chest, welcoming the anger at him. My stomach fluttered at the contact with his perfect skin.

"I love you, Raina," Damien replied. "Can't you feel the truth in that."

"Your love is a poison," I spat, trying to push him away. "You are rotten inside, like those trees at the palace."

"A poison you can't resist," he said, playfully pulling me toward him. I frowned, confused at his lack of urgency to chase down the escaped men. Damien's lip rose in a half smile, as if he knew what I was thinking. "I will catch them eventually. With the princess dead, they have no one to lead their rebellion."

I cringed, hoping he couldn't really read my mind. "Then why did you hunt us down?"

"You, of course," he replied, as if it was the most obvious answer in the kingdom. "I need you, Raina. The sooner you submit to me, the sooner we can be happy."

"Why?" I threw up my hands, striding away and pacing between the trees. "You have what you want. You killed Lucas, Niv is—" I choked on the words, feeling more human than I had in days. "Why do you need me?"

"I told you," Damien said impatiently. "To help me take the rest of the kingdoms. We are linked forever. When you released me from the mirror, you tied both our fates. This is our destiny."

"Destiny," I screamed. "This is not destiny, Damien. This is not love. You *used* me."

He gave me a wicked smile. "You can now use me for your

pleasure. How could this have not been fate? You felt the pull to the mirror. We were always meant to be."

I sighed, dropping my hands and staring at him. I bit my lip, thinking about what he'd said. "What did you mean we are linked?"

"You're too clever for your own good." Damien laughed. "There is no me without you. There is no you without me."

"Are you saying that if one of us dies, the other will too?" The realization caused my heart to lurch. Could it be that simple?

"Well, yes. But the plan is neither of us will die," Damien wrapped his arms around me, pulling me toward him in a possessive embrace. "We could rule, *forever.*"

The blood in my veins turned to ice as he held me. The idea of him ruling with his creatures, me by his side forever. I wouldn't have to fight what I was. It would be so easy to give in.

"I will not stand by and watch you destroy the world," I spoke before I could think.

"I wouldn't be destroying it. I'd be making it better," he told me. "People need to be led. They need to be told what to do. I make sure the humans are comfortable if we are fed. There will be no needless loss, no war. The kingdoms will be at peace."

"That is a perversion of peace," I spat, searching around me as I spoke. There must be something around here that could help me. When Damien stepped toward me again, I raised my hands, willing the blackfire to life.

"You know that won't hurt me," Damien scoffed. "Come with me, Raina. Stop being stubborn when you know I'm right."

"Never," I hissed. Desperately I pushed the flames toward him, my heart sinking when they licked around him harmlessly. Even his clothes didn't burn as I tried harder to destroy him.

I cut the flames off, crying out in frustration. "I will end you."

"You can try, Raina, but it won't work. There is no way to kill me, and I don't think you want to anymore."

I thought about what he had said about us being linked as my eyes finally found what I had been looking for—a way to escape him and finally be free. A dagger glimmered in the moonlight, discarded in the men's escape or brought by one of the creatures. I didn't care which. I looked up into Damien's eyes.

"I may not be able to kill you, but I can destroy you." I sprang for the dagger, turning to face Damien before I plunged it into my chest, straight into my heart.

CHAPTER 23

RAINA

*P*ain, like no other I'd felt before lanced through me. The metal of the dagger pierced my flesh easily, but I was not dead. My aim had been true, the dagger had plunged into my heart, but I remained standing. My heart jerked, trying to beat around the sharp steel. I looked over to Damien, who had collapsed, and for one moment I thought I had triumphed until he rolled over and groaned. I ripped the dagger from my chest, crying out at the second surge of pain, and watched Damien jerk on the ground.

I strode over to Damien as I reached for my chest to clutch at the wound, a pulling sensation spreading across my chest. I pushed him with my foot so that he rolled onto his back and sighed when I could see his chest moving. I thought about stabbing him through his own heart but knew it wouldn't do any good. I could see a wound on his chest healing as my own chest healed.

I flung the dagger into the trees, cursing as I rose from a crouch next to Damien. I would need to leave quickly if I hoped to escape him. Without hesitating further, I burst into a run hoping I could outrun the draw I felt to him. I headed back toward the mountain and along the trail I guessed Asher and Brigsten had taken when they fled. I could see the hoofprints clearly in the soft ground as I ate up the distance between me and the men.

I was conflicted, torn between returning to Damien and getting to Niv. The pull to Niv was stronger but only just. I shook my head, not able to understand why I let Damien have this hold on me. It felt good to run, exerting all my strength into a physical task. I kept watching for signs of the horses on the trail, following Asher and Brigsten's tracks back toward the mountain. As I ran, unease slithered up my spine as I saw signs of Damien's creatures following them. A growing dread blossomed in me as the night wore on. My limbs started to drag, even as I ran, pulling me down. I knew I would have to stop soon, especially with daylight near.

I skidded to a halt at a noise up ahead. A primal shriek made my entire body lock up as I strained to listen to which direction I needed to go to find the source of the noise. I narrowed my eyes, peering into the shadows of the trees around me and counting my heartbeats until I heard another scuffle. Then I shot toward the sound.

As I approached, I slowed my steps to listen and stalk closer through the trees to where I thought they might be. Carefully, I picked my way through a rocky area, steadying myself on a tree. I could no longer hear the fight. I looked up to meet the end of a sword, pointing at my face.

"How did you get away?" Asher demanded, his words laced with suspicion. I bared my teeth at him, lowering myself into a crouch until he backed away.

"Stabbed myself in the heart," I said truthfully, swallowing and trying to make my muscles relax. I watched my prey take another step back.

Asher's brow furrowed as he lowered the sword, examining the blood stain on my tunic.

"You're joking...right?"

I shrugged nonchalantly and stalked closer, swaying my hips. I told him about what Damien had said and how the blow hadn't killed me. I left out the part about how intimate we had been before I stabbed myself, not needing to give him another reason not to trust me. I looked over his shoulder to see if the rest of the group were uninjured. Nodding at each of them, I finally managed to relax.

"We should keep moving," Asher said.

"Yes we should," I replied.

"Good to see you too," Mal grumbled as Keres handed him the reins to his horse.

I kept listening as we traveled but didn't hear any of Damien's creatures following us. The men had dispatched the ones that had caught up to them, and I'd hoped that Damien was injured enough to give us a head start. I mulled that thought over, wondering why he had been more injured than I had been.

"Are you okay?"

I stiffened, only relaxing when I saw the concern on Keres's face.

"Sure," I told him.

"You don't look okay." We were walking along a road, trying to rest the horses but still moving.

I coughed, shaking my head. "How did you meet Asher and Niv?" I asked, changing the subject.

Keres chuckled. "We must seem like a strange group to you. Mal and the rest of my brothers lived in a village further north of here. Let's just say village life didn't suit us. We thought we could leave and make our fortune. Even become famous."

I raised an eyebrow. "Did you?"

"Find our fortune or become famous?" Keres laughed. "Neither. Yet."

We fell quiet for a moment, only the sound of our boots crunching the stones on the road.

"What is Niv like?" I asked quietly. I had always known she would grow into a magnificent woman and was saddened I'd never seen that.

"She's incredible, most of my brothers are in love with her though no one would cross Asher and make a move." Keres shuddered. "She's strong, fights just as well as Paxon, and listens to all of us. She looks out for us and keeps us from killing each other."

He gave me a genuine smile, and I felt my heart warm at the companions she had found. I must make sure each of them survived when this was all over. I looked at Asher, realizing that Niv's loss must have devastated him more than I'd thought. "I will bring her back to you."

"I think you will." Keres looked at me curiously. "I'm still not sure where you fit in to all of this. I've heard Asher and Niv argue about you over the years, but you're not what I expected."

I stiffened, ice taking hold in my chest. "Just because I'm in control now doesn't mean I'm not dangerous," I warned. "I might not always be on your side."

I picked up my speed, striding away from him faster and taking the lead. I scolded myself for relaxing around him. They must have seen me for the monster I was. I felt human now, but the draw to Damien, the need for blood, the temptation to give in and only think of myself… It wouldn't take much for me to give in to the evil in my heart and destroy them. They couldn't trust me, and I couldn't trust myself. I needed to harden my heart and remain the villain in their eyes. It was the only way for them to end Damien's reign, and it would be easier for them if they didn't hesitate. They needed to remember what I'd done and what I was capable of.

～

Avilar was larger than I ever realized. It was rare for anyone to travel from Lestoria. Usually, only merchants and traders came in and left. It had taken us nearly two days to reach it, and during the night hours, it had been as if we all held our breath, waiting for Damien to appear or his creatures to find us. The day before we arrived, I could feel the group's agitation and their need to get to Niv. My whole body hummed with trepidation, whether the cure would work or not. The cloud cover that had allowed Damien and his creatures to chase us had vanished, and I hoped that meant we were safe during the day at least.

I fought the hunger for blood, not sure how much longer I could hold it off. Every time I even thought about blood, I had to shake my head to clear it, fighting a presence within me and the temptation of my companions.

I admired the abandoned tavern Asher said they called home. Despite its disheveled appearance, I could imagine Niv growing up here. I tensed when the door swung open and a giant of a man approached.

I still didn't relax when Keres called out to the man. "It's just us Som."

He clasped the larger man's hand, pulling him into an embrace. Even Mal's lips twitched into a smile as we approached the tavern. Brigsten studied the building curiously, coming to stand next to me. He looked out at the surrounding areas, always alert. We stood back as the brothers greeted each other and Asher. They were a spirited group, and their enthusiasm made me smile, despite everything.

Eventually their attention fell on me, and I wasn't surprised to see the wary expression on the others' faces.

"Where is she?" I demanded, emotion leaking into my voice.

"What is *she* doing here?" Galen asked calmly, though he scowled as he spoke, clenching his fists at his sides.

"She can cure Niv," Asher said to him, clasping Galen's arm when he took a step forward. Though he turned back to narrow his eyes at me. "She better cure her."

"I will," I said firmly. "Now where is she?"

"Inside," Asher told me. I took a deep breath before moving forward, watching the seven men between me and Niv.

Niv was laid on a large table in the main room of the tavern. She was dressed as the men in Lucas's army had with completely black clothing, pants, and a tunic that would move easily with her during combat. I took a few steps closer to her, touching her cold skin.

She didn't look shriveled or decayed, as Harold had. Her skin was smooth, her face peaceful. She looked as if she was sleeping.

I brushed the hair off her face, her skin so pale it looked translucent. "Your bloodline, your family. They're not like us. It's how Lucas looked younger than his years. Why he was never ill and how one of your ancestors became the vampire king. That is why you didn't die immediately like Harold. When I fix this, it'll be up to you to end this," I whispered to Niv. I waited while a kettle was set up over the hearth. My eyes didn't leave her face until Brigsten handed me the cup of boiling water and the true love's kiss petals. "How long?"

"Another minute," he told me. We all waited in silence, each second drawing out seemingly longer than the last. We all watched the surface of the liquid lighten slowly from purple to a pure golden color.

"That's it?" Paxon asked. "Is it ready?"

I nodded and lifted a hand to separate Niv's lips, I gently

put the cup to them and allowed the liquid to trickle into her mouth. Being careful not to pour too much at a time, I continued until the cup was empty, massaging her throat to encourage the elixir to go down.

"Now what?" Asher demanded.

"We wait," I told him, hoping I was right. The book only mentioned the cure, not how long it would take.

I waited in the corner of the room, welcoming the shadows. Asher held Niv's hand, and the brothers were seated at the table.

"Are you sure this is going to work?" Brigsten said, pacing along the wall near me. "It's been hours."

"I told you what the book said…and didn't say." Like how long it would take to work. My fingers drummed on the wall behind me. "You'll have to trust what I've told you."

"Remember that time Niv managed to trick Paxon into chasing after that goat for two days?" Keres chuckled. "She'd tied boots to its feet and let it off in the woods. Then told him someone had stolen our goat."

Asher snorted. "He was gone for two days before he caught up with it."

"And then it took him just as long to bring it back," Som added.

I smiled, watching the group as they each told tales of Niv. Some were funny. Others had me leaning forward in fear for their lives, even knowing they were all alive and safe in the tavern. At least most of them were. My eyes fell on Niv and I peered closer. Was that a bit more color in her cheeks?

"How did you all meet?" Brigsten asked, taking a seat at the table.

The men looked at each other before bursting out in

laughter once more. "It involved a misunderstanding," Galen said.

"Niv had been to petition the king again," Asher started. "She had a temper...still does, to be honest."

"At least she does when it comes to those she cares about," Gunvor said quietly.

Asher looked at Brigsten. "She was a little frustrated, and on her way back to the tavern, she was gesturing wildly," Asher waved his hands, acting out the irate movement.

"And she knocked Mal's drink clean out of his hand." Keres slapped his hand on the table. "Mal being Mal started to face off against Asher, seeing how Niv was a girl."

"This was about a year after we escaped the palace," Asher said to Brigsten. "Niv and I had been training with the king's army. Figured we would need the skills. Niv was better than me, though."

"In no time at all Niv had Mal on the ground and was sitting on his head," Keres spluttered, laughing so hard he could barely breathe. He smacked the table again, ignoring the glare Mal was directing his way.

"We were all so shocked we just watched her until she politely asked Mal if he would behave," Galen said. "When he declined, she offered him training to improve his chances of being able to defeat her next time."

"I lost it at that," Keres said, holding his stomach. "We just waited with Asher until Mal gave up. At which point Asher handed him a replacement drink." He wiped tears from his eyes. "We'd only arrived in Avilar that day and hadn't found anywhere to stay."

"It was the Evesday Festival," Galen reminded him. "Bad timing on our part, all the way houses were full."

"Niv offered to let us stay here," Mal grunted.

"We had nothing to pay for lodging and once we cleaned this place up it was perfectly livable," said Asher.

"She used to invite strays over all the time. This lot never just left."

"Better than our parents' house," Gunvor added. "Bigger anyway, I get my own room here."

"Niv has had us training with the king's army since that day," Paxon told Brigsten. "We haven't missed a day until recently…"

"Some of us took to it better than others," Galen said, gesturing at Som who let out a soft snore from the end of the table.

His chin was propped on one hand, leaning on the table with his elbow. He looked oblivious to the attention he was receiving, and the others continued with their tale as if this was normal for him.

"They called us Niv and the seven, being as there's seven of us and she's the only girl," Keres explained.

"I'm sure he could have figured that out himself, Keres," Mal grumbled.

"You all believed her about the vampires and what happened. It gave her new hope." Asher was picking at a loose thread on his sleeve. He turned to glare at me, shaking his head. "It shouldn't have happened."

"You're right," I said simply. "It shouldn't have."

Guilt churned in my chest, looking at the group. A pang of jealousy sliced through me at how they acted like a family. Even Brigsten had been accepted by the group and included. I would forever be on the outside if I survived facing Damien with Niv. I knew I deserved to be alone, but the idea of never being part of a family brought back the old ache I had from growing up with my mother. A pit in my stomach formed, my thoughts spiraling. My actions had caused this, my choices.

Som jerked, suddenly awake, pulling me from my reverie. He tilted back falling back off his chair. "What was that?"

Galen frowned at him. "What was what?"

"She moved," he exclaimed.

"No. She didn't," Mal said, leaning over Niv's body on the table. "She looks the same."

"I swear she moved," Som cried.

I held my breath, taking a few steps closer to the group.

"He's right," said Paxon. "Her eyes just fluttered."

I closed my eyes in relief as I saw Niv's hand twitch. When I opened my eyes, I strode over to the table, reaching out to touch her face. Heat had returned to her, and she was no longer cold to the touch. My fingers tingled where they touched her skin in relief, a loosening of the tightness in my chest.

"Niv?" Asher pushed me aside, and I let him.

I took a few steps back to stand against the wall as the men crowded around her.

Niv pushed herself onto her elbows, looking around at the group at the table. "Why am I on the table? Oh gods, did Mal decide he'd finally try cannibalism?"

"You don't remember?" Asher took her hand in his, pulling her up into a sitting position. I watched as the group of men smiled and two of the brothers cheered. Niv swung her legs around, shaking her head at their antics. Asher helped her off the table, gripping her waist and pulling her into an embrace.

"Can't breathe," she squeaked, smiling when he let her go.

He still touched her, his eyes capturing hers. In that moment I saw a thousand words pass between them without a sound being made. Their love shone for us all to see, and my heart ached, thinking of Lucas. I sighed with relief at the same moment my heart broke at what my actions had caused. I stared at them, unable to look away. Lucas's loss settled deeply within me, and I knew he would have loved to see Niv so happy.

Galen coughed. "I'll need to examine her fully, to make sure there's no lasting effects from the apple."

"Apple?" Niv turned, Asher not letting her go as she studied us. "What's going on? You're worrying me."

She looked around the room, stiffening when she saw me. Her eyes widened when they met mine. She mouthed my name, her face pale.

"Hello, Princess," I spoke softly, but the words jolted her out of her stupor.

In a flash, a dagger was in her hand, and she lunged toward me. I did nothing to stop her as my back collided with the wall and cold steel was pressed to my throat.

"You will pay," Niv growled.

Asher appeared behind her, doing nothing to stop the outburst.

"I know," I whispered, staring into her eyes. The experience made me uncomfortable.

Niv slammed me against the wall again. Wood jutted uncomfortably in my back, yet I did not move. I waited.

Niv's eyes scanned my face, searching. Eventually she narrowed her eyes and released me, shaking her head. I knew not to expect a warm welcome. I was the villain, after all.

"You have control?" she asked.

I nodded. "There is no changing it." I hardened myself. Every part of her rejection vibrated through me. "But I brought you a peace offering." I nodded toward Brigsten, who stepped into view from behind Keres.

Niv grinned, her smile changing the harsh disgust on her face. She was beautiful, more so than when she had been a girl. The glimpses of her through the mirror did not do her justice.

"Brigsten!" she exclaimed. Throwing herself into his embrace as he stepped toward her. "How are you alive?"

"It's a long story," he told her. His eyes met mine and he

nodded. The brothers and Asher crowded around, their joy at Niv's recovery spreading through the room.

I walked to the door, taking a moment to look over my shoulder at them. A sourness surged from my gut, and I took a deep breath to push away the dark impulses. I was once again on the outside. I clenched my fists. Looking at a world I could never be a part of. Without speaking, I left the tavern and strode into the darkness of the night.

CHAPTER 24

RAINA

I stared at the sun, the bright disk peeking over the top of the treetops. Rising on the new day.

"What are you doing out here?"

My entire body jerked, turning to Brigsten.

"You shouldn't sneak up on me," I said, coldly.

"Sorry. We need you inside."

"You don't need me, Brigsten. I can't help you."

"Come back inside. We need you to help with the planning. You know Damien best," Brigsten held the door open for me. I looked at him dubiously before I walked through. The group consulted papers scattered over the table. I had listened to the plans from the doorway, feeling isolated from them. I wasn't one of them, not sure what I could add.

The day passed slowly, dragging as they went around in circles. When my part in the attack came up, Brigsten spoke on my behalf. He had explained what had happened, and Asher had told Niv about my connection to Damien. I'd thought about not telling them, but in a moment of human weakness, I'd given the knowledge to Brigsten.

"Why don't we just kill her then, and put an end to this?" Mal had grumbled, unsheathing his sword.

"It won't be as simple as killing her," Galen told him. "It doesn't appear she can be killed by normal means. A knife to the chest didn't work, so what makes you think your sword will?"

I snorted as they casually discussed my demise. I shouldn't have been surprised to hear no objections to experimenting to see what would kill me. I leaned against the wall in my usual spot, biting my lip and allowing myself to sink into a dark depression. As the sun set, I pulled the curtain aside to look out into the surrounding area.

As the darkest part of the night closed in, I slipped outside again to stare up into the starry sky. I had barely spoken and wasn't helping, despite what Brigsten had said. With no light from a large holding nearby, beautiful specks of light dusted the sky, showing off a cascade of starlight. It was hard not to eavesdrop from outside with my superior hearing as the group noticed my absence.

"I know I can't trust her," Niv told Asher. "She destroyed my kingdom and my family. We need her, though. It's that simple."

"She's charming and you're too kind for your own good. I know you'll never forgive her, but don't let her creep back into your heart. You haven't seen how ruthless she can be. She can destroy those creatures in an instant. Imagine what she would do to us if she felt like it."

Niv's laugh was hollow. "You think I don't remember what she is, what happened that day?"

"No, it's just—" Asher paused. "She's helping us now but we don't know what she will do tomorrow. How do we know we aren't helping her destroy Damien so she can take control instead."

"We will cross that bridge later." Niv's feet scuffed along

the ground. "We have this moment now. Let's not fill it with talk of *her*."

I moved away from the tavern, wanting to give them privacy. I walked slowly along a broken wall, trailing my fingers across the rough surface and tracing along the cracks. I whirled around as a branch broke behind me, only relaxing when Galen showed me he carried no weapons.

"That's foolish. You should have something to defend yourself. Especially from me," I spat, bitterly.

Galen rolled one shoulder in a half shrug. "I wasn't sure how you'd react to that."

I sniffed. "Can I help you with something?"

"I'm...curious about you," he said simply. "I have heard what Niv has said and listened to Keres and Mal talk of your journey. However, I'd like to hear from the horse's mouth, so to speak."

"There isn't much more to tell," I answered, pausing when I realized that wasn't true. Galen watched me, studying my posture. I sighed. "I have my own story, but I'm not sure it deserves to be told."

"We learn from the mistakes of others by understanding why they reached the crossroads they did and why they took the path they chose." Galen rubbed his chin.

"Niv knows enough not to repeat my mistakes."

"Are you sure?"

I thought about my grandmother and Kiara. I wondered if we would be in this situation if they had both been more honest with me. I close my eyes, wanting nothing more than to tell my story. If only so another soul knew of my struggle and how I had become what I was. Before I could second-guess myself, I let my words pour free. Galen listened patiently, taking notes on pages of parchment he'd pulled from his pocket. He waited until I'd finished to ask questions, prompting other memories to surface.

"Do you know what happened to your parents?" he eventually asked.

I nodded, swallowing. "Both dead. I killed my mother."

Galen bit the end of his pencil. "Well…erm."

I laughed at his discomfort. "Remember, I'm a monster." I bared my teeth at him and he paled, scribbling again on his parchment.

"Guess that just leaves how we get rid of Damien," Galen commented.

"Do you really think we can kill him?" I picked at a stone on the nearby wall, unable to look Galen in the eyes.

"Anything is possible with enough effort and thinking."

"That's not really an answer."

"I know," he said, nonchalantly. "I'm going to record what happened to you. I think it's best that others can learn from your mistakes. Documentation is the best way to ensure we don't repeat them."

I looked back at the tavern. Knowing Niv was alive gave me a sense of peace, but I wondered how long that would last. "Does he make her happy?" I asked Galen, turning to look at him.

"Well…I erm." I chuckled when Galen dropped his eyes, a flush creeping up his neck. "They are good for each other."

I let myself laugh, leaning against the wall. "You don't sound certain."

Galen reached up to rub his neck. "They are."

"Galen," Mal called from the side of the tavern. "What are you doing out here with *her*?"

I sighed. "Truce is over." I pushed off the wall and walked back to the tavern.

❧

I was shocked when I saw Niv walking toward me. I hadn't tried to talk to her yet, not entirely sure what to say. A thrill surged through me until I looked at her face, which was hard and cold as she approached. My heart sank when I saw she held the book, questions in her eyes. I was in the garden at the back of the tavern again, choosing to stay out here rather than with the group inside.

"Do you know what this means?" She thrust the book at me.

I hissed and the book dropped from my hands. My heart was hammering against my chest when I saw the burn on my hands where I'd held it.

"What in the gods?" Niv exclaimed, taking a step back from the book.

"The power I wield is too corrupted..." I shook my head, closing my eyes and clenching my injured hand. I hissed at the pain. When I looked down, the skin had started to lighten, no longer an angry red but the pink of healing. "You should be able to pick it up."

"I think I'll just leave it there." Niv crossed her arms, giving me a hard look. I shook my hand out, waiting for it to return to its normal color.

I looked up at Niv, my heart swelling at the sight of her. "It's good to see you."

"Don't make this harder than it has to be, Raina," Niv groaned. "We are both here because of your actions. Let's figure out how to end Damien, so I can go home and salvage what I can from the kingdom you destroyed."

"It wasn't like that," I snapped as anger reared up in me. "I loved you and your father more than I have loved anyone. I would never have chosen this."

"As you say," Niv spat back at me. "I loved my father. We took you from your cruel mother, but you are just as bad, Raina. Maybe there was a reason she treated you as she did."

I took a step back as if she had physically struck me, hand on my chest trying to quell the simmering rage just beneath the surface. "Why am I even here?" I said without thinking. "You're a spoiled brat. Born into an easy life and no idea what true hardship really is."

A part of me regretted the words immediately, but the hungry part of me applauded. Weakness was spreading through me with the gnawing hunger. Even though I hadn't used my powers while here, I needed blood. The creature I inhabited could smell the brothers and Niv, hungering for them. I clenched my fists, fighting the urge to release my power and be done with it.

Niv's laugh sounded hollow. "There she is. The creature of the dark you have become. I was beginning to think you were holding on to the meek persona you put on while you courted my father," she sneered.

I growled, only just managing to stop myself from jumping forward to grab her. I clenched my jaw closed and swallowed thickly. "Careful, girl."

We glared at each other before Niv looked at the book. Reaching carefully for it, she flipped the cover and thumbed through the pages. "Tell me what this means?"

Tension still in the air, it was an effort to concentrate. I scanned the page, surprised to see more to the passage I'd discovered back at the palace. The message Grandmother had left changed into a proclamation.

True love's kiss and power untainted.
The choice of the undying widow is key.
Between good and evil, the final battle awaited.
Only through her is victory a guarantee.

I frowned, reaching for the page and only pulling my

hand back at the last moment when I remembered my scorched palm. "This is new."

"Brigsten and I saw it appear. He can't read it, but I can. He gave the book to me at your request." She raised her brow in question, tilting her head when I nodded.

"I knew you would need it, and it's no longer mine."

"You must be the undying widow. What choice do you have to make?" she muttered.

I shook my head, sighing as some of my anger drained away. "It never makes it easy. I won't know until I make it. True love's kiss and power untainted. You have the cure from tainted power and my power in you." I let out an exasperated growl. "I don't know."

"How does this work? I know you've taught me from it, but I didn't realize how sentient it was." Niv shivered.

"Do you have a plan?" I asked her, still battling to keep my anger and hunger under control. The passage at the forefront of my mind, I concentrated on that. Niv may not have cared about riling up my temper, but I didn't want to lash out and harm her.

Niv shrugged. "Avilar won't send troops so it's just us. Other than charging in and seeing what happens, we don't have much of a plan."

"The final battle must be," I quoted.

"That's if we trust the book. It hasn't exactly led any of us down the right path so far." Niv reached up to brush a loose strand of hair out of her face. My eyes shot to her neck, and I licked my lips. She narrowed her eyes and put a hand on the sword at her hip. "Just because you're undying doesn't mean you can't feel pain."

"I need to feed," I reluctantly admitted. "Especially if we are going to face him."

A flash of disgust crossed Niv's face. "Great, don't count on any of us helping you out with that."

"I won't." I told her.

"I will."

My head shot to the right and we both whirled to face Brigsten, who had managed to approach us unheard across the yard as our attention was on each other.

"I'll be inside." Niv grimaced, walking back toward the tavern without another word.

"She will come around," Brigsten said sympathetically.

"She shouldn't." I was a monster. Since taking possession of my body, I hadn't truly been myself, and I wasn't sure if I hadn't always been a monster. It worried me that he had started to relax around me. "Let's get this over with."

"We are really going to just charge right in," Mal exclaimed. I was leaning against my wall near the door, my arms crossed over my chest as the men adorned themselves with weapons. My eyes wandered over their lithe bodies, mind wandering to inappropriate places as they strapped on their weapons.

"That's all we have," Niv told him. Mal continued to grumble incoherently, not particularly pleased with her words.

"Everybody knows where they are going when we arrive?" Asher asked as he sheathed a dagger in his boot. He looked at Brigsten, who nodded.

"I'll follow and go where I must," Brigsten told him. "I am your best chance for clearing out the cells. I lived there, after all."

His eyes held a haunted look when I turned to him.

"What's *her* role?" Mal glared at me.

"We don't know yet," Niv said.

The brothers and Asher didn't understand what the book wanted. None of us did. We were acting on faith at this point, and unease crept through me at the thought. At least this would be over soon, one way or another.

"Are the horses ready?" Brigsten asked.

The group looked at each other, and he shook his head, walking toward the door.

"Won't get far without them," he called back, giving me a smile as he walked toward me.

A huge explosion rocked the room, and I was thrown against a wall. I heard a sickening crack and crippling pain, lancing through my side as I hit the wall. Jarred further as I sprang to my feet, I put myself between the door and the others. I looked around frantically, searching for any sign of Brigsten through the dust and debris. A small hole had been blown open where the door had been; since I'd been standing next to the door, I had taken the full force of the explosion.

"Raina."

"Raina."

"Raina."

I shuddered as a group of Damien's creatures slowly prowled toward the opening, hissing my name. I reached out with my arms in a useless gesture to create a wall between the creatures and Niv. "Do you have Brigsten?" I called without looking behind me.

"Yes, but he's not conscious," Galen, I thought, called back.

"Get him out of here," I told him. I let the power draw forward, heat spreading down my arms as purple blackfire appeared in my hands. I grinned when Damien's pet, the tall vampire with dark hair stepped forward. Damien had called him Lewis back at the palace.

"I have a messssssage from our massssster," he hissed, smirking at me.

I stared at him waiting. "Well?" I asked when he didn't

speak. My fingers twitched. My entire being begging to release the power.

Damien's voice came from Lewis's mouth, causing a shiver to crawl up my spine. In my shock, I dropped the flames in my hands. "Come back to me, Raina. We can accomplish the incredible together. With you by my side, we could rule the world, and I will love you as you've never been loved before."

Even without him here, I could feel the draw I'd felt to the presence of the mirror all those years ago as a child and as an adult. That attraction and pull had started all of this. It was an effort to suppress the need to go to him, and I gritted my teeth. "Never," I spat, bracing myself. I counted four of them in the doorway, but I knew others might be outside.

"You will come to me, Raina. You're mine!" I knew the moment Damien's presence departed the creature, leaving me facing the vampires. They did not move to attack. They stood staring at me with hollow eyes.

"What are you waiting for?" I said, taking a step forward and daring them to attack. They still didn't move.

Cold washed over me, and I turned to look around the room to make sure the others had escaped. A crash from outside had me sprinting toward the back entrance to the building. I glanced back to see the four vampires hadn't followed me and were nowhere to be seen.

Panic gripped me as I darted out the back of the building and jerked to a halt. I needn't have worried. Niv landed a blow on the nearest vampire, sending him flying away from her while the brothers and Asher protected her back. They wove between the attacking creatures, engaging only when necessary and efficiently taking each one down. I stared as the group carefully picked off vampires, one by one, until only one remained.

Asher brought his sword down, severing the creature's

arm and causing it to release a high-pitched shriek. His legs were kicked out from under him by Mal, and the creature was shoved face down into the dirt.

"Why were you sent?" Niv demanded, crouching next to the vampire, which gargled and sputtered incoherently. "Why?"

"Dissssstraction," it replied.

"For what?" Niv said.

The creature looked up at me as I approached, smirking. When Niv turned to face me, her face was unreadable. She turned back, nodding at Asher and Mal who released the creature. Before it had time to react, she touched its shoulder and we watched as flame quickly spread over it. The vampire disappeared in a cloud of ash.

"Are you with us, Raina?" Niv asked me, brushing her hands together as she rose.

"Of course," I told her.

"You better be. You may be undying, but I will find a way to end you if you betray us. What happened after we left?"

"Damien wants me back," I said truthfully. I didn't tell her how I could feel a longing to be back with him, that I was struggling to hold back my desire to be with him. To race back to the palace and stay.

I took a deep breath. "We should move. He was sending these creatures to die. They would never have made it back to the palace before sunrise, but he may send more."

Butterflies swarmed in my stomach as I thought about seeing Damien again. Longing and dread warred within me.

CHAPTER 25

RAINA

"*A*re you ready?" Asher asked Niv, who nodded.

It had taken us more than a day to reach the cemetery entrance to the secret tunnels, but we hadn't seen any of Damien's creatures during the night. As we prepared to exit the tunnels, my heart quickened before we stepped out into daylight. The cemetery around us was quiet, and a light fog carpeted the grass, swirling around our legs as we walked through.

"Creepy," Keres whispered as we reached the edge of the cemetery. I turned at the sound of a scuffle to see Paxon stumble forward. He managed to right himself and looked around the group with a sheepish grin.

"Sorry," he whispered.

I saw Niv roll her eyes and shake her head. We moved forward, picking our way through scattered rubble and making our way to the residential streets.

"Everyone know where they are going?" Niv held her chin high, eagerness gleaming in her eyes.

We all nodded. I hesitated, watching her walk away into

the streets. I turned and scowled when I saw Brigsten watching me with an understanding smile.

"She will be fine," he told me.

"Let's get going," I huffed, pushing past him and heading toward the palace. We made our way back to the entrance we had escaped from a few days ago; it felt like years had passed since I was last here. The kitchens looked the same as when we had left them, empty and dark.

"This way." Brigsten gestured toward a door I'd never been through.

I didn't say a word as we quietly crept through the dark hallways, only cobwebs and bare stone decorating them. I felt Brigsten reach for me, and with only a little irritation, I allowed his hand to settle on my shoulder as I led him deeper underground and into darkness.

"How far do we need to go?" I whispered.

"A little farther. There will be a fortified door and it'll be lighter once we get past that."

The darkness enveloped us as we continued, and it was more time than I thought before I finally saw the large door to the entrance of the dungeons. Brigsten stiffened when I stopped to reach for the handle. I gripped it and tugged, not surprised when the door didn't move.

"Are we there?"

I turned to see Brigsten, eyes wide and flitting around the space at the end of the corridor. I reached up and guided his hand to the door. "It won't budge."

He smiled. "It will if you have the key." He groped around his belt until he pulled a large iron key from a small pouch. "Here."

I carefully took the key and inserted it into the lock below the handle. With some difficulty, it turned, making a grinding sound as the mechanism clicked open. My shoulders relaxed, the tension draining away as the door opened. I winced at the large creak as it widened, craning my neck around the door to see the other side. I blinked rapidly until my eyes adjusted, the bright light painfully harsh after the gloomy corridor.

Brigsten sighed as he took a step forward, moving more confidently now that he could see. "This door hasn't been used since Damien took over. They won't expect anyone to come this way, but we should still be careful."

We didn't speak as we stepped carefully down another short corridor, which opened into an antechamber around the corner. The smell hit me first.

My nose wrinkled at the odor of too many people crammed into a small area. The rank smell of sweat, odor, and human refuse slammed into us, almost knocking me back a step. My heart sank as I realized the men we had come to rescue may not be in much condition to follow us out of here.

I gagged, shaking my head as Brigsten approached the door on the other side of the antechamber. Reluctantly I followed, seeing the men divided into three small cells with twenty in each.

"Where are the women?" I asked.

"They don't last long in here." Brigsten looked disgusted. "Either they die from the conditions or they're taken away by the creatures.

"Why isn't anyone on guard?"

"Would you want to guard them?" Brigsten raised an eyebrow in question. I shook my head, swallowing and looking forward to fresh air.

"You're back," one of the men said eagerly. "Men, Brigsten came back for us."

The men slowly gathered around the entrances to the cells, clasping Brigsten's arm as he passed each cell door. Brigsten used the large key to unlock it as my eyes swept over the men who hadn't yet noticed me. My chest tightened when I didn't see my father. I had hoped my mother had been lying to me or wrong. That he was still alive, but looking at the men now...not one of them was over twenty-five.

I shrank back away from the scene, shocked to see my heart could still break. I stumbled back into the antechamber, my hand slapping against the stone as I leaned against the wall taking deep breaths.

The realization that I would never see my father again crashed through me, the taste of bile reaching my mouth. I swallowed thickly, taking one last deep breath, and turned to face the door to the cells as Brigsten came through. He gave me a questioning look, and I shook my head.

The men behind him halted with wide eyes when they saw me, the tension in the air palpable as Brigsten stepped forward.

"She's with us."

"She's one of them, the vampires," spat one man behind him.

"Do you want to get out of here or not?" I snapped harshly, whirling to open the door that would lead us back to the kitchens. "You have one way out of here, and we don't have time for your fear."

Brigsten didn't wait, passing through the door I held open. "Follow me, men, or do you not trust me."

A few of them glanced at me, and I ignored the venomous looks as I stared straight ahead still holding the door for them. Hesitantly they followed Brigsten, marching past me one by one. I heard muttered curses as they passed, but no one dared to speak directly to me. I pushed away the simmering anger at their hate and disgust, waiting until the last one had stepped through before I followed.

～

"It was too easy," Brigsten said to Niv.

We were gathered in a large hall, used by the people in the kingdom for festivals and ceremonies.

"We didn't see one creature and we should have."

"Wasn't that easy," I grumbled. We had moved painfully slowly with the escapees after we left the kitchen, creeping through the kingdom until we reached the prearranged meeting point.

Niv had spent that time moving from home to home, rallying the kingdom to fight Damien. I thought she was on a fool's errand, but as the word spread that Lucas's daughter had returned, that Princess Niveus was here to take back the kingdom, many had joined Niv and the seven to fight.

I hid in the shadows, not wanting to alarm any of the gathered citizens. I pushed away the gnawing hunger that had started to pulse in my middle, wondering if I would be able to feed before we finally took back the castle.

I resisted the urge to place my hand over my stomach and turned to leave the building Niv was holding court in. I retreated to the flat roof, longing for some silence. A tug in my chest pulled me toward the wall facing the palace. I placed my hands on the cool stone, staring at the place I had once called home, where I had been happy with Lucas and Niv. I gritted my teeth, thinking of the time stolen from us by Damien.

A presence brushed across my mind, and I shook my head to push away the feeling, jerking when I heard my name whispered on the breeze. I looked around, searching the shadows behind me and looking down into the street.

"Raina." My name was clearer this time, and a shiver chased up my spine at the sound of Damien's voice.

"Damien?"

"I can feel you near, Raina. Why haven't you come to me yet?"

I bit my lip, hoping he had no way of seeing through me. "I do not want to."

"Liar," he said with mirth in his tone. "I can feel your need for me, even without you next to me. You will come to me soon."

Elation rose within me at his words, and I tried to feel disgust at my eagerness to see him. I reached up to brush away the loose hair twisting around my face, picked up by the wind. "Will I ever be able to escape this cursed life you've given me."

"I freed you, Raina, from a cruel life trapped by your mother. You should be thanking me."

Anger lanced through me. "Thanking you? Why would I ever feel grateful for what you've done."

"You will be a queen by my side for all eternity. Who doesn't want that?"

"I don't." I gritted my teeth as another wave of hunger swept through me.

"You should give in. Follow your instincts. It's curious. I expected to feel more anger from you after what I did to Niv." I tried not to think of Niv and our plans, but Damien must have gleaned some of my thoughts. "You still hope to cure her." It wasn't a question.

"I would do anything for her," I hissed, my outburst loud in the quiet night.

"Think what you could do with your power, Raina. She is gone, let her go and be done with it. You should be by my side."

"Go away." I pushed power into my words, grateful when Damien didn't reply. I watched the palace as Damien's presence moved away. Unease spread through my middle when I realized my presence endangered everyone here. I couldn't help but mull over the words in the grimoire. The ones Niv showed me after she recovered. The words burned into my memory, never far from my mind.

> *True love's kiss and power untainted.*
> *The choice of the undying widow is key.*
> *Between good and evil, the final battle awaited.*
> *Only through her is victory a guarantee.*

It was my choice. Only I could stop Damien, and I needed to leave now to keep Niv safe. How could I stop him when his life was linked to mine, neither of us able to die? Reluctantly I stepped back from the wall, resigning myself to finding Brigsten and begging for blood. As I passed the hall, I looked toward Niv who was still taking her time to talk to each person in the kingdom who approached her. I would have to face him and trust that she could defend the kingdom long enough for me to end this, once and for all. A plan formed to leave before they attacked the palace to create a distraction and give them time to take it back by force. First, I needed to satiate my craving and tell Brigsten I needed to leave.

I left in the darkest hours of the night. Niv had stationed Mal and Keres as guards while their army rested. They planned to attack at noon when the vampires would be weakest. I needed to be inside the palace and in place before then. I would find Damien and keep him away from Niv.

"You're not going to say goodbye?"

I froze. Turning slowly to face Brigsten. I lifted my chin, staring at him straight in the eye. "It's for the best. You must keep her safe, Brigsten. She is the good that must lead this kingdom back into the light. I will find a way to trap him again, and then she must destroy the mirror. You know why I can't stay."

Brigsten sighed. "How do I know you aren't going to betray us again?"

"You don't," I said simply as I took a step toward him. "It's my choice, Brigsten. I don't know how I must choose, but I think the book was trying to tell me something…" My words trailed off lamely.

"I don't understand all this magic nonsense," he said, lifting his hand and running it through his hair. He narrowed his eyes at me. "You do right by us and make sure he can't hurt anyone anymore."

I nodded sharply and turned to slip away into the night, leaving Brigsten to join Keres and Mal. I barely felt the cold air biting into my skin as I walked slowly down the silent streets, my heart growing heavier as I drew closer to the palace. I was surprised not to see any vampires in the streets. Damien must have pulled them all back within the palace walls. Now he knew that Niv was alive and here, he would prepare for the attack.

I looked between the houses, wondering if Niv would try to evacuate now that the people weren't being guarded. I shrugged, figuring it wasn't my problem anymore and why should I care anyway. I was a vampire. They were human. I shook my head, not surprised that my humanity continued to bleed away. I hoped I wouldn't be alive much longer to see myself completely turn into the creatures I hated.

I forced myself to take each step forward, begging my will not to give in and hoping I could hold on just a while longer. The dark silhouette of the palace loomed in front of me as I walked slowly through the streets. A movement caught my attention to the left, and I saw a shadow stalking me. I swallowed hard, keeping my gaze ahead and continued slowly, not bothering to hide my approach. I needed to trust that the book, my grandmother's grimoire, wouldn't lead me astray.

I sensed rather than saw more shadows join the first, Damien's creatures surrounding me. I kept my chin high and ignored them. They wouldn't attack me now. Damien still wanted me, and here I was coming to him willingly. I prayed I was doing the right thing. I kept my hands at my sides as I entered the palace through the small entrance hall I'd used the first day I stepped foot inside.

Memories bombarded me of that first day, meeting Asher and getting to know Niv. How Lucas had treated me as an equal and been honest with me from the beginning. I had known little kindness from my parents, my mother more inclined to berate me and my father rarely available. It was the first time I'd felt like I could be part of a real family.

My tongue stuck to the roof of my mouth, which was suddenly dry as I walked down the corridor approaching the royal rooms I had shared with Lucas. I braced myself as I pushed the door open, a fluttering in my chest distracting me as I stared at Damien.

"Raina, my darling."

I frowned at his open smile.

"I knew you couldn't resist me, that you would come back to me."

I scoffed. "So sure of yourself, Damien?" I took a step toward him, a shiver running up my spine as he spoke again.

"Yes," he whispered. "I'm irresistible."

I tore my gaze away with difficulty, finally looking at the mirror that had started this all. If I could touch it, while touching Damien, could I trap him again? Would that even end this?

"Don't even think about it, Raina. You wouldn't know how to trap me, and it won't work a second time. I was fooled once by your grandmother but I won't be fooled again."

I bit my lip, trailing my hand along the wall. "It was worth a try. If you're so sure it won't work, why don't you show me how you can't be defeated."

Damien laughed, throwing his head back. "I can't wait to have these years with you. A battle of wills and an indestructible love. We will burn this world and enjoy it, together."

I shuddered. "Why are you so hell bent on destroying *everything*? What did this world do to you?"

"It did nothing." My breath caught as he was suddenly behind me, gripping my waist and pulling me close. His mouth trailed up my neck, his teeth scraping across my skin. "I do it because I can."

A moan escaped my lips as my body heated, silently begging him to continue kissing my neck. His breath tickled my ear as my hands moved of their own accord, covering his hands while they moved up my body. I opened my eyes, cold washing over me when I realized how close I was to the mirror. It was what I needed to shake the thrall he had over me.

Carefully I continued to follow his movements with one hand and reached for the mirror with my left hand. My fingers trembled as they inched closer to it. I had to stop myself holding my breath in case he noticed what I was doing. My fingers were a mere hair away from touching the mirror when his chest rumbled against my back.

"Raina?" He breathed.

"Yes," I answered breathlessly, pulling at the power within me as my hand touched the cool frame of the mirror.

"It's a nice try, but it really won't work."

I gripped his hand while I tried with my entire being to have the mirror swallow us both up. Trap us both and remove us from this world.

Nothing happened.

Dread pulsed inside my heart as Damien turned me to face him. My shoulders slumped as he laughed in my face, the laugh I had once found so attractive pierced my thoughts harshly. Why hadn't it worked?

"It would only work if you truly wanted it to, Raina." Damien chuckled, reaching up to brush his knuckle along my cheek. "You need me, my love, and you don't want to let me go. If you wanted me gone, I would be."

"No…I…" Was he right? I searched my feelings, knowing I would find the conflict within myself.

"Until you can decide one way or another, my dear, you will always live in turmoil." He backed away from me, approaching the door. "Don't worry. I'll leave you to figure it out, and I won't lock it. I know you'll always come back to me."

I could only stare as he turned his back to me. Leaving me with my traitorous, conflicted heart. I had failed Niv. I had betrayed them all again. For the first time since I could remember, I flung myself on the bed and sobbed. My heart aching and broken, my breathing became ragged. If I couldn't bring myself to stop Damien, what would become of the world?

CHAPTER 26

NIVEUS

"What do you mean she left?" Niv snapped at Brigsten, who had just casually dropped Raina's departure into his morning report. They were meeting in the office of what used to be a delegate's hall, where elected officials would work with the people of the kingdom to present issues to the king when her father had ruled.

Here they were, hours away from moving against their enemy for the final time, and the woman had abandoned them. She had never trusted her but knew it would be foolish to turn away Raina's help. It had been foolish to accept it as well.

"She felt she was being pushed to face him alone. She wants to take him out before you get there. I believe she is protecting you, Princess," Brigsten told her with a carefully blank face.

"Stop being so naïve." Niv breathed deeply, letting the breath out through her nose. "That woman can't trust herself. *We* can't trust her, and now we don't know where she is? If she was with us, the least I could do was keep an eye on her so she didn't do anything else to jeopardize the kingdom."

Brigsten shrugged one shoulder casually. "You haven't been with her since she betrayed you. I don't blame you, but something larger is at work here. I can feel us being driven by a force, maybe the magic. Maybe the book." He gestured at the large grimoire lying innocently on the office desk.

"We don't have time for this," Asher said warily, glancing around their surroundings to see who was listening. "We can't let them know anything has happened. The people have hope for the first time in years, and we need to make sure they trust us to lead them. The timing is bad, but as Brigsten said, we are going to win. I can feel it."

She knew he was right, but it was hard to push away the hurt and anger. Niv had just started to think that maybe Raina could help. She could never forgive her for what she had done to her father, but Raina could have helped rebuild the kingdom. Helped them take it back or at the very least kept the vampire king distracted.

Niv took in another deep breath, counting as she did so. "We can't do anything about it now," she said, resigned. "We can only think of what we need to do."

Her eyes fell on the grimoire, and she narrowed her eyes at it, scowling. Nothing further had appeared, and nothing had changed about any of the verses. All the words Niv hadn't been able to understand earlier in the book had slowly disappeared, leaving only the last paragraph on a blank page toward the center. She should have asked Raina more about how to use it; at least the traitor hadn't taken it with her.

Asher frowned as she approached the table, using one finger to flip open the cover. She stared at the final verse, the only words that remained in the book. Her eyes widened at the line that had appeared underneath.

True love defeats all, even the impossible.

"What does that mean?" she exclaimed, after reading the words to the group. Asher took a step to stand next to her and peered at the book.

Brigsten scratched his chin. "Seems like an old story, like the ones we tell our children when they are younger ..." his words trailed off.

"Tales that convince you that we all have a happy life and no one loses in the end. The enemy is defeated, and we all have a feast to celebrate," Niv scoffed. "If only we were that lucky."

"Something like that," Brigsten said, reaching up to scratch his chin.

Niv threw up her hands. "Nothing but riddles, I've had enough of this." Anger simmered under her skin and she reacted without thinking.

"What are you doing?" Asher paled as Niv picked up the book and approached the fireplace, which burned low behind them.

"This kingdom has had enough magic. I know how to use the power Raina has given me, and once this is over, I know how to give it up. We need no more magic, and this book is too dangerous. It's time we do it how my father did it, how each generation before fought for our kingdom. We need to have faith in ourselves and our people."

Niv looked at the book one last time and dropped it into the fire without further hesitation. The three of them watched as the flames engulfed it, faster than was natural. The book grayed and crumbled into ash in the hearth.

"What did you just do?" Asher whispered. "What if this doesn't work and we need more time or help?"

"We have ourselves," Niv said, striding to the window and gesturing. "We have our people. Now no one can use that book against us ever again. I am beginning to get the feeling the grimoire started this all to begin with."

"You might be right," Brigsten said. "But now we have no magical backup with Raina gone."

"We don't need it," Niv insisted, staring out the window and watching the sky lighten. "Let's gather the others. We need to be ready to attack at midday. I just hope Raina hasn't told that beast all our plans."

"Still a little abrupt, Niv. This isn't like you. You plan everything." Asher reached up to touch her face, which heated under his gaze. "Take a breath."

"I get the impression the book wanted us to do this alone. Why else was it being so vague?" Niv bit her lip, resisting the urge to kiss him one last time. Just in case.

Niv stared out the window, watching the six brothers she had come to love as her family. They all smiled and laughed with a group of children in a humble courtyard with a small fountain. Mal stood to one side with his customary scowl but she knew him well enough to recognize the brightness in his eyes. Keres, never far from Mal, was showing a young boy how to play a ball game.

"It's time we took the kingdom back. Even without Raina we will win," Niv said, knowing they had no other option. She stepped from the room, nodding at the brothers to catch their attention as she passed through the courtyard.

They each stood, alert and waiting for her to take the lead. The children watched in awe as they exited the court-yard. The group of adults who had agreed to stay behind and protect them, watched from a distance—those with little fighting experience but enough to protect those left behind.

It was a long walk toward the town square, one Niv hadn't visited often when she was princess. She took careful steps through the streets, ensuring she spoke to every person who approached her as she aimed for the very center of the square. She savored the calm with no vampires in the streets to attack them during the day. With a lightness she hadn't felt in years, she climbed up the few steps until she faced her kingdom. A swarm of butterflies in her stomach gave her a sense of urgency and nervous energy.

Niv smiled at the group gathered before her, finally facing the people of her kingdom. The sun was rising toward its peak without a vampire in sight. They had all gathered in the town square less than a mile from the palace, the only place they could all stand together before the final battle to win their freedom.

Silence fell as Niveus stepped up onto a platform erected in recent years for proclamations and speeches. She looked out at her people, the ones her father had led many years ago, now waiting to hear from her with bated breath as they waited for her to lead them now.

"We have been afraid for too long," Niv started raising her voice so that all could hear her. "I am proud of our kingdom. That we haven't fully crumbled under the rule of a vicious creature. Many would have given up, but here you stand with your hope renewed, and I am humbled to be here standing before you. I am here, not as your princess and not as your queen. I am here to help you take back your kingdom. What happens from here is up to you."

Niv paused, watching the faces of the men and women before her. A few were nodding while others looked tired and drawn. Pale faces looked back, gaunt from years of starvation and mistreatment from the vampires.

"You have been beaten into submission, but remember, you are still here. You still stand here with your lives and the ability to protect your families."

Niv let flames ignite in her hand, glowing red at first. She noticed the contrast from Raina's purple flames and pushed more power through her hands. She released the energy of the blackfire and let her senses guide the magic. The red slowly changed to gold as the power increased, and Niv grinned, knowing she was about to try something she hadn't before. She allowed the magic to spread and bathe her in golden light.

"I have the power to help you defeat our enemy, if you will have me."

Awed faces broke into smiles, and the whole crowd fell unnaturally still, watching her. The golden light spread across the faces in front of her, and Niv willed courage into her people. She willed strength to aid their cause and for them to survive what came next.

"Yeah!" she heard Keres cry out from behind her.

His shout was joined by his brothers and then the crowd in the square. The men around her, caught up in the impromptu spell, called out with ferocity and jubilation.

"Let's end this once and for all," Niv murmured, turning to face Brigsten and the seven.

All were caught up in the battle spell, creating a fortitude and eagerness to overcome the greatest evil.

"It's time," Brigsten told her, his eyes bright.

Niv jumped down, still allowing the golden light to shine from her and touch all those she walked by. It wasn't the blackfire that Raina had taught her, and she was acting entirely on instinct. It appeared to be working, helping her people overcome their suppression and fear.

The people eagerly followed, holding whatever weapons they could find, and Niv could sense the rightness of the moment. She was a princess of a broken kingdom, one destroyed by greed and power. She would take it back, rebuilding a new kingdom and introducing them to a new era of prosperity. Finally, without the overshadowing fear of the vampires. She would end every last one today, even if it took everything she had. She would give it gladly to see the vampire king fall.

Those in front with the better weaponry would cut down the vampires as the people took back the palace, and those behind would finish them off, bludgeoning until they were dead. She had stationed more experienced fighters on the flanks to protect those who would need it. Niv allowed a bubble of euphoria to pulse through her, and the light intensified, spreading from person to person in her army.

The people of the kingdom marched toward the palace, basked in sunlight and the power radiating from Princess Niveus. The gates were open as they approached, and they braced themselves to face the enemy who had ruined their kingdom for the final time.

CHAPTER 27

RAINA

I waited. I'd torn down the curtains and leaned against the stone balcony overlooking the kingdom from the royal chambers. Dark despair devoured me, gnawing at my insides. I hated myself. My naivety and trusting nature had doomed this kingdom, and I had been too brash, thinking I could defeat Damien. He had been ready for me and knew what to expect. How had he managed to stop me from pulling him into the mirror, trapping him as my grandmother had?

I snorted, watching the sun rise higher in the sky. Putting my head in my hands I groaned, tugging at my hair slightly to try and pull myself out of my dark brooding. I had to do something. The time Niv would attack grew steadily closer, and I could no longer stand here and wait for the outcome. I turned to face the mirror, scowling at it. It took three strides for me to stand before it, and I let out a frustrated scream at my reflection.

"Why didn't this work?" I clenched my fists, only just resisting the urge to punch the glass. My fingers trembled as I finally reached up with one hand to touch the glass. "Why didn't he destroy you? After all these years being trapped, why didn't he destroy you?"

"*Because he couldn't.*" The whisper was barely a caress at the back of my mind, more of a feeling than a voice.

I stilled, waiting for it to elaborate. I bit my lip, waiting patiently and hoping I would find answers. I breathed slowly for several heartbeats, nearly giving up on the voice speaking again when the presence brushed across my mind once more.

"*Between good and evil...the final battle...many years... this has been foretold. There will only be one moment...one decision...True love...impossible...*"

The words from the mirror trailed off as if I was listening to a conversation in another room and hearing words I wasn't supposed to hear. None of it made sense, and I gave in to my urge to punch the mirror. I heard a crack but none appeared in the glass. My reflection warped before returning to normal, the dark creature I had become staring back at me with hollow, angry eyes.

I needed to get out of here, find Damien, and help Niv. I turned to the door, releasing a cry as I raised my hands. Wood splintered, snowing down from the ceiling and showering the room with dust. I took a step through to the hall where the remains of a vampire lay. He must have been behind the door. I grinned wickedly at my handy work as I stepped over his broken body.

I met no other vampires in the halls as I walked through the palace. It was eerily silent as I entered the room where the apple trees now lay in decimated ashes. As I knew he would be, Damien was waiting for me there.

"My queen," he bowed his head.

I ignored the hand he offered me, walking past him toward the window. I could feel his eyes on me as I stood in the light, watching as the sun reached its zenith. "Have you decided?"

I turned to face Damien. "I choose love, which is something you can never give me."

Damien smiled, his features a beautiful nightmare. I tried to ignore the quivering in my stomach as his eyes devoured me. "Are you ready for the show to start? I want you by my side when I finally defeat the last of my people. Bring them to their knees."

"Why?" I said through gritted teeth. "I don't understand why you must destroy everything? What do you want?"

"You, Raina, I want you."

I rolled my eyes. "This started before I was even born. It was never about me."

"It was always about you." Damien threw the glass he was holding to the floor. "You were promised to me by your ancestor. You were supposed to be my salvation, my way to true power."

My mouth dropped open. "What are you talking about?"

"It wasn't supposed to be this way." Damien lifted his hand, brushing it through his hair, agitated in a way I had never seen before. "But I had to break you first. That was the deal. That was what I was told."

"Told by who?" I exclaimed.

"Marissa," he spat the word at me, and it took me a moment.

I had nearly forgotten, but it came to me when I realized I only had one other family member who could have made a deal with him.

"Grandmother's sister?" I reeled. "The one who helped you become what you are? The *creature* you are?"

Damien's lip curled into a sneer. "So easy to manipulate. So easy to lead down the path of darkness but weak. And here you are, so strong, and you are mine."

"I am not yours," I said. "Lucas—"

"Do not say his name." Damien stepped toward me, his eyes flashing with anger. "You were never supposed to love him. You were supposed to love me. Free me and then together we would rule."

I shook my head. "Saying it over and over will not make it true." I looked at Damien, really looked at him. Dark circles I hadn't noticed lay under his eyes, and his skin was paler than usual. I frowned and shook my head. "Why?" I whispered.

"Why does anyone do anything?" He looked deflated, staring out the window. "You were supposed to break when the princess died from the apple."

My frown deepened. "When Niv died?" He didn't know. He didn't know she was still alive.

"Ensure the death of the princess, and then you would be mine. That is what she said," Damien continued to ramble, his mind fracturing.

I couldn't help myself. I took his face in my hands and stared deep into his eyes. My hands warmed with a little power as I searched. I could not deny the connection between us. Even now I could feel myself drawn to him.

Being this close, our lips mere centimeters away, I leaned into him. His scent hit me, intoxicating, and surrounding me —sweet citrus and the breeze on a summer's day. I closed the distance between us, not being able to resist a soft kiss, though nothing like the ferocious and devouring ones I was used to from him.

I felt him tremble beneath my hands and whisper my name. I looked again into his eyes, looking past the monster he had become. I realized that since I had come back to the palace, since he had started changing, I had too. I couldn't feel the creature beneath my skin as I had before. It was calm, almost gone.

I pushed that thought away. "Had I met you in another life, Damien, it might have been true. But I am not yours."

His eyes shuttered, and in that moment I knew I had made a mistake. He pushed me away and I stumbled, only righting myself when I reached out for the wall. Damien turned on me, straightening. In a heartbeat, he was himself again, the Damien I had met in the mirror—confident, dark, and wicked.

He smirked. "Raina, good of you to join me here. You are about to witness me finally breaking this kingdom. I think it's time to move on to bigger and better kingdoms."

I blinked. It was as if our conversation never happened. "What are you talking about?" I said carefully.

"The rebels are attacking the palace. The princess's man, the annoying butler. He was spotted last night in the kingdom. No doubt coming here to avenge the death of the princess."

I gaped at him. Did he truly not remember what had just happened? Was the curse breaking? I searched myself, feeling the conflict and loathsome thirst for blood seeping back in. I swallowed, watching Damien as he returned to the cruel man that had ruled this kingdom for years. His attention was drawn to a vampire minion who had just entered the hall.

"It has started."

I tried to jerk my arm back when Damien grabbed me, dragging me after him as he led me to a window down the corridor. It overlooked the stables and the courtyard where Lucas used to gather his men before going outside the wall. I slid to a stop, looking at the large mass of people. It looked like every soul in the kingdom approached the palace.

Damien hissed, careful not to step directly into the light. I had no need to be careful, so I leaned forward, elation warring with anger as I watched the attack on what was once my home. The vampiric influence fueling my anger and hate toward the people now attacking mixed with sadness, wondering how many would survive. I tried to breathe slowly while I watched the crowd swarm into the area near the stables. A ghost of a smile crept into my face as I spotted Niv in the lead, determination apparent in her eyes.

Damien let out a gasp, and I turned to see him staring at Niv, who grinned when she met his gaze. "How?"

"You failed," I said simply, smothering my grin so as not to anger him further. He may not be able to kill me, but he could still take out his rage on the people I cared about. Niv directed the people around her, approaching several entrances into the palace, ready to fight in close quarters. "I hope you managed to make enough creatures to go up against such a force. Especially after I destroyed so many when I escaped with Brigsten."

Damien ground his teeth, his usual composure failing him. Suddenly, he smiled. "Never mind. I was starting to get bored of this kingdom. We should leave."

Damien strode off down the corridor, leaving me standing there with my mouth open. The sudden changes all in the last few minutes left me conflicted. I looked out the window, not seeing Niv but knowing she would be working her way through the palace soon. I was torn between going to help her and making sure I didn't lose sight of Damien. I turned and followed Damien, wondering where he was heading.

I found him in the royal chambers, staring at the mirror. His was reflection unmoving as I walked up behind him. I paused, waiting for him to react to my presence. His eyes met mine in the mirror, and they softened, surprising me. I licked my lips when he turned, and we stood in silence, facing each other. Several heartbeats passed before either of us spoke.

"What can I do to convince you to come with me," Damien spoke quietly, his voice barely above a whisper.

I closed my eyes, pain lancing through me as I thought about how everything could have been so different. If I hadn't found the mirror, if I hadn't met Lucas, if Damien hadn't hungered for power and nearly destroyed his family and mine.

"We cannot change the past," I told him.

"Can we not start fresh, work toward a new future together?"

"You hunger for power, Damien. That is your true love."

"Can I not have your love? Destroy this mirror and come with me."

I glanced at the mirror over his shoulder, my brow pinching. "Why do you want to destroy it now? What is the urgency when you've had years to get rid of it."

"Because of you." He took in a long shuddering breath. "You weren't whole while your soul was fragmented. I couldn't bring myself to destroy any part of you. Being able to control you so easily never felt right."

My laugh was hollow. "Didn't feel right? Since when have you had a conscience?"

He shook his head, slowly lifting his hand to cup my cheek. "What you must think of me."

He leaned in, slowly allowing me the space to step back if I wanted. I watched his eyes, not sure what I was searching for. I thought about stepping back, but my traitorous body froze, waiting for his lips to meet mine.

I couldn't deny my attraction to him, even though I hated him. But did I hate him? I hated what he had done, but having to fight my urges as a vampire, fight to be human, I knew how hard it could be not to give in. I had only had to cope with my internal battle for a few days. He had been warring with himself for centuries.

My breathing quickened before his lips met mine with another soft kiss, so sweet it was painful. My hands moved of their own accord, pulling him closer and imagining a future with him. If I let myself love him, truly love him, could that break this curse between us? The scattered words of the mirror came to me, it had mentioned true love. Was it a coincidence that the namesake of the flower that had saved Niv would also save Damien? Did he deserve to be saved?

Our kiss deepened, my body heating, not from anger but from the temptation of him. His hands slid up from my waist, caressing the skin on my arm and causing tingles to spread up me. I pulled back to gasp air, staring into his eyes and for a moment seeing a different man before me—the one untainted by his hunger for power and destruction. I opened my mouth to speak, not sure what I would say.

When a crash from the hallway had me turning. I stared into the reddened face of the daughter of the man I had given my heart to, her eyes blazing as she glared at the two of us.

I looked at Niv, whose eyes fell on Damien's grasp on my arm. I pulled my arm free, hoping she would understand. When I caught sight of the tightness in her jaw and her gritted teeth, my heart sank as I realized she thought I'd betrayed her again.

Pain flashed in her eyes for a moment before they hardened, full of hate, directed entirely at me. I trembled. Maybe I had betrayed her again. When she spoke, her words were directed at both of us.

"You have terrorized us long enough." She lifted her swords pointing at the two of us. "This ends today."

"Niv, it's not what you think," I said, reaching toward her and stopping when she growled at me.

"I don't know what game you are playing, but it is best for the kingdom if I just kill you both now. You have been a plague of destruction and torment."

Tears pricked my eyes, and I nodded. She was right. I had done enough, and this needed to end. Thoughts of running away with Damien, keeping him away from all the kingdoms, and helping him to become a better man faded from my mind.

"I understand." I waited for her judgment, the blow of her punishment when Damien chuckled behind me.

"How do you think this will end, Princess?" I could hear the sneer in his voice. "You couldn't defeat me before. What makes you think you can win now? My beloved has made her choice. She will always choose me and power."

The choice of the undying widow is key. The words sprang to mind, the words from the book repeating in my mind as time slowed. I stood between my darkest temptation and the girl I had grown to love with all my heart, so much so that she had given me strength to fight the monster that possessed me. I looked at her now, her beauty and love for her kingdom shining into the room. I turned my head to look at Damien, his face frozen into a cruel smile. My beautiful nightmare incarnate. I bit my lip as they faced each other, their anger making the air around me vibrate.

I had to choose.

Half turned as I was, my eyes fell on the mirror, its frame glowing softly and the glass shimmering. In that moment I knew which choice I would make. They continued to throw words at each other and I wondered why neither had attacked yet. Niv gestured with her sword but made no move to throw blackfire or her weapon at us. I became aware of Damien, still standing slightly behind me, almost using me as a shield. He still had a wicked grin plastered on his face, enjoying himself as he sparred only verbally.

"Enough," I called out, power radiating in my words. "Both of you." They fell silent, their attention turning to me.

"Enough," I repeated, softly.

I looked out the window at the light streaming into the room, laying itself over Niv. Only then did I notice the buttery glow coming from her skin. I sensed her use of power and shook my head, wondering what new trick she had discovered.

Damien and I lay in shadow, forever banished into darkness and death. We all waited, as if holding our breath and expecting one another to act. I barely had any warning; only my proximity to Damien allowed me to anticipate his movement before he struck, launching himself at Niv from behind me. The gleam in his eyes promised her destruction.

Time slowed once more. Damien reached for Niv and Niv braced herself for his attack, the glow intensifying. Positioned between the two, I had to choose who would be the victor. My heart beat hard in my chest, as my arms encircled Damien, pulling him with all my strength and using his own momentum to swing him around away from Niv. My eyes locked on to the mirror and I continued pushing him with me, plunging us both toward its surface. I could see Damien's face reflected on the glass, his eyes wide as we approached the mirror on the wall.

I stared at Niv in the mirror, her eyes widened in shock, and I hoped she would understand that I loved her. The shock of the frigid surface engulfing us drove the air from my lungs, ripping at both of us and yanking us apart.

The room filled with sunlight, and Niv's curious glow disappeared. My heart clenched now that I knew I would never see her again. I fell to my knees and looked around expecting to see the reflected room surrounding us, but all I saw was never-ending blackness.

"What have you done?" Damien asked, frantically.

He stumbled to his feet, taking a few steps away from me and whirling to look for the mirror. I followed his gaze, not surprised to see that it was not there, only the same infinite darkness, an all-consuming and never-ending world in every direction.

I breathed heavily, aware of the missing urges no longer driving me. The dark monster seeping away from me with each second that passed. The vampire I had become was gone. I was myself again, whole and entirely me for the first time since Damien had bitten me. I looked up at him as he fell to his knees. His shadowed features and pale skin were infused with color. His complexion became tanned, his black eyes fading to a rich hazel. He fell to his knees, crying out with such anguish I flinched.

"What did you do?" His head fell into his hands as I gaped at him, an entirely human Damien.

"I made my choice."

"Death would have been better than this." His entire body started to tremble.

I stared at him, closing my eyes and nodding. We were trapped together in this eternal world. I wondered what would become of us.

"At least they are safe from us. This is better than what was happening to the world," I told him, rubbing my bare arms as I shivered. I didn't say anything else, numbness washing over me. Damien stared at me with eyes dull, letting the horror of what I'd done sink in.

A prick of light broke through my despair as it appeared in the distance, spreading as it came closer. A soft lilac tinge becoming apparent as it got closer. I watched silently as it took the shape of a person, slowly approaching us. Damien sat cross legged, his head whipping between me and the light as its features became clearer.

"It is good to see you, granddaughter. It looks like you've had quite the adventure. You've earned a place with our kin."

I smiled at her, entirely calm for the first time in many years. My heart filled with love for the woman who had been my companion as a child. "Hello, Grandmother." I swallowed thickly, overcome with too many emotions to count. "What does all this mean?"

"I'll explain on the way."

I rose to my feet, cautiously passing Damien and standing with her. Both of us looked down at him.

"Now what will we do with you?" she asked him, keeping her face blank and turning to me. I looked between the two of them and gave my grandmother a smile.

"It is your decision, dear child." She told me. "Leave him in the dark, which is what he deserves, or bring him with us."

I looked at Damien, staring into his fear-filled eyes.

"Looks like I have to make one final choice," I said to him, crossing my arms over my chest. Our eyes locked, and we stared at each other as he waited for me to make my choice.

He blinked at me, as if waking from a trance. A fogginess I hadn't noticed cleared from his expression. "I understand if you want to leave me. I can't fathom what you must feel after what I've done. The years I planned and yearned for more." He shook his head. "The lives I have ruined."

Save the monster that destroyed or save the human who had craved power so much he turned himself into that monster. I resigned myself to walk away from him and leave him here. It was what he deserved. I closed my eyes, letting my anger wash over me and then releasing it.

"Why? I don't even remember why I craved more. I had a family," he spat, the venom directed at himself.

I crouched next to him, raising a hand to brush the hair

from his forehead. I stared into his eyes, assessing. Such human eyes, filled with torment and self-loathing.

I reached out a hand toward Damien. "Come on. Everyone deserves a second chance at peace." I pulled him to his feet.

"Where are we going?" I asked my grandmother.

"To meet our ancestors. It is unusual to bring a guest, one not of our kind, with us, but I think they will make an exception. He will be your responsibility, Raina. I hope you understand that." She narrowed her eyes at Damien.

I nodded briefly, not sure if I would regret the decision. "I understand."

Damien clung to my hand, and I gave it a squeeze.

"Our people, the charmarutha. We are not born of this world entirely. We have one foot in the world of the spirits, which is where we always return. We can choose to be reborn and live a life in the human world. Now that your time there has come to an end, we can return."

"Haven't you been back already?" I asked her.

"I was too involved in the human world. My mistakes and that of my sister…" She eyed me carefully. "Needed to be resolved before either of us could return."

"Your sister?" I gasped, my hand flying to my mouth. "I'm your sister?"

"Our relationship is fluid in the human world. We are all sisters in ours." She paused as we walked toward the welcoming glow of the light in the endless dark. "We chose to return together, and what a mess we caused."

I rolled my eyes at her chuckle. "Until I fell in love with Damien and helped him become the monster." It wasn't a question. It explained so much, why I had always been drawn to him. Why I hadn't been able to resist the temptation. "But I chose Niv in the end. I chose to save her."

"Is that all you chose to save?" Constance, my sister, my

grandmother tilted her head toward Damien. "Have you not also saved him? You considered yourself weak and naive to fall under his spell when he was in the mirror, but you were drawn to him through magic, the connection you forged when you helped him all those years ago. Only your sacrifice for Niv overcame that bond."

I turned to Damien who had been unusually quiet during our conversation. His gaze bore into me. "I don't remember you as you are now, but I remember you then. You gave me everything I wanted, and it corrupted me. I repaid you with death."

I let go of his hand. "It seems we both have a lot of healing to do."

Constance nodded. "We all do. We all made mistakes that we now must live with for eternity. I doubt any of us will be allowed to return to the human world for a very long time."

I shook my head as we bathed in the warm light, surrounding us. "I think that is for the best."

CHAPTER 28

NIVEUS

*N*iv stared at the empty room, her grip on her sword barely keeping it from dropping to the floor at her side. What had just happened?

One moment she was facing down Raina and the terrible creature that had nearly destroyed her kingdom, ready to finally have her revenge. And the next Raina had grabbed the monster, charging toward the mirror. Which swung slowly on the wall now, looking like any normal mirror.

Her entire body jolted as the mirror crashed to the ground, shattering into a thousand pieces at the impact as it hit the dresser below it. Even the frame had scattered across the room; entirely destroyed. Footsteps echoed loudly behind her, and she turned, raising her sword to meet her oncoming foe.

Breathing heavily, Asher appeared with his hand clasped against a wound on his side. He relaxed when he saw her, his eyes flicking over her to check she wasn't hurt.

"You're wounded," Niv commented, finally dropping her sword and stepping forward to help him into the room. She eased him down to the floor, settling next to him and leaning into his uninjured side.

"I'm fine. What happened here? I saw you run off into the castle once we had control of the creatures, but I couldn't get to you to follow. They all broke into panic, trying to scramble through us to get outside." Asher shook his head. "They ran into the sunlight, destroying themselves. Every last one."

Niv gaped at him. "What do you mean?" Her fingers gently touched his arm, reassuring herself he was alive and with her.

"What I said. They killed themselves. One of them caught me on the way out. I was too surprised to stop him." His face reddened at his admission. "Where are Raina and the vampire king?"

Niv shook her head, not daring to believe it. "It's over." She gestured at the pieces of the mirror cascaded over the entire room. "They're gone."

Asher's eyes darted around the room. "How?"

Niv shook her head, taking a moment to lean on his shoulder and close her eyes. "I don't know. I was here, ready to face them both, and they vanished. Into the mirror, I think."

"The mirror…" his words trailed away as he spotted the pieces on the ground. "You destroyed it?"

Niv shook her head again, not daring to open her eyes as a mild headache pricked behind them. "It just fell."

Her eyes flew open at the sound of stomping feet entering the room. She was on her feet in a second, only relaxing when she saw Keres and Mal leading their brothers into the room shouting a battle cry.

"All good in here," Asher groaned at Niv's feet. His face was pale, and she wasn't sure he could stand by himself.

"Are you not feeling well?" Keres asked, frowning and lowering his sword.

"I'm fighting fit." Asher waved a hand at him dismissively. "Just a little winded."

Galen approached, examining the wound on Asher's side. He gently lifted away the slashed tunic, and Niv watched carefully when Galen let out a concerned sigh.

"Well?" she asked.

"I'll need to take him back to where I'm treating the rest of the injured. It'll need stitches."

Asher grimaced. "I just need a moment."

"Better to get it over with," Mal said, reaching for Asher with a scowl. "You owe me a drink."

"Do not," Asher retorted, pain flashing across his features as he stood with one arm draped over Mal's shoulder.

Keres stepped in to help, and Niv followed them slowly away from the room. Her thoughts lingered on the royal chambers, the room where Raina and her father had lived together and where the worst event of her life had occurred.

"I think I'm going to knock this wing down and replace it with…" She paused, thinking of what they could build in its place. "What do you think? Medical wing or armory?"

"Armory," Mal and Keres answered as Galen and Paxon said, "Medical Wing."

Som and Gunvor just shrugged, their clothes grimy and their expressions drained. Niv gently touched Gunvor's shoulder. "Let's get Asher settled and then all cleaned up. We can celebrate with the rest of the kingdom."

"What will we do now?" Paxon asked her. "Now you've defeated the evil queen and her vampire lover?"

Niv shook her head wearily, careful not to stumble as they carried Asher down some steps and to where Galen was treating the rest of the wounded. Som shrugged at Paxon when she didn't answer. They continued in silence and Niv watched as Asher was settled onto a bench near a temporary workstation. They were in the ballroom, where she had first met Raina. Niv looked around, not surprised to see all the paintings of her ancestors destroyed.

"He really hated my family," she said, gesturing at the slashed artwork.

"It seems so," Galen agreed, preparing materials to stitch up Asher.

Niv looked toward Asher's pale face and gave him a knowing smile. Asher had never handled pain well.

"Let's go, boys." She nudged Gunvor, who turned bright red as her attention fell on him. She chuckled. "I'm sure we all want to get out of our dirty clothes."

They trudged back the way they came. "Where are we going?" Mal grumbled. "Back into the kingdom or do we stay here?"

"I'll show you to the guest wing. Hopefully it isn't in too much of a state of disrepair." Niv led them to the back of the palace to the rooms overlooking the garden. She had spent little time in them as a child, but it still pained her to see the broken furniture and aged linens.

"It'll take us a lifetime to get this place livable," Mal exclaimed, crossing his arms across his chest.

"We've lived in worse." Som shrugged and entered the rooms. He looked around curiously, opening each door and looking into the rooms.

"I'll meet you later," Niv told them. "I'm going to see if my rooms are still standing."

"Bye," Gunvor said shyly, waving at her awkwardly as she left them.

When she reached a junction in the hallways, she didn't head toward the rooms she had lived in. Instead, she headed toward a set of steps that would lead her onto the wall. She had one more task before she could rest.

The breeze twisted her hair away from her face as she stepped out, whispering across her skin in a reassuring caress. Niv strode toward the wall facing the mountains and stared out at the calm ocean of trees stretching into the distance. She placed her palms flat on the cool surface and took a deep breath. As she exhaled, the tension and fear she had tried to squash during the battle released into the air around her.

Holding the familiar ball of power at her center, the one Raina had taught her to use, she examined it. It waited almost peacefully, sensing what she intended as she peered into the darkness of the trees.

"It's time," she said to herself, pushing into the power one last time and muttering a single word. "Release."

The power she had borrowed and fought with to free her kingdom pulsed for one heartbeat before it skittered away from her, leaving her body as she gasped at its sudden absence. With it went the last of her anger, and she smiled a true smile for the first time in eight years. She turned, and in a few strides was on the other side of the wall, looking within the walls of her father's kingdom. Her kingdom.

She watched her people, not taking her eyes off them as they helped each other and chattered in groups. She watched as they spoke freely, buzzing with joy at their newfound freedom. Even when Galen arrived to inform her that there were only minor injuries and wondering aloud if it had something to do with the light she had used to rally the people. Where she had intertwined a protection spell within the golden glow.

She continued to watch as the light faded and her gaze over the kingdom only failed when Asher joined her, helped up the steps by Paxon.

"I thought I might find you here." He smiled at her,

looking younger than he had earlier that day. Gone was the tension in his face, the worried looks and careful eyes.

"It is a glorious sight."

"It is." He lifted his arm, and she leaned into his side, careful to avoid the injured area. "What will your first decree be, Your Majesty?"

Niv snorted in an unqueenly manner. "They might not want me as their queen."

"They are already talking about the coronation. I'm not sure you have a choice."

Niv sighed, tilting her head. "I haven't thought about being queen. Not since my father was killed."

"You will have to think about it now."

"I never thought this day would come." She waited a few heartbeats, thinking about what she would do, whether she even deserved to lead these people. She thought about putting it to a vote and how that would work.

"You don't have to think about it now." Asher leaned carefully and kissed her forehead. "We can have a night of peace."

Niv smiled, thinking about taking Asher back to her childhood rooms. Her smile faded when she looked out at the kingdom again. If she was to be queen, she knew one decree that would keep her people safe. "My first decree will be to ban magic. No longer will those who have the potential to destroy us be allowed in this kingdom."

Asher nodded. "I will ensure it happens."

They stayed together on that wall, even as the night took over and swallowed the sight of the kingdom before them. Only when Asher noticed Niv shivering did he gently take her hand, and they slowly made their way back inside the palace.

EPILOGUE

"*I* heard she used a spell to enthrall the king," said Sumi. "Wormed her way into the palace and then killed him off. She drove that young lass out. Jealous of her beauty, she wanted all the power to herself."

Sumi stirred a large container of stew, readying for the return of the hunting party. The whole kitchen listened as she went on.

"She hunted the young princess until she had nowhere to hide. Poor dear ended up taking up with a group of men."

"I heard they were from the north. They're a lot shorter there. She could have passed for one of them," Del piped up from the corner of the kitchen. She clapped her hands together with a puff of flour from the dough she kneaded. "She took care of them in return for food and lodging."

Sumi sniffed, ignoring the interruption. "Anyway, the queen hated that the princess had escaped. Offered rewards to huntsmen and assassins to discover the location. When that didn't work she enchanted every apple in the kingdom."

One of the young scullery maids, Darla, gasped. "She killed everyone?"

"No, don't be silly. The apple was enchanted so it would only kill the princess."

"Did she die?"

"The men she looked after loved her so much that the magic of their love kept her from death. She only slept once she ate the apple."

"What did the queen do?"

"She didn't know, too wrapped up in herself to realize the princess survived. Princes came from far and wide once they heard. A good fairy told them that only a kiss of her true love could wake her."

"Did she wake?" asked Darla.

"Only when a butler who had served the king loyally for many years came along did the spell break." Sumi beamed at the attention she was getting from the room.

"Then what happened?" Darla stood next to the basket of laundry she had abandoned at the start of the tale.

"When the spell broke, it backfired. And the evil queen was consumed by her power. She disappeared that day, never to return to the palace again. The princess and her butler moved back into the palace. Many of the people in the kingdom had been killed by the queen because they refused to serve her." Sumi turned to face the rest of the room. "The story goes that the evil queen haunts all the mirrors in the castle. That if you look long enough, you will see her reflected back at you."

"Mirrors," scoffed Del. "What a load of muck."

"It's just a story, though," Darla insisted. "She's not really in the mirrors."

"You'll have to look in one to find out. The queen was so obsessed with her own looks that she couldn't walk past one without staring at her reflection. Now her essence remains." Sumi shrugged, grinning when she turned her back on the room.

"What happened to the princess?" Darla asked.

"She built the kingdom up to be one of the most prosperous in the land. Many came to live there as it was the best in all the land, and the princess and the butler lived happily ever after."

Del chuckled, rolling her eyes. "That's all nonsense. I heard the queen's lover killed the king in his bed, taking her to be his consort. He had wanted the princess dead."

"It was all the queen. There was no lover," Sumi said. "Are you trying to tell me that she did all that for the love of a man? Pfft."

"When did this happen?" Darla asked, her eyes wide.

"Few hundred years ago. Way back in the king's line. When magic used to exist."

"Magic never existed. Now you're just being silly." Del waved a hand at Darla. "Don't you have better things to do than listen to her made-up tales. You have the whole guest wing to get ready before the ball."

Darla's eyes sparkled. "Is it true that even commoners are invited?"

"Yes." Del rolled her eyes. "Imagining yourself as the next princess?"

"Rumor has it that the king will allow the prince to marry anyone invited. It could happen."

"In your dreams, deary." Del turned back to kneading the bread while Darla picked up the laundry. She hummed a beautiful melody as she left the kitchen, wondering if she would finish the dress she had been working on in time.

That's the end of this tale, but watch out for more Tales of Darkness and Fate—coming soon!

AUTHOR NOTE

Wow, thank you so much for finishing our story. Anne and I really enjoyed putting this version of Snow White and the Seven Dwarves together. Though it didn't turn out as we initially planned, we grew to love the characters in this. You'll be pleased to know that we have plans for several books in this series. All from the villain's point of view. Raina did not take us where we expected, so who knows where our other villains will take us next.

Where Anne came up with the storyline for The Royal Pack Trilogy, it was me who planned out the plot for Rotten to the Core. Then threw it out halfway through, replotting the second half of the book about twenty times. Okay maybe eight times, but it felt like more.

Growing up I always had a love for fairytales, and I'm a huge advocate for happily ever after and what it is meant to be. There were so many small decisions that would have meant I wasn't where I am today and life would be very different if I'd taken one turn differently.

When it came to naming characters in this book, each of the seven are loosely based on the seven dwarves and one of the names came about by accident. We had already decided to name Asher before we intended him to be one of the seven. Then when we realized that he would be one of Niv's seven men it was a very "happy" coincidence to find out that

Asher means "happy" in Hebrew! The names of the rest of the seven are variations on the meanings for the names of the seven dwarves and it was great fun coming up with them.

We would like to thank all our readers, those who we see daily in the CWP community. You truly do inspire us to bring you more stories and your support means the world to us.

Love Liz
xoxo

REVIEW AND RECOMMEND

Thank you for reading the book. We hope you enjoyed it .

If you liked the book and want to share the love, we'd be thrilled if you could leave a review on Amazon and recommend it to your friends and family. As you probably know, reviews and word-of-mouth recommendations can make a huge difference for authors and readers alike.

With love,
Anne & Liz

CWP NEWSLETTER

At CWP, our mission is to help readers like yourself to discover new or less known paranormal romance (PNR) and paranormal women's fiction (PWF) authors and books.

Join CWP newsletter. You'll be the first to know about our new releases, and receive exclusive deals and special offers.

With love,
Anne & Liz

CWP AUTHORS AND BOOKS

We have more thrilling stories you can choose from and that are coming your way. Check out our authors and books 🤍.

With love,
Anne & Liz

CWP Authors: https://clanwhelanpublishing.com/authors/

CWP Books: https://clanwhelanpublishing.com/cwp-books/

Printed in Great Britain
by Amazon

21978621R00199